# PRAISE FOR *THE GIFTED G...*

"Hilarious and intensely moving…When you put the book down, you know you've been somewhere that mattered: into the heart of a family bound by (beautiful, annoying, riotous, bold) women in love. What a brilliant, original, powerful book."

—Heather Sellers, author of *The Boys I Borrow*

"A beautifully written, zesty family chronicle, THE GIFTED GABALDÓN SISTERS covers over a century of women's lives, pieced together like a Southwest quilt."

—Teresa de la Caridad Doval, author of
*A Girl Like Che Guevara*

"Funny, fierce, and wise."

—Judith Ortiz Cofer, author of *Call Me María*

"It has been a long time since I have cared for the characters of a novel as much as I care for the Gabaldón sisters. Their individual perspectives and personalities are woven together to create a three-dimensional world full of promise in spite of the daily obstacles familiar to us all. Lorraine López moves effortlessly between humor and heartache, opening us up to the possibility that what seems coincidental is truly magical."

—Blas Falconer, author of *The Perfect Hour*

"THE GIFTED GABALDÓN SIST... ...bout secrets and lies, dramas and scandals, big losses ... ...the very stuff that makes life worth livi... I've encountered such a rambun... characters. And in López's hands, ... prose, they lift off the page with dignity and soul, ... you root and ache for each of them until the very end."

—Alex Espinoza, author of *Still Water Saints*

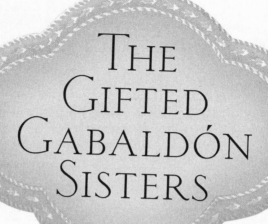

# THE GIFTED GABALDÓN SISTERS

## LORRAINE LÓPEZ

**GRAND CENTRAL**
PUBLISHING

NEW YORK    BOSTON

Copyright © 2008 by Lorraine M. López
Reading Group Guide copyright © 2008 by Hachette Book Group USA, Inc.
All rights reserved. Except as permitted under the U.S. Copyright Act of 1976, no part of this publication may be reproduced, distributed, or transmitted in any form or by any means, or stored in a database or retrieval system, without the prior written permission of the publisher.

Grand Central Publishing
Hachette Book Group USA
237 Park Avenue
New York, NY 10017

Visit our Web site at www.HachetteBookGroupUSA.com.

Printed in the United States of America

First Edition: October 2008
10  9  8  7  6  5  4  3  2  1

Grand Central Publishing is a division of Hachette Book Group USA, Inc. The Grand Central Publishing name and logo is a trademark of Hachette Book Group USA, Inc.

Library of Congress Cataloging-in-Publication Data

López, Lorraine
   The gifted Gabaldón sisters / Lorraine M. López. — 1st ed.
      p. cm.
   Summary: "Four sisters search for the truth behind a long-buried family secret"—Provided by publisher.
   ISBN 978-0-446-69921-1
   1. Sisters—Fiction.  2. Mexican Americans—Fiction.  3. California—Fiction.  I. Title.
   PS3612.O64G54 2008
   813'.6—dc22
                                                                2008004501

Book design by Stratford Publishing, a TexTech business

*For Debra López, Kenneth López,*
*Frances López Whyte, Sylvia López,*
*and in loving memory of Adelina "Luguarda"*
*Martínez de López*

# The
# Gifted
# Gabaldón
# Sisters

# PROLOGUE

# LOS ANGELES—1966

The Sea Breeze Bungalows, on Clinton Street off Alvarado Street in Los Angeles, were constructed in the early 1940s to provide housing for single working women and bachelors. Though the Sea Breeze units are some forty miles from the Pacific Ocean, the developer, clearly torn between Art Deco and beachcomber styles, compromised by constructing these peach-colored cottages with one porthole window apiece and then raising a sign decorated with painted seashells on the front lawn. The largest of the five bungalows, originally inhabited by the owner, sits at the tip of the pentagon, farthest from the street.

Two decades after construction, this three-bedroom home is now rented by the Gabaldón family: a widowed utility worker, with five children, and an elderly Pueblo woman. The four girls in the family share the largest bedroom, while the one boy, the middle child, sleeps in a youth bed in his father's room. The smallest bedroom belongs to Fermina, the aged housekeeper. Crammed into her quarters are a battered oak dresser with mismatched knobs, a flecked and clouded mirror, an oval hook rug at the center of the dark wood floor, and a single bed, heaped with folded quilts, near the wall. Beside the bed and aligned with the outer wall, just under the window, sits a bird's-eye-maple trunk.

The blond trunk is draped with a Navajo blanket patterned with red and black thunderbirds against an emerald background.

The house, empty of its inhabitants this Sunday morning while the family attends mass, sighs now with a gust buffeting the curtains and then groans at the joists, like an exhausted woman loosening her girdle in a private moment, as it settles into the foundation. The worn and lumpy pieces of furniture moan softly against rusted springs and frames. Even the maple trunk seems to slump, readjusting itself and resettling its contents. Among these are photo albums, framed family portraits wrapped in newsprint, wedding and baptismal gowns encased in plastic, quilts, shoeboxes containing letters, an ebony case holding costume jewelry and some turquoise and silver pieces, a scattering of cedar blocks, stacked high-school yearbooks, a manila envelope in which marriage, birth and baptismal certificates, high-school diplomas, and report cards are stuffed, and a parcel of yellowed pages, printed in fading ink and bound together with twine.

The first page in this stack reads as follows:

SUBJECT: FERMINA/WALPI
Work Projects Administration: 6-8-38—
  Data Collector: Heidi Marie Schultz
June 6, 1938
Words: 261

# FERMINA

Fermina is a petite woman with a corona
of braided gray hair coiled atop her head.
Unlike many ancianos in the Rio Puerco Valley,
her posture is upright and her neck long and
graceful. Yet she takes small, uncertain steps
when she walks, and she favors knee-length
gingham dresses and thick white ankle-socks.
Though she appears much younger, Fermina is
in her seventies. She was born in the 1860s in
Walpi, a Hopi village located on the First Mesa
in northeastern Arizona.

When she was a child, her father contracted
a fever and died. Soon afterward, her newborn
brother also succumbed to an unknown malady that
may have been measles. Her paternal grandmother
blamed Fermina's mother, a Tewa of Hano, for the
death, claiming the young woman had encountered
a snake. The Hopi believed a woman with child
who looks upon a snake will deliver a baby
born with spots. Raised blotches covered the
infant's body for the few days he lived. He died
before he could be sung into the clan, before
his grandmother could perform the head-washing
ceremony.

Fermina claims to remember stroking the
baby's cold, pimpled cheeks and whispering her
name in his ear, so he would know her when they
met in the underworld. Later, family members, as
dictated by custom, hurtled his swaddled corpse

over the edge of a northeast cliff. The blanket
unfurled like the wings of a hawk sailing a
sudden current. A sandy gust stung Fermina's
cheeks. She cupped a hand over her eyes, and
her brother was gone.

# Dog Party — Loretta: 1966

The best thing about Randy Suela was his dog, Flip, a lanky Dalmatian mix, with pink-rimmed eyes and a long, rubbery tongue. Flip would jig on his hind legs, wriggling like a belly dancer, when he saw me and then roll on his back, so I could strum his liver-spotted belly. I'd invited both Randy and Flip to my tenth birthday party, but only Randy, wearing a crisp madras shirt, appeared on the threshold that morning. I barred the doorway, my hands on my hips. "Where's Flip?"

"My ma said I couldn't bring him." Randy lowered his head. His black hair was so stiff with Brylcreem that combing had etched hard furrows clear to his scalp. He scuffed one loafer into the other, and brought his hands from behind his back to offer a cylinder-shaped parcel wrapped in pink paper. "I got you something."

My eyes on the gift, I said, "You aren't invited without Flip."

Randy shook his head. "But, Loretta, my ma says dogs don't go to parties." He leaned to the left, trying to slip past me into the house.

"Yes, *they do*." I shifted, blocking him. "Mr. Huerta's bringing his Chihuahua to my party, and he's the landlord, so he should know."

"But my ma—"

"Tell your mama it's *my* party, not hers. I can invite whoever I want."

"Get the dog, boy," called Fermina from the bedroom. Her voice scraped through the bungalow like a bad saw on green wood.

"What was that?" Randy backpedaled, stumbling on the black BIENVENIDOS mat.

"Never mind," I said.

"That was *spooky*." He peered over my shoulder into the house.

"It's just Fermina, her voice. She's a really old Indian."

Randy's eyes widened. "You have an *Indian*? Can I see?"

"Not unless you bring Flip. That's the deal."

"Maybe I can sneak him over." He turned to leave.

I grabbed his elbow. "Give me that first." Something sloshed against glass under the pink paper. "What is it?"

"Pickles."

My mouth went juicy. "Ooh!"

Randy smiled. "You like them, huh?"

"Dile gracias," called Fermina.

"Thanks," I said, ready to push the door shut. "Now, go get Flip."

When Randy returned with Flip, the dog lunged at me. His black claws raked my legs, scribbling chalky streaks on my thighs. I crouched, pulling him close, and he lapped my face with his fishy tongue. In the kitchen, I opened the box of dog biscuits I'd bought and tossed one for him before leading Randy to Fermina's room.

The door whined open, and the floorboards groaned under the carpet, as we tiptoed toward her bed. "¿Estás durmiendo?"

"No, venga." She propped herself up on the pillows. "Bring me my rosary, hija."

I opened the top bureau drawer. "Glow-in-the-dark or wood?"

"Wood. Glow-in-the-dark is for night."

I untangled the carved ebony beads from a nest of scapulars, thread, hairpins, and the greenish glow-in-the-dark strand.

"Dame agua, hija, with ice."

Randy stood frozen at the heart of the oval hook rug, staring. His jaw hung so low that silvery fillings glinted from the back of his mouth. I swung my gaze toward Fermina and imagined seeing her, as he was, for the first time.

To him, she must have made the gargoyles in fairy tales seem smooth as babies. Her skin was the color of cocoa, but the texture of oatmeal, puckered and bubbled with clots and lumps. Her pleated eyelids had avalanched over her eyes, leaving dark wet quarter-moons from which she peered at us. The few snowy hairs remaining on her head were tucked under a hairnet, which made her look both wise and weird.

I was used to Fermina, how she looked and the creaky way she spoke. I enjoyed curling up with her in bed and reading *Stories for Young Catholics* to her. But when I spied Randy wrinkling his nose, I, too, whiffed the sour mustiness of her sheets, the dry old woman smell that overpowered the joss sticks burning in her shrine to Our Lady of Guadalupe. The tang of spoiled fruit wafted from Fermina's mouth, like a cantaloupe husk at the bottom of the trash can. The same sweetish stench had risen from my mother's blackened toes.

I handed Fermina the glass, and she sat up to sip the water. Had she always made these strangled, gurgling sounds? I turned to Randy. "Okay, let's go outside."

He didn't move.

"Come on, Randy."

"Can I . . . *touch* her?" he whispered.

Fermina set the glass on her maple trunk. "No."

"How *old* are you?" Randy asked.

"Ten years old," she told him with a wink.

I leveled my gaze at her. "Tell the truth."

"Today is *my* birthday," she said.

"It is *not*. It's mine!"

"Entonces ven aca a recibir un besito."

I leaned in and her lips rasped my cheek.

"Happy birthday, hija," she said. "When I am gone, you will get a gift from me." On our birthdays, Fermina always promised my three sisters and me that we'd receive our present from her after she died.

"You know what I want," I said.

She nodded. "The glow-in-the-dark rosary."

"*No,* not that." Though I loved how the milky pellets absorbed light to gleam at night like the moon's own lonely tears, what I really wanted was for Fermina to find my mother in that underworld and tell her that she never said good-bye to me. The morning they took Mama back to the hospital, I woke up late and threw on my uniform. My father yelled at me to hurry, and I had no time to slip into my mother's bedroom and hug her before we piled into the car for school. She never kissed me, never said good-bye. I asked Fermina to find her in that place she calls Maski and tell her she has to come back, that she forgot something—something important. "I already told you what I want. Remember?"

Fermina nodded. She kissed the crucifix at the top of the rosary and mumbled her prayers. I tugged Randy's arm and led him outside, where my oldest sister, Bette, stood with a cluster of her girlfriends. They'd just arrived, handing her cards and presents because Bette had lied to them, claiming it was *her* birthday. For human guests, I'd invited Randy, only because of Flip, and two girls from school: Gloria Quon, who'd be late because of her violin lesson, and Nancy Acosta, a Jehovah's Witness, who would not come at all because celebrating birthdays was against her religion. Mr. Huerta promised to bring his Chihuahua, Baby, and our neighbor Mrs. Lucas said she'd let me borrow her golden retriever for the party.

The day before, my father had bought a bakery cake, a burro-shaped piñata, bags of Tootsie Rolls and butterscotch disks with which to fill the donkey, two packets of balloons, and party favors from Woolworth. When Randy and I slammed out the screen door, we found him tossing a clothesline to string the piñata on the avocado tree.

This was the first birthday party since my mother died in February, and my father was trying to do it right, though he'd never before given a party by himself. My mother had been the one to write out the invitations, bake and ice the cake, weave pastel-colored crepe paper into the trellis over the driveway, and blow up the balloons. It felt strange to see my father boiling wienies on the stove so early that morning that now they bobbed in the cold salty water like bloated fingers, odd to watch his hairy-knuckled hands measuring jelly beans into pleated candy cups. When he'd catch my eye, he'd wink, saying, "Real nice, ¿qué no?" He didn't even seem to mind that Bette had invited her friends, pretending it was her birthday. He was probably relieved to have more people for guests, as I had wanted to invite only dogs.

"Dogs?" he'd said when we first discussed it. "Like from the pound?"

"Not *strange* dogs—dogs I know, dogs from the neighborhood."

"You won't get presents that way," Bette had warned me, shaking her head. "Invite all the dogs on earth. Not a single one will bring a gift."

I couldn't care less for gifts, though the pickles were nice.

I shoved Randy toward my father. "Help him put up the piñata."

"Catch the other end of that rope, boy," my father said as I skipped toward the house, my shiny new Mary Janes stiff and slippery on the pavement. Flip panted behind the screen door. I pulled it open, and he shot out almost tumbling me. I caught his head in my hands and kissed his cold, salty nose. Then we bolted, racing around and around—the house, the carport, the patio. I shrieked, and Flip barked, stinging my shins with his thick, ropy tail when he overtook me near the trash cans, and then I charged after him. My seven-year-old brother joined in, but Cary, a husky asthmatic, soon grew pink in the face, huffing and wheezing until he had to stop.

My father called me to eat, and I begged a few more minutes, *please*. He hollered, "Get over here, girl!" And Fermina called from the side window, "Stop running with that dog. You will make him sick." I spun around to see Flip sink onto one haunch, panting. I tied his leash to a post near the trellis and refilled the water bowl for him to slurp while cooling his belly on the shaded concrete.

While Flip and I were racing, Gloria Quon had arrived. She, Bette, and Bette's friends had finished eating and were whispering together near the cuartito that housed the washing machine, not far from where my father had set up the picnic table for the party. At the patio, Cary helped himself to a second hot dog and more potato chips while Sophie kept him company. I had no idea where my younger sister Rita was.

There were five of us children, but once there had been six. With one exception, my mother named all of us for her favorite movie stars. First she named my oldest sister and me, Bette Davis and Loretta Young Gabaldón. Then she named the brother that followed me the English version of her father's name, Antonio Gerardo, to honor him, as he had died just before the baby's birth. But she switched back to movie star names when she lost Anthony Gerard, naming my brother and the two sisters that followed him, Cary Grant, Rita Hayworth, and Sophia Loren Gabaldón.

My mother used to say she "lost" Anthony Gerard—never how or why—when telling how many children she had and their ages. When she said it, her lips barely moved. Her voice seemed to come from another place, like she was hypnotized or as if she were a ventriloquist without a dummy.

My sister Bette and I wondered about this. Babies are not *that* small, we reasoned, but even if you did misplace one, soon enough it would start bawling, and then you'd find it straightaway. How *could* you lose a baby? How could our mother have lost a *boy*? When we asked Fermina, she said our mother should tell us what happened to Anthony Gerard. "It is her story," she said. "When it is time, she will tell you." Then she told us that she, too, had lost her brother when he was a baby.

"Really?" Bette's eyes grew round. "Where did he go?"

"Los riscos."

"The *cliffs*?"

She nodded. "He flew from them like a bird. Espérense. Your mother will tell you about your brother. Wait and you will know." Fermina would say nothing more about her lost brother or ours.

But Bette and I didn't like to wait, so we tried on our own to solve the puzzle of our brother's disappearance. We shut ourselves in our parents' closet, and Bette pulled a sheath of dry cleaner's plastic from my father's gray pin-striped suit. Maybe Anthony Gerard had gotten tangled in something like this, the plastic molding over his melon-sized head like a membrane, sucking into his nostrils and mouth as he gasped for air. Bette supposed he might have gotten lost this way.

"I'm going to visit Anthony Gerard," she said as we huddled in the leather-musky shadows between shoe trees. She pulled the plastic over her black curls and her face. "You coming?" She gathered the loose ends, knotting them under her chin.

I shook my head. "Nah, you go first."

The plastic puckered and dimpled before clouding with her breath. After a few minutes, she swayed and then slumped into my lap. I wanted to shout for help, but it was as though the plastic shrouded *my* head, stuffing my mouth and jamming my throat. I stripped away the clammy sheathing and slapped her face. She cried out, raised her hand to strike me, but I caught her wrist.

She said, "I saw him! I *saw* him!"

"Who?" I'd forgotten the purpose of our experiment.

"Anthony, Anthony Gerard! I *saw* him. He was wearing a sailor suit."

"*Sailor* suit?" I imagined the strutting Cracker Jack boy. "Where was he?"

"Long Beach." Bette nodded. "Pacific Ocean Park. I saw him holding an orange balloon on a string."

"P.O.P.? *Nah*-uh." I flashed on the chaos of hawkers in peppermint-striped jackets and straw boaters barking attractions, the tattooed and unshaven operators mutely churning rides—the Ferris wheel, the roller coasters, the small boats circling a moat of brackish water, and the bumper cars that sizzled overhead, showering sparks when they collided. I envisioned Anthony Gerard cracking open salted peanuts from a red-and-white sack and lining up to ride the roller coaster. The unfairness of it soured my stomach. "How come *he* gets to go there?"

"Stupid, *that's* where he was lost. I saw the Ferris wheel, the big one, near the water. *That's* where Mama lost him."

Being lost at P.O.P. hardly seemed a bad deal to me. "Is he still there?"

She shrugged. "That's where I saw him."

"What if he wandered out to the beach? What if he went too far out?" Even wading seemed treacherous. I would squeeze my aunt Nilda's freckled hand as I stood quaking, ankle-deep in foam, the wet sand worming between my toes after each slapping wave. If a slimy lock of seaweed brushed my ankle, I'd shimmy up my aunt's hip like a monkey. "Maybe he drowned!"

"Or maybe he flew off the Ferris wheel." Bette hooked her thumbs together, waving her fingers like wings.

I thought of my lost brother now, imagining him here at my party, strutting among the guests in his sailor suit, as I crammed the last wedge of bun into my mouth and watched Bette and her friends hoist Gloria Quon atop an upturned trash can. They strung a shiny gold ribbon from one of the gifts diagonally across Gloria's chest, crowned her with a tiara fashioned from tin foil, and sang, *"There, she is, Miss A-mer-i-ca..."*

Gloria was the type of child that adults make excuses to pet and fondle. She was chosen to play Snow White and Sleeping Beauty in fairy-tale plays, and she was the Virgin Mary for the Christmas pageant. Stage lights cast a bluish halo over her shingle-cut hair, bejeweling her dark eyes and glistening on her plump coral lips. When I met her, I was so moved by the creamy stalk of her neck that I wrapped my hands around it, sinking fingers into the warm skin. She'd cried for me to stop, and I pulled away, my face hot with shame. My cheeks still flamed with that memory.

My sister shot sidelong glances at me, and Randy Suela filled

Gloria's lap with poinsettia blooms, their scarlet veins milk-spotting his brown hands. Bette said, "Look, Loretta, look. We're making Gloria the queen!"

"Okay." I dropped my paper plate in a grocery sack my father had designated for trash. "I'll be right back."

Randy's tennis shoes scraped the cement as he rushed to catch up with me. The sound roused Flip, who whimpered, clawing the cement, straining at the end of his tether. Randy caught up with me when I leaned to scratch Flip's spotted ears. "Poor pup, you have to wait here."

"Can I go with you?" Randy said.

"I guess." I massaged Flip's ears until he sank to his belly, eyelids drooping. I gave him a final pat, and Randy and I trotted down the driveway.

"Where we going?" he asked.

"I got to get Sugar Foot for the party."

"Is that like a dessert or something?"

"No, he's a golden retriever with one white paw."

"*Another* dog? You sure like dogs, don't you?"

"I *love* dogs. And cats. And mice. And even bugs, but not worms."

"Do you like any people? Do you like any kids, say, in our class?"

I paused, thinking this over. "I like Gloria. She's pretty and she plays the violin."

"Do you like any of us guys? I mean, would you like someone like me, if that someone liked you?"

"Not if he didn't have a dog."

"I have a dog. So, do you like me?" He went silent, waiting for my answer.

I hesitated at the Lucases' ivy-covered gate. While I didn't mind Mrs. Lucas, whose thinning red hair flipped up, making her look like she could be Bozo the Clown's sister, I couldn't stand Ginger and Vicki, her teenaged daughters. Standing before their gate, I remembered the pigeon chick in the bushes near our house. Mama wouldn't let me bring the bird indoors, so I kept it in a towel-lined shoebox in the cuartito. I fed it rice cereal with an eyedropper. After several days, the tiny bird's stiff down grew plush, its breast round and sleek. The chick would trail after me in the cuartito when I came to feed him, and nest in my lap after eating, cooing with contentment.

"Don't show the Lucas girls that bird," my mother had warned me once as the sisters strolled past our house. "They'll take it away from you."

But I was so proud of the pigeon that I couldn't resist calling out to them the next time they appeared. "Hey, want to see something?"

I don't know how my mother knew it, but those lipstick-smeared girls, with their tight skirts and fat, smudgy knees, took the chick away with them. First they jabbered — one and then the other — their flat voices drumming like raindrops on a tin roof.

"What do you need a pigeon for, huh?"

"We can take better care of it. We're older."

"We even got a birdcage with a swing."

"That pigeon's going to die here."

"What are you going to do when it gets sick?"

"We got a friend who's a bird doctor. Take care of it for free."

Then they hefted the box between them, taking the eyedropper, the cereal, and the little bird away from me.

I didn't see them until weeks later, one Sunday after mass.

"How's the pigeon?" I asked Ginger.

"Huh?"

"How's that bird you got from me?"

She turned to Vicki. "You tell her."

"*No-o-o-o,* not me. You tell her."

"We had it in the yard next door," began Ginger, "and the neighbor was raking."

"Not raking," Vicki corrected her sister.

"That's right, not raking."

"Mowing."

"Okay, mowing," Ginger said.

My fingernails bit small white moons into my palms. "What happened?"

"Well, that's what we're trying to tell you," Vicki said.

"Blood everywhere." Ginger shook her head. "A real mess."

"Did you take him to the doctor?"

"What doctor?" Vicki asked.

"The head had already come off," explained Ginger.

"That's right," Vicki said. "The head was off."

"You can't put that back on. Not even with stitches."

"Why did you even let him out of the cage?"

"What cage?" Vicki had asked.

Now, if I saw either of the Lucas girls in the yard or even glimpsed one through the window, then I'd spin around, head for home, and forget all about bringing Sugar Foot to my party. But I wasn't likely to see them, as they'd taken to smoking cigarettes and riding around in cars driven by older boys with slicked-back hair.

"Well?" asked Randy as we stood before the Lucas gate.

"Well, what?"

"I have a dog. Does that mean you like me?"

"I guess so. Flip's a great dog."

"Would you want to go with me?"

"Go where?"

"Not *go* anywhere. I mean, like, be my girlfriend."

My stomach lurched. "No!"

"I thought you liked me."

"I like *Flip*," I said.

"Would you go with me if I gave you Flip?"

"You'd completely give him to me? He'd *live* at my house?"

"*If* I did," Randy repeated, nodding.

"Maybe I would." I tugged open the gate. Sugar Foot lifted himself out of his basket bed on the porch, shook all over, and loped toward us. Mrs. Lucas appeared at the screen door, bearing a jump rope. "Keep him tied up, Loretta, or he'll run off. There's a dog in heat on the corner, and you can barely control old Sugar, even with a rope."

I threaded the rope through his collar, and Randy and I started back for the party. As we walked in silence, I gave Sugar Foot plenty of lead to visit trees, but held firm.

Finally Randy said, "Look, Loretta, I can't do it. I've had Flip since he was a pup. I just *can't* give him away like that."

"I know." I liked Randy more than ever right then. "Let's race to the house, okay? On your mark, get set, *go*!" We bounded back to the party. Sugar Foot, though an old dog with a limp, won by the taut length of his rope.

My father had us gather up wilted balloon skins, crepe streamers, paper cups, plates, and tattered bits of piñata after the party ended. As we finished, I asked him if we could visit my mother before supper. He blew at the thin flap of hair that kept spilling over his forehead like a loose chapel veil. "¡Cómo molestas!"

"I want to see her. That was my only wish when I blew out all the candles."

"Never enough," he said. "The party, the balloons, the cake, and those dogs fighting—it's never enough for you, is it?" He gestured toward the patio with his bandaged hand, the one Sugar Foot had bitten, loose gauze trailing like kite string from his wrist.

I cast my eyes on my shoes. They were water-splotched now, and they pinched my swollen feet. Sugar Foot hadn't gotten along with Flip. My father and Mr. Huerta tried yanking them apart, but the dogs ignored them. Sugar Foot snarled, thrusting with such force that the rope burned my hands. Dad hollered for Cary to get the hose. When it was over, Mr. Huerta, his guayabera shirt sopping, shook a finger at me. "No more dog parties on this property, and I *mean* it!"

The disaster of the party opened a place in me so deep and dark and lonely that not even the coffee table piled with gifts—most of them for Bette—could fill it. "I never had a birthday without Mama."

"¡Cállate la boca!"

"Juan Carlos!" Fermina called from the porch. Her friend Irina was visiting. They swayed together on the glider, talking quietly. "Ven aca."

My father threw down the rope he'd pulled from the avocado tree. *"Cómo molestan"*—these were his favorite words; everyone bothered him.

But I bothered him the most. To tell the truth, I did it on purpose. The others acted like he was some friendly giant in a fairy tale. Bette and Rita would run to tackle his legs when he returned from work, as he was swinging his lunch box and humming, "I've Been Working on the Railroad," though he really worked for the city, fixing water mains and opening hydrants when there were fires. He'd toss my shrieking sisters into the air, one at a time.

Then he'd slam in the screen door and tickle the baby and give Cary a few friendly punches in the arm or muss his hair. All the while, I'd hide in my room or up in the avocado tree, staring down at the naked spot on his scalp and wondering why it had to be Mama. Why not him? "Where's la Loretta?" he'd ask. Bette would guess where I might be, and I'd hear him let out a sigh that whistled with relief.

Fermina's voice creaked like a rusted hinge as she spoke to my father, and Bette squinted at me, as though trying to figure out just how I'd become such an ass.

"We haven't visited Mama in a real long time," I said.

"Why don't you go to hell?" Rita balled her fists and scowled at me.

"Why should I?" I put my hands on my hips and swung my head from side to side as I'd seen the Lucas girls do when they argued. "To visit you?"

"Shithead," Rita said.

"Shut up, both of you," Bette hissed. "I can't hear what Fermina's saying."

"I miss Mama. I just want to visit her. What's so bad about that?"

"Dummy, you can't visit her. She's *dead*," said Bette. "All you can do is see the grave—dirt and grass. Her spirit's floated up to heaven. She's not even there." Bette often acted like she knew what she had no way of knowing, and, mostly, we ignored her, but this time she angered Cary.

"Liar! She is *so* there. I want to see her, too." Cary stepped beside me, twining his hot, chubby arm with mine. Sometimes I liked my brother almost as much as a dog.

My father fished in his pocket for the keys, yelling at us to get in the car, goddamn it. Bette hefted Sophie on one hip and lugged her to the car. Rita, tagging after them, turned to thrust her tongue out at me.

At the cemetery, we met the man who'd sold my mother's burial plot to my father. He claimed to be from the same part of New Mexico that my father came from, but he kept calling my father "paisano," and everyone knows that—where my dad's from—a *paisano* is a roadrunner. Even we, English-speaking children, called roadrunners *paisanos*. Until we saw the beeping bird in cartoons, we didn't have another word for them. To call our father *paisano* seemed silly, even insulting to him. Someone from his hometown should know better than this.

"Hey, paisano," the cemetery man said that afternoon as he strolled with us to my mother's grave.

"Why do you insist on calling me a 'roadrunner'?" my father asked.

"Ha-ha. You're a funny guy, paisano. But serious, that plot near your lady is still available, but not for long. You don't want no stranger sleeping near your wife."

My father stopped to light an unfiltered Camel. His sports shirt billowed as he sucked in a lungful of smoke. "I ain't planning to die."

"Serious, paisano, we all die. A small down payment will hold that piece of real estate for you until the time comes."

"Let me tell you something, paisano." My father flicked the ashes from his cigarette. "One, I am not a roadrunner, and two, I don't care who sleeps near my wife. She's dead. You got that?" He pivoted away, picking up the pace, and we trailed after him, trudging over the uneven tufts of grass as we searched for our mother's headstone.

When Cary and my sisters settled on their knees at the foot of the grave and my father stepped away to light another cigarette, I raced back the way we came. I found the cemetery man where we'd left him, kicking twigs from the walk.

"Hey, paisanita, you lost?"

I gasped, trying to catch my breath. "Look! I got five dollars." I reached into one of my shoes, where I'd stuffed my aunt Nilda's gift. "Here. Save that space near my mama." I pressed the folded bill into his hand.

He tucked it into his pocket. "What a good girl to save the plot for your papa."

I spun around to race back to my mother's grave. "Not for *him*!" I shouted over my shoulder. "For *me-e-e-e*!"

Not long after my birthday, Fermina developed what my aunt Nilda called a "wet cough," a hoarse whoop that rattled deep in her chest. To me, she sounded like a seal, all alone on a floe, barking in the fog, icy waves carrying her farther and farther out. As spring became summer, and summer, fall, Fermina grew worse. She developed bronchitis and then pneumonia. I spent hours lying beside her in her narrow bed, reading aloud from *Stories for Young Catholics*. The battered red book, a reader for older children, was filled with cautionary tales about characters like Jim D., a construction worker who neglected to have a full confession before falling to his death from a skyscraper, and Alice T., who skipped Easter duty before having a fatal encounter with a city bus. The book also had deliciously graphic stories about the martyred saints. I enjoyed best those that featured lions in coliseums. Fermina's favorite story was that of Saint Agnes, the girl martyr, who was tortured and killed while trying to protect her purity and refusing to renounce her faith.

One Saturday, after reading to her about Saint Agnes for

the fifth or sixth time, I told Fermina, "I'd have given up the purity—whatever it is—and renounced anything they asked me to renounce, wouldn't you?"

She thought about it for a moment, and then nodded. "No somos santas."

She asked me to read a story called "The Basement" next. This was about a man and his young son in a house under construction. The son, Johnny B., somehow got separated from his father in the unfinished house as darkness fell.

"Daddy!" Johnny B. cried. He wandered through the framing, bumping into a sawhorse and tripping over tools. "Where are you?"

Finally Johnny B. heard his father's voice from below. "I'm in the basement."

The boy bent over a square opening in the floor. "Where are the stairs?"

"There are no stairs, son. You have to jump."

Johnny B. stared into a black void. "But I can't *see* you!"

"It's okay. I can see you. I've got my arms open. I'll catch you."

He hesitated a moment. (I held my breath here. In *Stories for Young Catholics,* anything could happen.) But Johnny B. leapt safely into his father's strong arms. I read on about how Johnny B. was saved because he had faith, and how we should trust in our Father, who is not visible to us.

"How the heck did the father get down there without steps?" I asked.

Fermina shrugged.

"Well, I never would have jumped," I told her. "If that was my daddy in the basement, no way would I jump."

Fermina raised her eyebrows. "¿Por qué no?"

I clapped the book shut. "Now, if it was Mama—no problem."

She sighed and pushed my bangs from my forehead. A phlegm-clotted cough rattled at the back of her throat. Fermina spat into her handkerchief, wiped her mouth, and settled on her side to rest. It was warm and close in her room, in her bed. Soon I fell asleep beside her, my arm around her waist. Fermina had many days like this, when we could read and talk. But some days, she had no voice, and she remained in bed, rising only to use the bathroom with the help of her heavy, rubber-tipped cane. On days when she was strong, she asked my father to call Irina to visit her.

Irina was almost as old as Fermina, but she was strong and stout. She wore skirts made from old quilts, so worn that in places the ticking sprouted out. Into these skirts, she always tucked the same turquoise velveteen blouse, cinching the waist with a conch belt. She had large hands, stained purple with ink, and she carried a burlap handbag decorated with el ojo de Dios, the series of diamonds woven to keep the devil away.

"Uh-*oh*," I'd tease Rita whenever Irina appeared on our porch. "You better hide. Here comes Irina with that ojo de Dios to send you straight back to hell!"

Unlike Fermina, who understood much, but spoke only a little English, Irina was fluent, according to my aunt Nilda, "in everything." When Irina slipped into Fermina's room and closed the door, I'd put my ear to the keyhole to listen to them speak a language that sounded like they were gargling. Fermina once mentioned that Irina was helping her prepare my gift.

One afternoon, Irina stepped out of Fermina's room, nearly stumbling over me as I knelt by the keyhole. "You are the one who likes animals," she said.

I nodded. "I like all kinds of animals—kittens, puppies, even a golden hamster, long or short hair, would be great."

"Fermina has a good gift for you."

"What about me?" asked Cary from the front room, where he sprawled on his stomach before a comic book, *The Adventures of Superman*. "What am I getting?"

Irina pointed a thick-jointed finger at my brother. "Nothing for you." Shaking her head, she stalked out the front door.

Cary rushed to Fermina's room. I followed, but lingered near the threshold, listening where Fermina couldn't see me.

"How come Irina says I don't get a gift?" he asked.

"Niño, ven aca." She pulled him close and fingered his dark brown curls. She explained that he has a father to give to him what he needs, but the girls—las pobrecitas—have no mother for this. He didn't need a gift from her, but she gave him her blessing before saying, "Besito por favor."

He reached to kiss her cheek. When he stepped out of her room and closed the door, he looked at me. "I *still* don't get it. I'm good, aren't I?"

I shrugged. Sometimes he was, but there were plenty of times when he was a huge pain in the nalgas. I sure wouldn't give a single thing to someone who pestered as much as he did with questions. "Maybe Fermina's talking about desaguadero."

"What's that?"

"Remember what Mama used to say? She'd say that girls aren't supposed to get mad and yell. But you, she said, you're different. You're a boy. You don't have desaguadero like we do, so it's okay for you to have fits."

He scratched his head. "But what does that have to do with getting a gift?"

"I'm not sure," I admitted. "But maybe because you don't have it, you can't get a gift." Whenever Mama cupped a cool hand over my mouth, stifling a howl of fury, the injustice of it stung more sharply than whatever had angered me, because she'd let Cary bellow, kick, throw things, and carry on until he wore himself into a sobbing heap.

"You girls have desaguadero," she'd explain. "He doesn't."

Afterward, I asked Bette what the *desaguadero* was, and she said it was like a drain or an outlet. I figured it must mean that girls have the thing that makes them behave, that keeps them under control, and boys don't have this. I remembered how my father would wobble home after work, stinking like cough syrup. My mother never wobbled. And Fermina seemed to have the most control. Even I learned to make good use of my desaguadero. When my father behaved the way he did at the cemetery, I didn't make a fuss. I simply flushed his hairbrush down the toilet as soon as we got home. Later that night, he had to dig the pipes out of the backyard while Cary held the flashlight. Listening to his curses in the dark, I thought what a useful thing it is, this desaguadero. I didn't mind having it one bit, especially if it meant I would get a gift.

SUBJECT: FERMINA/BURIAL PRACTICES
WPA: 6-13-38—DC: HMS
June 12, 1938
Words: 243

## BURIAL IN WALPI

Fermina also recalls the burial of her Hopi father in Walpi on the First Mesa. She remembers how his body was prepared for the underworld the Hopi called Maski. Prior to burial, her paternal grandmother washed his head with suds from mashed yucca root. As she bathed her son, the woman wept and whispered words into his ear that no one else could hear. Then she and her sisters dressed the body in a blanket, shrouding the face with a raw cotton cloth that had holes cut for the eyes and mouth. Fermina's grandmother next tied a string around the top of his head, inserting into this four turkey feathers pointing downward. The women finally arranged the body in the grave, sitting upright and facing east, in order for him to meet the kind *"bahana"* (or white guide) who is supposed to provide well-being to the entire village.

Fermina shuddered at the sight of her father's prepared corpse. Her mouth went dry with fright, and she could not swallow the wafer bread (*piki*) and mutton stew served at the feast. She longed to add her bowl to those holding the sheep's heart and yucca roots upon his grave, under a nimbus of blowflies. She says now that she does not care how she is buried, but she hopes the little ones will see her face unmasked. Fermina wants them to see her as she is, in life and death, and not to be afraid.

# TO TELL IT SLANT—BETTE: 1967

True, I don't always tell it straight, but I *never* snitch. That's why people tell me things they don't tell anyone else. And that's partly why guys dig me, even older guys like Jesse Ramírez, a junior at Pope John's. Why else would he show up at my side as our eighth-grade class lines up before school? Just to deliver a carton of chocolate milk? I don't *think* so, though I take the chilly waxed box and shove it in my blazer pocket.

He touches my elbow. "Meet me in back of the church in ten minutes."

I flash him my deep-dimpled Cover Girl smile, the one I've been working on over Easter vacation. He shoves his fists in his pockets and lopes off. Since I'm the shortest and youngest (just turned twelve) in class because I was double-promoted in third grade, I stand at the front of the line, and the other girls about bore holes into my back staring at me. I turn to give them this ho-hum look, like I am *so* used to cool guys coming up to me that it's almost tedious. And Jesse is supercool. Check it out—he's Golden Gloves, like Lance Álvarez, who made out with me at Bertha Villalobos's party. I figure Jesse probably has some message for me from Lance.

Jesse knows I'd never run to my teacher blabbing about some guy who told me to meet him. Instead, I tell Miss Weidermeyer that I'm "indisposed" and ask to be excused. I don't exactly know what "indisposed" means. I read it in a book and remember it caused a lot of embarrassment. Sure enough, Miss Weidermeyer's mouth drops open, and her cheeks get all pink. "You go right ahead," she says.

And I'm off, strolling through the corridor, enjoying the clatter of the metal taps I've fastened to my saddle oxfords until I'm near the front office. There, I slip off my shoes, duck down, and creep out the front door.

Outside, I jam my shoes on and dart around the parking lot to the rear of the church. I could cut straight across the lot, but I have to steer clear of the tree with toes, dead center of it. It's an old shaggy tree with crumbly bark and fernlike leaves. The roots—shaped like long gray toes with thick, smooth nails—are yanking up from the ground. I stay away from that tree after what it did to Blanca Hinojosa last fall.

I wasn't there at the time, but other kids in my class saw the whole thing. Supposedly, the tree got even with Blanca for chasing my sister Loretta with a booger. They say that old tree lifted a heavy toe—dripping with hairy, dirt-clotted roots—to trip Blanca, and then it snagged her jaw with a drooping limb, tumbling her flat on her back. The tortoiseshell comb in her bun gouged her scalp like an arc from the crown of thorns. Blanca's pretty well-known for being mean to quiet kids like my sister. Still, what that tree did to the girl freaks me out. First of all, I can't stand goriness, and they say the blood spurted out. I would have fainted on the spot. And, if that tree is on Loretta's side, I hate to think what it would do if it ever got its branches on me.

The church is dark and cool. I dab my fingertips in the holy water and make a quick sign of the cross. Then I step over to the pamphlet rack in the vestibule. It kills me how many brochures on dating, heavy petting, and premarital sex are written by priests, nuns, and brothers. Most have these serious block-letter titles printed over traffic-sign shapes: *STOP BEFORE IT'S TOO LATE! THE DANGERS OF DRINKING AND DATING! THE POINT OF NO RETURN!* I pick up a copy of *NECKING AND SIN!* Corny as the titles are, Rebecca Chávez sure could have used these at her ditching party last month, where we huffed airplane glue and guzzled Boone's Farm wine like it was Orange Nehi. When I went for the bathroom at her house, I pulled open the wrong door and found all these guys huddled around Becca. She was slumped on the bottom bunk in her brothers' room, judging from the cowboy wallpaper, and she had her blouse off. Becca's pretty heavy, but still I was astonished at how large her chi-chis were—the nipples staring back at me, huge and pink, like wounded eyes. She blinked at me like she'd just woken up and someone shouted, "Shut the goddamn door!" So I did. Then I found the bathroom and spewed up every sticky drop of wine.

Even remembering this makes me queasy. I'm relieved when Jesse hisses, "Bette, over here" from the stairs to the choir loft.

I smile and approach the stairwell.

"I thought you might not come." He cups my shoulder with a hot hand, pulls me down beside him on the steps. "You're nice to come."

I'm thinking, *Boy, is he ever friendly, but maybe he wants to whisper Lance's message in my ear.* Next thing, though, he's got his slimy lips all over my mouth, and he's breathing like he's just run a race. Soured chocolate milk coats his tongue as he forces it, like a hunk of meat, between my lips. I push away. "Hey, wait a minute."

But Jesse wraps his arms around me, fingering the back of my blouse for bra straps, which he plucks, as if this will loosen them.

I wrench free. "That hurts!"

"Come on, babe. Lance says you're cool." He dives for my neck, while forcing a knee between my legs. He yanks open my blouse, popping the buttons off. These bounce down the stairs, pinging like beans tossed into a pot.

That's when I know he's trying to do me like my uncle used to before I put a stop to it. Jesse jams his hand up my skirt, and I try throwing him off, but he's too heavy. I clench my fist and pop him in the eye. He pulls away, covering his face. I sink back, so we're seated side by side. I suck in a deep breath and jab an elbow in his side.

"Hey," he says. "No fair. I can't hit girls. I'm Golden Gloves, you know." He stands, hauling me up to face him, circling me with his arms. "I could *really* hurt you, babe." And I jerk my knee up, hard as I can, between his thighs. He grunts and collapses on the steps, curling up like a pre-born baby in one of those anti-abortion posters.

My taps hit the floor like gun blasts as I race through the vestibule and into the church. As I'm sprinting up the center aisle, I glance at the Jesus nailed on the cross over the altar. It's a goofy idea, but I'm hoping I'll catch his eye, trade a look, as if to ask: *Did you see that?* But the statue stares off somewhere over my head with a puzzled look on the blood-streaked face. Maybe he's supposed to be gazing into heaven and wondering, *Why hast thou forsaken me?*

Outside, I tie the tails of my blouse together and button my blazer all the way up. My heart's thumping like some animal squeezing up from my chest to push out through my throat.

At my back, a gravelly voice makes me jump. "What are you doing here?"

I lean over, clutching my guts like I'm sick.

"What are you running from?" Monsignor Hartwell drops his

cigarette and crushes it out with his heel. He's seen me hightailing it, so he's not likely to buy that I'm all that ill, or even indisposed. "What's wrong?" he says.

Sure, he's acting all concerned, but if I fink on Jesse, I'll just get myself in trouble; so I go, "My grandma died." And I burst into tears.

Monsignor marches me straight to the school office. Weirdly, my sister Loretta is already there, hunched like an owl on the bench before the secretary, Mrs. Ortega, at her desk, and my father's standing by the window, gazing out the venetian blinds.

"H'ita," my dad says when he sees me. "Sit down. I got some bad news."

I sink to the bench beside Loretta.

My dad takes off his glasses and wipes the lenses with a handkerchief. "Fermina passed away this morning." Then he folds me into his arms.

"Why, Bette already knew," says Monsignor as he reaches under his cassock for a pack of Salem cigarettes. "Anyone mind if I smoke?"

Mrs. Ortega juts a thumb at the back office. "Mother Superior doesn't allow smoking."

Monsignor taps out a cigarette, extends the pack to my father. "Care for one?"

Salem is not his brand, so my father waves it away. "What do you mean Bette already knew? Knew what?"

"Bette already knew that her grandmother passed," Monsignor explains. He flicks his silver lighter and sucks the flame into his filter-tipped cigarette.

"You put that out, Monsignor, or I'm going to buzz Mother Superior." Mrs. Ortega pulls an orange plastic ashtray from a desk drawer and thrusts it at him.

He takes the ashtray, examining it as if it's some artifact from an ancient civilization. "She told me her grandmother had died."

My father shakes his head. "But how—"

"Sometimes children, like animals, can sense such things. It's one of the mysteries of life." The monsignor gestures with his cigarette, like he's making a smoke diagram to show how this works. Bluish spumes stream from his nostrils, reminding me of the brass dragon that Fermina—*oh, Fermina!*—uses for burning incense.

It hits me—she's gone! Thick, hot tears blind me, and I wail. My father hands me his kerchief and pats my back.

"My Lord," the monsignor says.

"That's it." Mrs. Ortega pushes an intercom button and then leans forward to speak into the box on her desk. "Mother, would you step out here for a moment."

The monsignor grinds his cigarette in the ashtray and then pockets it—ashes, stub and all—in his cassock. He reaches for the window, but he can't get it open, though he mangles the blinds trying.

Mother Superior steps out of her office, her pale, wimple-pinched face looking harassed, and then confounded. I can only imagine what she thought at the sight of us in that smoky room—me ratcheting up the decibels, my father thumping my back to get me to stop, Loretta hunched and rocking, and the monsignor working at the window, as though trying to fling it wide to escape the lot of us.


As Dad steers our red-and-white finned Chevrolet Impala onto Alvarado Street—me up front and Loretta, Cary, and Rita in the backseat—I let up on the crying, which is making my forehead ache.

As soon as I stop blubbering, my father says, "Why did you say that?"

"Say what?"

"About Fermina."

I draw a shuddery breath. "When I saw you and Loretta, I figured she died."

"Not that." He switches to Spanish, so the others won't understand.

"Then what?" I say.

"Dígame en español." My father lowers his voice.

"How come you're talking in Spanish?" pipes Cary.

Loretta and Rita can be so stubborn I have to pound bruises into their arms, but at least they know when to keep quiet. Not Cary. He's the all-time, family champion, blabbermouth king of the living pests, and no amount of sibling brutality can stop his questions. I give the old man credit for being patient with the kid. When he's fed up, Dad just says, as he does now, "I do *not* know. I just do *not* know."

When my father parks the car, he tells the younger kids to go inside and get something to eat. I reach for the door handle, but Dad grabs my arm. "Espérate."

So I stay put, my head bowed like I'm about to receive a blessing, or a blow.

The back doors slam shut, and the younger kids lumber for the house. My father says again, "Tell me why you said that."

I'm still confused, so I go, "Said what?"

"How come you told Monsignor your *grandmother* died?"

"He misunderstood or something. He probably just assumed she was our grandmother because she's old. What's the big deal?"

But he doesn't answer. Instead, he hauls himself out, leaving me alone in the car, staring at the glove compartment.

\*     \*     \*

In the living room, Aunt Nilda and my uncle José, The Nasty Thing, are on the couch. Nilda's crying on the phone while The Nasty Thing watches roller derby on television with the volume turned low, though everyone knows that when a person dies, we're supposed to observe luto, and that means no television, no record players, and no radio. Even the mirrors are supposed to be covered with towels, so you don't get distracted from your sorrow by trying out new hairstyles and lipsticks. Turning the volume down must be The Nasty Thing's one concession to luto. I'm surprised Nilda lets him get away with it, but she's all absorbed in her phone call.

The Nasty Thing sips whiskey from a Flintstone jelly glass. The smell of it stings my nostrils from across the room. In fact, he reeks like a bullfrog that's been swimming in a barrel of booze. Loretta says he looks like Hitler would have looked if he'd let himself go to pot, and I can see this in the razor-parted black hair, the broom-bristle moustache, and those fanatical eyes. But really, he's just a lardy, liver-splotched bullfrog in a gabardine suit. He's what would have happened if a princess kissed a toad and it became human in all its "toadishness."

Loretta slinks in from the kitchen and climbs onto Nilda's lap. At almost eleven, she's too old for this, but does she care? Her eyelids are pink and puffy, but she looks pretty snug, nesting her head in the hollow of Nilda's shoulder. The Nasty Thing stares at the skaters thundering around the rink, trying to throw one another over the rails. He sips his drink and strokes the ceramic panther with fake emerald eyes that we keep on the coffee table. When a commercial for Alka-Seltzer flashes on the screen, José's gaze slithers around the room. "Where's Rita and Sophie?"

I shrug. "No idea."

"Qué mentira," my father says, entering from the hall. "You

know they're in the kitchen with Cary, eating everything in sight." Lately, Cary, who turned eight in the fall, has been given the job of feeding Sophie and wiping up after her, since he's pretty useless otherwise.

"Pues, I *know*," Nilda says into the phone. "Es que, she was really suffering con el bronchitis and then the pneumonia. She could hardly breathe toward the end. But never did she complain. Nunca. Not even once." She smooths Loretta's wavy hair, listening a moment before repeating, "Pues, I *know*."

Rita and Cary, who's got Sophie by the hand, wander in from the kitchen. Cary has grape jelly commas in the crooks of his mouth, but at least he's run a washcloth over Sophie's face. Her dark curls are still damp at the hairline.

Rita flings herself into my uncle's lap. Loretta and I have a tough time getting through to her. We've told her over and over that even if it starts out all cozy—with him tickling your knee, squeezing your thigh—sooner or later the funny business starts. By then, it's too hard to get away. Though he tries to wait until he's alone with one of us, he'll start this stuff in front of anyone. I bet he's proud of how sly he is, pinching, grabbing, and wheezing like that busted harmonica Cary found in the park.

Loretta and I stay clear of The Nasty Thing. In fact, Loretta looks at him as though he's the dark spot on the carpet where Cary vomited after too much Halloween candy. She won't even talk to him, but I will, just to show I'm not afraid. It's been years since he's tried that crap on me. I never snitch, but I do bite, and he still has white scars from my teeth on his knuckle.

"Come on, Rita." I tug her arm, try to lead her away. "Time to go out and play."

"No." She burrows in The Nasty Thing's shirt, and he gives me a look that is the adult equivalent of *Nyahh, nyahh!*

*"Now,"* Loretta tells her. "You better go with Bette right now."

"Shut up, you sonamabitch," she says.

Nilda drops the phone and lunges from the couch. *"What did you say?"*

Wisely, Rita shuts her trap. Her eyes, already huge, bulge out more, as if ready to pop from the sockets. She *knows* she stepped in it big-time. Since our neighbor Shirley started babysitting Sophie and Rita, Nilda hasn't been around much. She doesn't know about Rita's latest habit: cursing. She picked it up from the construction workers who came to remodel the front bungalows before Mr. Huerta's daughters moved in. The old man thought it was cute at first to see this little kid swearing like a sailor, but the rest of us got tired of it mighty fast. He's finally getting fed up, too. "Don't talk like that," he murmurs from the recliner, where he's settled himself behind the newspaper. The headline reads: ALI WON'T SERVE; LOSES BOXING TITLE, and under it is a photo of that good-looking boxer, the one who used to be called Cassius Clay, arms up and fists clenched, in a boxing ring. I can just barely make out the words "cowardly," "stripped of title," and "criminal prosecution" in the column. None of it makes any sense.

Nilda shakes her head like she can't figure out why Dad doesn't paddle the kid on the spot. She's his oldest sister. Like me, she's used to taking matters into her own hands. Since he doesn't budge, she tears Rita off The Nasty Thing and hauls her into the bathroom to wash out her mouth.

Before Rita's feet hit the floor, she's sobbing. "No! No! I didn't mean it!" and *"Fermina,* help me!" Rita's howls shake the house. My father folds the paper, tucks it under his arm, and exits through the front door. His lighter clicks as soon as he steps on the porch.

"It's about time," Cary says.

Four-year-old Sophie wags a finger. "She's a weally bad wabbit."

"Come here, cutie." The Nasty Thing pats his lap. "Let me hold you a tiny bit."

"No!" I grab Sophie's arm. "Nap time. Loretta, it's your turn to read."

As I lead Sophie to the bedroom, I peek in the doorway at Fermina's room, her mattress already stripped and folded in half, and her maple trunk bound with hemp for storage. After that strange business in the car, I'm wondering, who was she and where'd she go? I always tell the younger kids that our mother flew up to heaven when she died over a year ago. But any dummy can tell that's pure bullshit. How the heck would I know where dead people go? All I can say for sure is that Fermina's not here with us. Only this morning, she gave me a dry peck on the cheek before school, and a few hours later, her bare mattress is doubled over like a fat man enjoying a joke.

"Here." I hand Loretta *The Story of Ferdinand* when we get to the bedroom we share with Rita and the baby. I kind of hate thinking it, but now that Fermina's gone, Sophie and Rita will probably move into her small bedroom. Loretta and I will have this room to ourselves. "You read," I tell Loretta.

She plops on her bed, opens the book. Sophie kicks off her shoes and climbs beside her. I sit on my bed, my face in my hands. "Fermina's really gone," I say to Loretta, who hasn't bothered to ask how I'm bearing up, let alone throw an arm around my shoulders to comfort me, as I would have done for her.

Instead, she begins reading, *"Once upon a time in Spain..."*

"Fermina's gone. Don't you get it?" I tell her. "We'll never see her again." But Loretta continues reading until Sophie's milky, blue-veined eyelids flutter shut.

"Don't you even care?" I whisper because Sophie's nearly asleep.

Loretta reads to the end, even after Sophie's slow breathing thickens into snoring. Then she shuts the book and smiles, as though pleased by the way the story turned out.

"Why are you like this?" I want to knock Loretta all the way back to Ash Wednesday. She was the same when our mother died. Acting all calm and well-behaved, so Nilda had to go on and on about what a good girl she was, what a *big* girl she was, while the rest of us—even the baby—acted like cartoon characters who'd had rockets shot through their stomachs, leaving only the landscape showing. But we couldn't grab our collars and shake ourselves out like those characters can to make themselves whole again. We had to walk around for months with that big gap in the middle and the ache of the wind whistling through.

One morning, right after our mother died, I rushed up and tackled Loretta from behind on the way to school. Books and papers scattered, her lunch box flew, landing with a splintery crack. I tore into her like a tornado—bloodied her nose, mangled her glasses, split her lip, pulled her hair until she cried like a decent person. Now I say, "I'm not going to kick your ass this time. You can choke on your tears, for all I care."

Loretta slips out of the bed and crooks a finger like she wants to show me something. I'm still pissed, but I'm curious, too, so I trail her out to the kitchen. She springs open the silverware drawer, and, naturally, a roach, fat and waxy as a date, plops out. She taps it with the toe of her shoe, making a crunching sound.

And I say, "So what?"

She stoops to touch the mess lightly with her finger. The cucaracha gathers itself up, shivers, and streaks toward a crack in the baseboard. Loretta looks up at me. "See?"

"You didn't kill it all the way."

"Fermina's gift," she whispers.

"*Come on.* That thing was barely stunned."

"At school," Loretta says, "I touched a fly trapped in a spider's web, and it wriggled free. And then, they called me to the office to tell me Fermina died, and that's when I knew I *cured* that fly. I'd gotten her gift."

"Ugh! Why would you touch a *fly*?" I never heard such bullshit. Why would Fermina give Loretta the gift of…gift of *what*? Curing bugs? What kind of gift is that? If she could *kill* insects, especially the mega-tropolis living under this roof, then *that* might be a gift worth having.

"She knows I love animals and bugs, so she gave me the gift to make them well." Loretta grins, looking all dopey and dreamy. "I bet you got a gift, too, maybe something to do with what you're already good at."

To be honest, I never believed poor old Fermina when she talked about our gifts, figuring she made it up because she had no money for presents and didn't want us to think she'd forgotten about us. I know how it is when you have to stretch things, slant them sideways, so you don't look bad—nothing wrong with that.

On the other hand, what if I did get some kind of gift? If Loretta got one, I would, too. What kind of gift would that be? I'm a pretty good fighter, but jeez, I wouldn't want boxing skills. How embarrassing it would be if I rose up the ranks in Golden Gloves! What if I had to climb in the ring with Lance and knock him cold? The world title's up for grabs now, and no one would try drafting me into the service. What if *I* stepped into old Cassius Clay's shoes?

Maybe my gift is love, true love, like between me and Lance, whose older brother, Frank—come to think of it—is also pretty cute. I shake my head. Sometimes my thoughts are so goofy you'd think *I* was the little kid who didn't know any better.

*    *    *

"Filth!" Nilda shrieks so loud that my back teeth ache. It's Saturday. The Nasty Thing dropped her off at our house superearly with her fuchsia travel case, and she's been going after the dirt in our house ever since. Rita and I linger over our bologna sandwiches, watching Nilda clean the kitchen. There's something weirdly relaxing about watching someone scrub, scour, and scream in horror, even if it hurts your molars. Now she's got her head stuck all the way under the kitchen sink, where she's wiping—of all things—the wall *behind* the pipes. "Filthy, nasty!" Every speck of grime shocks and thrills her at the same time. "I never seen such mess! I don't know what your father's paying that...that... marana cochina, that beatnik, but somebody should grab her by the ankles and shake every penny out of her pockets. It's a pigsty here. No wonder you got cucarachas galore."

"Tía," I say, remembering the exchange with my father in the car, "was Fermina *related* to us?"

*Bam!* Nilda conks her head on the bottom of the sink and crawls out backward from underneath, rubbing her crown. "Bah! What kind of nonsense is this?"

"Yesterday Dad said—"

"Fermina, rest her soul, was nothing to us." Nilda crosses herself and kisses her gloved thumb. "You know that. She worked for the family. That's all."

"Yeah, but—"

"She was la criada. And that's all there is to it," Nilda says, her voice rising.

It's pretty weird for a maid to stay in bed all day and have her meals brought in on a tray, the way we did for Fermina toward the end, but I say, "I didn't mean anything."

She points at me. "Don't you start spreading this around, you hear me? And you, too, Rita, you forget about these fairy tales." Nilda dives back under the sink. "Instead of making up stories, you girls ought to mix up some boiling water with Clorox…"

This is my cue to get the hell out, unless I want to find myself going at crud behind the stove with an old toothbrush. I tug Rita's sleeve. She's still sulky about yesterday's mouth-washing, but she knows what's up when Nilda mentions boiling water and Clorox. We tiptoe out the screen door, easing it shut so it doesn't slap against the frame. Loretta's in the bedroom—she can help Nilda wage the war on filth and keep an eye on Sophie, too, while the old man and Cary are getting haircuts. We make our way next door, where Shirley, who cleans house and babysits for us, lives with her old grandmother and her daughter, Cathy.

Our house is in this courtyard behind four stucco houses. The bungalows face each other, and ours, the largest, sits behind these and looks out onto the street. Shirley has the small two-bedroom bungalow on the right-hand side, which is identical to the one it faces on the left, where Ethel, a nice drunk lady lives. The front houses are occupied by the landlord Mr. Huerta's two grown daughters and their husbands.

Rita can play with Cathy, while Shirley practices on me. She's studying to be a beautician and needs all these practice hours for her certificate. Though she's already old—almost twenty-five—Shirley is more of a friend to me than a neighbor. We watch *American Bandstand* together and compete with each other to learn the new dance steps. Much as I love dancing, I look forward to the beauty sessions in Shirley's bathroom even more.

We round the courtyard toward Shirley's bungalow, and there's her grandmother Señora Trejo hollering her brains out in Spanish from the side yard. "¡Huevón, perezoso, sinvergüenza!" And I figure she's cornered another lizard with her garden hoe. The old lady is hell on lizards. She chops them in the middle, so the two halves writhe apart. We have a mess of lizards around here, and I have seen her chop at least a dozen, but I never heard her talk to one before, other than saying "¡tómalo!" as she brings down the hoe. We make our way around the side of Shirley's bungalow, and there's the old lady raising her hoe, but not over some doomed lizard.

A man I've never seen before lifts his hands in surrender. He's wearing a black bowling shirt with gray panels in the front, shiny pants, also black, and pointy patent leather shoes with—give me a break!—tassels.

"Oiga," he's saying. "Watch it with the hoe."

This releases a high-pitched stream of Spanish from Señora Trejo. She slices the air, promising to halve his heart.

He steps back, shouting, "Hey, Shirley! I got to talk to you!"

In the bungalow's front window, a beige curtain flutters and drops, like an eyelid blinking open, then shut.

Shirley's grandmother charges forth on her sturdy viejita shoes, black dusty leather jobs that lace all the way up the ankles. She raises the hoe over her tight nest of braids and brings it down—blade upturned—with a muffled *thunk* on the meaty part of his shoulder.

"¡Ay, vieja!" He spins around, and she strikes him again on the nalgas. "Stop, okay! I'm going already."

Señora Trejo lands a last blow to the ribs before the guy stomps off, muttering curses. Even after his car's engine churns, the old woman keeps waving the hoe, looking—except for her flower-print housecoat, support hose, and old-lady shoes—like Saint Michael driving off a dragon in Rita's *Catechism in Pictures* storybook.

Señora Trejo spits in the dirt. "¡Basura!"

Then she notices us staring at her, and her brown face softens, pleating like crepe paper. "Pues, vengan, vengan. Pasen p'a dentro." Though violent with lizards, and apparently with strange men, too, she's usually kind to us. Today she makes me nervous, especially since she's still armed with the hoe. I ask if we should come back later.

"Pues, vengan." She climbs the concrete steps and opens the door for us. "¿Tienen hambre?" Señora Trejo leans the hoe against the wall, so it will be handy for next time.

Rita and I shake our heads. "No, gracias." Watching a man beaten with a hoe does not make a person think of food.

Once inside the darkened kitchen, Rita heads for Cathy's room, while I exercise my Spanish with the old woman. I listen to her lo siertos y qué lástimas about Fermina's passing and ask about her reumatismo, until Shirley hollers that she's ready for me. Relieved, because I have run out of small talk at the same time as I have run out of Spanish, I slip into the bathroom.

Shirley points at her makeup tray, hairdressing kit, manicure bag, and stack of folded towels. "I saw you guys in front and started laying out stuff." She whips an old sheet over me, clipping it with a hairpin. "What'll it be today, Bette?"

"How about you?" I say. She looks so pretty with her black hair all fluffy around her pale powdery face and her dark eyes lined so they tilt like a cat's.

"*You* choose—geisha, Cleopatra, secretary."

"I mean I want to look like *you*—your hair, your eyes, everything." I'm thinking if she does me up good, I might look like I'm related to her.

She laughs. "Too easy. Man, I could do that in the dark."

"Okay," I say on a whim. "Let's turn off the light."

"Serious?"

"Yeah, let's see if you really can make me look like you in the dark."

"Not completely dark, though. I got these candles. It might be kind of nice, different anyway." Shirley paws through a drawer and pulls out a few long tapers. She lights these, dribbles wax to stick them upright on the counter. I flick off the light.

Usually, Shirley's bathroom is pretty awful-looking: greenish paint flaking off the walls, mold-peppered shower curtain, and chipped toilet seat. Now the flames flickering in the mirror shift and twist our shadows on the walls, making me feel like I'm in a magical otherworld, instead of a grubby, too small bathroom.

Shirley shakes a bottle of foundation cream. "Just the face or the works?"

I settle on the toilet lid. "The whole works."

While we're waiting for the foundation to dry, she takes a rat-tail comb and starts teasing out my hair. "Guess you saw him out there."

I nod. "Who was he?"

She goes, "Cathy's father, my ex–old man."

"*That* was Cathy's father?" The way Cathy has described her father—smart, handsome, generous, and kind—I pictured John F. Kennedy, Elvis, and Jesús Cristo all rolled into one, not some corny guy in pointed shoes.

"Hush, I don't want Cathy to hear." She brushes my cheeks with a fine powder, which tickles my nose.

"Your grandmother sure doesn't like him," I say.

"Because he doesn't pay us no support like he's supposed to. Sure, he gives Cathy tons of junk, but he won't pay support because we don't let him see her."

"Why don't you let him see her?"

"Because the cat won't pay support."

"You could let him see her once and then see if he pays."

"Oh, he'd *like* that, wouldn't he?" She rattles a can of Aqua Net, before hissing a cloud of it over my head. The smell of it coats my tongue with a sharp metallic taste.

After my hair is styled, Shirley brings out the nail polish. She lifts one of my hands, splaying the fingers. "You're peeling your skin again, aren't you?"

"Not that much." I have the habit of ripping my cuticles and shredding the top layers of skin from my fingers to the palms. This gives my hands a raw, marbled look, kind of like boiled ham, but it's no big deal. Some kids bite their nails; others stutter. I just happen to peel off my skin.

"I'm going to tell your dad to put those medicated gloves on you again." Shirley worries that I'll get an infection. When she gangs up with my father, they make me wear greasy Minnie Mouse gloves, which stink of menthol.

"Come on, Shirley. I swear I'll stop. I've just been nervous with Fermina dying and Nilda around, making me all jumpy."

"Man, what *is* her problem? When I took over empanadas last night, she acted like I'd come to rob the place." Shirley pushes back my cuticles. "Very uncool."

"She's okay, really," I say, thinking of my uncle The Nasty Thing and how hard it must be to put up with him, enough to turn anyone into a maniac about filth. "She just gets overexcited with dirt in the house."

"But that house is spotless! I keep it cleaner than I do my own place!"

"It's just Nilda. The filth's mostly in her head," I say, and then I pause before asking, "Say, Shirley, what do you know about Fermina?"

"Well, she was old, no? Over a hundred, wasn't she?"

"Yeah," I say, "but who was she? Like, where did she come from?" Maybe if I figure out who Fermina was, then I'll find out about that gift thing Loretta brought up.

Shirley shrugs. "Some kind of Indian, I think. She didn't talk too much about herself, but Fermina was cool people."

Sudden pounding on the bathroom door makes us both jump. "Mommy! Mommy!" Cathy cries on the other side. "Mommy, Rita said a bad word."

Shirley yanks open the door, and Cathy tumbles into her arms, bawling and blowing snot bubbles from her blunt little nose.

"What's wrong, honey?"

"Rita said a bad word to me!" Cathy blubbers. "She said the S-word."

"The S-word?"

"Shit!" Cathy buries her cowlike face in Shirley's sweatshirt, wailing like someone's whipped her with a tire iron. "She said I'm full of *shit*!" Over her shoulder, I spy Rita in the hallway, a pinched look on her face.

I unclasp the pin and pull the sheet off. "I better take her home."

Shirley's on her knees, rocking Cathy in her arms, trying to calm her down. She nods at me. "Come over later," she says, "so I can finish."

"I'll try." I step around her. "Sorry, Cathy, and Rita is, too."

"I *am* not," Rita calls from the hall. "I'm *not* one bit—"

I stopper her mouth with one hand and scoop her up with my other arm. She's tall for her age, but skinny and light. As I'm lugging her out the bungalow, and she's trying to bite my hand, I don't forget to thank Señora Trejo for having us over and I wish her buenas tardes.

When we're outside where no one can see, I dump Rita on the grass and push her down when she struggles to stand up. "You stupid," I say. "I can't take you anywhere." I sock her arm, which sends her into hysterics. What kills me about Rita is how she acts all big and bad, but when it comes right down to it, she's the biggest gallina in the family, next to Cary. I don't understand why a person who's scared of getting hurt is always talking such garbage that you have no choice but to beat the crap out of her. I throw a few last chingazos, real mild ones because she's such a freaking crybaby.

When she catches her breath, she says, "I'm going to tell on you."

"Yeah, you go ahead, Rita, and I'll really let you have it," I tell her as I head for the house. I open the screen door and close it behind me in a calm way, though I'm worried that Nilda might overreact. My aunt doesn't have kids of her own, so these scuffles freak her out, as if we're going at each other with chain saws.

Nilda's sitting at the table sorting beans for supper. *Ping, ping, ping*—she's dropping the good beans into the pot and plucking out dirt plugs, half-beans and rusty-looking bits. I put my arm around her shoulders and say, "You make the best beans, Tía." I plant a sweet kiss on her cheek. "No one gets them as tender and tasty as you do."

She smiles and glances up at me. "My *God,* what happened to your face? And your head? You look like a streetwalker!"

I pat my hair. "I was just playing beauty shop. That's all."

Outside, Rita is working up to a full-bodied squall for when she parades in.

"¿Qué pasa?" Nilda squints through the screen. "Is that Rita?"

She already sounds excited, so I say, "Yeah, she fell from the avocado tree again."

"Cómo molesta. She knows she's not supposed to be up there."

"I *know*," I say, making my voice rise from the senselessness of it. "I told her to come down, but she wouldn't listen."

"¡Dios mío!" Nilda rises for the door as Rita slams in, sobbing so much she's hiccoughing. Part of me wants to applaud; she's giving such a great performance. Nilda gathers the kid in her arms, saying, "Did you sprain anything when you fell?"

"I didn't fall. Bette beat me up!"

Nilda shoots me a look. I raise my eyebrows and shake my head. Nilda fingers Rita's head like it's a melon she might buy. "Where did you hurt yourself?"

Rita sucks in a huge breath and says, "I didn't hurt *myself*. *Bette* hurt me!"

"I did not."

Nilda glances from Rita to me, as though trying to decide which one to believe. She's likely leaning toward old Rita, since I am not exactly famous for telling the truth. Rita, on the other hand, is nearly a menace with honesty. But everyone knows there's always a first lie, and a lie to avoid getting in trouble is the usual first lie.

Then Rita blurts, "You big old bitch!"

"¡Jabón!" shrieks Nilda. "Run, get me the Palmolive!"

I sprint for the green bar on the edge of the tub. It's nice and soft, frothy even, from sitting in a puddle of water. I hand it to Nilda without even wiping off the runny parts. Rita's yowling makes my ears buzz like I'm sitting too close to the fireworks on the Fourth of July.

Sophie wakes and starts screaming, too, so I slip into the bedroom to get her, and there's Loretta, right on her bed nearby, reading a book and holding a pillow over her ears. She can't be bothered to comfort Sophie, even though she's just a few steps away. I calm the kid down, and Sophie gives me a strange look as she takes in the effects of my beauty treatment. She touches my cheek. "Pobrecita."

Loretta lets out a snort of laughter.

"You mean *bonita*." I'm always trying to teach Sophie the right Spanish words for things. "*Bonita* means pretty. *Pobrecita* means poor thing."

Sophie's brown eyes are sharp and alert, though her cheeks are flushed, damp with sleep. "I know," she says, patting my hand. "Pobrecita."

Of course, Loretta finds this hilarious, and I guess it is kind of amusing, so I laugh, too. I'd hate to give the kid a complex. Then I turn to Loretta and ask what she's reading. I don't like her taking my *Valley of the Dolls* without asking.

She mumbles, "Dog dizzies."

"Dog Dizzies?"

"*Dog Diseases.* It's a book about dogs and why they get sick. I got it from the library, if you have to know every detail."

I flash on what she told me earlier. She can't possibly believe that business about healing animals. No way. "Hey, you want to go to the store with me? We could take Sophie in the stroller." It'd be a shame to waste this makeup job and hairdo on just the family. But I wouldn't want to stroll down Alvarado by myself like this — even pushing a baby stroller. "I got some money. We could get an Eskimo Pie, split it three ways."

Loretta glances up, a suspicious look on her face.

"Maybe we could go over to Desiree's." Someone should see me like this, even if it's just my ex–best friend from way back in the fourth grade.

"Fermina's Rosary is tonight," she says.

"I know that, dummy. We'd be back in time. What do you say? Want to go?"

"Not really," Loretta says, turning back to *Dog Diseases.*

After dinner, Nilda steps into our room, all serious, to perch on my bed and talk with us. "Now, it's up to you girls," she says, "whether you want to go to Fermina's Rosary or if you want to stay here with Mrs. Huerta and the little kids, and you want to remember her as she was."

"Remember her as she was." Loretta sometimes repeats words or phrases she likes to herself.

"You want to stay then?"

"No, I want to go," Loretta says.

"How come Shirley's not watching the kids?" I ask.

"Pues, your daddy asked her, and she said the little girl is sick."

"Calfie?" asks Loretta, mispronouncing the name on purpose to emphasize the poor kid's resemblance to a small cow.

"Yeah, she's got trouble with her stomach."

"*Stomachs,*" says Loretta, who can be pure mean.

"I'm going to the Rosary," I say, ignoring her. To be honest, I don't enjoy seeing dead people in caskets, and I'm not wild about kneeling around the various hard parts of the church floor and praying at all the Stations of the Cross, though I can't remember if this is just a Lent thing or how we pray for the dead. But how would it look if Loretta goes and I stay home? It might seem like I don't care about Fermina that much or like Loretta's more mature than me.

"Bueno, if you want to go, you girls better clean up. You better comb out that, that rat's nest, Bette, and put in some braids," Nilda says. "Scrape that junk off your face, too." She stands, smoothing her skirt. "Afterward, we're going to Stella's, so you want to look decent over there. She's got that nice boy, that Norberto. Remember him?"

Loretta and I curl our upper lips. We remember Norberto all right. He's the kid who likes to strip the blouses off our Barbie dolls to touch what he calls their "titty bones." Last I'd heard, he'd had an operation for the growth in his nose, which caused him to whistle when he breathed. "I thought he was in the hospital."

"He's well now," says Nilda as she rises from the bed. "Hurry up and get ready."

"What are you wearing?" I ask. Of all my aunts, Nilda has the best clothes, though she doesn't make too much money working as a nurse's aide for an old doctor, and The Nasty Thing is mainly a bum.

"I'm wearing that black linen dress with the turban hat and my oxblood pumps and clutch. You think that's okay, for luto?"

I picture it all and nod my head, though I've some doubts about the oxblood pumps and clutch with black linen. But if anyone can carry these colors off, it's Nilda. Jackie Kennedy has nothing on my aunt, when it comes to style.

"Now, come on, you two better get ready. The Rosary's at seven," she says before stepping out of our room.

I stand before the closet, trying to decide what to wear, and Loretta puts a marker in her book. She strips off her shorts and shirt, pulls a navy shift over her head, kicks off her tennis shoes, and steps into black loafers. She doesn't even change her socks! The whole process takes a minute. Then she flops back on the bed and reopens *Dog Diseases*.

"You're going to go like that?" I ask.

She turns a page. "Yeah."

"But you didn't even look in the mirror."

She shrugs.

"You should at least brush your hair."

"Hmm," she murmurs.

"You look weird. Your glasses are crooked, your legs are too skinny, those socks don't match that dress, and your knees are grimy."

She doesn't even bother to answer, much less jump up and make herself more presentable. What's the point of being a big sister to someone like this? She never listens, never takes my advice. I might as well nag at a brick. The worst thing is, once we get to the Rosary, it will be "la Loretta" this and "la Loretta" that and "qué bonita" and "qué linda" all over the place. It's enough to make me puke. All of the aunts and uncles will be practically standing in line to pinch her cheeks. "Peaches and cream," they'll tell her, or "que rosita." While I'm so freckled and brown, I might as well be coated with invisible paint.

Though I hate to, I duck in the bathroom to undo Shirley's beautiful work. I have to really scrub, too, because it never occurs to my father to buy stuff like cold cream. I can't wait to turn fifteen, so I can work and fill the medicine chest with Noxema, Clearasil, Aqua Net, Dippity-Do, and some deodorant other than Right Guard, and Kotex, for when the time comes, and Nair, or at least some decent razors.

I brush out my hair, making it as dull as a dead cat's fur. I hope people at the Rosary will think mourning has taken a toll on its luster. As I'm pinning it into a bun, I hear Nilda's voice buzzing through the wall. She's in my father's room. I barely make out what she's saying, but I hear my name. I crack the door open without a sound.

"What were you thinking, hombre?" Nilda says.

"I didn't tell her nothing," my father says.

"Por Dios, cállate la boca," Nilda warns him. "Do you want everyone to hear?"

"Déjame solo."

"This is not a good time. Leave it alone. That's all I am saying."

"Ay, Nilda." My father sighs in such a way that I know he will do as she says. His doorknob jiggles, and I ease the bathroom door shut.

I claim the front seat for the ride to the church. I usually sit up front and try to keep my eyes off street signs and billboards to avoid car sickness. Reading these even from up front can make me lose my dinner in a flash. Plus, my father drives at such a crawl that every stop, every start, every turn, feels like the swell of a wave in the middle of a lazy sea. I swear the man relies on the earth's rotation for momentum. And, naturally, he's puffing on a stinky Camel.

I say, "Hey, Dad, can't we roll down a window?"

"Nope, can't do it."

"The smoke's making me sick. It's like a gas chamber in here."

"Can't do it."

When we finally get to the church, the lot is full, but my father circles and circles like a vulture, until a pickup truck pulls out of a choice space in front, and Dad swoops in. He stubs out his cigarette, turns off the engine, and says, "Okay, get out."

As soon as we step into the church, I about gag on the incense clouds boiling up from the thurible. Loretta claims to like the stuff. She's sniffing at it with such pleasure that I want to punch her arm. The hot, stuffy church fills with the same faces that I saw for my mother's Rosary and funeral over a year ago.

This group is mainly a herd of oldsters who speak a lilting no-pause Spanish that jams paragraphs together to sound like a single, superlong word. The women are overly perfumed. They wear hazardous costume jewelry that jabs you when they hug, and they are always hugging. The men are devoted to cheap, shiny suits and ugly ties. Needless to say, there are zero cute guys among them. Stella's son, Norberto, with his vast nostrils and connecting eyebrows, is the only young one in the group.

As we make for a front pew, the priest is setting up. He's new to the rectory, just came over from Spain. He rides a motorcycle and owns a leather jacket. People freak out and scream "Hippie!" when an ordinary male lets his hair get shaggy, but a priest can get away with braids like Sitting Bull. This guy's sun-streaked locks touch the collar of his cassock, and when he forgets something from the vestry, he shakes his head, cracking a long-dimpled grin. Yep, it's pretty sad when the hottest guy at church is the priest.

Sadder still is Fermina's coffin in front of the communion altar, the powder blue lid propped open. I catch a glimpse of the cream-colored satin lining, the stiff lacy trim, and that's all. I don't want to see more.

I wish Rita had come with us. With the stink of incense, the heat, and the gallons of scent dousing the women here, I know I'd be able to count on her to faint. She is a first-class fainter, even at age six, and church is her element, where she does her best work. Whenever Rita keels over, I haul her to the bathroom in back, where we happily wait out the service.

I expect we are going to sink to our knees and start the praying, but my father and Nilda lead us past the first pew and up toward the coffin. The last time I looked in a coffin, my mother was inside, holding a prayer book; rosary beads threaded through her long fingers, but she looked nothing at all like my mama. I stare at the floor as we file toward Fermina's coffin, but my eyes wander over and I see her. "Fermina. *Fermina?*"

The church full of faces, the coffin, the altar boy swinging the thurible, Jesus on his cross with painted blood dripping to his chin—all of it swirls and dips like I'm riding the whirligig at Pacific Ocean Park. I hear people speaking, but I don't understand what they're saying. Voices break apart. And then Loretta whispers, in a slow, strange voice: *"Remember her as she was."*

A cool, sparkling darkness covers me, like I'm wearing a dazzling cloak of stars strung together by loose black webbing. Maybe I'm dead? But I hear a siren whine, cars whooshing past, and Loretta scoffing, "No, you're not dead, stupid. You're in the car."

"What happened?" I feel groggy, but rested, like a shipwreck survivor washed onto the broad upholstered lap of the front seat.

"You had some kind of fit," says Loretta, nose-deep in *Dog Diseases,* my father's big ring of keys nested in her lap.

"I fainted?"

"I guess."

"Did you bring me here?"

"Heck, no. Dad lugged you out. He made me stay with you until you feel better. I'm missing the beginning of the Rosary," she says, turning a page.

"I fell *all* the way down and everything?"

She nods. "You kissed the floor."

"Down," I ask, "you mean straight down, right? Not sideways?"

"Yeah."

"And...nobody could see my underwear?"

"Nope."

I let out a huge sigh. Accidentally showing panties is the kind of thing a person never stops worrying about.

"Nobody saw a thing when you fell," continues Loretta. "But when Dad carried you to the car—whoo-ee!—free showtime at Sacred Heart of Mary."

"You liar!" I sock her shoulder.

"Knock it off," she says. "I'm kidding."

"Honest?"

"Yeah, honest. No one saw your underwear."

I straighten my dress, smoothing down the hem to make sure it would have been long enough to cover my nalgas even as I fell.

"We better go back," says Loretta, not knowing the first thing about fainting in church.

"You're nuts. After a person faints, no one expects them to return to church."

"Fine, you stay. I'm going back to pray."

"Since when do you pray?" I remember how Loretta became so disgusted when she didn't turn into a saint and fly up to heaven during her First Holy Communion that she gave up on religion.

"I didn't get to say good-bye to Fermina."

I snatch the keys from her lap. "You can't leave the person who's fainted, dummy. It's not safe."

"You seem fine to me."

"Look, Loretta," I say, dangling the keys. A spark, an idea is catching. I run the keys through my fingers like coins. "I bet I could drive us somewhere, and we'd be back before the Rosary ends."

"You can't drive."

"Sure, I can."

"Lie," says Loretta, biting on a cuticle.

"Really, I can drive. I drove last summer when Dad and the uncles got real loaded that time at Octavio's ranch. How do you think everyone got back to Tía Beatriz's?"

"That was just in the country."

"Once you do it, you don't forget, like riding a bike. I'll show you."

"So you're going to steal the car?"

"You can't steal a thing that belongs to you, right? And this is our family car, right?" I say. "Now move over."

She slides over me, and I slip into the driver's seat. "What about Fermina?" she says. "I didn't get to say good-bye."

"There's always the funeral." I stab the key in the ignition and stretch my leg for the gas pedal. I can barely reach it, so I scoot the seat up as far as it will go. Driving in the city is way better than bumping over country roads. Once I maneuver out of the lot, the paved street feels smooth as butter under the Impala's fat tires.

"You have any idea where we're going?" Loretta asks.

"I was thinking we could go to Elysian Park. It's close," I tell her.

"Yes, the park!"

After a few blocks, we head up the twisty road that spirals into the park. It's superdark, even with the headlights on, and I'm driving at a crawl, so we don't flip over a guardrail and tumble down the hill. Finally we reach the picnic area, and I glide the car into a parking slot. I pull out the key, flip off the headlights, and sink back into the seat. Driving can make a person pretty tense.

"It's like being blind," Loretta says, "when the moon is gone."

Without moonlight and streetlamps, there's barely enough light to make out the barbecue pits and picnic tables. I scroll down the window to a cool, damp breeze that smells of eucalyptus and burnt charcoal. I slide open the ashtray to find whatever butts might still be smokeable.

"What's that?" asks Loretta, cocking her head.

"Don't try to spook me. You're always—"

"Shush! *Listen.*"

Something feeble whimpers in the distance. I can barely hear it, but I can tell this something feeble is *not* human. And I start to freak out. But Loretta swings her door open and leaps out like we've just arrived at Disneyland.

"You can't go out there," I tell her.

She races through the picnic area toward the trash bins. Then I lose her in the shadows. Jesus, I'm thinking, they're really going to be pissed at me if she vanishes like those people in this book I read called *Disappeared!* I fish out a half-smoked butt, straighten it, and plunge in the lighter on the dashboard. No point in *my* vanishing, too. The lighter pops and I put the butt to my lips, drawing in a raspy lungful. Besides, I *know* Loretta is too big a pain in the nalgas to disappear this easily.

Sure enough, she's already striding back to the car, bearing a cardboard box like she's a peanut vendor at Dodger Stadium. "Guess what I found!"

"Money?"

"No, dopey, look. Look!" She rests the box on one hip and opens the car door on my side to shove it in my face. Under the dome light, I see two wet-looking black things, writhing like miniature seals on a greasy rag.

"What are those? Rats? Ugh, get them away!"

"Puppies! They're newborn puppies!"

My eyes focus. "They're sick," I say. "What's that on that one's eye?" Rice grains fill the hollow of the smaller pup's socket, but these grains are twitching. My stomach plunges. "Worms!"

"They're just maggots," says Loretta. "Let's take them home. I can cure them."

"Put them back, Loretta. I'm not driving maggoty dogs around in the car."

"You have to! Or I tell that you stole the car and kidnapped me and"—she sees the butt burning between my fingers—"and *you're smoking*!"

"Like they won't know something's up when we come back to church with a box of puppies." I crush the cigarette out.

"I already thought of that. We can drop them off at the house. I'll hide them in the cuartito, and then we can go back to the Rosary." She glances at her wristwatch. "We've got just enough time."

"I do not drive with maggots."

"Come on, please, Bette. I swear I'll be your friend forever."

"I already have plenty of friends."

"But you don't have me," she says, standing there and holding on to the box so tightly that I can tell she's never going to let it go.

"Put them in the goddamn trunk." I hand her the keys, and she practically skips, rounding the car to stow the creepy things.

Turns out, she's right. We do have just enough time to stop home to drop off the puppies. Just as we're about to make a clean getaway, though, we run smack into Señora Trejo trudging up the driveway with an apronful of weeds. She spills these when she sidesteps to avoid crashing into us. Loretta and I help her scoop them up, but it's so dark we can't see too well.

"Yerba buena," she says, raking the cement walk with her bony fingers.

I ask the viejita if Cathy is still sick. She nods and hurries away.

"Poor Calfie," says Loretta, clucking her tongue.

Then we run our asses to the car and tear back to church.

People haven't even started filtering out yet. I pull into the front parking lot, feeling smart and wicked for getting away with this, when Loretta groans. "Oh no!"

"What?" I ask, but then I notice the problem, too. A Volkswagen Beetle is hunched right in our parking space. There are no other places to park in the front of the lot. But do I lose my nerve? I do not. I just cruise around and around like my father did earlier, searching for a spot. Nothing turns up. There must be some Holy Roller event at the social hall, because although we loved her, Fermina really wasn't popular enough to fill a parking lot. "We'll have to use the lot across the street."

"How will you explain how the car got there? Strong winds?"

"I'll think of something," I say, not sure I have time to come up with anything really inspired. "You just go along with it, okay? Whatever I say, you got to act like it's God's own truth, got it?" At least with Loretta, the good kid, on my side for once, I might be able to get away with this. We practically have to fly across the street to get back to the church as the mourners trickle back to their cars. We don't have to wait long. I make out Dad's pin-striped suit and Nilda's black shift emerging from the vestibule.

"How are you feeling?" my father asks, handing us each a holy card, a funeral keepsake—the picture of the Virgin Mother on one side, Fermina's name, the date, and a prayer on back.

"Still dizzy," I say, working for sympathy, "a little feverish, and headachy."

"You go straight to bed when we get you home," says Nilda, putting a cool hand to my forehead. "All that makeup you had on, no wonder you're sick."

"Hey," my dad says, already sounding worked up, "what's going on here?"

"Where?" asks Loretta. She tucks her holy card in her pocket.

"Where's the car?"

Nilda scans the lot. "Dios mío!"

"They had to move it," I say.

"Who? Who moved my car?"

"Delivery men."

My father narrows his eyes. "*Delivery* men?"

"Yeah, well, they needed the spot to bring in the...delivery, so they had to move the car." Not great, I admit, but better than nothing.

"They needed to bring the delivery," Loretta says.

Dad swells up, but since he's right outside the church surrounded by people, he controls himself. "Qué delivery, ni delivery?"

"Doughnuts!" I say. "Doughnuts for the social hall. They're having some kind of thing in there, and they needed all these doughnuts and coffee."

"Tons of doughnuts," Loretta pipes in. "Loads of coffee."

"Doughnuts," repeats Nilda in a doubtful way. My father just shakes his head. But a gaggle of Holy Rollers wander out of the social hall and right past us, bearing doughnuts on paper plates and steaming cups of coffee. "Hmm...," murmurs Nilda. "We better stop at the bakery and pick up something to take over to Stella's."

Dad shakes his head, but he doesn't say anything more as we lead him to the basketball court to find the car. Despite my queasy gut, he and Nilda ride up front, so she can jump out—if there's no parking—to buy the sweets at the bakery.

"Who changed the seat?" my father barks.

"The delivery guy," I say. "He was real short, so he moved it."

After that, he and Nilda ignore us as they talk about who sent what flowers and who showed up and who was too lazy to bother.


When we're in bed, Loretta whispers, "Soon as everyone goes to sleep, I'm going out to the cuartito to take care of the puppies."

"Seriously, Loretta, they look real bad," I tell her. "They'll probably die."

"No, they won't. I can make them well. That's my gift from Fermina."

"Come on, you don't really believe that."

"I do believe it, and I believe you got your gift, too. You can tell lies that people believe. That's your gift, almost as good as mine."

"Get out," I say, but this gets me thinking about how well that doughnut bullshit played out. "They only swallowed the delivery story because you went along with it. Plus, those guys showed up with doughnuts."

"That's not why. You're the one who told the lie they believed. Try it out tomorrow. Whatever you say, I bet people believe you."

We both go quiet. My father's slippers shuffle in the hallway, and the newspaper rattles. I remember today's headline, that article claiming the world champion boxer is, of all stupid things, afraid to fight. Everyone lies. But some lies are way more idiotic than others. Maybe my gift is to tell smart lies—lies that are not an insult, like the one in the paper. Maybe I can tell lies smart enough to be believed.

Loretta whispers, "Listen, I don't want anyone to know about the puppies. Not while they're sick." Then she goes on about how she's going to cure them. She has a sack of stuff: eyedroppers, peroxide, tweezers (I'll never touch *those* again), gauze, and adhesive tape.

I turn on my side, so Loretta can't see, and give my pillow a little hug and a kiss.

"How come you do that?" she asks.

"Do what?"

"Kiss the pillow like that. I see you do it every night."

"You're crazy," I say, and turn away from her, pulling the covers over my shoulder. The pillow thing is just something I started after Mama died. This used to be her pillow, see. I swapped it with my old pillow right before her funeral, when everyone was too busy to notice. Even now, when I bury my face in it, I can still smell her hair oil and the crushed fern and coriander scent of her. I cuddle the pillow to me like a baby as I drift off to sleep, and sometimes I sneak it a little kiss. It's not like I can't fall sleep if I don't—just takes a superlong time, is all.

Loretta tiptoes out to the cuartito, and I think about Fermina and the gift thing. Who was she, really? I feel like I should know, like I need to know. Before long, I'm kind of whispering to Fermina, like she's right here with me, asking her this and that. I pat my pillow, and since Loretta's gone, I slip it another kiss. *I love you, too. Good night.*

SUBJECT: FERMINA/FOLKTALES
WPA: 6-17-38—DC: HMS
June 14, 1938
Words: 539

## OWL CHILD

Of the folktales Fermina heard when young, one that stays with her is the story of an owl that claimed a human child. In this tale, parents of a temperamental girl would put her outside when they could no longer bear her tantrums. Late one night, while the father was worshipping at kiva, the girl raged when her mother tried to get her to sleep. The exasperated mother cursed the child, threatening to put her out if she did not settle down. She refused, so her mother cast her into the night. The child sobbed until she fell asleep. An owl flapped to her side and nudged her, hooting gently. This roused the girl. She reached for its feathery breast, and the owl carried her off.

When the girl's father returned, he asked where the child was. Her mother admitted putting her out. But the man had not seen his daughter outside when he returned from kiva. Alarmed, her parents summoned the other villagers to help them hunt for her. They searched until dawn without finding a trace of the child.

After several days, a hunter from Oraibi stooped to drink from the spring in Hotevilla, when he heard a child laughing. Following the sound, he found a girl in an owl's nest. She sprouted short brown feathers on her arms, her chest was furred with down fuzz, and her small nose had begun to harden and crook like a beak. Her dark-ringed eyes glowed amber from the shadowy nest, and when the hunter called to her, she hooted in reply.

The hunter returned to his village on the Second Mesa and described what he'd seen. Soon the news reached the girl's parents, who sought the hunter. He described the place where he had seen her, and the girl's father led a party of men to retrieve her. When they found the nest, the owl was perched in it. It surrendered the girl to her father, explaining it had claimed her because she had been cursed and cast out. "When you return home," the owl said, "you must seal the child up in a room for four days. You cannot look upon her during this time. The fourth day, after sunrise, you can look in. Fail this, and you will lose your child forever."

The father agreed, and the party returned to the village with the feathered girl. The parents shut her in a room and sealed the door. They followed the owl's rules until the morning of the fourth day. Before dawn, the woman woke the man to ask if she could open the sealed room. He forbade her and went back to sleep. But the mother reasoned that since this was the fourth day, what difference would an hour make? She broke the seal, and the door burst open. An owl emerged, flapping from the home toward Hotevilla.

The commotion woke the man. He was furious and then heartbroken to learn that they had again lost their child. The woman wept for days, but received no consolation from the villagers, who realized that one should neither curse a child nor cast her out, for an owl may snatch her and never bring her back.

# CURSED AND CAST OUT—
## RITA: 1967

Rita sits cross-legged on the floor of her neighbor's bedroom as Cathy opens a plastic case and shakes her dolls out: five Barbies and two Kens, with felt hair that rubs off like moss. Though Rita is a year older than her five-year-old neighbor, the two girls usually play whatever Cathy chooses, since she owns the toys, a roomful of them, in fact. Rita had hoped they would roll Cathy's Radio Flyer outside to give each other wagon rides, but when she entered Cathy's room, she found the girl lying on her side on her canopied bed, stroking her round stomach. "It hurts," Cathy said, and she lifted her paisley-print blouse with floppy sleeves, the "butterfly" blouse, as Rita called it, wanting one of her own. Cathy's flesh underneath was mottled, blue-veined, hard as a volleyball. Rita reached to touch. "Don't," Cathy said. "I can't make."

"Make what?" Rita had asked.

"I'll be okay in a minute. It hurts hard and then it stops."

"Tell your mama."

"No, then she won't let me play. Get my doll case, will you?" After a moment, Cathy had lowered herself, with a groan, to sit beside Rita.

Now Cathy peels a shiny black gown off her champagne-blond

Barbie, and Rita thinks of the indigo snake she's seen shedding skin at the zoo. Cathy lays the nude Barbie on the floor and tugs the psychedelic-print bell-bottoms off a patch-headed Ken. Then she settles the Ken doll on top of Barbie.

"Now, if he touches her with his pipi," Cathy says, breathing through her mouth, "they'll get a baby."

Rita lunges to her feet, her face hot. "Nah-*uh*, that *never* happens."

"It's true, ask anyone," Cathy says.

Rita flashes on her uncle José unbuckling his belt (*Want to see the birdie?*) and wonders about Cathy's hard blue stomach. Does her uncle take *her* for ice cream? Does *she* have a baby there? She shakes her head. "Know what, Calfie? You're full of shit."

The younger girl's brown eyes fill. "Maw-*ma*-aw!" She bawls like a cattle-labeled novelty can when upended.

"Calfie's full of shi-*it*!" Rita sings in a low voice. "Calfie's full of shi-*it*!"

Cathy scrambles to her feet and bursts from the bedroom. She pounds the bathroom door. Her mother opens it and takes the girl in her arms. Something catches in Rita's throat as she looks on at the two — Shirley cradling Cathy, stroking her back — just before Bette hauls her out, trailing apologies in their wake. After Nilda punishes her for cursing again, Rita has to play alone the rest of that long day, blaming Cathy — the damn crybaby, the *liar* — for her boredom.

By morning, though, Rita's ready to forgive Cathy. She heads next door, after breakfast, and knocks. The door cracks open, and the old woman, Señora Trejo, appears, her silvery hair uncombed, straggling over her shoulders in a witchy way. Rita steps back, but says, "Can Cathy play?"

"She no here."

"Who am I suppose to play with then?"

"Berry sick. Cathy no here." The old woman shuts the door.

Rita rounds the bungalow, tiptoes to peek in Cathy's bedroom window, but the shade is drawn. She returns home to find Bette and Loretta whispering together on the porch.

"Uh-oh," Bette says when she sees Rita. "Now you've done it."

"Done what?"

"*You* put a curse on Cathy and made her sick."

"Get out of here." Rita looks to Loretta.

"You should watch what you say," she tells her.

Bette says, "You told Cathy she was full of shit. Now she really is."

"Is *what*?"

"Full of shit," Bette says. "*That's* what! You made her sick."

"You lie." Rita shoots another look at Loretta, who nods.

"It's true," Bette says. "Cathy's in the hospital now. She can't make number two. Something's stuck in the pipes, and she's all blocked up."

"She has a bowel obstruction," Loretta tells her.

But Rita hears "vowel obstruction" and thinks of the workbooks Nilda provides to keep her busy during the day. She wonders if Cathy's consonants are okay.

"She can die from it," Bette says.

Rita flashes on the younger girl's swollen stomach. "Nah-*uh*, her panza already hurt before I said anything bad."

"Doesn't matter," Bette says. "She could have just had a stomachache, but you made it worse. If Cathy dies, you'll be a *murderer*."

Loretta's eyes are serious. "That's right."

"You shut up! I didn't do that." Rita's sure Cathy lifted her butterfly blouse before the angry words, but the fixed accusation on her sisters' faces and their insistent voices plant a tiny seed of doubt. Maybe curses can fly back and forth, like the swing at the park when Rita pumps her legs to make it go faster and higher.

"It's what you got from Fermina. It's your gift," Loretta explains. "You cursed her. They can put you in the electric chair for what you did. Strap you down—your legs, your arms—so you can't even wiggle a toe, and then *zzzzzzt*!"

"I said *shut up*!" Rita cries in confusion. Why would Fermina want her to hurt people? "Or I'll make *both* of you full of shit!"

Bette and Loretta charge into the house, slamming the screen door behind them. They barrel through the hall, Rita on their heels. Before she catches up, they slam into their bedroom, the bigger room they share now that she and Sophie moved into Fermina's room. The bolt scrapes into the lock. Rita studies the closed door—its chalky whiteness, grimy knob, the scuff marks at the base. She puts her ear to the keyhole. Rita can't make out the words, but she *knows* they are saying bad things about her.

She wanders outside again, settles on the front steps, and plays with the ballerina flowers that grow nearby. She twirls the red stems between her fingers, making the ballerinas kick higher and higher. Bette and Loretta will be sorry if a kidnapper turns up to offer Rita some candy. She gazes at the street with longing. Soon enough, she's sure, Bette and Loretta will fight—they always do—and one or the other will emerge to play ballerinas with her.

But this time her sisters don't quarrel. They don't leave their room until noon, and then they won't speak to her. They whisper to Cary, and he gapes at Rita, wide-eyed and silent, while they eat lunch. Even Sophie will have nothing to do with her. As Rita winds tepid spaghetti strands on her fork, she imagines Cathy's intestinal tubing—twisted and knotted—her potbelly cramping in pain. She crams the pasta between her lips. Without thinking, she bites down on her tongue, splitting the skin. Blood floods her mouth, tasting like the sun-warmed sea.

After a few days, her father comes home—nose swollen, glasses fogged—and takes her hand. "H'ita, I got bad news," he says. "La Cathy passed away this morning." Rita's head feels loose, then heavy, and everything turns black. When she wakes, a wet towel on her forehead, Rita clenches her teeth until her jaw aches. She pictures the shelf in the cuartito that holds a blue-and-yellow tin of lighter fluid, brown bottles of insecticide, and an aluminum flask of turpentine—all with their skull-and-crossbone labels. She belongs perched behind cobwebs on that stained, splintery plank: *Dangerous. Hazardous. Lethal.* Her words have poisoned Cathy as surely as a swig of bleach.

Every time sirens wail, even on television, dread jolts through her. Rita expects a squad car to screech into their drive, the police to hammer on the front door, cuff her, slam her in a cell, and then strap her in the electric chair. She's seen a movie about this: the murderer yanked from bed, arrested, and then hauled, screaming and begging all the way to The Chair. The image of that wood-frame seat, with its tangle of wires and worn leather cuffs and straps, is seared into Rita's memory, along with the hair-raising howls of the condemned.

Rita's convinced she, too, will be arrested in the night; so after the others are asleep, she rises from bed. She tiptoes to the doors to make sure they're latched and checks all the windows before slipping back in bed and rubbing her cold feet. Just as she drifts toward sleep, she rouses herself to try the locks all over again. One night, Rita isn't satisfied with checking and double-checking. She pushes her father's recliner to block the front entry and wedges a dinette chair under the knob of the kitchen door. Still, she can't sleep, so she rises to lodge sofa cushions in the living-room windows and blockades the door to her and Sophie's room with a nightstand.

In the morning, her father grumbles about the furniture against the doors, the cushions in the windows. Sophie crashes into the nightstand when she gets up for the bathroom. But Rita can't help that. Night after night, she repeats the ritual. By day, Rita dozes over her lunch, her head in her hands. She naps in front of the television and falls asleep once in the bath. Finally her father takes her in his arms. "H'ita, what's wrong?"

Rita shrugs.

"You want to see the doctor or something?"

She shakes her head.

"Then you got to stop getting up in the night like this."

Rita nods, swearing to herself she will stop.

But that night, she twists and turns in bed, like a fish caught in a net. Her legs twitch and her feet tingle with the urge to kick the covers off so she can check just one door, one window. Shadows in her room swell, guttering as thin shredded clouds scud by, veiling and unveiling the bland face of the moon. On the news, Rita has seen photos of the moon sent by the *Surveyor* to planet Earth. In them, the orb looks even more like a face, sallow and blemished, impassive and cold. She imagines this uncaring mask unfazed by the sooty cumulus swirling below. A slow-moving cloud casts an umbra near the ceiling that sharpens into her mother's silhouette, but her expression is hard. Rita turns toward Sophie, whose snoring signals her deep, enviable sleep.

Rita struggles, ready to give in and check the house, when she faces her mother's profile again. The shadow has shifted, transforming the silhouette into an owl with horned feathers and a crooked beak. The owl tenses, poised to strike. But a fresh bank of clouds dissolves the image. Now Fermina's bumpy profile issues from the shadowy stucco. Her mouth moves: *M'ija, you know what to do.* Rita bolts upright in her bed, smacking herself on the forehead—it is so simple.

"Goddamn police," she whispers. "You won't ever catch me." Her muscles loosen, and she sinks back into bed. Then she shoots up again. "You'll never put me in the electric chair." She falls onto her pillow, feeling light enough to float, like she could raise the window, push out the screen, and loft out into the night.

That September, Rita starts first grade at Sacred Heart Elementary. She should have gone to kindergarten the year before, but in the confused time after her mother's death and Fermina's long illness, no one bothered enrolling her in school, so Rita stayed home an extra year with Sophie. Born in spring, Rita is well over six when her father finally registers her. Even so, the mother superior hesitates to accept Rita as a first grader. She peers at her over wire-framed glasses, her doughy face pleated with doubt. "She'll have to pass the entrance test. Very few youngsters who don't attend kindergarten can pass." She sits Rita at a desk and hands her a sheet of paper and pencil. "Write the alphabet, young lady."

Rita writes quickly, both in upper and lower case. She's about to begin another set in cursive when the nun stops her. "So she knows her letters."

Of course, she does. Her mother taught her before she died, and both Fermina and Shirley harped on Rita to practice these during the long days they watched her. When Nilda took over after Shirley quit, she was even stricter about Rita's written work.

"Now write your name," Mother Superior says.

*My name is Rita Hayworth Gabaldón,* Rita prints at the bottom of the page.

"Turn the sheet over and draw a picture of a girl."

Rita reverses the paper and draws a straight horizontal line, then two angles dangling from each end of that: a roof. Then she sketches a rectangle, places two windows and a door within it.

"That is not a girl," Mother Superior observes. "That is a house."

Her father leans over to regard Rita's work.

"Where is the girl?" the nun asks.

"She's right in there." Her father presses a nail-blackened finger on the page.

The nun squints. "Where?"

"She's inside with her daddy. They're eating chicharrones and watching the fights on television. Right, h'ita?"

Rita nods.

Mother Superior barks with laughter, clears her throat. "Can the child speak?"

"Well, she don't talk a whole lot. She used to talk more, but these days, she's pretty quiet. It's kind of nice. The rest of my kids—except Loretta—talk both my legs off, so I enjoy the quiet from this one."

"Ah, Loretta," the nun says with a smile, "now *Loretta* behaves very nicely." She pulls out a packet of forms, and Rita's father enrolls her in first grade.

Rita's teacher is a petite, girlish woman. She wears the modern-style habit—shortened skirt and, instead of a wimple, a head-band veil that reveals her pink ears and mouse-brown curls. Sister Rose Ellen chirps when she speaks, punctuating her sentences with "honey" or "sweetie pie." She often wears her guitar, strung on a strap and banging against her backside. She sings folk songs when the mood strikes her.

"But she's *s-o-o-o* big!" Sister Rose Ellen says when she meets

Rita. "She's absolutely *huge*." Her tone suggests Rita ought to be unloading trucks instead of entering the first grade.

"Why won't you talk, honey?" Sister Rose Ellen asks after a few days. "Little girls have to let out that sugar and spice sometime."

Rita stares until the nun's smile flattens.

"Let's hear what Rita has to say," Sister Rose Ellen tells the class at reading time. "Rita, what color is Harold's crayon in the story? Surely, you can answer that."

Rita gazes from the nun's grinning face to the book's cover, where the boy displays a deep purple crayon. Then she looks back at Sister Rose Ellen. The nun's face pinkens, and she calls on another child.

Sister Rose Ellen corners Rita after class, saying, "Maybe you'll sing with me, if you don't feel like talking. How about 'Blowin' in the Wind'?" She toots a recorder for pitch before strumming the first chords. Rita sinks into a too small desk, lips compressed. After a few verses, the teacher dismisses her.

One afternoon while the class is having an art lesson, Sister Rose Ellen announces the forthcoming Christmas pageant. "Everyone will have lines to say—nice and clear—for all the families and other students to hear." She smiles. "That goes for *everyone*." Rita paints a boat while the teacher speaks. She dips her brush in blue tempera and strokes wavy ribbons under its hull.

"If you're not in the pageant," Sister Rose Ellen says, "you will miss the Kris Kringle gift exchange and the party—cookies, punch, candy—and that's just too bad."

Rita swishes her brush in a water-filled coffee can, tinting the water sapphire.

"Does *everyone* understand?" The nun looks at Rita.

"Yes, Sister," the other children reply.

Rita paints the sun, swirling a thick mustard-colored blob.

She streaks the ball with orange, painting a sun fiery enough to ignite the classroom, hot enough to turn it into a dustpan full of ash.

The morning before the pageant, Rita wakes up retching. She vomits in bed. Bette helps her out of her soiled bedclothes, and Loretta wipes her face. Rita's father gathers her pajamas, linen, and blankets and hauls them to the cuartito to wash, before calling his work. Rita spends the day huddled in a quilt on the couch, watching game shows and soap operas.

"Ah, the life of Riley," her father says when he brings her ginger ale and saltines.

Rita flashes him a weak smile.

During Lent, Sister Rose Ellen orders Rita to stay after school nearly every day. Rita's penance: she must kneel while Sister Rose Ellen sits at her desk, "silently praying." One rainy afternoon, her father leaves work early, driving the utility truck out to pick up Rita and the others from school. He ducks into her classroom, his yellow slicker dripping. "What are you doing?"

"Praying," Sister Rose Ellen says.

"I got the truck running out here, so we better go. Come on, get your books." He notices Rita's reddened knees. "How long you been kneeling?"

"Oh, not that long," Sister Rose Ellen says quickly. "She's just begun praying."

"How come no other kids are praying?"

"They aren't stubborn like Rita. They speak when spoken to."

"Is that right? How come you ain't kneeling? You're a nun. I'm sure the prayers would fly higher from you with all your training in the church."

"I am praying, but I can't kneel. I have a condition—my back."

"Is that right? Well, tell you what, Sister, I got a condition, too. It's kind of a thing where I get mad when you mess around with my girl, you understand?"

"If that's your feeling, Mr. Gabaldón, I can't be responsible for her progress. Children who won't speak aren't adequately prepared to pass to the next grade."

He shrugs. "Then I guess you'll have her again next year. But I think she knows her lessons. She does fine on her tests and that homework you give. I never noticed no section on the report card for how much she talks. I could ask the principal about this, but I think she's probably going to pass." He takes Rita's hand, and they dart out of the classroom, dodging sheets of rain sluicing from the roof.

The next year, Rita has Sister Albert George, a tough nun in full habit and wimple. Her missionary years in the Sudan have leathered her face. Now it is the texture of turkey wattle. A yardstick dangles from her belt like a sword. Sister Albert George appreciates tall, quiet children much more than the spritelike chatterers who irritate her ancient nerves.

Though her silence agrees with the old nun, Rita finds no pleasure in school. She keeps to herself, dreading what she might blurt in a flash of anger, and the other children avoid her. Somehow they sense that she is hazardous, and they don't dare tease the large, mute girl. But there is no way they can know she's killed someone with poison so potent it has contaminated the dead girl's mother and the old woman, too. La vieja rarely leaves the house since Cathy's funeral, and almost overnight, Shirley has become elderly herself—hunched and pale as a specter as she wanders from her bungalow to the mailbox at dusk, her nightgown billowing like vapor with each step.

## PIPTUKA: THE NON-SACRED CLOWNS

Fermina tells of clowns, painted and dressed in ragtag costumes, that would appear on rooftops in Walpi as though descended like spirits from the clouds. They would immediately bicker about how to climb down to the ceremonial grounds. As they tumbled down ladders, these clowns insulted one another, while onlookers howled with laughter. Once on the ground, the clowns performed comic skits before the kachina dancers arrived.

Fermina remembers four groups of ceremonial clowns. Her favorite of these were the *Piptuyakyamu*, or *Piptuka*, which she translates as "those who keep coming back, who will not stay away." These were not sacred clowns and had no set routines or traditional costume, apart from painting their bodies. The appearance of the Piptuka depended upon the object of their satire. They would mark their faces with stripes if mocking the Navajo, wear masks if poking fun at the Paiute, or don women's dress if burlesquing women.

The Pitpuka's skits satirized outsiders or the outlandish behavior of certain villagers. A routine that Fermina remembers well is one wherein they mimicked a married couple whose loud arguments disturbed the peace of their neighbors. One clown, attired as the wife, hectored the clown acting as her spouse, who, in turn, berated her. The two bellowed over petty matters, such as who had let the fire die out and who had more

of the blanket when they settled down to sleep.
At one point, the clown wife tossed a gourd of
water at her goading husband, and missing him,
she drenched the clown portraying her visiting
mother-in-law. This skit reduced Fermina's
own mother to tears of hilarity. For months
afterward, whenever Fermina wanted to amuse her
mother, she reminded her of the water flying at
the clown mother-in-law. In the aftermath of that
performance, the village couple mocked by the
Piptuka became more subdued, their marital spats
no longer public spectacles.

Fermina says that when she was young, she
believed the purpose of the clowns was simply
to make people laugh, but now she sees they were
teachers, showing the Hopi how to behave by
ridiculing outsiders and those whose behavior
was inconsiderate of others. The kachina
dancers, she observes, were always the same,
like the seasons, but the clowns were like
children—rude, impulsive, and unpredictable.
All clowns were believed to prevent evil by
confounding witchery. The Piptuka were the
lowest order of this society. But for Fermina,
this band of buffoons was the most memorable and
enjoyable of all that she witnessed performing.

# 4

# Once a Pint of Time — Sophia: 1968

This is *not* a funny story. The princess is going to *die*! So how come your daddy hides behind the newspaper, silent laughter bubbling over the top like the busy water he puts in his whiskey? And your big sister Bette, on the telephone, winks and grins from across the living room. You settle Suzy, Woozy, and Doozy in your lap. They never laugh at you. They just stare. (Loretta says Suzy isn't a Suzy, but a Raggedy Ann. "Well, she's a Suzy now," you tell her.) So what if Woozy is a plastic yellow horse and Doozy a Gumby with one chewed leg? These are your babies. You'd never make fun of the tiny moon marks on Doozy's foot or the jelly stain on Suzy's apron. You would never, ever laugh at your children.

You start the story again. "Once a pint of time —"

Cary stomps in from the kitchen. "Hah!" he says. That's how he laughs — a single burst that makes you jump. "What's that? Like two cups of days?"

You glare at him — those chubby cheeks, that gaping mouth. The princess will have a greedy brother, and the Invisible Dragon will sneeze, lighting his hair like a match head just *before* the poor princess dies.

"Or sixteen ounces of hours?" Cary says, and Daddy can't take any more. He crumples the paper in his lap and laughs outright. Then he says, "Leave her alone. Let her tell her story."

"It's 'once a *pond* of time,'" Cary tells you.

"I know that," you say, wondering for a moment what a "pond" of time is. Less than a lake? More than a puddle? "Can't you see I'm telling a *silly* story?" And you start again. No dead princesses, no dead princess brothers. "Once a pint of Tide," you say, "was poured into the river, so all the goggling fish and all the wiggly worms could have a bubbly bath...."

"Listen to this," Bette says. "My kid sister, she's just five, but she's hilarious!" She holds out the phone while you tell a silly story to make them really laugh.

Loretta says this is what the old woman Fermina gave to you: you can make them laugh and laugh with your squeaky voice, your crossing eyes, your jokes, and silly stories. Sometimes you drop down on all fours, bark, and pant like a dog. "Rover," they call you, and pat the socks you've clipped to your hair for droopy ears. You sniff shoes and lift a back leg, pretend to squirt Cary's sneakers, or lunge to snap at Rita's butt. Even she giggles at this. Mostly, you like making them laugh. It gives you a ticklish feeling deep in your stomach. Their laughter rattles in your ears, like pink-and-white candies bouncing in a box. But sometimes, you get tired, "cranky," Bette says. Still they laugh when you stick out your tongue, and when you stomp out of the room, they clap.

One dark Saturday afternoon, thunder booms, lightning flashes, and now hail hammers the roof—perfect weather for watching horror movies on television. Loretta's real dogs, the ones she found in the park, whimper under her bed, but everyone else lounges in front of the TV. Arms out like a sleepwalker, the Mummy staggers through the night. (Rita runs to hide in the bathroom, the way she always does when the music gets scary, and Cary says, "Isn't anything else on?") The Mummy wants to strangle a sleeping lady, so he kicks open her door, shuffles to her bed, and then, and then—a hoarse, whispery blizzard fills the screen.

"Now it's broken," Cary says. "I told you to change the channel."

Loretta snaps off the set. "Like that would've helped."

"Gina? *Gina?*" Bette says into the phone. "Damn, it's dead."

Rita skulks back into the living room, her eyes big as a bug's. "Where's Daddy?"

Bette shrugs. "He's working overtime."

"Well, what are we supposed to do now?" asks Cary.

They all look at you. But you don't feel like making them laugh this time, so you say, "Tell me about Mama. What was she like?"

Loretta's eyes shine. "She was beautiful."

"She was big," Bette says, "and heavy. She had huge arms like a wrestler."

"She made the best food." Cary licks his lips.

"Are you *kidding?*" Bette snorts. "She burned the meat, scorched the beans."

"She was better at cakes and cookies," admits Loretta. "Mama was always nice."

Bette shakes her head. "She never let me do anything, never let me go anywhere. And she could smack pretty hard."

"You're crazy," Loretta says. "She never hit me."

"You don't remember that time someone stole the last piece of lemon pie, and no one would admit it, so Mama got that old razor strap. You remember, don't you, Cary?"

Cary nods. "She got me after you. She *did* hit pretty hard."

"She never hit me," Loretta insists. "I was supposed to get it after Cary, and then the phone rang. She forgot all about me."

"Who ate that pie anyway?" Cary asks.

"*I* did," Loretta says. "I loved Mama's lemon pie."

"But what was Mama *really* like?" you want to know.

"She was tough," Bette says. "She didn't let me get away with anything."

"She read to me," Loretta says. "She liked to sing to me."

"And me," Rita pipes in her rusty voice.

Bette winces. "Terrible voice, though, like a cat being skinned alive."

The more they talk, the more confused you become. The mother you are picturing keeps changing, her face growing hard, then soft, then hard again. How could she be so many different people? Who was she? Does anyone know?

"She loved me best," Cary says.

No one argues with that.

Just the lights come back on, you are hungry again. It's all that talk about Mama's baking and lemon pie, but the truth is there's always a yawning feeling in your stomach. You imagine a deep hole like the one your uncle Santi, the baby of his family just like you, dug to put pipes for an indoor bathroom in your grandparents' house in Río Puerco. There's something dark and earthy like that carved deep in you, something you can't possibly fill, though it feels pretty good to try. You tiptoe to the old, ticking Amana and ease open the door. You go right for the cold-cut drawer—pimento loaf, your favorite! And there's a long yellow brick of Velveeta cheese. But only a heel of Wonder bread left, so you scoop out a small handful of cheese, roll it into a slice of pimento loaf, and devour the salty, waxy cigarlike mess of it, standing like a horse before the opened refrigerator. Tastes so good, you whinny and paw the linoleum floor with one foot, before preparing another snack, this time with bologna. You neigh happily before biting into this.

Loretta startles you, saying, "Why are you standing there making horse noises?"

"I'm Silver," you say, "the Lone Ranger's great stallion."

"More like Tonto," she says, "or tonta, letting all the cold out like that."

"Do horses like lunch meat?" you ask.

"No, dum-dum, they eat hay and oats."

"Well, I'm a meat-eating horse." You pop the last bite into your mouth and slam the refrigerator shut. You wipe your chilled, greasy fingers on your shorts and break into a foot-stomping dance. "I'm the meat-eating, tap-dancing horse of the Lone Ranger, the first and last of my kind!" Your arms shoot out, your hair flops about, and your cheeks burn, but those feet tap-tap-tap like you're stamping out a raging forest fire. If you stop, the bad guys will remember to shoot the Lone Ranger. Then they'll strip off his mask and spit in his dead face. (And Loretta will say, "Why are you eating again, so soon after lunch?") So you're dancing, dancing, dancing for all you're worth—

"You know what," Loretta says. "You're nuts," but she laughs anyway.

That night, Bette crawls into your bed with a few snapshots. One you recognize right away: an old woman in a shawl. "That's my fairy godmother," you say, wriggling a loose tooth. You picture her flitting about your room at night with a silver dollar.

"No, it's Fermina. She stood in at your baptism when Grandma couldn't come, so she's like your godmother. Fermina gave you the gift to be funny." Bette shows another photo. It's of a woman so large she fills the doorway she's standing in. She's wearing a housecoat, a kerchief over her hair, and glasses with dark frames shaped like sideways teardrops. Her face is lifted to the sunlight and she's squinting. Her mouth is open like she's ready to speak, about to introduce herself to you.

"*That's* Mama," Bette says. "That's her when she first married Dad."

"What was her name?" you ask.

"Esperanza," Bette says. "That means 'hope.'"

"She's big," you say, fingering the photograph's scalloped edges.

"Big *and* tough."

There's a heavy gilt-framed portrait of your great-grandparents with your grandfather as a baby in the front room, which is identical to the one hanging in your aunt Nilda's house. There's even a photo of that old woman you don't remember, the one who made you be funny, in an oval frame in Bette and Loretta's bedroom. Though you love monster movies and scary stories, that picture spooks the heck out of you. Fermina looks so grim in it that you can hardly believe she would think to put this laughing gift on you, like an itchy sweater you can't ever take off. "Why don't we put these pictures up?"

Bette shrugs. "Ask Dad."

There's something in your mother's sunlit face, her squinched-up eyes and bunching cheeks. She's not about to speak; she's going to laugh. She's looking straight at you, ready to hoot. "Do I miss her?" you ask Bette.

"Yes," she says, "yes, you do."

their families would ever grow desperate enough to sell them.

That night before sleep, Fermina's mother warned her to keep away from the man called Chuka while he stayed in the village. His flesh smells of Maski, she said, of bone ash and sulfur. She claimed he had been expelled from the underworld, not wanting to believe his story that a family would trade a member for cornmeal and meat.

This was the first Fermina heard of the People taking the Hopi from their villages. That is what the Navajo called themselves, *the People*. The Hopi called them *the Tavasu*. Fermina's mother told her the Hopi used to trade with them—corn for sheep. The Hopi always had corn or cornmeal to exchange for mutton. But later, cattlemen from the east filled the plains with their herds, and the Navajo had few places for sheep to graze, so they raided others, seizing food, horses, and captives. Fermina spied Chuka from a distance during the few days he remained in the village. She did not fear him, though; he was too frail and haggard. If he had not come from Maski, he was headed there soon. Fermina worried more about the Navajo raiders. In weeks to come, news of assaults on neighboring villages became so frequent that many no longer wondered if the village in Walpi would be attacked. They speculated instead on when, and this filled Fermina with dread.

SUBJECT: FERMINA/SLAVERY
WPA: 6-17-38—DC: HMS
June 6, 1938
Words: 496

## RETURN OF A SLAVE

Fermina learned of the enslavement of the Hopi not long after her father had died. One night, when the village was enjoying a feast, a man emerged from the shadows and limped toward the hearth. The villagers stood in surprise. "Chuka," one of the men said. "Where have you been?" Fermina did not recognize the newcomer. Later her mother explained he was from another mesa. He had relatives living in Walpi, so many villagers knew him.

The man was sooty with filth and emaciated. "Let me eat," he said. The women filled a bowl for him and handed him a gourd of water.

"We thought you were dead," someone told him.

"I was in the south herding sheep for el Señor." He told the villagers that el Señor was a kind man who had treated him well. But weeks ago, Chuka led the sheep to an alkaline pond, and many fell dead. Afterward, el Señor decided the slave should return to his village. He was on his way there when he stopped in Walpi for food.

The men asked when he was captured. Many had heard the Navajo would seize Hopis and trade them to the Hispaños or the strangers from the east or keep them for themselves as slaves. But Chuka said he had not been captured. He was sold by his own clan during a famine on the Third Mesa. He shrugged, as though this was a bit of misfortune, nobody to blame for it. The villagers glanced at one another, probably wondering if

# THEY WERE LIKE THIS—
## LORETTA: 1971

The day of the earthquake, I woke to the attic bedroom shuddering and rolling from side to side, like a ship tossed by steep swells.

I had been dreaming I was in a movie theater, stumbling, searching for a seat. I bumped knees and stepped on the feet of people already seated in the row. They hissed at me, whispered curses. "Sorry," I said, "sorry, sorry" as I guided myself with the worn velveteen seat backs. These were stiff to the touch, cool and inert like the shorn pelt of dead animals. The movie, an old film in sepia and cream, had already started. But the celluloid, scribbled with luminescent streaks, ticked and stuttered out of focus when the projector stalled. Still, I'd recognized the actresses, though I couldn't name them—famous, all of them, stars of the fifties. They wore flowing dresses that cinched at the waist, tapered at the wrists, and draped to the floor like sculpted ivory. My eyes on the screen, I fumbled forward and trod on a small booted foot. "Excuse me," I said, glancing at an old woman, in a shawl, huddled in the seat.

My hand reached out, lifted the rebozo. *Fermina!* She compressed her lips in a sympathetic smile. I knew this look well, and my heart contracted. "What's wrong?"

Fermina turned to the person beside her. I followed her gaze and gasped. I slid past Fermina and sank to my knees. "Mama!" I buried my face in my mother's warm lap, encircling her legs with my arms. "You're here," I said. "You're whole."

"Can I stay with you?" I asked.

Fermina strokes my shoulder. "No, mi'ja."

"You don't belong here," my mother said.

"Let me stay," I begged. "I can't lose you again."

My mother swayed to shake me off, and the floor trembled with the force of it, tumbling me from that dim theater into the sunlit attic bedroom I shared with my sister.

Bette, in the twin bed beside mine, yanked a blanket over her head and murmured, "Leave me alone, will you?"

"This is *not* normal," I said.

My bed vibrated, jostling me. Books slid off the shelves, and the bookshelf itself seemed to take a few steps from the wall. From the window, I glimpsed power lines snapping from their poles near Queen of Angels Hospital on the hill. These flashed and sparked like fireworks. Framed posters rattled against the walls, water sloshed out of my fish tank, and somewhere deep in the outer attic, glass shattered.

Bette jackknifed upright. "What the *fuck*?"

"Maybe it's the end of the world," I said. The attic grew still. Sirens shrieked in the distance. "Or an earthquake." I remembered my dogs in the backyard. Storms and loud noises spooked them. I bolted from bed. The closet was a tumble of clothes. The hanger rack had collapsed, heaping skirts, sweaters, dresses, and jackets. I dug through the mound for my huaraches.

Bette climbed out of bed and knelt on the love seat under our window. "Look at them running out of the hospital," she said. "See that smoke? Must be a fire."

I peered over her shoulder. Nurses, doctors, and attendants in white or aquamarine scrubs, along with patients in smocks, streamed down the steps from the hospital on the hill, their movements herky-jerky, nearly comic. "I wonder who's getting the newborn babies out," I said, "and what about the sick kids?"

Bette shrugged. "Great chance for the loonies to escape from the psycho ward."

Our room, an officelike enclosure in one corner of the attic, faced eastward and was painted with yolky enamel. The room was well-lit by the rising sun, but deep shadows shrouded the outer attic. I stepped out of our room and flicked on a switch to light the stairwell. Nothing happened. "No electricity," I called to Bette.

"Cool," she said. "Maybe they'll cancel school."

The door at the bottom of the stairwell flew open, bathing the steps with bluish light. "You girls okay up there?" my father shouted. His voice was taut with strain. Storms and emergencies made him anxious and irritable, as high-strung as Rita.

I stomped down the steps. "Leave that door open, so I can see."

"Is Bette all right?" my father asked, his forehead creased with concern.

"She's fine." I made for the stairwell to the backyard.

"Where're you going?" The old man was barefoot and shirtless, his chest worm-white in stark contrast to his leathery neck and ruddy face. His comb-over flap—more salt than pepper—hung askew, and the pockets of his khakis stuck out at his hips like miniature flags of surrender. His hands shook as he fumbled for a cigarette.

"Check the dogs."

He narrowed his eyes and clucked his tongue. "Are you crazy? That was an earthquake. You can't go outside for some stupid dogs."

I brushed past him and leapt down the back steps two at a time. "Fuck you, too," I murmured once out of earshot.

The long backyard was empty. The mulberry and magnolia trees still and silent, only the freeway roared intermittently beyond the back fence, and a tire strung from a mulberry branch swayed above the tall grass. Though I appreciated the vast overgrown yard, the worst thing about moving from the bungalow on Clinton Street to this big house on Bellevue was that the landlord, our family doctor, allowed no dogs in the house. Anthony and Gerard barked incessantly when they were spooked, until I came downstairs to calm them.

I clapped my hands, whistled, and called, "Here, boys, here!" I expected the dogs to leap out from the side yard or wriggle out from the crawl space, but there was no sign of them. I paced the length of yard, clapping and calling. No dogs. In the side yard, I saw that the tall ivy-covered gate was wide open, the hasp pried from its post. Tears stung my eyes. I glanced over the fence and caught sight of our neighbor Ambrose striding across his yard, brushing his hands together, as though he'd just taken out the garbage. He had on the soot-colored suit and burgundy vest he always wore, whether going to work at the bank or mowing the lawn. His puffy cheeks, as usual, were shadowed with greenish stubble. A timid man, Ambrose flinched and flushed pink when he saw me, but managed an awkward wave.

"Have you seen my dogs?"

He shook his head. "No, but I'll keep an eye out." Ambrose stepped through the back door of the house he shared with his mother, an invalid whose hectoring voice sounded from their opened windows all day long. Though he'd once complained to my father about the dogs barking, I pitied Ambrose. I didn't blame him for always wearing the same dusty suit and not remembering to shave. The old woman gave him no peace, except when she slept.

The ground grumbled under my feet, the magnolia tree trembled, leaves rattling like maracas—an aftershock. I imagined the dogs wide-eyed with terror, racing through the streets, as though to outrun the quaking earth.

I rushed back upstairs to dress. I suspected one-eyed Gerard of leading the gullible Anthony in this escape. Gerard more than compensated for his lack of sight with cunning. I once caught him with a hot dog stolen from a picnic table, smearing its mustard on the slower dog's muzzle, so Anthony would be blamed for the theft. Sharp as he was, Gerard didn't like being separated from his food dish for long. I pictured both dogs leaping with joy when I found them.

I passed my father again in the hallway on the main floor. He'd thrown on a shirt and was sipping from a cup of coffee. "They called me to work," he said. "The V.A. hospital collapsed. There's people buried in the rubble."

I was amazed the phone worked, but I just shrugged.

"Make breakfast for the kids, okay? You and Bette take care of them while I'm gone. Nilda's on her way."

"I have to find the dogs first." I made for the attic stairs, but the old man grabbed my arm and pulled me down with unexpected strength. His cup fell, shattered on the floor. I slipped, banged my knee on one step, and scraped an ankle on another.

"I don't tell nobody nothing," he said, his face hot and close. "But I'm telling you to make breakfast for those kids *now*."

I twisted free. "No!"

I swear I didn't even see it coming. I thought I'd slammed my cheek into the wall, but when he drew his hand back, his eyes inky pinpoints of surprise, I knew. I touched my cheek and couldn't feel my fingers on it. I raced upstairs.

"Loretta," he called after me. "Listen, h'ita, please—"

I shot into the attic bedroom and slammed the door.

Bette was dressed and brushing her long hair. "What's the racket about?"

"Dad's insane," I said, fingering my cheek.

"You know how freaked out he gets with earthquakes and fires and shit. He's always getting called to work, and it drives him nuts to have to worry about us."

"He's a goddamn lunatic."

*"And?"* She rotated her hand, indicating I should get to the point.

"Anthony and Gerard ran away." A sob tore from my throat. "They broke through the gate, and they're gone."

"Ah, shit, Loretta," Bette said, stroking my shoulder. "After breakfast, I'll help you find them. But I bet they'll come back on their own. Dogs that aggravating don't just disappear."

By the time I dressed and came downstairs to boil water for oats, my father had left for work. Cary told me the old man had been summoned to open water mains all over the city to douse fires ignited by the quake. "Without Dad," he said, "the firemen can't do a thing." He grinned, and for a moment, he was transformed from a heavy, sullen twelve-year-old into a beaming young boy. His sleep-tousled brown curls framed his plump face, making him look almost cherubic.

"Anyone can open a water main," I said. "All you need is a wrench."

Rita sat at the kitchen table in silence. Her wide eyes stared out at some invisible focal point. And eight-year-old Sophie swished into the kitchen wearing her "grass skirt"—narrow plastic strips gathered into an elastic waistband—pink pearls and a yard of yellow yarn clipped to the top of her head and streaming to her shoulders for "long blondie hair." She began strumming an invisible ukulele and yodeling *"Little old lady whoooo,"* with such seriousness that Cary and I had to laugh. Even Rita broke her trance to grin.

"Listen," I said when Bette appeared in the kitchen. "Pour in two cups of oats, will you, when the water boils, and then stir. I've got to go."

"Jeez, Loretta, I know how to make oats."

"Where you going?" My nosy brother had to know.

"I've got to find Anthony and Gerard. They got loose."

"I'm coming with you," Cary said.

But before he rose from the table, the front door creaked open and scrabbling sounds echoed through the hall. My great black dogs streaked into the kitchen, whipping their thick tails and shimmying with joy. "¡Válgame, Dios!" Nilda cried, following them in. "¡Qué bárbaro! Those dogs nearly knocked me over, pushing to get in."

I dropped to my knees, hugging one and then the other. Their coarse black coats smelled of eucalyptus leaves and fresh-mown grass. One-eyed Gerard nudged Anthony's moist snout out of the way to lap my face, and Anthony circled around to approach me from the other side. Both whimpered with pleasure.

"Take them outside, Loretta," Nilda said, "the filthy things. And wash up with soap and *hot* water—you hear me?—before you come to eat."

I had no choice but to tie the dogs to the mulberry tree until I had a chance to repair the gate. They howled all during breakfast, and I tried to eat as quickly as possible, though the oats Bette made were thick as paste and peppered with scorched bits.

"Did you feel the earthquake, Tía?" Sophie asked, speaking into the saltshaker, as though interviewing our aunt. She tilted the shaker toward Nilda for her answer.

"Don't talk into the salt," Nilda said. "You'll get germs on it. Of course, I felt that quake. It shook the apartment like a washing machine in the spin cycle. I thought the roof would fall in." She pulled her gold cross from her blouse and kissed it. "Thank God we weren't hurt. But I can't take no more. I told your uncle. That's it."

"What do you mean?" Bette asked.

"We can't stay in this crazy place," Nilda said. "We're moving back home."

Sophie spilled the salt, and Rita's spoon clattered to the floor.

My chest grew tight. "But you can't. You can't just *leave*." Nilda was all we had left, and there was so much she hadn't yet told us about our mother, about Fermina. I couldn't bear to think of her leaving us and taking her memories, those untold stories away with her.

"It's okay, honey. I'll still visit, and you can come see me in Río Puerco." Nilda patted my arm. "You girls are older now. You can take care of each other pretty good." She shot a look at Sophie. "Pick that up. I told you not to mess around with the salt."

"Are you really, *really* moving?" Cary asked.

Nilda nodded. "I can't take this, this, this...*earthquakes* and traffic and thieves and things." Last month, a cholo had snatched Nilda's purse while she was waiting for a bus. "It's too much. Es que, I'm not young no more. It's time to go back home."

Sophie brushed the spilled salt into her palm with a dish towel and set the shaker upright, sparking an idea for me.

"What about Uncle?" Bette asked. "What'll happen to him if you leave?"

Nilda looked at her as if she'd lost her mind. "¿Qué piensas? He's coming, too."

After breakfast, I helped Nilda wash dishes. My fear of losing her made my tongue thick and clumsy. I couldn't find the words to ask her directly what I wanted to know. It seemed babyish, even pathetic to beg for stories about my mother and Fermina, so I elaborated on the plan triggered by Sophie's saltshaker microphone. I would pretend I had a class assignment that required me to interview her about the past, about my mother, about Fermina. My aunt, who was prouder than my father of my good grades, would never refuse to help me with schoolwork. "Tía," I said, "I wonder if you could help me with a homework project."

"No sewing," she said.

"No sewing, I swear." Last year, I'd enlisted her help with an apron for my stitch-craft elective. By the time we finished trimming away the crooked seams and frayed edges, it was no bigger than a pot holder. "It's an interview," I said. "I have to ask you about the past and family and make a tape recording."

"Tape recording? Where are you going to get a machine for that?"

Good question, I thought, but said, "Maybe I can borrow one?"

"Father Knox has one, I think." On top of her main job as a nurse's aide, Nilda worked twice a week at the rectory, helping out the daily housekeeper. "I could ask him. But why interview me? I never did nothing interesting. You should interview your father. He was in France during the war and Nuremberg for the trials. Now, *he's* had an exciting life."

My father was not too well-known for sticking to the facts, but I couldn't tell my aunt her favorite brother, the second to the youngest, the one she—the oldest girl of ten children—claimed to have helped raise, was a liar. "I need the *real* truth, a woman's story."

That Saturday, I hiked from our house on Bellevue Avenue clear to my aunt's building on Boylston, near downtown. The dogs howled with disappointment when they saw me climbing the steps near the hospital on my own. I had fixed the gate, securing it with bicycle chain and combination lock. Now Anthony and Gerard leapt at it, begging to be taken along. No way could I bring those two large dogs to my aunt's tiny apartment. The last time I'd tried this, they'd stampeded upstairs so noisily that Helen, the manager, threatened to call the police.

The sky, like on so many winter mornings in Los Angeles, was an amber-tinged gray. The chilly breeze, dense and sooty, brushed my face and arms like barely perceptible cobwebs. I trekked from Alvarado to Temple Street, past mercados, taquerías, dime stores, and newsstands, crossing thick streams of traffic parted at red lights. More people thronged the streets than I'd expected just a few days after the earthquake, though Bette had told me many immigrants—campesinos in their own countries—believed they were safer outdoors, should another strike. As I trudged the cracked sidewalks, sidestepping broken glass and rubbish, I framed the questions I would ask Nilda during our interview.

She had borrowed the recorder from the rectory on Friday to keep through the weekend, but I hoped to ask all my questions in one day and not to have to make the long trip again on Sunday. By the time I turned right onto Boylston, my feet throbbed and my calves ached. The familiar street followed an incline toward my aunt's apartment building at the dead end. Rows of tenement buildings and dilapidated houses lined both sides. Last year, Sister Anselm brought my eighth-grade class here by bus to sing Christmas carols for the "poor and destitute." I was relieved neither Nilda nor José appeared to acknowledge me among the carolers. Remembering this, I hurried along the street and up the splintery stairs to my aunt's door.

Nilda had set out a bowl of purple grapes for me and greeted me like an adult visitor, rather than her fourteen-year-old niece, smiling shyly and smoothing her linen skirt before sitting beside me. The tape recorder was set up on the bird's-eye-maple chest that once belonged to Fermina. I was relieved that my uncle was nowhere in sight.

"You want some tea?" Nilda asked.

"Maybe later." I clicked the recorder on and taped myself saying, "testing, testing, testing." Then I rewound the tape, which spooled with a *scritch-scratchy* sound, before playing back my voice—high and clear as a child's.

I figured I should ask my first questions about Nilda, her experiences, before getting to what I really wanted to ask. "Tell me about your childhood," I said.

Nilda pulled back, an astonished look on her face, as though no one had ever asked her such a thing. "Bah, I thought you were going to ask me about history, about the Depression and the war, and things like that."

"It's personal history," I said. "That's what the project is about—*personal* history. Don't you want to talk about your childhood? Was it hard?"

Of course, Nilda jumped right in to contradict. "Qué hard, ni hard," she said into the microphone. "I had a beautiful childhood. I was the second oldest of ten, the first girl, but I didn't have that much work until your dad and Santi were born. I helped raise those two. I fed the sheep in the mornings, gave them oats. They would graze all day, but we fattened them with oats. That was my job. I loved the lambs. When the ewes wouldn't feed them, I'd fill a bottle with cow's milk and stuff a rag in the top so they could suck."

"I thought you didn't like animals," I said.

She shrugged. "Qué like, ni like. Animals are filthy, but it's not their fault. Mostly, they're work, pure work."

I thought of my dogs, how they ordered my day, beginning with their first meal at daybreak, continuing through walks and the evening meal, the intermittent yard cleanup they entailed — not to mention my part-time job at the pet clinic on Glendale Boulevard, which I enjoyed, but kept mainly to pay for their food, shots, and vitamins.

"Tell me about your mother, about Grandma," I said.

"Your grandma ruled the house," Nilda said with a smile. "She was short, just a tiny thing, but she was tough. She told everyone what to do, just once, and they did it. No messing around. She loved sugar, you know that? I remember her slipping into the pantry again and again to dip her thumb in the sugar and lick it off. Filthy habit, ¿qué no? But no one was going to tell her nothing. She liked a drink, too. 'Dame un traguito,' she'd say, and you'd jump up to pour her a shot of brandy, just one or two a day."

"How did she get along with Fermina?" I asked, leading to where I wanted the questions to go.

"They got along good. Con respeto. You couldn't back-talk neither one of them. You didn't even try. They spent a lot of time together, and they got real close." Nilda entwined the index and middle finger of her right hand. "They were like this. When your grandma got married, her mother died, so Fermina was like another mother to her."

"What was Fermina like when she was younger? Did she ever go anywhere or have any friends?" I wanted a sense of what Fermina's life was like and to understand how she managed to endow us with these strange gifts.

"Fermina didn't go too many places. She was already older when we were growing up, and women didn't run all over the place like they do now. Besides, she didn't drive or gallop around on horses. She stayed home. But, I remember, she had one friend, a lady named Heidi Schultz, who used to visit her. She came to the house a lot one summer, with this neighbor's boy—Pepe was his name. He translated for her because Heidi didn't speak no Spanish."

"Really?" I'd never heard this before. "How did she know Fermina?"

"She heard about her somewhere or another, maybe church. I think Heidi was writing a book. She asked Fermina all these questions, like you're asking me, to write the answers down for this book." Nilda squinted, straining to remember.

"Did you ever see the book, Tía?"

"No, I never did. Maybe she didn't finish it. I remember she got married to one of the Vigils—Óscar, the oldest one—and moved to his ranch just west of Santa Fe, so she stopped coming to visit, and Fermina was kind of sad after that."

"She missed her."

"Yes, she did. Heidi was writing this book or whatever, but they became real close during those visits." Nilda entwined her two fingers again and held them up.

"Is she still alive?" I asked. "That woman, Heidi Schultz?"

"Heidi *Vigil*, you mean. She was much younger than Fermina, so she's probably still around."

"What else do you remember?" I said in a casual way. "Do

you remember, say, meeting my mother? What was she like back then?"

Nilda nodded at me, as if to say, *now I get it.* "Your mother was different from anyone I ever met. Pues, she was big, you know that. I never saw a woman that big, tall and heavy, and your father, you know, is a skinny little thing, so I thought they looked kind of strange together. Plus, your mother, rest her soul, was plain, plain, and Juan Carlos was muy guapo. He was even cuter than Santi, the baby. He still is. But back when he had hair, all the girls chased after him. You've seen those pictures."

I nodded. My father photographed well. He resembled a young Clark Gable, but without the jug ears. No doubt that had attracted my movie-loving mother to him. "How did they meet?" I asked.

"On the bus," she said. "They were coming from Albuquerque. Your mother was just fourteen, like you, and your dad was nineteen, about to go in the army. I was twenty-nine, just married. I married late, you know. Esperanza, your mama, was with her girlfriends in the back, and he was up front, wearing this Panama hat he just bought. He was *so* proud of that hat. But your mother and her friends, oh, they thought it was hilarious. As a joke, she went to him, grabbed the brim, and pulled that hat over his eyes. Esperanza laughed so hard, she fell into the seat beside him. He took off that hat and they got started talking, just like that." Nilda's eyes shone and her cheeks grew rosy. "Your mama loved to kid around and joke, just like la Sophie—exactly like her."

"I didn't know that," I said. I'd always imagined my mother silent and thoughtful like me. "I thought she was quiet."

"Ay, no, Esperanza was bien popular. Always talking, always laughing. Everybody liked her. Your dad was the quiet one, muy callado, and obedient—oh, he would do anything he was told to do. Once she met him, he didn't have a chance. They were engaged before he shipped off."

"What else do you remember about her?"

"Well, she was honest, even what they call blunt. If you were drunk, she'd tell you. Esperanza didn't like drinking. If your skirt was too tight or you had too much lipstick, she'd say so. And she was honest about other things, too, like if they gave her too much change at the store, she'd hand it right back. One time she drove all the way back to Bullock's when they forgot to charge her for some stockings."

"What was she like after she married my father?"

"Well, she changed a little. Esperanza loved children, wanted a baby more than anything. But it was nine years before Bette was born, and your mama didn't have too much to do. She went to beauty school and learned to cut hair. Used to cut my hair." Nilda fingered her brown tresses. "They'd moved out here, away from family and friends. That wasn't good for her. She went to the movies all the time by herself because your dad doesn't like going to the show. He likes cards and horse races, things like that."

"He could have gone with her."

Nilda shrugged. "I was afraid she wouldn't make it after losing the twins."

"*What?*" For a moment, I thought I'd misheard my aunt. "What twins?"

"I shouldn't say this, but you're older now, you can understand. About a year before Bette was born, your mother got pregnant, and she lost those babies."

"Like my brother Anthony Gerard?" I asked.

Nilda nodded. "Miscarriage in the sixth month. The doctor said they were girls. Válgame, Dios, I never seen anyone so heartbroken. She wouldn't leave the bed. They lived right in this building, across the hall. She got that pleurisy and then pneumonia. I had to work. I couldn't be with her except on weekends, so she stayed alone in bed, with a pillow against her side for the pain." Nilda crossed her fingers again. "We were like sisters, like this."

"Poor Mama." My throat thickened.

"Esperanza was strong, though, stronger than I thought," Nilda said. "Next year, she had Bette, and you right after that, then Cary and the little girls. She was a good mother. She cared about all of you. La Bette is like that, too, you know. She takes care of you. Your mama would be proud of her. She'd be proud of all of you."

Footfalls sounded in the outer hall, my uncle's familiar, heavy-footed gait. I still hadn't found out what I wanted to know. "Tell me about Fermina again," I said. "Did she, say, know any, um...magic?"

"Now, don't *you* start on that silly business. La Bette already asked me about those gifts, or whatever, Fermina talked about. It's a bunch of nonsense." Nilda cleared her throat, pushed the microphone away. "That's enough, m'ija, that's enough for now."

The door swung open, and Uncle José appeared in the doorway, swaying on the balls of his feet and reeking of liquor. He glanced at me and at the recorder on the table. "What's she doing here?"

"She's interviewing me," Nilda told him. "It's for a school project."

José rolled his eyes and shrugged off his jacket, a new leather blazer, to hang in the closet. "I want to eat," he said.

"Stay for lunch, m'ija," Nilda told me.

José combed his hair in the mirror mounted on the closet door.

"I better go." I wound the tape onto one spool. "Can I take this? Or will we have time for another interview before you move?"

*"Move?"* José said over his shoulder. "Who's moving?"

"We are, hombre. Don't you ever listen?"

"Qué loca," he said.

Nilda handed me a box for the tape.

I hugged her and stood to leave. "Bye, Tía." I slipped out the front door and heard Nilda say, "I told you we're moving back home."

"Shut up. We ain't moving nowhere!"

As I walked home, I thought about my mother. Who she must have been and who I'd thought she was seemed two completely different people. And the mother I remembered was distinct from both the giggling, friendly girl Nilda knew and the quiet, reflective woman I'd imagined. She was twenty-nine when Bette was born and nearly forty when she died that winter before I turned ten. What I recalled most about her was the music of her voice, lilting and inflecting like song when she spoke. Her scent also stays with me, the aroma of corn masa, fresh cilantro, and lime. Food smells, warm smells. I loved to cook, to conjure up my mother's fragrance. Her face and body were likewise imprinted in my memory. That she was tall and heavy, everyone knew. I remembered the details: the strawberry birthmark on her forearm, her well-shaped dark eyebrows, the way her nose protruded at the tip, and how long, lean, and shapely her legs were for a woman of her girth. And I'd never forget her pillowy softness, the comfort of her embrace, like slipping into a warm bed for the profound absolution of sleep after a troubling day.

I shook my head to clear these images and focus on the streets. It was easy for me to lose myself in thought and take a wrong turn or miss one. Cars whooshed by, occasionally honking or shrieking to stop at intersections, the sidewalks were crowded now, especially near bus stops as I approached Alvarado and Sunset. Many people gathered around the kiosks chattering in the Spanish my ears no longer registered, it had been so long since I'd spoken it. I stole glances at these people, many far from home and separated from family, and I thought again of my mother, envisioning her in that apartment across from my aunt's, by herself in an unmade bed, clutching a pillow to her side. I'd had pleurisy once. I knew the knife-twisting pain in just drawing breath. But Bette had been with me while I was sick, and we'd stretched out on the sofa watching television together. What had it been like for my mother so far from family, so completely alone, while she grieved for the baby girls she'd lost?

I nodded at a harassed-looking woman pushing a stroller past me. A short, emaciated man stepped toward me. His windbreaker was dingy and his linty corduroys torn and grimy. He revealed a row of rotted teeth, brown pinholes dotting the yellowed enamel, when he smiled. "Perdóname. ¿Hablas español?" I shook my head, fearing he needed directions, which I had trouble giving in English, let alone in Spanish.

He thrust a piece of notepaper at me, and I glanced at him in sympathy, thinking how frightened I would be to find myself lost and alone in a place where I could not communicate with others. I opened the note: *Will you fuck with me?*

I balled up the paper and flung it at his feet. Bile roiled up to my throat. I swallowed hard and shoved past him, running without stopping until I'd flown down the steps near the hospital. My lungs flamed. I had to stop to catch my breath before trudging down the steps to our house. Of course, he wasn't chasing me.

No doubt someone had given the man the note as a cruel joke. If he couldn't speak English, he surely couldn't write, or even read, what was written in that note. I wondered what he made of my reaction to what he likely thought was a request for directions. As I approached our yard, a curious silence greeted me. The dogs didn't throw themselves at the fence, barking in glee at my return. Had they escaped again? I hurried to the side yard. The bicycle chain held tight. I tumbled the lock and pulled open the heavy gate. "Anthony," I called. "Gerard!"

High-pitched whimpering sounded from the crawl space. I crouched and reached under until I found a collar, and pulled at it until Anthony emerged, dust-covered and rigid, but whining, his muzzle foamy with spittle. "God, *no!*" I thrust my arm again into the shadows. This time, I hauled out Gerard, his thick, bullet-shaped body inert and his one eye walled, frozen in its socket. I turned back to Anthony. His eyes rolled back, and he was struggling to breathe. His muzzle emitted a heavy, chemical stench, a hot noxious fog. I reached into his mouth to clear his windpipe. In panic, he bit my hand hard, but there was no obstruction in his throat. Blood dripped from my knuckles as I rushed for the hose. They'd been poisoned, I knew it. I had seen a poisoned cat at the clinic. I'd watched helplessly as she convulsed before dying. But I thought I could save Anthony. I would force the nozzle into his throat and flush his stomach out. When I rounded the corner with the hose, Anthony took a few stiff steps and toppled over, his legs scissoring spasmodically. I sank beside him and laid my palms on his cool fur. "I will cure you," I said over and over. "I will make you well."

Anthony's head jerked as though he'd been called to attention. Then it lolled in my lap, his tongue spilling out with a wash of sticky froth, as his muscles released and a last foul gust whooshed from his mouth.

Bette cleaned my wounds with peroxide and bound up my hand with gauze and adhesive. "You should go to the doctor," she said. "You could be in shock." I shook my head, my arms felt rubbery, and I couldn't shake that phosphorous odor. It thickened my mouth and scorched my throat. But I said I'd be fine. My father wanted to call Animal Control to dispose of the bodies. When I heard this, I stormed out of the house to the toolshed for a shovel, Cary following at my heels. "I want to help," he said.

We had only one shovel. "I'm using this," I told my brother, and I searched for a spade or pick for him. On the shelves over the lawn mower, I spied a row of dusty jars and cans, among these I found a brown-tinted bottle. I turned it to read the label: RODEN-TICIDE. It was nearly empty.

"I can use this," Cary said.

I turned to face him. He held up a hoe. "Where should we dig?"

"Way back," I said, "near the ivy by the back fence."

We dredged up the coffee-colored earth in silence until Cary said, "What do you think made them sick?"

I shrugged, stabbed my shovel into the ground.

"Maybe some dog virus," he said. "Or asthma." Asthmatic himself, Cary stopped hacking at the ground, put a hand to his chest. "Do you think it was asthma?"

"No," I said. "They didn't have asthma." Something in Cary's wide eyes and trusting face kept me from telling him that the dogs had been poisoned.

"How come you didn't cure them? I thought you could make them better."

My shovel clanged against a buried stone. "I do *not* know."

By sunset, we'd scooped out a grave deep enough for both dogs. I wanted to bury them together, so they would never be alone. We hammocked empty burlap sacks to carry Anthony and Gerard to the hole. Cary and I placed them side by side in the earth and covered them with more sacks before spading earth into the small pit.

When the grave was covered—a mound of mealy earth and weed clods—Cary leaned on his hoe and looked at me. "You should say something, like a prayer."

But I shook my head and dragged the shovel back toward the house.

In the weeks that followed, I nearly quit the clinic. I almost couldn't bear to handle the dogs that were brought in for vaccinations and well care. The only reason I stayed was that I couldn't imagine what I'd do with my afternoons without the job, without my dogs. When the vet offered me a spotted puppy from a litter of strays, I looked at him as if he'd lost his mind. It was as though I was just recovering after a fall from a skyscraper, and he'd asked me if I'd care to leap off a cliff this time.

Ultimately, José had his way, dashing Nilda's plans to move home. They stayed in the tenement building on Boylston Street, but after the dogs died, I didn't have the heart to do much more than work and go to school. I lacked the energy to return to ask more interview questions, and Nilda, in disbelief and disappointment over José's refusal to move, never inquired how the project had turned out. I shoved the tape deep in a drawer up in the attic bedroom I shared with Bette. Besides, I had no machine on which to play the tape. Soon I nearly forgot it altogether.

But I never forgot finding that bottle of poison in the shed. He couldn't have done this, I told myself again and again. But what if he had? Before the morning of the earthquake, I hadn't realized that his dislike of me had hardened into hatred. And I hated him, too, in a cool and cautious way. I would never strike out at him, but I wouldn't speak to him or look at him or touch his things, as though he were an invisible, contaminating presence, foul and deadly as a poison gas.

On his part, he continued going to work, coming home, eating meals, watching baseball games, doing charitable work for Saint Vincent de Paul, and gambling with his friends in the Loman Club on Saturday nights. Except for working and gambling, he usually dragged Cary along with him when he left the house, especially when he hauled donated furniture from wealthy or deceased parishioners to poor people in our parish.

One Saturday, they returned earlier than usual from Saint Vincent de Paul activities, and Bette, who'd slipped out to meet her boyfriend, Luis, hadn't yet returned home. I worried she'd be in trouble for leaving without permission, but my father was too tired and preoccupied to register that she was missing. Cary, holding an ornate birdcage, trailed behind him into the house. "Look what we brought you, Loretta," he said before I could pick myself up to vacate the room my father had entered.

I stood and peered in the cage at a large, molting green-and-yellow parrot with a crusty beak. "What's this?" Rita and Sophie drew near.

"Mr. O'Toole died," my father said, his first words to me in weeks. "This was his bird. I don't know the name."

"Dumbshit," the bird said.

"I am *not*," Sophie told the parrot.

My father shook his head. "He's got a bad mouth."

"We brought it for you, Loretta," Cary said.

"Como sueño." My father yawned and collapsed on the couch, likely to shore up strength for that evening's card game.

Cary and my sisters helped me clean out the cage. I lifted the bird out to examine it. It was a male and not very young, though such birds can live long lives. We shut the bird in the bathroom while I scrubbed out the bottom tray and the girls shredded newspaper. Cary scoured the rusted bars with a Brillo pad. The bird cried from the bathroom. "Asshole! Asshole!"

"What are you going to name him?" Cary asked me.

I shrugged. The bird was old. He probably already had a name he was used to, though I hoped it wasn't one of the words he knew.

"How about Polly?" Rita suggested.

"No," I said.

"Call him, 'Cusser,'" Sophie said. "Dirty Cusser."

"No." I would call him Saint Vincent, after the charity, something that might help steer him in a better direction.

When the cage was clean, I retrieved the parrot from the bathroom. Despite his foul mouth, the bird had a sweet disposition. When I lifted him, he rubbed his balding head under my chin. "Vincent," I said as I ran a finger down his shabby breast. Parrots can molt year round, but this case was severe. I would keep him quiet and calm in my attic bedroom and feed him hard-boiled egg whites, cottage cheese, nuts and vegetables with plenty of flaxseed oil, so his plumage would come in thick and glossy.

"That's a good name," Cary said. "You come up with good names, like Anthony and Gerard. They lived up to their names. They were like friends, like brothers."

Rita opened the cage door. I maneuvered Vincent inside and snapped it shut.

Cary continued, "Everybody liked those dogs, not just us. You know who gave them food when you were gone?"

I froze. *"Who?"*

"Ambrose from next door," he said. "I saw him giving them hamburger that day you went to Tía's house. Man, they loved it. You should have seen." Cary peered in the cage. "They were going to send this bird to the pound. Mr. O'Toole's son was ready to take him over there, but Dad said you might want a bird, so they gave him to us."

I met the bird's beady stare. "Dumbshit," he squawked.

For the next several weeks, I would rouse myself at the first streaks of daylight, throw on a robe, step into my huaraches, and slip downstairs and out the back. I'd lean on that ivy-covered gate and howl at our neighbors' yard until it was time to dress for school. I returned at intervals during the day, to stand at the gate and bark myself hoarse. What the other neighbors made of a fourteen-year-old girl baying in her backyard, I can't say. Only Ambrose knew what this was about, why I made a racket loud enough to rouse the Devil slumbering in hell, let alone a bitter old woman, from fitful bouts of sleep.

If my father minded this behavior, he never said a word. But once as I headed for the stairs during a rainstorm, I passed him in the hallway, and he thrust his yellow slicker at me, saying, "Here, h'ita, you might need this."

SUBJECT: FERMINA/WEDDING CUSTOMS
WPA: 6-17-38—DC: HMS
June 16, 1938
Words: 499

## MARRIAGE ON THE FIRST MESA

Fermina witnessed few weddings on the First Mesa, but her mother often described her own marriage ceremony, remarking on how difficult it was for her. Because Fermina's mother was Tewa of Hano and not Hopi, her father's clan was reluctant to accept her. Warfare between the Hopi and the Navajo had driven the Hopi to seek support from the Tewa, who lived near Taos at the time. The Tewa agreed, in return for land and membership in the Hopi village. Land was granted, but the Hopi did not readily accept newcomers, and Fermina's father met much resistance after choosing his bride. His clan agreed to the match only when they saw that he would not relent. Fermina's father then asked his prospective bride's mother for permission. She consented, and the bride-to-be spent the next day making *piki* (wafer bread). Afterward, she and her mother took piki to the groom's family, who offered meat in exchange. Then everyone knew the couple would be married.

Leading up to the ceremony, Fermina's mother had to grind enough corn to fill twelve large pots. This took her almost a year to finish. The two stones she used to grind corn on the metate slab raised blisters that toughened into calluses on her hands. On hot summer days, when no one was looking, she would toss corn dust on her neck and between her breasts to absorb sweat as she worked.

After she filled the dozen pots, the women

returned to the groom's house to announce
their arrival in four days. The bride's family
dressed her in a *manta* (a ceremonial blanket)
and wheeled her hair in butterfly whorls for the
visit. All the groom's relatives gathered for
this occasion. The bride's uncles told them that
they brought this girl to grind as much corn as
she could, and the groom's uncles replied, "Good.
We are glad to have her."

Early the next morning, the bride ground corn
at the groom's home. The bride spent three days
grinding corn, kneeling all the while before
the metate and stopping only to eat and relieve
herself. On the fourth morning, female relatives
washed the heads of the bride and groom,
twisting together strands of hair from both and
saying, "Now that you are woven together, you
will share a long life and become old together."

Fermina's mother also explained that after
the man and woman were married, it was customary
for the women in the groom's clan to heave mud at
his mother's home, shouting insults at the bride.
They called out that she was lazy, that she did
not grind corn well, and that she was Tewa, not
Hopi. Traditionally, the groom's mother tosses
mud in return, arguing her new daughter-in-law's
virtues. And the attack would end. But this
time, the mother-in-law remained silent, so the
women jeered until early evening. The bride, her
calloused hands throbbing, listened to the women
howl like coyotes until long after the sun had
flattened beyond the mesa.

# REAL, DEEP, AND TRUE—
# BETTE: 1974

Just as I've rolled myself a nice fat number and settled on my bed with *Siddhartha,* the goddamn phone blurts a half-ring, jangling my nerves like a freaking fire alarm. I ignore it, light my joint, and it stops after a bit. I suck in a sweet, burning lungful, then another, focus on the page, and there it goes again. *Motherfucker!* I stub out my smoke, throw the bedspread over the ashtray and stash box, and stomp over to answer the blasted thing. I pause, clear my throat, and say, "*Hel*-lo," in my sweetie pie voice because I know exactly who it is. There's only one person with this tele-pathic knack for disturbing my rare moments of peace.

"Oiga, m'ija, it's me Ceci," my future mother-in-law says in her breathless way, like she's been running a marathon, instead of sitting on her plump ass cradling her princess phone to her ear. "I just came from Safeway, and they got those Betty Crocker potato flakes on sale. On sale, m'ija! This week only!"

"Really?" I say, wondering what the fuck she's talking about.

"I know Nilda wants to use real potatoes, but think about it, m'ija, does that make sense? The instant are so much faster and way more economical!"

"O-*kay,*" I say, recalling the gist of the potato conflict: Ceci's championing the flakes for the wedding buffet, but Nilda, the purist, wants to peel a thousand potatoes herself, bubble them up in a cauldron, and cream the pulp by hand, preferably with a bent fork. If it's hard work and makes no sense, Nilda's behind it 100 percent.

"Pues, there I was at the store, and I didn't know what to do," Ceci says in a tone that suggests she knew *precisely* what to do. "So I bought twelve boxes."

"Twelve boxes," I say. "Hmm."

"Do you think that's too many, m'ija? We don't have to use them all."

One box is too many, as far as Nilda's concerned, but I say, "Sounds okay."

"So we're going with the instant." Ceci's voice is rich with triumph.

"It makes no difference to me."

"Okay, m'ija, just checking. I don't want to do nothing to interfere. This is *your* wedding, not mine or Nilda's. It's all about you and Luis." She makes kissing noises. "I'll call you later, if anything else comes up."

After we hang up, I wish I'd asked *her* to break the news to Nilda about the potatoes. I hate being in the middle of this petty shit, and there's no end to what Nilda and Ceci can find to argue about. Last week, they skirmished over the carne asada, and yesterday it was the salad. Side dishes still loom on the horizon. I don't even want to think about the fucking cake!

But apart from that stupid hassle, getting married is a dream come true for me. A beautiful dream from that moment at Pearl Gomez's quinceañera when I first spotted Luis in the Knights of Columbus hall and true love struck like a sneaky uppercut. I had just turned sixteen, and Luis was twenty-two. He was wearing this cool white suit with a vest and a black shirt. (Who'd have guessed he had a mother obsessed with instant potato flakes?) He looked so fine, I tingled all over. Once, I slept over at a friend's house where they had this piano that mice nested in. Late at night, the mice scrabbled over the hammers and wires, making this eerie plinking sound. That's how I felt when Luis lowered his shades, smiled at me. When he cruised over later to ask me to dance, those damn mice went wild.

We danced every dance. After the band quit and the lights came on, we got a good look at each other, and he scribbled my phone number on his wrist. He kissed me lightly before taking off with these other guys, also wearing white suits and sunglasses. Loretta brought me my purse and said in her sarcastic way, "Who was that masked man?"

"That's the guy I'm going to marry," I said.

"Yeah, *right*."

Now, three years later, after I turned nineteen, we *are* getting married. Naturally, I'm thrilled. But sometimes—I have to admit—I stroll to the bus station on my breaks from work at the bindery. Day after day, I wander over there, though it's a nasty place crawling with sleepy old drunks, stringy teenagers with bad skin, screaming babies and their desperate-looking mothers. And I find myself checking the board where they post the fares and destinations. It's only forty dollars to Phoenix, fifty-five to Albuquerque. Then my break is over, and I'm back at the bindery, telling how I'm having artificial seed pearls sewn onto the bodice of my wedding dress. I have to holler over the roar of the presses, but anyone can see how ecstatic I am.

Despite her cynical attitude about my wedding, I've asked Loretta to be my maid of honor. Of course, she has to know *every* detail before she'll agree. Any other eighteen-year-old would be flattered to have been chosen, but oh *no,* not Loretta. She has to know all about the best man, the other bridesmaids and groomsmen, who the ring bearer's going to be. She even wants to control what the fucking priest is going to say.

She says, "If he tells you to 'obey' even once, I swear I'll walk out."

I tell her I have no idea what the priest will say—no one listens to priests anyway. Besides, he's fresh from the Philippines; his accent's so thick, I doubt anyone will be able to understand him, whatever he says. But that's not good enough for old Loretta. She wants me to tell him to say what *she* expects. And another thing—she wants Cary to be one of the groomsmen.

"It's too late," I tell her. "Luis already asked his friends and a cousin."

"I think you should have Cary in the wedding. He's gotten friendly with Luis lately. I'd think he'd want him in the wedding, too."

It's true. My fifteen-year-old brother's glommed onto my fiancé, like he's some substitute big brother. "What if he's an usher?" I was kind of planning on this anyway.

"Well," she says, "let me think about it."

I know she'll agree, but first I have to grovel. I really have no choice, because I hate pissing off any of my close friends by singling one out for the honor. They'll all understand, though, if I choose my sister.

If that's not enough pena, Ceci's stepped up the phone calls, pestering now about the flowers. Seems she knows this person who can do them cheap. He did the flowers for Father Gillespie's ordination and they were *so* beautiful and *reasonable.* Just let her make the call and that will be all settled, one less thing to worry about, m'ija. Now, I've tried being nice, I swear, but I have told this woman *all along* that I am doing my own flowers. I don't care if they serve cat litter from the buffet table or if the priest declares me Luis's slave for life— *I want to do my own fucking flowers!*

She's just uptight from all this wedding junk. That's what it is—stress. Why else would she hang up on her daughter-in-law-to-be?

Weirdly, the more his mom yaps at me, the less Luis has to say. It's like he turned the chore of talking to me over to her. When he comes by the house, he just stares at whatever's on TV. It can be *Soul Train* or *Romper Room,* he doesn't give a shit. He's all mesmerized, like the picture tube's going to reveal some deep truth, like it's those cave walls of Plato's that bounce off shadows of what's really going on for people too lazy to turn around and see for themselves.

Last night, he actually passed gas in front of a rerun of *Bonanza.*

"¡Menso!" I hit him with a throw pillow. "We're not even married yet! I could still hop a bus to Phoenix, and nobody would be able to say a thing."

"What's wrong with you?" he asked. "Huh?"

"Forget it." I stalked off to bed as he gawked at a bunch of guys chasing around on horseback.

The next day, I'm still pissed at him in a vague way, but I try to be cool, tell myself it's just nerves, like Ceci says. I focus on the wedding, what a blast that will be, though planning it is a huge pain. For instance, it's a church requirement, or some such shit, that we meet with the priest ten days in advance of the ceremony. Before that session, we head to Luis's apartment, where we drink beer and argue about his hair.

His cousin Bianca gave him the stupidest haircut imaginable. It looks like she clapped a bowl on his head and hacked around it. I'm marrying Bowl-Clip in less than two weeks. He's all proud because she cut it for free. He's saved a whole five bucks and looks like a comic strip character—*pretty* good deal. I try explaining that you're not supposed to *economize* when it comes to how you look at your wedding. But it's like arguing with an onion; he'll never get it. I give up and chug my tall boy.

We drive to the rectory without talking, Luis burping the whole way. If I wasn't so in love, I swear I'd kick his ass out on the Hollywood Freeway and hijack his car at least to Phoenix.

The priest sure has a load to say to us, but I can't absorb too much of it. After the beer, I seriously have to pee. I cross my legs at the knees and ankles, one foot bobbing like crazy. I'm afraid if I ask to be excused, Luis will blurt something idiotic and Father Muñoz will call the whole deal off. My eyes tear up, and I bite down on my tongue, praying silently: *Wrap it up. Please wrap it the fuck up!*

My intended, the mute, grows entranced with his own shoes.

I finally interrupt the guy. "Listen, just be sure you don't say anything about the wife having to obey the husband, okay?"

This unleashes a freaking tsunami of unintelligible words, and finally, around an hour later, the priest stands up and says, "Go and piss," and I bolt for the door. Only later does it strike me that he must have said "go in peace."

I try, but I'm not always patient with Luis, though he's so fine that anyone would be glad to marry him. I swear. For one thing, he's a musician. He plays lead guitar with a band called Sabor. They perform at high-school dances and quinceañeras and what-not. They do a lot of pop numbers and oldies, but Luis writes the original tunes they play. His strongest piece is called "I've Got the Four-Oh-Five Blues," which he's dedicated to the San Diego Freeway (the 405) at the start of rush hour, a little after four — as in 4:05, get it? It goes on a bit long, especially when he's been drinking and ad-libs lines, but it's catchy. He's working on a tune for me, too, a love song, and *that* will be his best ever. Maybe some producer will turn up at a quinceañera, hear him play it, and sign him to a huge contract. Then people will listen to it on the radio and wonder who inspired the haunting melody, the unforgettable lyrics. Of course, I'll have to help him out with the words, like I did with the "Four-Oh-Five Blues," and there's only so much you can do with a person who thinks "zost" is a word.

"What's this 'zost'?" I asked him when I read his lyrics.

"You know, that black stuff that comes out of tailpipes, smoke, or whatever."

"That's '*ex*haust,'" I had to tell him, "emissions, car *ex*haust, not 'zost.' There's no such thing as '*zost.*' Jeez." And I penciled in the correction.

Clearly, he needs me like Sonny needs Cher, except that I'm short with curly hair and I can't sing, but I *can* spell and I've got a good vocabulary. He needs me, plus he's sweet. Really, he is.

For no reason, he'll bring me a couple of avocados in the pockets of his chinos. "Alligator pears," he calls them, and he rolls them in my lap. If they're soft under the skin, I'll shave them with a paring knife and mash the green flesh with a fork. Then I squeeze half a lemon over it, toss in some salt, and scoop it onto saltines that I eat while Luis strums his guitar. Times like these, I know I'll always love him, even if he never gets that recording contract and my song never gets played on the radio, even if he ends up pumping gas in the Mojave Desert and wearing an oil-stained shirt with his name misspelled — LEWIS — on the pocket.

And though we nodded like bobbleheads when the priest asked if we'd been pure, we *have* made love, plenty of times, and that's what's so perfect about us, always perfect. I try explaining this to Loretta, who's never even taken a phone call from a guy, let alone gone on a date, so this is like describing color to a blind person.

She rolls her eyes. "Right, the earth moves."

"It's beautiful, like losing consciousness in a fantastic dream, better than tripping on the best grass you can buy."

"I don't like dope."

"Better than wine then."

"Now, *that's* doubtful," says la borracha, who has a taste for the sauce.

As the wedding draws nearer, old Ceci's gone from being all smiles to strictly orders. Most of her sentences to me begin with "you have to," as in "you have to meet the photographer" and "you have to order the cake" and so on. I have *no* peace. When the goddamn phone rings, I cringe, knowing she's thought up a dozen more things for me to do. It's not my fault that when she married Luis's father, they had to elope and they were so poor they couldn't even afford pillows. This is her justification for tormenting me with wedding plans.

"I just want everything nice for you," she says whenever I complain. "When we got married, we didn't have a thing, not even pillows."

(I imagine shipping a truckload of pillows to her just before buying a bus ticket.)

She'll probably go insane with fury when I miss today's fitting. My brother, Cary, has asked me to go with him and some friends to a baseball game at their high school, so I'm off. And it's fun in a nostalgic way to smoke pot on the bleachers. I don't give a shit about baseball, but I enjoy seeing people I know, like Steve Reyes, who sits by us. He used to be in love with me for ages. He was a big jock in high school, and now his younger brothers are on the team, so he's swung by to watch them play.

When he grins at me and says hello, it's clear he's still nuts about me.

I remember he wanted to study art. When we were dating, he gave me a canvas striped with all these shades of color, like a rainbow. Later I found out it was just an exercise for design class, but still it was nice. I bet if I'd stayed with him, he'd have painted my portrait, and it would have been so good they'd put it up in some gallery, like they've got that Pinkie up at the Huntington, where everyone goes to gawk, wondering just who that delicate beauty was to old Thomas Lawrence.

"You still paint?" I ask Steve. He used to be a funny-looking guy, but his beaky nose and bulging brow have smoothed into a more regular face. And he has a *much* better haircut these days. No bowl-clip here.

He nods. "I paint houses. I work for my uncle now."

"You didn't go to college?"

"I take some courses at East Los."

"Any art classes?"

He laughs. "Nah, I'm sick of paint by the end of the day."

Maybe it's the dope, but I feel like the mice might start skittering in the piano again. Since I'm about to get married, I keep it friendly, but not overly so. I'm even nice when his girlfriend shows up—a stick insect with big hair—bearing two tall Cokes.

I have a decent time with my brother, despite his lame friends, whose conversation is about as dumb as a person can imagine. I ignore them and enjoy the dope, the faraway, muffled feeling it gives me. All muy tranquilo, except I keep flashing on that fitting appointment. No way will I go all red-eyed and stinking of weed to zip myself into artificial seed pearls. Talk about a downer. Just thinking about it creates this pressure in my shoulders and neck. In fact, since I've known Ceci, I've had this stiff neck from tension, a pain like you get when your beloved pillow falls off the bed and you end up sleeping all crooked.

A week from the wedding, and I have to admit there are some things about Luis that kind of disturb me. Like his drinking. He's only twenty-five, but already he's a huge lush. He even admits it. There's a long tradition of badass drinking in his family. His father holds a job and doesn't drive around collecting DUIs, but the man puts away nearly a fifth of Jack Daniel's a night. Even my dad can't keep up, and the old man's no piker. Luis, himself, easily polishes off a six-pack while watching baseball on television. Now, I like a drink myself. I even have a favorite wine—Chateau La Salle—which only costs a few dollars and requires no corkscrew. But Luis doesn't understand the concept of having a glass of wine only now and again.

Tonight he brought over a six-pack for dinner. Two beers remain in the fridge when we decide to go bowling with Cary and Loretta. Typically, when a guest brings drinks, he's supposed to leave the undrunk portion for the household, but Luis makes a big deal of helping me clean up after dinner and taking out the trash. With it, he lugs out the beers. I assume he's throwing them away, hope maybe he's giving up drinking. But as we're about to climb into the car, Luis digs the beers out of the garbage to drink on the *way* to the bowling alley.

"You *diehard*!" I let out a laugh, but I have to force it.

Loretta shoots me a look, though she doesn't say a thing.

But when we get home, she starts in on that gift business.

Seated before the vanity, she's rubs in her Noxema real casually and says, "You ever think about Fermina and the gifts she supposedly gave us?" She's trying to be offhand, but I can see she's taking it somewhere. "I admit I've got my doubts, especially when I couldn't save the dogs. I believed it for a long time, and it *was* real to the extent that I believed in it. I know I do have some ability, some skill, in treating animals. But I have to do the work, to educate and train myself. It's not the gift I thought it was."

"What are you getting at?"

"Well, what if it's the same for you? What if, say, you're telling yourself a lie and making yourself believe it. It's never going to be true, just because you want it to be. You have to do the work to keep believing it." She screws the lid back on the jar and wipes her hands on a washcloth. "For instance, what if you're telling yourself you love Luis, but you're just settling for him? He drinks a lot, doesn't he? And he's not all that smart. I mean, you could try it out, not force yourself to believe, and see what happens."

"Cut the crap!" I tell her. "I'm not lying to myself. I love Luis. Of course, I don't expect *you* to understand that."

Her nasty parrot whistles and squawks from its cage. "Bullshit!"

"Will you cover that fucking thing up?" I tell her.

She throws a quilt over it, and then stares at me like I'm a specimen in an experiment that's showing some unusual effects. She leaves it alone, though.

I'm *not* lying to myself. I think about things as they are, and I am worried. I'm about to marry a guy who drinks way too much. But I also believe in the power of love. That's probably my real gift, not telling lies. With love, people can handle whatever shit comes their way. If, for instance, Ceci was capable of loving her husband—instead of being fixated on instant potatoes and pillows—why, I bet he wouldn't drink at all. That's what Loretta doesn't get. My love for Luis is real, deep, and true. No lie!

I plan to spend my last day on earth as a single person with my family. I'm thinking I'll cook them a special dinner, spend time with each, and say my good-byes, that kind of thing. But, first thing in the morning, there's Ceci on the phone with her list of things for me to do before the rehearsal this afternoon. "M'ija, good thing you took the day off. We got tons to do."

"What about my family?"

She says, "Family is forever, but we got to pick up that punch bowl before noon."

So, whoosh, off we go in her little car, Ceci yammering the whole way about boutonnieres and where to put the table favors and how she doesn't know why Nilda insists on boiling the beans when the canned are just as good, ask anyone. I stare out the window, wondering how badly my face will scar if I swing open the door and hurl myself out. Then I sneak a look at old Ceci, trying to find some resemblance to Luis. There's very little of my intended, *thank God*, in this dumpy woman with coppery sausage curls. But what if Luis and I have a baby who looks like her? As I'm picturing a miniature version of my future mother-in-law kicking in a bassinet, she turns to me and says, "You know, I'm going to be your mama now that you're marrying my son."

My face gets hot. *"What?"*

"Well, your mother's gone, m'ija, so I thought—"

"My mother's not gone," I tell her. "She's still with me."

She reaches over and pats my hand. "It's just nerves."

I close my eyes and see my mother's face. Her short, curly black hair, pink cheeks, the bulbous tip of her nose, her glasses, her pale lips parted, and her small dark eyes softening with compassion.

*Of course, I'm with you, always with you,* my mother whispers to me, *but you can still be nice.*

We were supposed to have a rehearsal dinner at a restaurant, and my dad would have paid for it, as our family tradition goes—the groom's family picks up the tab for the wedding; the bride's pays for the rehearsal dinner—but the old man approached us a few months back, saying he'd likely shell out a couple hundred for the dinner, so could we use the cash instead and skip the dining out? Luis thought the money would be better. We could buy grass with it and earn us another two hundred back for our honeymoon dealing it. We took the money and bought the dope, but it turned out we ended up smoking so much that we didn't make much on the investment, just enough to buy a couple tabs of acid for tripping during the celebration. Luis says we'll have our honeymoon trip on our wedding day. And that's cool.

After we finish doing all the useless junk Ceci is so desperate to accomplish and get through the wedding rehearsal, I finally head home to fix a meal for my family. Luis and his best man, Jorge, insist on coming over to eat with us. I prepare my specialty—liver and onions fried in bacon drippings. With the extra two people, I have to chop the meat in smaller portions, but there's enough. More than enough because people don't go for liver like they should.

Cary, of course, scarfs it down, pausing only to say, "Can I have your radio when you move out?"

Dad eats without mumbling one word of thanks. Sophie will devour anything, but Rita and Loretta make big displays of pushing it around their plates without touching much. This, naturally, pisses me off, so I throw down my fork, spring from the table, and slam into the bathroom. My Last Supper—why couldn't they at least try? Truth is, they'll probably be relieved when I'm gone, less competition for the hot water and telephone. But you'd think *someone*— Sophie, Cary, or at least my dad — would be all broken up about me leaving. Loretta, alone, seems to think I'm making a mistake, but she's not trying too hard to stop me.

Only my dad bothers to come after me. "H'ita, what's wrong?" he says through the bathroom door. "Did you burn your tongue?"

"I should have stayed in college," I say through the keyhole. "I was smart in school. I could have majored in psychology or something. You could have made me finish school instead of working at the bindery."

"Pues, hija, if you want to go back to school, then go. You don't want to get married, fine. That's up to you."

Then I hear Luis. "She don't want to get married? Shoot, I won't marry her. She's the one that asked me."

"Shut up! Shut up! Leave me alone. Everyone just leave me alone!"

And they do. I sit on the toilet lid, crying and honking my nose into tissue from the roll. Then I splash my face, all swollen and blotchy — perfect for wedding photos — and emerge to find my dad talking quietly with Luis in the kitchen.

"They get nervous, you know," he's saying.

I go for a glass of water, and Luis gives me a wary look. "Are you better or what?"

I nod. "I'm sorry, I just—"

"It's okay, h'ita," my father says. "Just take some Anacin and go lie down."

So I do.

Though he's at his folks' house and I'm with my family, Luis and I agreed to swallow our hits at eight on the morning of our wedding. So here I am in the shower, gaping as the spray of water splinters into ice chips and then tiny diamonds webbed on glimmering strands, and I see how everything is attached to everything else, like the luminous beads on Fermina's favorite rosary. This reminds me of her spirituality. When I'm straight, I don't dwell on shit like this. But now, I sense how her spirit connected itself to people and to the world. This isn't about God, and it's sure as hell not about the church. It's about being part of a chain or a web that keeps her whole and a part of me, the way my mother is after all these years. We are linked, and the links—if you could see them—are golden, not hard like metal, but more like light. Everything *is* connected, I realize as I towel myself off. But something's missing, something I can't name, though I know it's about Fermina—something to do with who she was and how she lived.

In the bedroom, Loretta's applying the only cosmetic she uses: ChapStick. Seated before the mirror, she looks like the Evil Queen in *Snow White,* her nose and jaw sharp as blades. "*Mirror, mirror, on the wall,*" I say, and my words reverberate like I'm speaking into a well.

The Evil Queen glances at my reflection and caps the tube. "You're stoned."

I shake my head, and then I nod, laughing until I shudder and sob.

"Christ, Bette, do you want some coffee?"

"Wine, I need wine."

Of course, we have to argue about that, but eventually she brings me a mug of cooking sherry, horribly sour shit, but I gulp it down, holding my nose. Then I rush to the toilet, throw up half my brains, and feel immensely better.

I finish dressing and slap on my makeup. I don't do much with my hair, though. It's pretty thick and curly, so it looks best when

I leave it alone. As I finish applying mascara, I remember I have to wear burnt shoes, the pair I'd drunkenly tossed into the fireplace at a nightclub last week after Luis and I toasted our wedding and chinked in the champagne flutes. Sweet Luis singed the hair on his wrist pulling them out before they burned too badly. I examine them—blackened bottoms, char-marbled heels—and slip them on under my dress. The hem almost covers them pretty well, but Loretta takes one look and says, "How come your shoes are burned? They smell like smoking tires."

"Never mind. No one can see them under there."

"*I* can see them."

"No one notices shoes."

She raises an eyebrow.

"It's too late, isn't it?"

Loretta shrugs. "There's always divorce."

Though it's my wedding day, there's the usual bickering over the bathroom and the breakfast stuff. I can't eat a thing. Instead, I watch the others scrapping like it's just any old day—Cary jabbering while pulling a tortilla away from Sophie, who's slapping at his hands, and my father hunting for his lighter. Suddenly their jaws elongate and their foreheads melt back. Their faces darken with fur and their teeth sharpen into fangs. They become wolves. Of course, it's the acid, but tripping tends to reveal underlying stuff about people, their true natures. Rita pops on the scene and howls about some missing panty hose—a tall, girlish lycanthrope in a striped bathrobe.

Often my trips will take on a theme, and today's is "People Who Turn into Animals." I'd hoped for a fairy-tale theme after seeing Loretta become the Evil Queen. After all, it's my wedding—what could be more appropriate? But animals, it turns out, rule the day, though Loretta remains the Evil Queen.

When we climb in the car, it fills with the rank stench of wolves, but I control my queasiness all the way to church.

Naturally, we're ten minutes late, but when we arrive, there's no sign of Luis. How fucked up is that? I head back for the car, parked across the street, ignoring all the gawkers milling about.

"Hey, where you going?" my dad calls.

"He's not here. I'm going home."

"Knock if off, mensa," he says. "There he is driving up right now."

My heart drops like an anvil chucked over a cliff.

The priest is frantic, probably has another wedding right after ours and doesn't want to get backlogged, so we hustle into position. The organist starts up, and my dad, the weepy wolf, and I parade down the aisle. Most brides would be touched by seeing their fathers cry. But my dad bawls over anything. I never take it too seriously when my father turns on the waterworks.

The church floor is what gets to me. It's this dark blue linoleum with white snaky swirls like ghostly serpents writhing in mire. Imagine picking your way to the altar, in charred shoes, over all these phantom snakes. Mighty distracting, take it from me. I make it to the altar, though, and the priest starts mumbo-jumbo-ing. We mumbo-jumbo back. More priest, more parishioners, more priest, and then I sense Loretta stiffening beside me, so I tune into the blabber.

The priest—though a thin guy—has these fat cheeks, puffed all the more by his high collar. Gray stripes streak back from his temples, through his closely cropped hair: he's a friendly chipmunk chirruping in a dell: "...and as the church follows the leadership of Christ, our Lord, so must the wife follow her husband."

My heart squeezes. I shoot a sideways glance at the Evil Queen. She trembles with wrath. Worried she'll bolt or maybe even smack the priest, I concentrate on the chipmunk, willing him to stop. But he continues on, a cheery woodland creature, lacking the sense to wriggle his velvety nose for danger.

"In the way the church obeys the will of Christ, the wife must bend to the will of her husband in marriage."

Loretta is about to blow, when Luis grabs my hand. "I, Luis Reynaldo Hernández, take thee, Bette Davis Gabaldón, to be my lawful wedded wife, to have and to hold..."

What's a chipmunk to do, but twitch his whiskers and go on from there?

And so we are married.

At the reception, Nilda and Ceci get into it in front of the punch bowl and have to be separated by some ushers—not Cary, though. He spends most of the afternoon hiding out in the restroom from Sophie's nutty friend Aracely, who's got some crush on him. I score nearly six hundered bucks from the dollar dance, just enough for first and last on a rental in North Hollywood.

The house, our first home, used to be an office for this orange grove, so it's smallish. And it's filled with dark wood paneling—all horsy and masculine. The kitchen is like a closet, and the wood in there is painted navy blue for some reason, so it's superdark. Actually, the whole place is short on lighting, but that's okay. We'll get lamps. In the meantime, I stick lots of fat, drippy candles around and string amber-colored beads in the kitchen doorway. Luis found this huge cable spool that we're using as a table in the living room, since there's no room in the kitchen for it.

I love this house and having people over, which is fine because Luis enjoys company, too. He works the early shift and almost always has guys over when I get home. They'll be sitting around, listening to music or strumming their guitars, huffing on a bong, and drinking beer. I change into jeans real quick and mash some avocado and deep-fry some cut-up corn tortillas for chips. Then I join them with my glass of Chateau La Salle. And I am the woman of the house, a real person with bills and everything.

I couldn't be happier, unless, of course, Ceci would leave us alone. She visits a wee bit too often, if you ask me. Just today she brought me yet another housewarming gift: a tall, spiky plant with sharp points at the tops of the leaves. "Sansevieria," she says it's called. "Mother-in-law's tongue. When you have kids, you have to put it up because it's poisonous at the root."

"Gee, thanks," I say, and get rid of her fast because I have an appointment.

Soon as she splits, I haul ass to Planned Parenthood for my pills, and I get the shock of my life when the doctor tells me I'm pregnant! Now, I know I've been not too regular about taking the pills, but I didn't think that'd be a problem. I try to take two or three to catch up. I thought they had carryover strength. Turns out, they don't.

I rush home to tell Luis, and he's like, "Cool, we're going to have a kid."

I flip out. "You dumbass, we can't have a kid! How about the acid I dropped? How about the smoking and drinking and taking the fucking pill the times I did remember to take it? All that will hurt a baby. Besides, I'm not ready to have a kid. I don't know how to be a mother, and I don't have anyone around to show me."

"How about my mom?" he says.

"Get serious." I roll my eyes. "And what kind of father would you make? Drunk on your ass all the time?"

Good, sweet Luis takes me in his arms and says it's normal for pregnant women to get uptight. He wipes my cheeks with his shirt-tail, tells me not to worry. Everything's cool. I repeat this to myself like a prayer, so everything will be cool—really, deeply, and truly.

SUBJECT: FERMINA/FOLKTALES
WPA: 6-21-38—DC: HMS
June 20, 1938
Words: 386

## BAD CATS

Fermina remembers another folktale she heard on the First Mesa: the story of cats that made trouble for villagers in Old Oraibi. They played with the weavers' yarns, tangling and soiling them, and they got into the sheep's innards being prepared for feasting. The Hopi shooed them with curses. This so enraged the cats that they decided to build their own village. There, the cats lived well. The cat men hunted, and the cat women cooked mutton stew and made piki. The cats didn't behave as they had in Old Oraibi. Here, they were industrious and treated each other with respect. They worked together before the Piktotokya celebration, preparing for the dance performance. They helped one another with costumes, lending this and that.

The day of the dance, the cats were delightful-looking in their costumes. The cat dancers emerged from kiva to sing and dance. But because they were only cats, they had just one song. This is how it went:

> We, we are little cats
> We protect your food—
> Corn and peaches.
> We would be kinder,
> But you were cruel to us,
> Women and men.
> Poor us. Poor us.
> We dance delicately.
> Cat, cat
> Meow, meow, meow.

Cats from far away arrived at the cat village.
There was plenty of food for these newcomers.
But other visitors came, too. Several frogs
hopped into the village. The sleek, graceful
cats looked down on the bumpy, oily frogs. These
creatures were not welcome. But the cats could
do nothing about them during the ceremony.

The performers continued dancing, and the
frogs enjoyed watching, but the cat dancers were
furious. They decided to alter the song to reveal
their feelings, so this is what they sang:

    Cat, cat is ripping
    Cat, cat is ripping
    Cat rips frog's back legs
    Cat rips frog's back legs
    Cat, Cat
    Meow, meow, meow

The frogs wondered why the cats threatened
them in the song. Was this a joke? One of the
frogs suggested they all croak, which is how
frogs laugh, as the cats sang. Together they
croaked and croaked. No one could hear the cats
over the frogs.

Then clouds rolled over the mesa, blocking the
sun. Rain fell in heavy sheets. The downpour
flooded the cat village, flushing out drowned cats
while the frogs swam away, croaking merrily.

# BENDÍGAME, MADRE
# PURÍSIMA — SOPHIA: 1977

If you are like me, you wake up every morning with the same prayer stamped in your heart that is burning on your lips: *Dear Virgen Madre* (you don't believe in God, never have, but you don't dare ignore la Virgen), *help me shed some weight here! Please! Oh, and while you're at it, can you do something about my eye?* So you have two prayers really. But you try to collapse them into one, so you won't seem greedy, like you were last night, smuggling buttered tortillas into bed. Now, if you are like me, you've got grease spots on your pillowcase, which will probably never come out. So you throw in an extra part to the usual prayer: *And, Virgen, help me remove the stains from the pillowcase, if you can. But more important, work on the weight thing and the eye. Blessed Mother, I humbly beg your intercession.*

Then, being like me, you roll out of bed and fumble for your eye patch and glasses on the nightstand. The patch, a beige-colored adhesive job, is quite the fashion statement. It's meant to look natural, like a flap of skin that just happened to grow over your eye, but it goes with your shock-white face about as well as a splash of cocoa on snowy linen, but even worse than the patch is having that wild eye show. Lazy eye, the optometrist with abundant nose hair, told your father. The truth is — that eye is about as lazy as a hummingbird on Benzedrine. It jumps and flinches, priming to leap out of the socket and bounce like a Super Ball for Tijuana. It's the only part of your slothful body that isn't lazy. It's not a lazy eye; it's a crazy eye. You pull the plastic backing off the adhesive and stick the patch over the wild eye and slip on your glasses.

Now, you have begged the Virgin Mother (and your father) for more attractive "granny-style" wire frames that every self-respecting glasses-wearing person owns. After all, this is the late seventies, and people — especially fourteen-year-old girls — don't want to look that much like Walter Cronkite anymore. But Fuzzy Nostrils has vetoed this. While your exposed eye is neither lazy nor insane, it is quite peaceably, even legally, blind, requiring a lens of magnifying-glass density. So you had to choose between a mannish tortoiseshell and industrial-strength pink-plastic deals. The pinks are rhinestone studded, but no doubt safe for welding in. The horn-rims resemble those worn by Clark Kent, the glasses he tears off when he turns into Superman. The very act of ripping these from his face signals his transformation from a timid frank-furter into a Man of Steel. Having little desire to resemble Clark Kent, the wienie, you picked the pink plastics, which, with the patch, suit you to seek employment as Captain Hook's maniacal secretary.

"Ahoy, matey," Cary says when he emerges from the bathroom. He doesn't dare tease you about your weight because, truth is, he is even fatter than you, and though you are more than four years younger, you can fling weight insults with greater zest than he can muster. But, if you are like me, you avoid slitting open that particular vein of discussion.

Instead, you say, "What do you *do* in there?" Your brother

spends more than half his time in the can, but he doesn't flush, run water, or turn comic book pages. You know this because you've knelt with your ear pressed to the keyhole. "What do you *do* in there anyway?"

Of course, Cary won't say. He just starts singing, *"Yo-ho-ho, and a bottle of rum..."* These are the only words to the ditty he knows, so he sings them over and over.

You ignore this, fill the tub, and try to enjoy your bath, likewise paying no heed to Rita, who pounds on the door. If it's urgent enough, she'll burst in to piss while you shave your legs. But when your father starts yelling "Sophia Loren, please, h'ita. I got to go!" it's high time to grab a towel.

What a sour joke it is for your mother to have named you for one of the most gorgeous women to grace the planet. She died (your mother, not Sophia Loren) when you were a tyke, so you don't remember her much. You can't even cry for her when the others get to boo-hooing on her birthday, especially not with this *tontería* of a patch threatening to curl off at the first trace of moisture. But you'd like to meet the woman and trade a few words on this subject. It's not so bad for your older sisters to be named Bette Davis, Loretta Young, and Rita Hayworth Gabaldón. Even your brother can pull off being called Cary Grant. But when people find out your full name is Sophia Loren Gabaldón, they just have to laugh.

Your eye patch wilts with the steam. You press it back, but it sags away from your damp skin. You'll need another before school. You hate waste, but it'd be worse if Cary, or your father, catches sight of that wacky eye and starts feeling all sorry for you.

"Híjole, muchacha, I thought you'd never come out." Your father gets a load of your flushed skin and toweled hair, and emits a snort of laughter.

"Hey, what's so funny?" you ask, imitating Minnie Mouse, so he will have something legitimate to laugh at.

Here, he yuks it up as he pushes past you.

You make a beeline for the nest of bills atop his dresser. You pluck a dollar for lunch, just in case. You're committed to fasting all day, but you never know what'll turn up in the cafeteria. If it's taquitos con guacamole, forget it, you're a goner, even though the guacamole is as thin as gruel and a shade of green that suggests some level of radioactivity.

On the way to the kitchen, you stop in the laundry closet and flick on the iron. You wash your uniform at night and iron it every morning. For sure, you are the neatest, best-groomed, overweight, eye patch–wearing teenager in the world, though you don't know why you bother. Maybe you hope people will be so blinded by the brilliance of your blouse, so mesmerized by the razor pleats in your skirt, that they will overlook the eye patch and the sixty pounds you need to shed.

But wait, what's that buttery aroma wafting from the kitchen like a vaporous finger beckoning hungry cartoon characters? Can it be? Yes, your sister Loretta is diabolically sizzling slices of batter-dipped bread—French toast, your favorite food in the world, especially the way she prepares it, with finely grated orange peel, cinnamon, and nutmeg beaten into the egg. You hustle to the kitchen, determined to commence fasting tomorrow.

Already seated at the table, Cary juts a thumb at your towel. "You going to eat in *that*?"

"I'll take it off, baby, if that's what you want. I'll take it *all* off!" And you begin humming the striptease song while plucking at the knot. *"Ta-da-da DUM, ta-da-DA-DUM, DUM, DUM, DUM-DA-dum-dum-dum!"*

This cracks Loretta up, but Cary, suddenly transfixed by his plate, turns blister red to his hairline. You drop the towel at your ankles and start gyrating, wiggling your boobs like a tassel twirler having a seizure. You grab up the towel and swing it over your head. You consider hopping on the table, but it may not take your weight. When the towel catches on the light fixture overhead, you interrupt the performance for a brief tug-of-war, which you win when the mothy globe loosens and shatters on the floor.

"What are you doing?" Nilda asks as she enters from the back door. Her face is blanched with horror. "Válgame, Dios. You're naked and you're breaking the lights! Are you *insane?*"

Now, you and Nilda have a lot in common when it comes to praying. She talks to God at least as often as you summon the Virgin, but she never asks for anything. She just tells God to appreciate her. *"Válgame, Dios"* is her favorite saying. Literally it's "value me, God," meaning: *You must notice, God, how I'm surrounded by lunatics. That* must *count for something.* Really, she's saying, "Save me, God. Save me from this bunch of nuts. And send me to heaven when the time comes."

But just because you and Nilda are prayerful people doesn't mean you're chums. Bette says that Nilda just doesn't "get it" about you. Most people laugh their heads off whenever you open your mouth, or just step into a room, which can be disturbing. Only Nilda is immune to your jokes and funny faces. This is why you think Loretta was full of baloney when she used to go on and on about your gift, supposedly from Fermina, the old woman you barely remember, the one you thought was your fairy godmother. You'd like to catch up with her in the afterlife, and ask, "Hey, what gives? Is this some kind of joke?" At odd moments, you catch yourself thinking about the old woman, wondering just who she thought she was anyway, saddling you with this ridiculous gift.

And if you're so great at giving everyone a laugh, why is Nilda just staring at you and shaking her head?

Never in a million years could you explain why you were nakedly pulling down the light fixture with a towel. You're not quite sure yourself, but it's not something that bothers you the way it upsets her. She's calmer now, after a cafecito and a plate of French toast—*your* serving—which she eats while Loretta sweeps up the glass and you iron your uniform, hoping to erase the earlier impression with superior laundry habits.

When you return to the kitchen fully dressed, Nilda takes your hand and looks into your good eye, which is also a bad eye, and says, "Looks like I'm just in time." She hands you a flat package.

"What's this?" You're pretty sure it has something to do with dieting. Nilda's a great one for telling you how much you've gained since she saw you last. Her favorite greeting: "My God, you're so *fat*!"

"Pues, it's a record, one of those albums. Go on, open it up."

You pull off the bag to reveal a bald priest smiling at a bunch of zombielike teenagers on the cover. The neon yellow print under the photo reads: *Father Cochran—The Straight Dope on the Birds and the Bees.* Great waves of laughter roll to your throat, but you swallow them back because Nilda is so wholly embarrassed.

"It's about the—*you know*," she whispers, "the facts of life."

The title alone makes your eyes sting with merry tears. "Thanks, Tía." You bite the soft skin inside your cheek, so as not to giggle. "You want to listen to it with me?"

"Oh, no, no, no." Nilda shakes her head. "*Absolutely* not. You and la Rita listen together. You can get some good information for teenage girls. You'll see why you shouldn't be fooling around naked in the kitchen, breaking lights. Válgame, Dios."

Maybe Rosa and Aracely can drop by today for a few laughs. "I'll play it this afternoon."

"You mind what it says, muchacha," Nilda says.

Cary laps at the syrup on his plate. "Maybe I ought to listen to it, too."

"No," says Nilda, "this is not for boys. This will only give them ideas."

"But I need ideas," your eighteen-year-old brother says, and, boy, does he *ever*. He lunges for the record, but Nilda smacks his paws away.

Now, if you're like me, it's not enough for you to have an appalling appearance; you must have grotesque friends as well. Owing to their bizarre looks, it doesn't take you two seconds to spot Rosa and Aracely in the crowded school yard before first bell. Rosa is over six feet tall in her bare feet, and Aracely's lucky if she reaches five feet in heels. It's not just size that makes them odd. Rosa looks like she could be Frankenstein's monster's fraternal twin—not his bride, because her black braid hangs lank and dull as a dusty theater rope. But she could easily be his sister. Her olive skin is so seamed and pocked by acne scars, pits, and blips that she produces susto, when encountered unexpectedly, until she opens her mouth, that is, and the whining starts. Yes, she's the monster's cranky sister, the one who almost didn't escape the laboratory because she was so busy complaining. Then there's Aracely, a brown terrier of a girl, who gets so worked up shooting off her mouth that she actually pants, the tip of her pink tongue pulsating. *A-huh-a-huh-a-huh.*

These are not easy friends to be saddled with, but what can you expect? The three of you blend in about as well as a trio of clowns at a Junior Miss pageant. *Mother Mary, how about some new friends, say some normal-looking humans to hang around with? Would that be too much?* Today Aracely has a new hairstyle, or maybe she's just had some misfortune with her cream rinse. Her short blue-black tresses spike up from her scalp, giving her the look of a startled hedgehog.

You amble over as they're gabbing about their favorite subject — sex.

Rosa whines, "But my mamá says the only reason to do it is to get babies."

"I'd say that's a sad commentary on your old man," you observe.

Aracely laughs, but then says, "Like you're an expert. You never even got a hickey before." Her one claim to sexual expertise: Javier Rivera planted a love bite on her during *Rocky* when he returned from the restroom and mistook her for his date in the darkened theater.

"Well," you say, pulling Nilda's record out of your book bag, "I'm no expert, but check this out — *The Straight Dope on the Birds and the Bees.*"

"What's that?" Aracely asks.

"A sex education record," you say.

Rosa sulks. "My mamá won't let me listen to sex records."

*Virgin Mother, about those friends, could you snap it up?*

"Ooh!" Aracely grabs the record and turns it over to read the back. "When can we listen to it?"

"After school," you suggest.

"I'll get in trouble," Rosa says. "I know it."

"But where?" asks Aracely, panting in excitement. *"Where?"*

"Mamá will find out, and she'll tell Papá, and I'll get a punishment. You and Aracely don't care, but I'm always on punishment because of you guys."

"Let's go to my house after sixth period. We can use Cary's record player."

"Will Cary be there?" Aracely's fascination with your brother is as profound as his dread of her. *Will he?*

"If he is, he'll probably be in the bathroom."

"They'll all be pissed off and make me watch my sister's kids the whole weekend. You guys don't even care if I get in trouble."

You and Aracely turn to Rosa at the same time. "Shut *up!*"

"Okay, okay, but where are we going to meet after sixth?" she asks.

You plan to meet by the Chalice Hidalgo Memorial Bench—named for a studious lesbian, a junior who was beheaded when a semi jackknifed into her family's Volkswagen on their way to Chula Vista. This bench—shunned by most due to morbid association and because some girls fear contracting lesbianism from its wrought-iron seat—is obscured by a huge willow. From there, you can observe who gets picked up by whom and in what, without being seen in the company of your oddball friends.

After first bell, the three of you separate for class. You climb the stairs for college preparatory English, while Aracely, in business careers, trots off to typing class on the main floor. Rosa, la pobrecita, slinks down to the basement for manual arts, where she will weave lanyard key chains until lunchtime. On your way to the stairs, you make a brief stop to collect your books. You share a locker with Lydia González, a petite sophomore, who keeps things like leg makeup, lip gloss enhancer, and sun streak alongside the thin picture books on her shelf. While you don't despise Lydia, you're suspicious of anyone who thinks to put makeup on her legs. *On her legs, Virgen!* You can't imagine what she makes of your eye patch, bizarre glasses, and thick body.

And today as you brush past her and her band of similarly

attractive friends, she makes a show of greeting you, "Sophia, girl, how are you?"

You smile, baring teeth. "Hi, Lucretia."

"It's *Lydia.*"

"Right." You twist the combination lock.

"How's it going?" asks Elizabeth Montoya, the prettiest girl in the sophomore class, with her honey-blond hair and tilted green eyes. She takes advanced classes, and you suspect she'd be somewhat of a decent person, if she didn't run with this bunch.

"So, Sophie, who're you bringing to the Spring Fling?" Lydia asks with a glance at the sniggering group.

You shrug, as though oblivious to the banners that have been hanging in the corridors for weeks, and you grab a literature anthology. "Do you need your *Stuart Little,* or anything, before I lock up?" You estimate Lydia has accumulated over a hundred dollars in library fines on the children's reader that she checked out at the start of *her* freshman year. "Need anything for first period? Remedial reading, isn't it?"

She stares straight ahead, biting her lip. You slam the locker shut. "*Stuart Little*—let me know how that baby turns out, will you?" You hold up the anthology, thick as the Sears catalogue. "I have to read all these big books without pictures."

Lydia's face clenches like a fist. "*Bitch.*"

"Cool it, Lyddie," whispers Elizabeth.

"I ain't going to cool it. She's trying to make like I'm a dummy or something." She turns to you. "Girl, why do you got to act all smart? Don't you know everyone's laughing at you? Don't you know what a joke you are?"

"*Shush, Lyddie. It's Rita.*"

As your sister strides across the hall, Lydia and company clam right up. Rita, aside from being silent and scary, is a forward on the basketball team. She's notorious for fouling out through rough play. If she's not afraid to throw someone across the court in front of a hundred witnesses, who knows what she'd do if you pissed her off before a mere gaggle of girls? Elizabeth and the others slip away, but Lydia stays rooted, swinging her head from side to side like a demented cobra. She probably does need one of her basic books for first period, or she'd scram, too.

"Need money, Soph?" asks Rita, keeping an eye on Lydia.

"I'm okay."

Rita sniffs at Lydia. "You smell like shit."

You also wriggle your nose gamely. "Phew!"

Rita says, "You must have stepped in it."

Lydia glances at the thick lip of grass-bearded stool adhering to one heel. "Shit!"

"You stink." Rita shakes her head.

"Really bad." You wonder why you didn't smell it earlier.

Lydia winces, gives a frustrated shrug, and limps off, favoring the crap-encrusted shoe as though she has twisted an ankle.

"What's that payasita's problem?" Rita asks, using her favorite name for a girl who applies cosmetics excessively—a little clown. "Why was she picking on you?"

"Who knows? Maybe her leg makeup itches."

"Leg makeup?" Rita grins. "Do they really have leg makeup?"

"Leg makeup, scar eliminator, nose putty, butt-vanishing cream..."

Rita laughs, glances at her watch. "Catch you later."

You check that the coast is clear before dashing to first-period English. You're on the lookout for Sister Barnabas, a huge hunk of nun who has made up her mind to "counsel" you for "body image" issues. She's hoping to get you to join her "group," fatties all, who gather together to lament that nobody likes them. She's singled you out because you are not only overweight, but you present the added psychological challenge of being half an orphan. Now you know that Barnabas probably cares—she's that type—but you also know she's working on a counseling certificate in order to get her butt out of the classroom and into a cozy little office. You can't see how on earth—*explícame, Virgen*—this nun, who is larger than you by two, and, let's face it, a *nun,* thinks she can help you.

Nevertheless Barnabas stalks you, relentlessly skulking around, lurking in corners, and tiptoeing up behind you. But you give her a good run for her money. Though you're big, you're slippery as hell. You slide into supply closets, crawl under bleachers, and dive into crowds without a ripple, ever dodging her massive shadow. Until today—*Madre mía, things have got to go better than this*—when she claps a meaty claw on your shoulder outside English class. Then in a moment of nunnish playfulness, she cups her other moist hand over your glasses, smudging the lenses annoyingly.

She disguises her voice with a lilt. "Guess who?"

"Hmm . . . Sister Barnabas?"

Barnabas squeals, "How did you guess?"

"Wow, Sister, what a coincidence, I was just thinking about you."

"Really?" Her blue eyes are deceptively normal behind stylish granny frames.

"I was planning to come by and have our little chat after midterms."

"You don't have to wait that long." She pats your arm. "You might even do better on the tests if you had a chance to get a few things off your chest."

"After midterms, Sister, I swear I'll come by to see you." Naturally, after messing with Lydia, then horsing around with Barnabas, you're late again for first period. Sister Cleophas, a musty old nun who resembles a garden gnome in full habit, reels her pocket watch from the folds of her habit. "Third tardy this week, Miss Gabaldón."

"Well, maybe the second, but even then you shouldn't count the time I slipped on the stairs, and today I got held up by Sister Bar—"

"*Third* tardy this week, Miss Gabaldón." Cleophas scribbles out a pink slip. "You must see Mr. Barresi before returning to class."

You snatch the slip and begin the sad march to Barresi's office. Cleophas has had it in for you since you refused to kiss her before Christmas when one of the suck-ups strung mistletoe over her desk. The entire class lined up—one by one—to buss her dried apricot of a cheek, but you acted so engrossed in "Araby" that you didn't notice. You thought it worked, too, but she's been so pissy ever since that it's clear you've only been fooling yourself.

You try ducking into the bathroom to hide out, but there's Lydia González at the sink, spritzing herself with Jean Naté in a fury. You hold your nose and back away.

So now you have to deal with Barresi, a failed hairdresser who lucked into the vice principal gig at Sacred Heart. As a result, he believes he rules the known world. *Maybe* he was handsome once, but now he's so bloated and old, not even Cleophas would give him a second look. Of course, this doesn't affect his certainty that all the girls—especially unattractive ones—are mad with love for him.

Once inside his office, you determine not to look at him, not to flatter the conceited boor with your gaze. You stare instead at the dusty books on his shelves.

"Why are you always late?" he grumbles after a pause.

You decide to pull "a Rita" and keep your trap shut.

"Do you hear me? What happened to your eye?"

That he's never noticed you before strengthens your resolve.

"I asked you some questions, young lady, and I want answers."

Your tongue curls, resting in your mouth like a slug in a stony crevice.

"You'll speak when you're spoken to." His voice rises, and though you're not looking, you can tell he's up from behind the desk. His feet pad the carpet. Maybe he'll slap you, so you can go home early, catch the soaps, and later sue the school. "Am I going to have to call a parent conference?" he asks. "Because I promise I will, young lady, and you can take *that* to the bank."

Not your fault that your father's working in the Harbor area and can't be reached, so your oldest sister has to be called instead—and certainly not your doing that Bette arrives at the school falling-over drunk. She whispers—as you head for the conference room—that last night she dropped acid, and she's just gulped sangria that morning to take the edge off. But when she got this call, she says, she knew she had to come, even though the streets keep pulling apart like taffy. She just couldn't find good shoes, so she had to wear her wedding heels.

But being stoned out of her mind and stumbling along on burnt and noxious-smelling white pumps doesn't keep your sister from defending you before the semicircle of nuns congregated with Barresi in the conference room. Normally, Bette's well-groomed and attractive, with long, curly black hair and a sweet, dimpled face. She was a cheerleader, senior class president, and a prom princess at this very school. But since her miscarriage, she's kind of gone to pot. Today her hair is as strung out as she is, her cheeks gaunt and sallow, and her eyes glassy, huge, and spooky.

Sister Barnabas nearly smacks her lips at the sight of your depraved sibling, while Barresi makes it seem like you were trying to instigate insubordination. *How can someone like you instigate anything but mildly creepy feelings in others, dígame, Virgen?*

Some of the nuns, your teachers, pipe in with positive remarks about your grades. But Bette blurts, "Where are your balls? You don't have any, do you?" This seems absurd since: a) it is completely out of context following comments on your decent grades, and b) apart from Barresi, she's addressing a group of testicle-less nuns.

"You have *no* balls!" Bette smacks her palm on the table. "And I mean it to the maximum!"

You don't dare laugh. Instead, you cough and fiddle with your glasses. Faster than a rattlesnake can strike, Barnabas thrusts a Kleenex box at you.

That's when you break down and talk. You suggest calling a taxi to take Bette home. You'll have your father drop off Cary later to retrieve Bette's car, as that roomful of wimple wearers, plus Barresi, have nary an idea how to cope with the smashed older sister of a snotty, one-eyed freshman.

The dang conference takes the whole lunch period; so after they've sentenced you to detention next week, you go straight to class. When the final bell rings, you are so hungry that the hookworms in your biology text look mighty tasty. But, as arranged, you stop by your locker for the Father Cochran record and then head to the Chalice Hidalgo Memorial Bench. You are the first to arrive. Your friends are slow as mud, and they're forgetful, too. They may not show up at all. Ten minutes pass, fifteen, then twenty.

You tuck the record into your book bag when Elizabeth Montoya slips between the willow's fronds. Her stride is loose and lazy like a pacing tiger's, her hair stippled by sunlight slanting through the droopy branches. She's puffing a cigarette and blowing perfect smoke rings.

Most of the other girls have gone by now. Only Maria Spinetti, the freshman who never bathes, sits out front, waving off flies and scratching her grubby knees while she waits for her equally filthy father to collect her.

Elizabeth moves closer until she's standing beside you, casting her cool shadow over your thick white legs, as she pulls a pack of Marlboros from her bag. "Want one?"

"Sure," you say, your voice high and squeaky. "Thanks, Elizabeth."

She laughs, revealing a row of even teeth that are so white they seem unreal. "You're funny, you know that?" She taps out a cigarette. "Your voices, your jokes—you got a sense of humor. You could be on *Johnny Carson,* I bet, telling jokes. That *Stuart Little* stuff was hilarious, but I couldn't laugh or anything 'cause Lydia was right there. It was a real gas, though."

"Thanks." You hold the unlit cigarette casually between two fingers.

She pulls out a matchbook and snaps a flame. "Hey, you hungry? I got my boyfriend's car. You want to drive over to Tommy's for a hamburger or something?"

You swear your stomach has ears because as soon as Elizabeth utters the word "hamburger"—before your brain can register the information—it bawls like a water buffalo. "Sure."

"Come on, then. He parks it around the block for me, so I can drive it while he works at this body shop on Alvarado. I've got my own key."

You're barely listening. You are like Popeye's friend Wimpy when it comes to hamburgers, and Tommy's burgers—nested in steamy buns, slathered with chili, and topped with warm pickle slices—are the best around. "Wait," you blurt. "I don't have enough money." The dollar in your pocket won't even get you a full order of oily fries.

"My treat." Elizabeth crinkles her cat eyes, baring her luminous teeth. "Come on." You approach a primer-colored Chevy, and she unlocks the passenger-side door. "It's a bomb, I know, a real cholo-mobile," she says. "But it drives."

"Oh, it's fine." Her boyfriend is one of the older dudes who turns up at school dances, basketball and volleyball games, like a jackal on the prowl, always waiting for some simple thing to stray from the herd. Pedro, Pito, Pepe—something like that—already has gray hairs threaded in with the black, and acne scars you can see from across the street. "He's nice to let you use his car."

"Yeah, well, it's convenient. But I'm definitely going to break up with his ass once I get my license and my parents buy me a car." She twists the rearview to check her lipstick, smoothing over her lower lip with a pinky finger.

"Sorry to hear that."

"Nothing to be sorry about. Have you ever seen him? He's pure cochino—ugly and gross. He keeps wanting me to touch his chorizo, and you *know* that ain't never going to happen." She shudders and stabs the key into the ignition. "You mind if we stop at my house so I can change first? I hate wearing this school shit."

"No. Go ahead."

"I live up near the park. Hey, can I show you something? I have this favorite place—a special place—I want you to see it. Do you mind?"

"No, no," you say, silently warning your stomach to shut the hell up. *Virgencita, can you help me here?* You cover it with your book bag, hoping to muffle the sound. But the roar of the engine does a pretty good job as you and Elizabeth Montoya wind up the twisting streets into the park to see this special place.

You have to laugh. Of course, Lydia González, Suzy Gómez, and Marina Verdugo are waiting at Elizabeth's "special place." What did you expect? That Elizabeth Montoya, the sublime, would inexplicably befriend you, Sophia, the ghastly. No reason for the jolt of surprise when the other three emerge from a copse of eucalyptus trees. You're not too worried, but you wonder why they look so odd approaching you. Then you realize they're holding sticks behind their backs. A chill slides up your spine, but still you have to laugh.

"What's so funny, huh?" Lydia draws her stick from behind her and hits it against one palm. "Now there's no big sister here to protect you."

Elizabeth Montoya drags on her cigarette, releasing a couple of perfect rings from her well-shaped lips. "Look, I got her up here, but I don't want no part of this." She turns her back and hikes down the hill.

Lydia lands the first blow, stinging your upper arm. The trio hoots. "Take off that patch!" shouts Marina. "Come on!"

You have to laugh.

But another blow breaks against your shins, and you stumble to your knees.

"Think that's funny?" Lydia asks. "Take off the patch."

"Okay, okay." You peel it off. "There."

"Ugh," cries Suzy. "That's *ug*-ly!"

"Put it back on," Lydia says.

"It won't stay now," you say. "The adhesive—"

Lydia raises her stick and a hot-white surge rushes from your nose to the base of your skull, blinding you. Your glasses dangle from one ear. "I can't see." With a dull rain of thumps, the glasses spill to the grass. It's not that bad, almost as though it's happening to someone else or to some thing. Like these girls are pounding a dusty tapestry strung on a line far away, in another city, at another time.

You hear them grunting and cursing. Through the bitter odor of blood, you whiff their sour sweat, the Jean Naté, the dog shit, and hairspray. You almost taste menthol from the trees and the warm fresh-cut grass pressing under your nose when you tumble. Rolling feels good, in fact. The knoll ahead is curved like a lap. You imagine your mother's broad, warm lap, then Fermina's, and now this. You roll down, down, down. The trees, the grass, the wind-torn clouds overhead, churn, like you're a marble spinning in a kaleidoscope. Your skirt hikes to your waist, and you're sure you will never, ever get the grass stains out of your blouse, your panties. But still you let yourself roll. For a while, they are after you, thumping your back, legs, stomach, with their sticks.

You roll harder and faster and someone says, "Shit!" And they grow silent. But you keep spinning, snagging your hair and clothes on twigs, bushes, rocks, but these don't stop you, and you can't stop yourself. You don't even try. Not even for the stone embedded near the bottom of the hill, or at the sickening sound of a bone splintering above your wrist when you strike it hard. The hill ends and you finally grow still. A fierce jolt shoots from your elbow to your fingertips when you stand. You cradle your mangled arm with the good one, and squint up at the others.

Of course, they are gone.

You smooth down your skirt and hike to the park station for the telephone booth. Once there, you call home collect. Loretta answers, and you say, "It's me. I'm at Elysian Park. Can you come pick me up?"

"What are you doing *there*?" she says. "What happened? Are you okay?"

You open your mouth to explain before realizing there's no way to say what happened and why.

You just have to laugh.

SUBJECT: FERMINA/NAVAJO RAIDS
WPA: 6-21-38—DC: HMS
June 21, 1938
Words: 451

## LEAVING THE VILLAGE

Fermina estimates she was about nine years old when the Navajo raided her village. She was asleep, but woke to shouts and sounds of struggle. Her mother pulled her from her blankets and lugged her toward the woods behind the village. Howls and war cries rent the autumn night. Navajo horsemen encircled the village, clubbing anyone in their path. When Fermina's mother stumbled over a fallen body, one of the raiders caught her in his arms. Another grabbed Fermina's ankle and dragged her, scraping her elbows and knees. He bound her with rawhide strips and propped her on horseback beside her mother. When the villagers were killed, captured, or driven away, the Navajo ransacked their homes, stealing or breaking what they found. They shattered crockery, splintered looms, and set heavy mantas aflame. They piled their plunder onto horses, along with the captives. The wails of survivors, who had climbed to the rooftops, filled that moonless night as the Navajo finally galloped from the village. They rode all night, stopping only at daybreak to rest.

Fermina and her mother had been captured with other children and women. One was large with child. All were young, healthy, and strong, while hunger had whittled the Navajo so that the knobs of their joints and notches of their spines jutted through loose flesh, but they shared what dried meat and meal they had with the captives.

Fermina and her mother traveled with the Navajo for days. By daylight, they hiked eastward, and at night, they slept under the open sky. They climbed to a place where snow fell and camped in canyons surrounded by tall iron-streaked boulders. One night, the woman with child confided to Fermina's mother that this baby would be her first. The next morning, she escaped. The Navajo sent a party after her. When they retrieved her, the woman was no longer big with child.

Later, Fermina overheard her say she had slipped away as the pains started that night. She discovered a lair and rested in it, but the cramping wouldn't stop. She cried out for help, but no one came, so she had to bring the baby herself. She birthed an infant girl on the floor of that cave and covered her with leaves, saying, "If I take you, I will lose you, so I must leave you here." She slunk away, cupping her ears against the baby's soft cries. When she had hiked some distance, the mewling sharpened into shrieking. The woman turned back. A thick cloud of crows hovered over the mouth of the cave, and soon the baby grew silent.

When the Navajo found the woman, she was wading into the river, large stones knotted into her skirt.

# Like Falling in a Dream —
# Rita: 1978

At noon, Rita slips into the Woolworth on Sunset for a grilled cheese and milk shake before heading to the hospital. Faculty meetings at the high school free her until basketball practice at four. The hike from Woolworth to the Queen of Angels, and later back to school, will fill the time exactly. Rita climbs onto a counter stool, trying to catch the waitress's eye, when someone calls, "Rita, Rita Gabaldón, is that you?"

Rita spins to face a pale pregnant woman wearing a stylish helmet of lacquered black hair. A navy leotard stretches over her huge abdomen, but the woman's arms and legs are spindly, spider thin. She's pushing a shopping cart, a small boy installed in the toddler seat. Rita stares at both of them blankly.

"It's me — Shirley. Don't you remember? We were neighbors."

"*Shirley*," Rita says, her heart thudding in her throat, "but I thought you —"

"I know." Shirley nods. "I'm okay now, really."

The boy bangs his heels against the cart. His hair stands straight up on his small head, like shorn porcupine quills.

"This is my son, Russell," Shirley says.

"Hi," Rita says to the boy, who thrusts his milk-coated tongue out at her.

"Behave now," Shirley tells him. "He's just turned three, still needs his naps, and it's almost time right now."

He kicks at the cart with force. "No, no, *no*!"

"Your grandmother," Rita asks, over the din, "how's she doing?"

"Stop and I mean it." Shirley puts an arm over the boy's legs, holding them until he keeps still. "Grandma died over a year ago. How's your family?"

"Fine," Rita says. "We're living on Montana Street now, up that big hill."

"How's Bette? You know, she used to come over in those days and sit with me. I really *wouldn't* have made it without her. I hope she's doing well."

Rita doesn't want to say that her sister dropped out of college years ago to work in a factory assembling phone books, that she's still messed up from the miscarriage, that she's been drinking too much and doing drugs. "She's married now."

"Really," Shirley says, and she smiles. "I hope she's happy."

"I want to go!" the boy says.

Shirley fishes in her purse, finds a pen and paper, and scribbles on it. "Here's my phone number." She hands it to Rita. "I'm Shirley Tanaka now. We live in Silver Lake, not too far from you. Tell Bette to call me, will you? Tell her I asked about her."

"I will."

"Great seeing you, Rita, you look…so grown-up." Shirley clears her throat, backs away. "Wish we could talk more, but I better get this little guy home," she says, and wheels the cart to the register, one wheel screeching in complaint.

"Shirley," Rita calls after her. "Shirley, *I*…"

Shirley barely glances over her shoulder, flutters her fingers, and rushes up front.

The hospital sits atop a steep hill overlooking Bellevue Avenue, where Rita's family lived for a few years after moving from the small bungalow on Clinton Street. She stands at the summit of the cement steps leading down to the dead-end street and gazes out at an apartment complex constructed where their house had been. It had been a large, drafty three-storey, with temperamental wiring and unpredictable plumbing, but to Rita, it had been like a castle with intricate molding, turrets and gargoyles, prism-glass windows, hidden chambers, and a wild, overgrown yard in place of a moat. The landlord, though, sold it to developers, who'd razed the structure and those next to it to construct the boxlike apartments. Rita squints, but finds no trace of the old house, no evidence it ever existed, and no hint of the home Ambrose and his mother lived in next door. Erased, she thinks, completely erased.

Relieved, after seeing Shirley—alive and well—Rita nearly skips the long blocks to the hospital. But it strikes her now that Shirley never mentioned Cathy when they spoke. How can that be? Rita thinks of Cathy every day and imagines what she would be like if she had lived. She'd be sixteen, now, just a year younger than Rita. They might even be friends, trading phone calls and sleepovers. "Hey, Cath," Rita might say, "want to go to the movies?" Or "Let's ride bikes up to Elysian Park."

As Rita enters Queen of Angels Hospital to visit her uncle, she's reminded all the more of Cathy, who died here. And now the doctors have told Nilda that José will end his days here, too, predicting he will succumb any time now, though he might slip into a coma and linger for weeks. After all the harm he's done to her sisters, this doesn't depress Rita too much. Rita imagines her uncle literally slipping and falling into darkness and silence so complete that she nearly envies him. She pictures him tumbling, his hospital gown flapping as he dives through nothingness.

That afternoon, she finds Nilda in a chair outside José's hospital room, skimming a *McCall's* magazine. "I get nervous in there with him." Nilda lilts her chin toward the door. "Like I'm just waiting for him to hurry up and go." But as she flips through the magazine, her brow is smooth, her eyes untroubled. Even the waves in her brown hair seem softer, more relaxed than usual. "You think Sophie would like this?" She points at a magazine photo of strawberries with whipped cream. "Only seventy-two calories a serving—the topping is sugar-free."

Rita shrugs, and Nilda asks if she wants to see some of the newspaper she has folded on the seat beside her. "How mean they are to that Hearst girl," she says. "La pobrecita was kidnapped, and brainwashed. You'd think they'd have sympathy. But no, they want to throw her in prison." She gestures at the editorial page, an article with a headline decrying plans to commute Patty Hearst's sentence.

But Rita's not interested in Patty Hearst's troubles. She scans the front page for news of space travel. She longs for the day when she will travel to the moon and stroll across its broad, bland face, her feet scuffing the moon dust comfortably, as though this is a homecoming. Nothing here, except a short bit about some jailed Russian physicist, a canceled trip to Moscow in protest. Delay, and more delay, she thinks. Rita refolds, replaces the paper, and Nilda squeezes her arm. "Except for your dad, you're the only one to visit."

"Maybe they'll come later," Rita says, knowing this will never happen.

Nilda shakes her head. "They despise him. Everyone does. My brothers laughed at him because he never went to school. Did you know that?"

"He seems smart enough to me," Rita says. Despite what he'd done to her as a little girl and her sisters — now that he is dying — Rita admits to herself that he must have been a clever man. Her uncle got by from job to job with a trunk full of painting supplies and a collapsible ladder. He'd mock her father's job with the city, bragging that *he* worked only when *he* felt like it.

"Did you know his mother was a prostitute? She worked in one of those houses in Tijuana, raised him there. Made him like a slave in that house. She hired him out, too, when he was just a kid, sent him to work on a rancho. He didn't have no easy life." Nilda juts her chin toward the door again. "Go in and see him."

"Is it a good time?" Rita nearly wishes she'd gone to school to practice free throws, instead of yielding to this pinch of duty.

"He ain't going anywhere, is he? If he's asleep, just hit his foot a little, like this." Nilda nudges Rita with the magazine. "He's in that first bed there."

At the threshold, Rita draws a deep breath, as if to dive into murky water. The aquamarine drapes around her uncle's bed are parted, and she slips through the gap. A monitor beeps nearby. The room is thick with disinfectant fumes. Rita grows light-headed, confused, wondering how this shriveled, jaundiced body can be her uncle's. Only when she spies the familiar brush of his moustache does she recognize him.

He'd been a heavyset man with a thick mane of black hair and bristly eyebrows. When he strode, floors shook. His fleshy jowls wobbled like gelatin when he laughed or coughed. Now at his bedside, Rita searches the loose skin — puckered like a deflated balloon — for her uncle's features. His head, chest, shoulders, and arms have withered and shrunk, only his belly is distended, over-sized like an insect's abdomen.

"Uncle, can you hear me?"

His eyes are shut, but sparse, sleep-crusted lashes twitch. He opens one eye.

"Blink, if you hear me."

He closes his eye, and both open.

"Do you want me to take your hand?"

Again, he blinks.

Careful of the tubing inserted in his wrist, Rita lifts his hand and encloses the cool yellowed fingers in hers. His thumb jerks, and Rita feels the pressure of his touch. She gasps, her heart thrashes against her ribs.

In an instant, Rita is six years old, astride his ankle, which he bobs for her "pony ride." Then he draws her into his lap. His fingers are little men, Snow White's dwarfs marching from her ankle to her knee. He whistles their work song. But his whistling is labored, as though he's climbing steep stairs, straining under a heavy load. Rita giggles because the dwarfs' footsteps tickle inside her thigh as they make their way to the mine. Rita, weak with laughter, twists to get away. The tickling hurts now. She can't squirm away. The fingers keep marching. *Stop! Please stop!*

Rita drops his hand, stumbles into a chair alongside the bed, shivering. Perspiration crawls between her breasts and under her arms. The tile floor whirls crazily and her stomach plunges like an elevator that's snapped its cables. She puts her head between her knees, struggling to replace this memory with others.

He used to work at the now-defunct amusement park by the sea, Pacific Ocean Park, where he leased a stall to sell water turtles and neckties, on which he painted tropical flowers and palm trees. He also sketched portraits in pastels, and he cut silhouettes from thick black paper for people who waited in long lines. And at home, he would draw cartoons for her on the backs of envelopes, on napkins—pictures of ducks smoking cigars, cats dancing, and pigs driving cars—that made her laugh. As his pen flew, his breath grew ragged the way it did when his fingers marched between her legs, and he'd huff his inhaler. The greedy sound of his breathing didn't bother Rita then.

But Bette says he bellowed once at their mother because she had served salad on the same plate with roast beef, beans, and mashed potatoes. *Only the pigs eat salad on the same dish with the meat.* Mama had taken his plate to the sink and pulled open the back door. She held it wide until José stumbled out, cursing in Spanish. Her mother had called after him, "You would be the one to know what pigs do."

When Rita's breathing steadies, she leans to look into her uncle's eyes. "I can't remember that many good things about you."

He blinks.

"I should feel bad for you and want you to get better. But I can't do that, Tío. I forgive you, though, what you did to me. To all of us. I have to, because if I don't, you'll always be there, like a splinter in my heart. Do you know what I'm saying?" Rita draws near, takes his hand again. "I can help you."

His eyelid twitches, but he doesn't blink.

She leans close, cups his hairy ear. "I curse you to die, Tío. Nothing will hurt you anymore." Rita brushes his clammy cheek with her lips and stands upright. She parts the curtains, and she slips away.

After practice, Rita sinks into a hot bath. She's filled the tub almost to the rim. Only her knees and face surface the steamy water. Though her ears are submerged, she hears the telephone ring through the thin walls and raises herself to listen.

"Hallo? Yeah, well, we knew it was coming." Her father pauses. "Okay, Nilda, ya me voy." Then he knocks—two somber thumps—on the bathroom door. "H'ita, that was Nilda. José passed away."

Rita remembers a word she's read on a sympathy card: "condolences."

"I'm going to bring Nilda over here to stay the night." His keys jangle.

"You want me to come with you?"

"Nah, just tell Loretta, Nilda's coming for supper, okay?"

"All right." Rita listens to his footfalls, wondering why he won't speak to Loretta himself. Since her sister started college, their father has become—not afraid—but wary of her. And Loretta, twenty-two now, about to graduate from college and already accepted into veterinary school at the University of Georgia, seems to regard this as deference, as her due.

Rita dries herself and pulls on a sweatshirt and jeans. She winds her hair in a towel and emerges from the bathroom. Loretta's door is shut, as usual. Rita knocks. "It's me," she says before entering.

"What do you want?" Loretta's reclined on her bed, her textbooks and notes spread on the quilt. Her shabby parrot paces the headboard. When it catches sight of Rita, it whistles and squawks, "Shithead!"

"José just died, and Dad's picking up Nilda to stay over tonight."

Loretta's glasses, glinting in the lamplight, make her look eyeless, expressionless. "I don't suppose you had anything to do with that."

Rita shrugs. "He wasn't going to get better."

"Bullshit!" the parrot shrieks.

"Right, so you helped him along."

Rita wonders if Loretta is teasing her. "You don't believe in that stupid gift business. I mean, look at you, reading a science book."

"So what?" Loretta says.

"There you are. Why not go around like Saint Francis of Assisi himself healing animals, right and left, instead of moving all the way to Georgia for graduate school? You really don't believe that stuff at all, do you? How can you after the dogs died?"

"It was too late for them," Loretta says, shaking her head. "Even at the pet clinic, I could never do much for animals in their death throes."

"Besides, if it were true, it would be brujería, witchcraft. You don't buy that." Rita's not sure what to believe, wishes she had some way to know. She often rakes her memory for traces of Fermina, for answers, even clues about this.

"Maybe I do." Loretta yawns, stretching. "Maybe I don't."

Rita suspects that behind the blank expression and flat voice, Loretta is laughing at her, amused at the hold this childish belief has over her. But despite Loretta's mockery, or maybe because of it, Rita struggles for her older sister's favor. Rita likes to believe they are closer, that she has more in common with the orderly, self-disciplined Loretta than with her other sisters or Cary. In Loretta, Rita sees her future self as she would like to be. They are both reflective, serious types, who usually limit themselves to expressions of fact. They are as unlikely to exaggerate or embellish as Bette and Sophie are to stick to the truth, so her implicit ridicule stings Rita much more than a flat-out insult from anyone else. Loretta purses her lips, arches her brow, and Rita knows her sister is having a bit of fun with her. "What are you going to fix for supper?" she says now, to put an end to it.

"I'm thinking arroz con pollo and tortillas."

"We've got tortillas in the freezer. I'll stick some in the oven."

Grateful for this excuse, Rita hurries from her sister's room to the kitchen.

"Shithead," the parrot cries.

In the kitchen, she pulls a frosted sack of tortillas from the freezer, and Bette steps in the back door. "Ooh, tortillas," she says. "Did Loretta make those?"

Rita nods and says, "José died."

"Oh, my God!" Bette's almond-shaped eyes fill. Rita knows her oldest sister detests their uncle, but she rarely passes on an opportunity for a good cry. Right after losing the baby, weeping was all she did for days on end.

"Come off it." Rita cracks apart the frozen tortillas with a butter knife. "You never even bothered to see him in the hospital."

"I'm thinking of Nilda." Bette's voice breaks. "Poor Nilda, all alone."

"Nilda's fine," Rita says. "Stay for supper and see for yourself."

"I can't. I've got to be somewhere. Where's Sophie?"

Rita shrugs. "Who knows?" Since her accident last spring—she weirdly fell down a hill at the park, fracturing her wrist—and the eye operation that summer, fifteen-year-old Sophie spends most of her time with her friends, Aracely and Rosa. Except for meals, she's rarely home. "Where's Luis?" Rita asks.

"Working graveyard." Bette pulls open the refrigerator door.

"So why can't you stay to eat?"

"Mind your own business." She slams the door shut.

"Guess who I saw today?" Rita says.

"Who?"

"Shirley. Remember Shirley?"

"Shirley!" Bette's cheeks dimple. "How is she?"

"She looks great. She's married now, has a kid and another one on the way. She gave me her number, said you should call," Rita says, but Bette's not listening.

"Cool," she says with a glance at the wall clock. "Hey, since Sophie's not here, could you do me a favor?"

"What kind of favor?"

"If Luis calls, will you tell him I'm taking a nap?"

"You mean *lie*?"

"Not lie, just tell him I'm taking a nap."

"Do I look like Sophie, or even as stupid as Cary? This is me, Rita, and I do not lie, not for you, not for anyone. Tell your own lie. You're the expert, after all."

Bette pauses, an uncertain look on her face. "I don't like to overdo it."

*So they both have doubts.* But Rita loses this thought in a dizzying rush of precognition. This scene: the kitchen, the ticking clock, the frosty tortillas in her hands, her face reflected sideways in the butter knife, this conversation with Bette—all of it has happened before. She can almost predict what is coming next. Almost.

Loretta enters the kitchen, glances at Bette, and says, "What are you doing here?"

"Jesus, I'm still a member of this family."

"Aren't you supposed to be at work?" Loretta reaches for the canister of rice.

"I traded shifts with this girl."

"Staying to eat?"

"No, I can't. I've got to be somewhere."

Rita can't resist. "She just dropped by to find someone to lie to Luis when he calls here looking for her."

"I'll do it." Loretta pulls a pot from a cupboard.

Rita gawks at her sister, and Bette narrows her eyes. "What's the catch?"

"No catch. I don't mind lying. It's nothing to me." Loretta pours water into the pot. "I'll just say they picked you to replace the pope, and you had to fly out to Vatican City for the induction, or whatever. I'll tell him anything you want."

"Just tell him I'm taking a nap. That's all. Don't embellish, don't complicate."

"I think I can handle that," Loretta says.

A car honks from the alley. "I've got to go," says Bette, her face shiny and eyes bright. "Thanks, Loretta."

"You forgot to say, 'I owe you one.'"

"One what?" Bette asks.

"A lie."

"Of course," Bette says. "Anytime you want." She pulls open the door and rushes out.

Rita races to the kitchen window and lifts the curtain. Some dude with slicked-back hair and wraparound shades sits in the driver's seat of a red Triumph that's pulled into their drive. He leans to kiss Bette when she slides into the seat beside him. "Who's that?" Rita asks.

"Some criminal, a drug dealer," Loretta says, "and a fence, I think."

"A fence?"

"Someone who sells stolen property."

"How'd she meet *him*?"

"How else?" Loretta asks. "He's a friend of Luis, like everyone else in the world."

Bette jokes that her husband is the Chicano Will Rogers; he never met a guy he didn't like, or who didn't like him. And no one has become a closer friend to him these past few years than

Cary. Watching the car pull away, Rita almost feels sorrier for her brother than for Luis. "But why?" she asks.

"Because he's stupid and dangerous, so he's just right for Bette—after stupid, but boring, Luis." Loretta's the anti–Will Rogers, Rita thinks. Except for their brother, Cary, Loretta's never met a guy she likes. She continues, "At least, the Criminal doesn't drink himself into a coma every night."

Loretta's stirring rice into the boiling water when the phone blurts a half-ring. She strides across the kitchen, lifts the receiver. "Hello...yes, but she's taking a nap right now.... Okay, sure, I'll tell her." She hangs up and returns to the stove, stirring the bubbling pot once more before covering it tightly with the lid.

At supper, Nilda's still preoccupied with Patty Hearst, the editorial she'd read in the paper. "Bah, there's no compassion anymore, no forgiveness for that girl."

Rita's father has little to say on the subject. But Loretta weighs in. "You'd expect forgiveness," she tells Nilda, "after suffering all that time."

Nilda nods. "And being brainwashed—how could she know what was going on?"

"I'd forgive her," Rita says, without knowing why, and she takes her aunt's hand.

But her aunt blushes and pulls away. "Déjame sola. I'm trying to eat."

"What about the funeral?" her father asks.

"We'll have it over at Saint Viviana's. I don't like that priest at Sacred Heart. Last Sunday, he criticized women for dyeing their hair, said they could be putting that money in the collection plate." She strokes her own Miss Clairol Medium-Ash tresses.

"Besides, Saint Viviana's is pretty rinky-dink," Sophie says with a wink. "It won't be that obvious that we're like the only mourners."

"Cállate la boca." Nilda turns to Cary. "You're going to be a pallbearer."

"Me, Luis, and Dad, but you need more than three."

"I heard you can hire altar boys," Nilda says.

Rita flexes her bicep. "I'm strong. I could do it."

Loretta peers at her over the top of her glasses. "Nothing you'd like more than burying José," she says in a low voice so only Rita can hear.

"Absolutely *not*. Girls can't be pallbearers." Nilda purses her lips and shakes her head. "At least, it was quick in the end."

"What happened anyway?" Rita asks.

"I went to check on him after you left. He was sleeping, just like a baby. Then he moved real quick, like in surprise, and that was that." Nilda scrapes back her chair and stands. "Oígame, Sophie. I want you to take forty dollars from my purse to buy a nice black or navy blue dress and get that hair cut, you hear me?"

"I bet it was like falling," Rita speaks her thought aloud, "like falling in a dream."

Nilda dips her head, crosses herself. "I hope so."

SUBJECT: FERMINA/CAPTIVITY
WPA: 6-28-38—DC: HMS
June 27, 1938
Words: 531

## BARTERED AT THE RIO GRANDE

The captives traveled with the Navajo to the Rio Grande. Many strangers gathered there. They spoke strange languages, their speech sounding to Fermina like dogs barking. These people had buffalo hides, blankets, sheep, sacks of meal, and many more women and children—begrimed, weary, and roped to one another, as Fermina and the others taken from her village had been bound just before reaching the riverbank.

The Navajos loaded their horses with sacks of cornmeal, hides, and dried meat, leaving their captives with a yellow-haired man. This man herded the Hopi women and children onto a wagon, which they rode for several miles. When they reached a settlement, he led the captives into a mud barn that he sealed with a metal latch. Darkness fell, and the captives pushed on the door until the latch pried out. They slipped out of the barn, racing for the cottonwoods near the river. Then they separated. Some continued eastward. Others headed for the mountains. Fermina and her mother hurried toward the wagon road that brought them from the river. They hiked all night. Before daybreak, Fermina's mother stoned a jackrabbit, which she skinned and roasted. The meat was stringy and tough, but they devoured every scrap and sucked on the bones.

The next day, horses appeared on the wagon road. Fermina and her mother hid in the brush, but a rider spotted them. One seized Fermina,

trussed her with his lariat, and loaded her
onto his horse, while the other struck down
her mother with the butt of his shotgun. Blood
pooled on the sand beneath her. The riders
quarreled before remounting their horses. They
rode off with Fermina, who stared—stunned and
silent—after her mother until she disappeared
from sight.

The men took Fermina to another settlement
and locked her again in a darkened adobe barn.
After a long time, the door swung open and an
old woman scuttled inside. She spoke to Fermina
in Tewa, her mother's language. The woman told
Fermina her name was Pacencia and explained
this was Chato Hidalgo's farm. She said Fermina
should stop weeping, that she should save her
strength. She handed Fermina flatbread, and while
the girl ate, the woman said Hidalgo was a lazy
man, who liked to sleep all day and gamble at
night. He was not a good man, she said, but if
the girl worked hard, he would feed her.

Over the next months, Fermina stayed by
Pacencia's side, learning her tasks. She helped
the old woman bake bread in the horno, gather
brown eggs from under the hens, sweep the floors,
and wash clothes by boiling them in a tub over
an open fire. She traveled with her weekly to
draw barrels of river water.

One day, men in dark blue shirts rode out to
collect Hidalgo. When he returned, he landed a
hard slap on Fermina's cheek. Then he took a jug
from the cellar into the cuartito and slammed
the door shut. Too stunned to cry out, Fermina
fingered the stinging skin. Pacencia spat on the
floor and warned Fermina to keep her distance
from Hidalgo: even a lazy man can be dangerous
enough to destroy a life.

# THE MINI-MART AND THE
# TEMPLE — SOPHIA: 1981

After hunching over the sales tables at the kids' clothing store where you work, you stretch and massage your forearm, the dull ache a reminder of the spill at the park four years ago, the cracked ulna that should have knitted by now, and those girls. Where are they now? Married, you bet, pregnant with toddlers. Aracely sees Elizabeth at church, says she's gotten fat since her husband split, leaving her with twins, and her hair's falling out. As you finish refolding the neon green and pink short sets in sizes 4 to 6X, you wonder if she'll turn up here to shop for her toddlers. What would you say to her? *We have some darling knit caps, Elizabeth. True, they're for children, but they stretch. And by the way, did I mention my boyfriend?...* You picture Harold, his back, his buttocks, and his phallus, thick as a tree root, but warm and pulsing.... Your stomach tightens with desire before you can push the image away to get through the afternoon.

The store has sold only one of the pink sets — no doubt to a customer blinder than you. Somehow, the Wee Folks buyers have overlooked the fact that the psychedelic era ended, but even if it were in full swing, not that many people can stand the sharp headaches caused by staring too long at these aggressive colors—headaches like the one hammering behind your eyeballs as you lumber up front to find Lourdes, propped in a seat behind the counter.

You reach for the inventory binder. "Well, we only sold one set."

Lourdes groans, shifting creakily in the folding chair. God forbid you should sit during your eight-hour stint. Once you leaned your rump against the counter, and she nearly exploded with rage. But Lourdes is pregnant, and what's more, she's the store manager. She could string a hammock in the stockroom for napping if she wanted. "You guys aren't 'suggestive selling,' like I showed you."

"I'm always telling customers their kids have the perfect complexion for these daring colors, but they take it like an insult." You push your glasses up. They still feel new—delicate wire frames and smoke-tinted lenses that hide your odd eye, less spastic since the operation, but still not quite right.

"Then I guess Fatima's not pushing stuff like she should," Lourdes says.

"Give her a break. She barely speaks English." Poor Fatima just arrived from Iran, which she calls Persia, and she's just figuring out that dimes, though smaller, are worth more than pennies and nickels.

"I'm not sure she's going to work out," Lourdes says.

"It's just that she doesn't speak English that well, not that she's a *blockhead*—"

"Hey, that reminds me. Is your boyfriend still looking for a job?"

"Yeah?"

"Wee Folks needs a truck driver."

"What happened to Boots?" You're fond of the aging black man who, along with racks of hideous clothing, delivers cornball jokes at the back door—*Knock-knock. Who's there? Lettuce. Lettuce, who? Let us in, and you'll find out.*

"His wife caught him screwing around on the overnights. She's making him retire."

"No way. He's a *grandfather*. He's *never* come on to me."

Lourdes just gives you a look. "*Any*way, they're looking for someone to replace him, and I thought maybe Harold would be interested. The pay's not bad, and drivers get all kinds of benefits we don't get here on the floor. I've got an application somewhere." She opens a drawer and paws through the sticker guns, price tags, charge slips, and pens.

You hesitate. "Um, is there a test for this job?"

"Huh?" Lourdes slams the drawer and yanks another wide. "Here it is."

"Like, do the applicants have to pass a written test?"

Lourdes furrows her brow. "I doubt it. He *can* drive, can't he?"

"Sure, he drives all over the place." You fold the application into your purse, and your ever-rumbling gut goes silent, like somebody finally pulled the plug on a faulty air-conditioning unit. "Thanks, Lourdes," you say with such feeling that it sounds phony as hell. "You want me to receive that shipment of pajamas in back?"

"Oh, leave it alone, or we won't have anything to do tomorrow. Help me decide on a theme for the nursery." Lourdes pulls wallpaper swatches from another drawer. "I'm thinking 'Noah's Ark,' but Hector likes the 'Cow Jumped over the Moon' stuff."

You glance at the patterns. A couple that needs a theme for a baby's room is about as far removed from you and your jobless boyfriend as Prince Charles and Lady Diana are in planning their royal wedding in July. Even so, as Lourdes arranges the samples on the counter, a pinprick of envy jabs you.

Marriage, or even moving in together, is unfathomable on what you earn. Harold desperately needs a job, but who would ever hire such a gangling dope? About the only thing he *can* do is drive. That's why this opportunity feels like such a blessing—*gracias, Virgencita*—you imagine the application glowing in your purse, imbued with heavenly light. If Lourdes had let you work in the back room, you'd have cut a jig between the shipping cartons and shot a private prayer to the Blessed Mother, who surely arranged this. Instead, you say, "I don't know, but this giraffe/giraffe, elephant/elephant, monkey/monkey thing feels redundant to me. And cows jumping over moons might not be the most *soothing* thing for a little kid." You hold the swath away to focus on the sharp black hooves, the swollen pink-tinged udders. "I mean, *I'd* wonder, like, *where* do they land?"

"Harold," you say as you climb into the cab of his turquoise truck after work, "do you know what time it is?" You like to give him the benefit of the doubt because he doesn't do too well with visual stimuli like clock faces. His glasses are even thicker than yours. (Your children will likely need seeing-eye dogs from birth.)

"Uh-h-h, after six?"

"Do you remember what time my shift ends?"

"Five-thirty, right?"

"Why didn't you come for me on time?" You smile to let him know you're not angry, just curious.

"*Oh,* I'm late. You're not mad, are you?"

"*No-o-o,*" you say, determined not to spoil the evening.

"Let's get take-out burritos over at Taco King." His voice rises in anticipation of the treat.

You hate to disappoint him, but you won't have money for take-out food until payday. "Why don't we eat at my house instead?

This is Loretta's last weekend home before she heads back to vet school. I bet she'll fix something pretty good."

"Do you think she'll make burritos?"

Loretta would no more serve burritos for Sunday dinner than she'd boil up hot dogs on Thanksgiving. "She *might*."

In fact, Loretta has roasted a Boston butt, with pearl onions, quartered red potatoes, thick chunks of carrot and celery stewed in bubbling broth. As soon as you step in the back door, aromatic gusts from the oven caress your face like a lover's touch. You'd like nothing more than to pull the roasting pan from the oven and ladle a bit of browned potato and caramelized onion into your saliva-flooded mouth. Instead, you lead Harold toward the front room to tell him about the job. *That's* how excited you are about it.

But Harold isn't so thrilled. "Driving a *truck*?"

"That's what truck drivers do, honey."

"I don't know, Soph."

"The pay is good, and you get benefits. Have you ever had benefits before?"

"No, but—"

"You can't turn your back on benefits. And, what's wrong with driving a truck?"

"Nothing, but you know my mom—"

"What about your mother?" You can't imagine the stoic Mormon woman being anything but relieved if Harold found work. "She wouldn't object to you driving a truck? She's a bus driver after all."

"It's just she has that thing from her work, that problem."

"*Oh-h-h,* that. It's not hereditary, honey, is it?"

"No way do I want to go through that. You should hear her moaning on the can."

That Harold will never have benefits hits you like a pan of ice water tossed in your face. "It doesn't have to be like that. We can get doughnut pillows."

Harold shakes his head. "The body's the temple, you know." And that's it—discussion over. Harold's favorite phrase works both as end punctuation and an indisputable reminder: *his* body *is* a temple. Below that straw-colored mop and the thick tortoise-shell glasses affixed at the bridge with a Band-Aid, underneath those futuristic velour V-necks and threadbare corduroys, stands the impeccable architecture of sturdy bone and rippling sinew, sheathed in the smoothest, tawniest skin imaginable. Stroking Harold's bare chest is like running your fingers over sun-warmed silk that happens to be as sweet to the tongue as honey butter.

You can barely believe that this temple is yours, all yours. In fact, it's the only thing of physical beauty you possess; because if Harold's body is a temple, yours must be a mini-mart, a squat concrete square, shelves bulging with canned Vienna sausage, Cheese Nips, Fig Newtons, Tab, Ivory soap, Kotex, Right Guard, and cases and cases of Metrecal. So you fold the application back into your purse. You can almost see the benefits—whatever they might be—flapping out the window like winged monkeys.

Depressingly, most everyone is home for dinner, most everyone being Loretta, of course, who's prepared this—her last supper before flying back to school in Georgia—your brother, Cary, and your old man. Bette is likely at her apartment, serving charred meat and leathery potatoes to the Criminal while caring for her newborn baby, and Rita has just moved to Northern California to clear hiking trails and clean up state parks with some outfit she joined after earning an Associate of Arts degree in environmental science.

With luck, Harold will eat swiftly, and you can slip away before the family acts out too much. But early on, your brother starts in with the air typing. Since he was hired as a typist at an insurance company downtown, Cary has become obsessed with developing his skills.

"What's he doing?" Harold asks.

"Typing," you say without looking up from your plate.

"Huh?"

"He's typing," Loretta explains. "He wants you to pass the B-U-T-T-E-D, the 'butted,' whatever that is."

"The last letter was an R," Cary says. "That was a clear R, Loretta."

"No, it wasn't. You used your left middle finger, which is reserved for the E, D, and C, and you dipped a bit, so it was a D."

"You *lie*! I didn't dip. I *lifted*, and you're supposed to use the middle finger for the R." He holds up his middle finger, pressing an imaginary R over and over for emphasis. "Besides, why would I ask for 'butted'? There's no such thing."

"No, there's not," Loretta says. "I wouldn't pass you a thing, even if you typed a proper word. Typing at the table is rude. I never notice you bothering to type 'please.'"

Harold slides the butter dish toward your brother.

"You know they're hiring guys at the yard—loaders, unloaders." Your father points the tines of his fork at Harold. "Bet they could use a strong guy like you."

"Bad for the back." Harold stuffs his mouth with meat.

"Hah?" grunts the old man. "You got back trouble?"

Harold shakes his head, swallows. "And I don't want none."

"Shoot." Your father peers over his glasses at Harold. "Young guy like you worried about your *back*? Are you kidding?"

"If you lift properly," Loretta says, "bearing weight can benefit your entire skeletal frame."

"The body's the temple, you know," says Harold, and you squeeze his thigh under the table, transmitting a silent prayer to la Virgen: *Help me out here, please!*

Loretta arches an eyebrow. "Interesting."

Cary's fingers take flight while your father grabs the shaker and issues a hard rain of salt onto his plate. "Stop that typing. Just tell us what you want."

"Can't you see?" Cary retypes his sentence, slowly and emphatically.

"Don't give him nothing," your father says.

"How is, uh, Rita doing up north?" asks Harold.

"Fine," you say, afraid no one else will answer. "She calls once a week."

*C-O-L-L-E-C-T,* types Cary.

"She must like it up there, eh," Harold says, stabbing a carrot, "so green and all that. They don't got too many niggers up there, neither."

Now, you have heard about people who can spontaneously combust during moments of intense emotion, and you wish with all your heart that you were one of them, so you could ignite, incinerating the household before anyone has a chance to react. Or even that the Blessed Mother would make one of her unexpected appearances to the faithful and lift you speedily up to heaven. ("*You have suffered enough, my child. Take my hand.*") But another part of you—not the heart—feels detached, even curious about who will be the one to savage poor Harold.

Your father is the likely candidate. Most of his coworkers and buddies at the utility company are black, and he knows better than any of you how stupid and dangerous that word can be, but he just picks up his plate and silverware. Balancing his glass of iced tea against his chest, he heads for the door. He will eat the rest of his meal on the back steps, a retreat reserved for times of most profound disgust, like when Bette first separated from Luis and brought the Criminal home for Christmas dinner.

Cary's fingers are frozen in the middle of a word. He looks like a magician halted while casting a spell because he's forgotten the incantation. You rack your mind for some painless way to chastise Harold before Loretta gets a crack at him.

Her chair scrapes. She stands and takes Harold's plate.

"Hey, I'm not done."

You put a finger over your lips. "Shh."

"I believe you are," Loretta tells him. "In fact, it's time for you to go now." She carries his plate to the sink.

Cary's hands drop to his lap. "Man, I can't even *believe* you said that."

"*What?*" Harold is mystified. "*What* did I say?"


The entire drive to Harold's house, you tell yourself you shouldn't love him. He's a dolt, stupider than Lydia with her picture books. He *says* he graduated from high school, but have you ever *seen* his diploma? He's just an idiotic white guy with a gorgeous body, and you shouldn't love him any more than rich geezers ought to fall for buxom strippers who have trouble stringing two syllables together.

But when he flops on a hassock (his well-formed buttocks at a pert angle) and tosses you the *TV Guide,* so you can tell him what's on, you know you can't help *but* love him. And after his mother goes to bed, when he's got you in his arms—skin to skin—on the musty quilt covering the springs hatching from the sofa, you realize you never had a choice about not loving him. If you stopped loving him, you would shut the door on this flesh and these lips and this solid chest—heart thudding—as it rubs against your bare breasts. You would lose this world of supple skin and salt kisses. And losing it, you would be lost, too.

(Maybe there's a way you can be smart enough for the both of you.)

When Harold drives you home, you have him kill the engine and coast through the back alley. You slip off your shoes on the porch as he rolls off in reverse. But as soon as you pad in the door, the kitchen light flicks on, and your father, Loretta, and Cary file around the table, as though assembling for an impromptu committee meeting.

"What's up?" you say.

"We want to talk to you, h'ita." Your father's voice is grave.

"Me? What'd *I* do?" You aren't responsible for the words that come out of Harold's mouth. In fact, one could argue that *he's* not entirely responsible, either.

"It's about Harold," Loretta says. "Don't you find he's a low-level person?"

Your father shakes his head. "Level ain't got nothing to do with it. He's a lazy no-good." He props his elbows on the table. "Remember Severito, now he was a real baboso, a true low-level, but he had this cousin Nuncio, and Nuncio was always after your mother because she was real smart, and she could write good. He wanted her to write letters on how he was so slow, he should be tested." Your father raises his eyebrows, as though he finds his own story hard to believe. "He wanted to be *found* retarded. He didn't want to work, but he played cards, and he was a cheater, a *cheater's* cheater."

"Harold's not a cheater," you point out.

"Oh *yes,* he is," Cary says. "Me and Luis play basketball with him. We've *seen* him cheat."

"This Harold, h'ita, he's a sinvergüenza. He don't even feel bad about himself."

"What Dad is saying," Loretta says, as though your father has just rattled off in some obscure dialect she must translate, "is that Harold seems to be taking advantage of you." She peers at you over the frames of her glasses. "You know I don't like to get involved in what you people do, but I'm making an exception because you're the only one who comes close to me in terms of academic potential—"

"Gee, thanks," Cary puts in.

"But you meet this, this—well, he's just a goof, isn't he?—and you don't apply for college." Loretta starts counting on her fingers. "You're eighteen, working full-time at that shop, but you never have money, and you don't have plans for the future."

"I have plans, lots of plans."

Your brother gives you a doubtful look. "Like what?"

"I want to move out, get my own place."

"With Harold, right?" Cary nods, as if he knows it all.

"It ain't a good relationship," says your father.

"So, are you forbidding me to see him?"

His eyes widen. "Qué forbid, ni forbid. I don't forbid *nothing*."

"Then what's the point of all this?" you ask.

"The point is," Cary says, "you need to wake up, Sophie. The guy's an ass."

"Funny, I don't remember the meeting we held for Bette after she left Luis to move in with that Criminal. How come no one ever told her to wake up?"

"I don't tell Bette nothing because she don't listen," says your father.

"And I *do*?" You slide your chair out from the table and stand. "Well, thank you for your input. I *have* listened, and my thinking is that this is *my* business, not yours." You stomp to your room, wishing you had the maturity not to slam your door. Lacking that, you bang it with such force the house shakes.

You regard yourself in the clouded dresser mirror. Your face is full, red as a beefsteak tomato that's ripe enough to burst a seam, but your smoke-tinged glasses give you a certain élan. "Yeah, that's right — the hell with them."

Bette or Rita should be here to put in a few words on your behalf. You think of *la Virgen* and of Fermina, how you once believed she was your fairy godmother. You could sure use some intercession here....

The phone rings, and someone knocks on your door. You inch it open.

"It's for you," Loretta says.

Joy sparks. With a lover's clairvoyance, Harold must have sensed the trouble. "Hey," you say warmly, even sexily, when you pick up the phone.

But Bette's voice, not Harold's, buzzes in your ear. "Are you high?"

"No, I just, I thought you were someone else."

"Listen, I meant to call earlier. Loretta said they were going to talk to you."

"Thanks, I *could* have used the heads-up. I was just now wishing you were —"

"I have to tell you something," Bette says, her voice thick, like she's been crying. In the background, you hear the baby fussing.

"What is it?" You hear the Criminal's low voice grumbling in the background, and Baby Elena is howling now.

"I got to go, but I wanted to tell you that I love you, Sophie, whatever you do, whomever you're with. You are still my sister, still a part of me. Call me later," she says, and hangs up.

*     *     *

"So, Harold," you say, stretching out on the beach towel beside his long golden temple, clad now in burgundy Speedos. "What kind of job would you like?" On a Tuesday, Paradise Cove above Malibu is deserted, except for stout mothers with toddlers, and retirees in sagging swimsuits. Alongside these bumpy, blue-veined oldsters and chubby moms, you look only slightly plump, if you don't peel off the oversized T-shirt, that is. "I mean if you could do anything at all."

"Golf," Harold says.

"But, honey, golf is *recreation,* isn't it? It's not really a job."

"Golf pros get paid lots of money. Look at Jack Nicklaus. *He's* rich."

"Yeah, that's true." You can see Harold has put some thought to this matter, and you want to encourage this. "Good, that's right. But, honey, don't golf pros have to, like, enter tournaments and travel around and win money?"

He scratches his head. "Yeah, I guess."

You squirt Coppertone onto his shoulders, rub it in. "It's not like someone will show up and—*poof*—make you a golf pro. You got to take steps."

"Huh?"

"You need money to hire a caddy, pay tournament fees, and travel around." The coconut scent makes your mouth water.

"I could get a sponsor." Harold rakes a dried seaweed bulb over the sand.

"You *could,* but you've got to get noticed first. You've got to win tournaments."

He drops the bulb and yawns. "I suppose."

"Okay, then. What would you like to do so you could enter and win tournaments? I mean, if you had to have some kind of job, what would it be?"

He thinks about this. "I don't want to work for nobody. People always get all mad at me, make me do stuff I don't want to do."

"Well, how about working for yourself, then? That guy who started that carpet-cleaning business and became a millionaire isn't much older than you."

"The one on TV? *He's* a millionaire?"

"Yup."

"Bet he gets to play golf whenever he feels like it."

"Sure he does." Momentum builds. The discussion is going somewhere!

"I could do that," Harold declares.

"But you can't, Harold, because of the greens fees." You hold your breath, scoop a handful of sand, and let it stream through your fingers, casually.

"I mean I could clean carpets." Harold sits up. "I could get me one of those…"

"Carpet cleaners?"

"Yeah, one of those. I could get me one, put it in my truck, and drive around cleaning rugs. When I made some money, I'd get more machines. I could even hire some wetbacks, pay them almost nothing, and spend serious time on the golf course."

"That's right, Harold, exactly right." This flash of ambition is so encouraging that you say nothing about his plan to exploit "wetbacks." Instead, you begin curling shut the mouth of the potato chip sack, gathering soft-drink cans and sandwich wrappers.

"What're you doing?" Harold asks.

"Cleaning up. Aren't we leaving?"

"*Leaving?* You got somewhere to go? Thought this was your day off."

"I thought you'd want to leave, maybe look at some carpet cleaners," you say, tipping your hand big-time.

"Nah." Harold draws you into his arms. "Not right now that I got me a sexy woman here."

"Where?" You make a big deal of looking around to make him smile, but he burrows his head in the crook of your neck, commencing a series of stinging love bites. Feels nice, but clearly, hell has *got* to be the place where no one gets your jokes.

The carpet cleaner, a gleaming, steam-snorting monster that Harold wants, costs more than eighteen hundred dollars. You've tried talking him into a more modest home version of this machine, but he's attached to the industrial-purpose apparatus, arguing that he can do office buildings as well as homes with it. So as not to stifle his ambition, you say, okay, that makes sense. But spending eighteen hundred dollars makes no sense at all. He'd have to clean forty-five carpets at forty bucks a pop to break even. The millionaire on television and his fleet of employees can do them for half that, and people can rent shampooers themselves at Safeway for ten dollars.

Worse than this, Harold expects you to loan him the money, which you don't have. You're always broke a week before payday, even though you're paid twice monthly. You tend to eat out a lot now that Harold's persona non grata at your house. You practically hemorrhage money when the two of you go out. Just last Sunday, you dropped a cool hundred at the Pomona Fair, not including gas. You'd never realized how expensive having a boyfriend could be.

(And it's a serious business, too. Two nights ago, you went shopping with Aracely and Rosa, and your face still hurts from laughing. You never yuk it up like this when Harold's around. Having a boyfriend is no laughing matter.)

After that family intervention, there's no way to ask your father or even Cary to lend you the money. Loretta would no more give you eighteen hundred dollars than she'd take up quail hunting. You doubt Bette, living with the Criminal, even gets to *see* money, and Rita, just starting her job with that environmental group up north, is likely poorer than you. Nobody you know would contribute to what even you realize is a piss-poor investment.

When the millionaire in the television commercials says, "Every stain has its solution," clearly he's talking about solving problems. This you can do, so you apply your mind to the matter every day, especially at work, where you are aggravated beyond sense by the back-to-school rush of mothers and spoiled, whiny kids, all of whom you hate with a thrilling passion. Plus, your period is due, and anticipating the tidal flow of blood and rib-racking cramps makes you fierce enough to snarl and snap. To top it off, last night you discovered some kid — surely not an adult! — shat in one of the dressing rooms. You gagged cleaning up that nastiness as best you could, but today the whole shop still stinks like an outhouse.

"Put more Pine-Sol in there," Lourdes keeps telling you.

"I already poured on so much that I'm going blind from the fumes."

She marches to the employee bathroom and emerges with the pine cleanser to slosh about a few jiggers herself, while mumbling this curious refrain: "*I ask you to put Pine-Sol, you better goddamn put Pine-Sol.... You want to work here...get paid to do what I say...when I say it.... Stupid motherfuckers let their kids act like animals, goddamn it.... Hate this shit!*" before stomping off into the bathroom.

"What's that, Lourdes?" You lift the sticker gun from the pile of lavender culottes you're pricing. "You talking to *me*?"

But she's already slammed the door. If only you had the cojones to dump the culottes and walk out. Instead, you shoot adhesive tags on garment tickets, building up an angry rhythm, when Fatima comes through the mall entrance, holding a dark green checkbook.

"Hey, aren't you off this afternoon?"

"Afternoon off, sure," Fatima says, handing you the checkbook.

"Don't tell me you're going to buy something."

Fatima eyes the jumble of purple plaid you're stickering. "Pooh, not here."

"What's this then?" You hold up the checkbook.

"Customer leave this. I put in purse and I forget. Call to customer, okay?"

"Sure, thanks for bringing it back," you say before she rushes off. You turn the checkbook, flip it open. According to the register, the balance is over three thousand dollars—*whew!* Nobody should have that much money just sitting in the bank.

"Where's the goddamn soap?" Lourdes yells from the back.

"Under the sink!" You slip the checkbook into your purse behind the counter. "You have to open a new bar!"

Amazingly, every problem does have its solution.

"Is it my imagination or was the carpet just cleaned again?" Cary asks as he enters the front door and catches you sprawled on the couch eating a grilled cheese and finishing off a family-sized bag of Fritos while watching *All My Children.*

"No and yes," you say. "In contrast to your imagination, the carpet's just been cleaned."

"Wasn't it shampooed last week?" He loosens his tie and kicks off his shoes before negotiating the carpet with stocking feet. "Yikes, still wet."

"You have to walk on the furniture," you tell him. "Climb on the armchair over there, then jump to the hassock. It rolls, so pull yourself on the drapes to the door, if you have to get to the kitchen."

Cary mounts the armchair. "How come you're home in the middle of the day?"

"Stomach flu," you say, stuffing a fistful of corn chips into your mouth. "You?"

"Bomb threat—we had to evacuate the building."

"Did you get the mail?"

"Yeah, Dad got a letter from Nilda." He holds aloft an envelope. As much as you miss your aunt, who moved to New Mexico to live with her youngest brother, Santi, on the family farm soon after José died, and would like to open the letter, you know your father, though laid-back about most things, would have a fit if you tampered with mail addressed to him. Cary tosses the mail on the coffee table, leaps for the hassock, and grabs the drapes. "How come you keep shampooing the carpet?"

"Not me—Harold."

"But why?"

"He enjoys it."

After reeling himself to the hallway, your brother turns to say, "He better not think he can get in good with us by cleaning the carpet every few days."

"He just wants us to have nice rugs." But the truth is—in the month he's had the machine, he's cleaned carpets only at your house and at his mother's. He's shampooed your family's wall-to-walls three times, and you've paid him—fifty bucks!—each time, but his mother paid him only once. (She refused to pay the second time, saying it wasn't necessary to shampoo again a week later.) Though you thought that once Harold got in the habit of making money, he'd want to earn more, so far this has not happened. In fact, the more Harold makes, the less he wants to work. Poor Harold, you sigh and lick the salt from your fingertips. The new business has overwhelmed him.

Last week, your father complained about the damp floors. "I don't want that boy cleaning these rugs no more," he'd said, folding his arms across his chest.

"It's not costing you a penny," you pointed out.

"That ain't the problem. The durn rugs are always wet. We're going to get athlete's foot. It's stupid to keep cleaning them when they're already clean."

"So you're forbidding me from having the carpets cleaned?"

"Qué forbid, ni forbid. I don't forbid *nothing*. I'm just telling you enough is enough. No more rug cleaning, period," he'd said.

Cary pokes his head in the doorway. "What's Dad got to say about all this?"

"Oh, he's cool."

Someone pounds on the front door, and you jump. Harold? Surely, he doesn't expect to shampoo the carpets twice in the same day. You stand on the couch to peer out the window: a tan uniform leg, leather belt, holster, hairy forearm, and clipboard. Your heart seizes. The room whirls. Maybe you'll faint and fall into the wettest part of the carpet and, with luck, drown.

"Who's that?" Cary's feet make squishy sounds as he pads to the threshold.

"Don't open it," you say, but it's too late.

Fingerprinting, photos, officers barking orders, but the worst part for you is the waiting. You wait hours before you're led into the courtroom, where the old judge's eyes are so recessed in his puffy lids that you're sure the codger's asleep until he sets bail, naming a figure so high the room spins. He raps the gavel and calls, "Next!" You're herded to a holding cell for more waiting. Nothing to read, nothing to see but the dejected faces of the others grouped with you. Except for you, everyone here could have been arrested for filthy hair. You have never seen such a collection of oily, uncombed locks. You hope to distance yourself from the others through superior hair hygiene, and through crying.

You will beg Harold to go on with his life. You can't expect him to wait for you to be released, a hardened woman of uncertain age. You see your future self emerging from the prison walls. Dated street clothes hang on your gaunt frame. You've lost weight in prison, so you look pretty good, sadder but wiser...

"This is a mistake," a woman with bad skin says to no one in particular. Everything about her—from her stained turtleneck sweater to her paisley bell-bottoms—is a mistake. She should be more specific.

You dread what Rita and Loretta will have to say about all this. You hate to even think about how your father will take this, and remembering how Cary's jaw dropped when you were cuffed and led out to the squad car prompts a fresh flow of tears. Bette, at least, will understand.

Someone shouts your name. You follow a guard to the desk, where a clerk says your bail is paid and gives you a form with a trial date on it.

"I don't have to stay?"

"Not unless you want to," jokes the clerk.

You picture Harold swiftly shampooing scores of carpets for bail money, but reality shuts down that image, and fast. Your father, no doubt, dug into his retirement for bail. But when you step into the visitors' area, you behold a most stunning sight: Cary slouching before the wanted posters, his thumbs in the belt loops of his Levi's.

"*You* bailed me out?"

"I went to this bondsman, so I only had to pay like ten percent."

"Still, that's a lot of money."

He shrugs. "Savings." Cary has wanted a Mustang convertible since he started building model cars as a kid.

"Was Dad too pissed-off to get me out?"

"I didn't tell him, didn't think you'd want him to know."

"I wish no one had to know."

"Don't tell anyone then," Cary advises.

"What about the trial? What about a lawyer?"

"We'll figure that out when the time comes, okay?" A deep flush rises from your brother's neck to his forehead, suffusing his jowly cheeks with violent color. "You got to pay me back, you know."

"Of course, I will." This may take time. No doubt you've lost the Wee Folks job.

"And this has to be the last time this kind of shit *ever* happens, got that?"

"Never again, I swear!"

He pulls open the door. "Better be. 'Cause, Sophie, this ain't funny. Not one bit."

SUBJECT: FERMINA/SERVITUDE
WPA: 7-7-38—DC: HMS
July 5, 1938
Words: 817

## CHILDBIRTH AND MANUMISSION

To pay gambling debts, Hidalgo sold Fermina, sending her off to the Rio Puerco Valley to work for Inocencio and Yrma Gabaldon. Devout Catholics, the couple named the servant girl "Fermina," after San Fermin, on whose feast day, the 25th of September, she had arrived in their house. Later, Fermina learned that the date marked the martyrdom of San Fermin, first bishop of Pamplona, who was strapped to a bull and dragged to his death.

The childless couple treated Fermina well enough in the beginning. Yrma Gabaldon taught her to cook and serve meals. But la señora had a reputation for stinginess. Early in marriage, Yrma had delivered two stillborns. It was rumored that she was too selfish to get a living baby out. When Fermina came to the Gabaldons, Yrma was again with child. The midwife advised her to offer the poor food to assure a safe birth. But Yrma refused. After a long labor, a lifeless boy—a frown stamped like a boot heel on his blue face—emerged from between her thighs. Inocencio buried him beyond the apple orchard and Yrma never conceived again.

Over time, Fermina learned Spanish, forgetting much of the Tewa and Hopi she once spoke. On trips to town, she would see men and women from the other Pueblo tribes. These people reminded Fermina of ghosts, they were so emaciated and haggard. She felt fortunate not to have to live as they did. So when Yrma cuffed her for dropping an egg, she dared not complain, and when Inocencio came to her at night, she did not cry out, though at first, she feared he was murdering her, ripping her insides out. In time, it became *"como una mosca caminando sobre mi mano"* (like a fly walking on her hand), and before long, Fermina grew round in the abdomen.

One morning, her back flamed with pain. She sank into a chair and warm water gushed between her legs. Yrma sent Inocencio for the midwife, who arrived in time to help birth the baby. To cut the umbilical cord, the partera set the infant, a boy, on Fermina's stomach. He blinked at her and croaked. Fermina called him "rana" because his legs were bent like a frog's.

Fermina was about thirteen years old when she delivered her son in 1882. Yrma and Inocencio claimed him as their child, naming him Decidero for Inocencio's father. After his christening, the Gabaldons invited the priest for dinner. The curate noticed Fermina and grew agitated. He explained that people could no longer keep such servants. The president had said that the Moqui, the Hopi slaves, must go back to their people. Yrma readily agreed, but Inocencio refused to send the girl away.

The next time Inocencio rode into town on his own, Yrma ordered Fermina to return to her people. Decidero, Yrma said, was old enough to drink goat's milk now. Not sure where her people were of if they remembered her, Fermina gathered her few belongings and trudged toward the ditch. After wandering a distance, she doubled back and slipped into the Gabaldons' adobe barn. From there, she heard the baby wailing and Inocencio cursing Yrma when he returned before nightfall. Finally he emerged, called out Fermina's name, and whistled for her, the way he would summon a dog. She hurried from the barn and followed him back into the house.

The baby was red faced, rigid with cramps and weak from diarrhea. Fermina nursed him through the night and he recovered. Though Yrma agreed to let her stay, things changed in the household. Yrma would pull Fermina's hair and slap her without provocation. Fermina worked harder than ever because she feared Yrma would again cast her out, especially once the baby was weaned. After the priest's visit, the Gabaldons were ashamed to attend mass, prompting the curate to return to their home. He found Fermina outside boiling lye for soap and questioned her. She explained that she wanted to stay. Then, he said, she must be baptized to become a member of the family.

So it was that Fermina was taken to church for the first time to be baptized and have her name written in the records. Though it was the custom of the time, Yrma refused to give her their surname, and Inocencio induldged his wife in this matter. Instead, they christened her Fermina Hidalgo, after the man from whom they acquired her. Now Fermina could attend church with the family. This infuriated Yrma, but at least she and Inocencio could bring the boy up in the sacraments. Sunday mornings, Fermina enjoyed sitting in church and watching the parishioners, who squirmed in stiff clothes and tight shoes, much more than cooking alone in the hot kitchen. Besides, the priest had said the man on the cross was the son of God, who was all-powerful, so Fermina prayed to him for help.

# 10

# MIASMA — RITA: 1982

*Assholes,* Rita thinks as she scans the other crew members on the bus to a work site one summer morning. The ranks of the California Environmental Maintenance Corps are filled with repeat shoplifters, chronic truants, druggies, minor gangsters, and underage drinkers. These low-level lawbreakers have been given a choice: lockup in a detention center or join the CEMC. Though they chose the corps, they nevertheless groan at reveille, gripe at mealtimes, and complain while digging trenches and pulling up brush — the good-for-nothing malcriados.

There are a few exceptions like Rennie, who sits across the aisle from Rita, strumming his secondhand guitar, his rust-colored afro ablaze now in the sunlight streaming through the windows. Although serving a stint for dealing, Rennie claims he *likes* working for the CEMC. Definitely a step-up, he says, from peddling hashish at the high schools. There are also a handful of genuine volunteers who start out with Rennie's attitude, but the inland summer heat, the manual labor, and the low pay soon weed out these workers. And most that remain are lazy and aggressively stupid, like the slack-mouthed Jackie snoring in the seat in front of Rennie, his mullet tapering to a rat's tail along the back of his thick neck.

So far, Rita hasn't met anyone like herself in the corps, a mature twenty-one-year-old volunteer who doesn't complain and doesn't quit. Deep in the woods, she savors the fragrant sanctum of pine straw, fern, and moss under the canopy of loblolly, incense cedar, and redwood—all of it so insistently green that her throat tightens with pleasure. She prefers working alone, so she can imagine a solitary life in the forest, at least until a shovel clangs nearby or curses echo through the woods when one of the petty criminals bursts a blister. Even this stream of shaggy eucalyptus and tall rippling grass scrolling past the bus window lends Rita a few calm moments before she finds herself eavesdropping on a conversation between the two girls seated behind her. She's familiar enough with them to dislike them in a vague way, though she doesn't know much about the two, except that they're cholas who've been in the corps almost as long as she has.

"Hey, you seen that new guy this morning?" Lupe asks, her voice loud and gruff.

Rita pictures the girl's flabby face, wiped clean of the heavy makeup she applies for trips to town. Without the caked-on foundation, glittery eye shadow, thick eyeliner, and clumpy mascara, Lupe's wan face resembles that of a pretreated corpse.

"Yeah, I seen him dragging his duffel over to the guys' dorm," says Belinda, a whittled-to-the-bone cholita, who struggles to ingratiate herself with the tougher, louder girls, like a small dog wriggling abjectly before larger ones.

Lupe smacks her lips. "That's one fine dude, mmm-mmm-*mmm*."

"He ain't bad," Belinda says, "for a gabacho."

"Check it out, eh, he's supposed to be on the bus with us, but he tells the director he's got this *lawyer* coming out here and he's got to wait for him at the office."

"You talked to him?"

"Yeah, I went up to him, and I go, 'What's with you, dude? How come you ain't in khakis?' Says his name's Andy and gives me all this crap about the lawyer—biggest pile of mierda. I'm surprised Noah bought it."

"Well, he ain't on the bus," Belinda points out.

"Eh, did I tell you about the time we crashed that party in Echo Park? We didn't know nobody there, and we was drunk, I mean off our asses..."

Rita tunes Lupe out, wondering who this new guy thinks he is, slacking off the first day. This takes her mind off the road. Rita's been tense on bus trips lately, especially when she can see enough from the window—like now—to second-guess Rafe, the driver. The narrow highways often wind around steep mountain face, and as the bus climbs, the drops grow dizzyingly sheer. When she sits at the back of the bus, Rita doesn't dwell on this too much, but here in front, she wonders if Rafe might be hungover, sleepy, or otherwise impaired. To distract herself, Rita works herself up against the newcomer. Just who the *hell* does he think he is?

After a week, Rita, though curious, still hasn't met the new guy, who probably works with another crew. Some teams clear hiking trails, while others reforest burn areas. It's common not to see male coworkers, who sleep in a separate dorm, for several days, if they have a different mess rotation. But Rennie mentions to her that this Andy has been in the infirmary the whole week.

"What's his problem anyway?" she asks.

"Malaria."

"*Malaria?* How'd he get that?"

"He's some kind of rich kid. Parents take him all over the place, private jets and stuff. Supposedly, he contracted it in Nairobi, and now he has to take it easy."

"Yeah, right," Rita says.

That Saturday, Rita rides the bus into Sebastopol with the other corps members. Most can't wait to blow their small stipends eating out, drinking if they have ID, or shopping in overpriced specialty stores that fill in the touristy, wine country town, but not Rita. She hoards her money, though she will treat herself to a movie at the discounted matinee price and buy herself a burger afterward. These outings never cost her more than ten dollars. Except for laundry funds, the remainder of her pay she socks away, literally knotting the bills into an old green sock, which she keeps in her footlocker.

After eating, Rita hikes back to the kiosk, where Rafe has parked the bus, waiting to return the six o'clock group to camp. At nine and midnight, he returns to pick up corps members who want to stay out later. Rita is usually the only one to board the early bus. She likes having it to herself, except for Rafe, a slender black man, who respects her privacy on these companionable, but silent, rides from town.

This afternoon, though, someone else is sitting up front, just behind Rafe. The two are chatting. Rita avoids the other passenger's eyes, but nods at Rafe and makes her way to the back. Rita flips through a shoppers' circular she's picked up as she listens in on their conversation. Rafe whistles, pointing out a dark green Lincoln parked across the street. "Now, there's a sweet car."

The guy shrugs. "It's all right."

"You wouldn't want a car like that?" Rafe says.

"Why would I? I got myself a nice candy-apple red Corvette with a V-8 engine."

Rafe shakes his head. "Get out of here!"

"Just got it from my old man, for my eighteenth birthday," the guy says.

"You expect me to believe *that*?"

"It's true." Dusky sunlight reddens his ears, which stick out slightly from his head. Rita spies a manufacturer's tag peeking from his collar and longs to tuck it in.

Rafe churns the engine and the bus rumbles from the kiosk. They ride in silence for a few moments.

"No lie," the guy insists. "I do have a 'Vette."

"Your dad must be a millionaire," Rafe says.

"That's right," he says.

Rafe turns to give him a suspicious look, and Rita gasps as the bus wanders over the yellow divider. Rafe steers back into the lane.

"Ever hear of the Silicon Valley?"

"What about it?" Rafe says.

"My dad and some buddies started that. They made shitloads of money. Before my parents got divorced, we were living in Beverly Hills."

"Only one house, huh?"

"No, but that's where we lived most of the time. We have one in Marin, too. That's where I live now with my mom. We got a mansion there, twenty bedrooms, an indoor pool, hot tub, and sauna. It's on about five hundred acres."

"Yeah, *right*," Rafe says.

"It's true." He turns to Rita. His wide gray eyes, dense lashes, well-shaped eyebrows, and bow-shaped lips strike her as childlike, even feminine, as he appeals to her. "You believe me, don't you?"

She shrugs, looks away. Outside of television or films, Rita's never before seen a face as pretty as this.

"If you're so rich, how come you're stuck pulling weeds here?" Rafe asks.

"I had some trouble, see."

"Why didn't your old man pay off some judge or something like that?"

"That's *why* I'm here. It could have been a lot worse."

"Get out of here." Rafe tunes the radio to a local station, cranks the volume up, and whistles along with "Hey There, Lonely Girl." No one speaks the rest of the way back to camp.

Later, before the sun dissolves behind the tree-line, Rita lugs her clothes to the laundry, and that movie star face stops her short. He's perched on the aluminum bar fence before the men's dorm. "Where you headed?"

She lifts a box of detergent in reply and continues on her way.

He leaps from the fence and hurries to catch up with her. "My name's Andy," he says. "I'm new here. Will you show me where you wash clothes?"

Rita points ahead, and Andy follows her into the small stucco building that houses four washing machines and two industrial-sized dryers. The dry warmth of the laundry room—the soft linty-ness of it, the throaty rumble of the machines, and the perfumed fragrance of fabric softener—usually cocoons Rita cozily. But now, with this newcomer staking claim to her attention, the room's scented snugness grows hot and cloying. And surreptitious glances at that film star face fill her with a weird sense of unreality, as though she's in a waking dream with a celebrity she can't place.

"I notice you don't talk much," Andy says as Rita inserts quarters into two of the washers. "Hey, if I get my clothes, will you help me with the machines?"

Rita shrugs, and he bolts for the door. She starts the washers, tossing in a cupful of soap flakes before loading her clothes. As she reaches to flick off the light, Andy reappears, bearing two stuffed pillowcases. "So how's this work?"

Rita indicates the printed instructions on the wall. "See."

Andy laughs. "So you *can* talk." He stuffs a jumble of jeans, jockey shorts, white socks, and towels into a washer. "What's your name?"

Rita shakes her head. "Sort them, or the whites will get dingy, the colors fade. Don't you pay attention to commercials?" She pulls his clothing out of the machine, but Rita's not about to sort his laundry for him. "You have quarters?"

Andy pulls a twenty-dollar bill from his wallet. "Where do I get change?"

"Nowhere," Rita tells him. "It's the weekend. Nobody's here."

"You have change?"

"I can't break a twenty." No matter how good-looking this joker is, Rita has no intention of returning to the dorm for change.

Andy drops his eyes, and his lower lip protrudes, prettily, as he gathers up his clothes.

"I guess I can *lend* you quarters," Rita says, relenting. "You can borrow some of my detergent. Sort your stuff, and I'll start the machines."

"You know you're really nice." Andy grins, baring teeth lustrous enough to appear in a toothpaste ad. "You're not like the rest of them, are you?"

Rita slams the coin trays into the machines and sprinkles in detergent. "This one has hot water," she says, pointing, "for the light stuff—underwear and towels. Put the darks in the other machine. That's set on cold."

"You're cute, too, in a natural way. I bet you could be a model with your height."

"Yeah," Rita says, parroting Rafe's tone, *"right."* She wheels out of the laundry room and strides back to the women's dorm.

The next day, Sunday, Rita arrives at the canteen early for breakfast, hoping to eat alone. The malcriados are usually too hungover to show up before ten. And her head start is rewarded—no one in sight. She's almost finished with her meal when Andy enters the dining area and grabs a tray. Rita gulps water to slosh down her last mouthful and gathers her utensils. Before she rises from the table, Andy catches her eye and grins. "Mind if I join you?"

"I'm done."

"Come on. Stay and have a doughnut with me, okay?"

Rita shakes her head. "I don't like sweets."

"There's fruit. Everybody likes fruit." Andy lifts a crescent of cantaloupe. "How about this, or an orange?" His shining eyes remind Rita of her brother, Cary, begging her to play cards with him. She returns to the serving area, picks out an orange, and follows Andy back to the table.

He grins. "You didn't want me touching your fruit, did you?"

"What if I didn't want you to *pick out* my fruit?"

"Look at that orange." He points his fork at the thing. "It's half green. It's got to be hard, sour as a lemon. You didn't want me *touching* it."

While Rita pries the stiff peel from the fruit, Andy tells her about himself. He lowers his voice to talk about his parents' divorce, his father's philandering, and his mother's lover. He mentions a young sister, her scoliosis, her dream of becoming a pediatric nurse. He even brings up an old girlfriend, tells how they "drifted apart."

After Rita scrapes off the last bit of peel and divides the orange's leathery segments, Andy grabs it from her hands. "There," he says, "I've touched it. Now you don't have to eat it."

Rita wipes her mouth with her napkin and stands. She turns for the exit, but Andy rises and blocks her. "You're funny, you know that? You don't want me touching your food, you wipe your hands like a million times, and you won't even breathe in my direction. What are you afraid of?" He grabs her hand, lifts it to his lips. "Think I've got cooties?" His pointy pink tongue flicks out and he runs it over her knuckles.

Rita freezes, too stunned to move.

"I wonder what it'd be like for you if we kissed. Germ warfare?"

Rita wrenches her hand free, wipes it on the seat of her Levi's. Her face burns. "Malaria," she says. "Supposedly, you have malaria. Or is that bullshit like everything else that comes out of your mouth?"

His smile fades. "Malaria, for your information, isn't contagious. You get it from mosquitoes, but don't trust my word. Look it up. I get bouts, and I have to take quinine tablets and rest. I can't *infect* anyone."

Rita steps past him, hurrying out of the canteen.

"Sorry I *bothered* you," he calls after her, "with bullshit."

In the dorm, Rita quietly scrubs her hands with soap and hot water, so as not to disturb the snoring girls. Surely, there are different strains of malaria, some contagious, some not. Afterward, she reaches for her dictionary. *Malaria,* she reads, *is transmitted by infected anopheles mosquitoes.* Symptoms include chills and fever. This is just a paperback dictionary, an abridged edition at that. And even if scientists believe malaria is passed strictly by mosquitoes, they don't know everything. New discoveries contradict common beliefs every day. Rita shivers against the cold clamminess of the dorm. She bundles up in blankets and re-reads the entry. The secondary definition interests her this time around: *any foul, unwholesome influence or atmosphere—miasma.*

That afternoon, Rita calls home collect from the pay phone outside the canteen. Bette answers. "How's Elena?" she asks.

Bette says, "Sick a lot from day care. Germs, you know."

"I *know*," Rita says with feeling. "How are *you* doing?" She worries about her sister, who's moved back home after the petty gangster she was living with was locked up on charges ranging from dope dealing to selling stolen property.

"Well, it sucks, of course, living back at Dad's, and with the baby. But, what can you do? I'm going back to school, working, and saving to move out." A match scratches and Bette inhales noisily. "I hope to get my ass out of here by fall but who knows?"

"And what's-his-name?" Rita asks.

"Nothing to say." While avid about her sisters' lives, Bette keeps them in the dark about her business. Rita recalls her astonishment when Bette left the laid-back and genial Luis for the seedy thug she started seeing after a few years of marriage—a marriage that Bette, up to that point, had insisted was "perfectly happy."

"How's Sophie?" Rita's youngest sister is another source of concern.

"I shouldn't tell you this," Bette says, "so act surprised when she breaks the news, but Sophie's pregnant."

Rita nearly drops the phone. *"What?"*

"Yeah, she says she wants to start a family with Harold."

Rita pictures a household of lanky dopes—vacant-looking blond mop tops in thick glasses. "Is she insane?"

"When it comes to Harold, she is," Bette tells her. "I don't get it. The guy reminds me of a long yellow straw, something that fell out of a broom. Plus, he's never around. He disappears for like days. I bet he's seeing someone else. Sophie pretends everything's great all the time, but I know stuff is up."

"Like what is that business going on between her and Cary?"

"She owes him a ton of money," Bette says. "I'm not supposed to be blabbing about this, either, but she was arrested for forgery."

*"Forgery?"* Rita is aghast. How is it she knows so little about her younger sister?

"Yeah, she did something stupid, but it was first-offender stuff, you know, no jail time. She just had to repay the money and fines and shit, so she borrowed a bunch from Cary. Right now, that's the least of her worries."

"What should we do?" Rita wonders if she should request leave and take the Greyhound down to L.A. to talk some sense into Sophie.

But Bette says, "Nothing we can do, and you're not supposed to know, so don't even call. She's nineteen now, thinks she knows it all. She won't listen to anyone."

Rita has trouble imagining Sophie pregnant, and then with a child. The unreality of it makes her queasy with regret, and—though this is hard to admit—envy.

"Hey, listen," Bette says, "maybe me and Elena will drive up to see you. I seriously need to get away from this place."

*"Really?* Don't get my hopes up if you're not really coming."

"What's up with *you*? You sound all tense."

"I'm okay," Rita says, but hesitates. "I'm just, you know, worried."

"About what?"

"Well, germs, illness," Rita says. The afternoon sun has filled the booth with syrupy heat, so she nudges open the door to let in some cool air. "Malaria."

*"Malaria?* Like the disease?"

"Yeah."

"Why would you worry about that? You're not in the fucking tropics, you know. You can only get it from a mosquito bite."

How does everyone but Rita know all about this disease? "I know," she says.

"If you want to worry about diseases, you could try syphilis or gonorrhea."

"What's that?"

"It's venereal disease. You know the kind of thing passed through sexual contact." Since Bette's enrolled in coursework for a psychology degree, she's become a font of information for Rita and her sisters.

"No risk there." Rita breathes deeply in relief. "What happens if you get it?"

"Basically, if you don't get treatment—all kinds of bad shit can happen if you contract syphilis or venereal disease. It starts with like sores and lesions, but they can lead to blindness, paralysis, even dementia."

"Jesus!" Rita puts her hand to her throat. "Where'd you hear this?"

"I read. I watch the news. Don't you have television up there?"

"In the rec room, but I never go there—too many stupid assholes."

"Read the paper then," Bette says. "Yeah, if you want something scary, try venereal diseases. Listen, Dad's going to have one big-ass phone bill."

"I'll let you go."

"Hey, don't worry about stuff so much, okay?"

"I won't," Rita says, dredging her memory for the precious little she heard about such diseases in high school. As she heads back to the dorm, she's tempted to drop into the rec room and flip on the news. Preoccupied with this, she doesn't react when Andy calls her name. She doesn't even look up until he shouts, "You in some kind of trance?"

"I'm thinking about stuff," she says, guiltily remembering their last conversation.

But he doesn't seem to hold a grudge. "What stuff?"

Rita turns away, quickens her pace, but Andy catches up. "What do you say we take a walk or something?"

"Nah," Rita says.

"What else were you going to do? Go back to your dorm and sit around? Wouldn't you rather be out on a day like this?" he says. When he puts it like this, the thought of lying in her bunk, worrying about syphilis and gonorrhea, loses appeal for Rita. Since corps members are forbidden from hiking into the woods alone, she rarely has the chance to roam beyond the camp. It's been a while since she and Rennie hiked to the pond to the east. And after a week of overcast skies, this sunny afternoon feels like a reward.

Rita hesitates as she assesses Andy. "I guess so," she says at last. They arrange to meet by the fence after filling canteens and grabbing day packs. "Bring a swimsuit," Rita says. "There's a pond we can swim in."

Andy pulls at the waistband of his khaki shorts and peers in. "I'm wearing it."

Rita doesn't say much as they trudge the hard-packed trail wending through the woods to the pond. Wind ripples through the trees and tall grass, and scudding clouds cast intermittent shadows. Gooseflesh rises on Rita's arms and neck. *Miasma,* she thinks, silently mouthing the word. As if encouraged by her utterance, sooty clouds thicken overhead. Rita points to a rise. "Just over there's a creek. We can follow it to the pond, but it looks like rain. Maybe we should turn back."

Andy shakes his head. "Let's hustle. I want to see this pond."

As they reach the water, a light rain sprinkles from the swollen clouds. Rita settles her pack on a boulder, and Andy pulls a bottle of wine and a corkscrew from his.

"Where'd you get that?" Rita asks.

"I brought it from my mom's. It's pretty good. I think you'll like it."

Rita shakes her head. "I don't drink."

But after a while, she accepts a swig from the bottle, screwing her face up at the bitter taste. "You *like* this?" Rita frowns, but tries it again—taking small sips when he hands her the bottle—as they sit watching the mist rise from the pond. When the wine makes her cheeks hot and tongue thick, she refuses more. "Want to swim?"

"Sure." He tips back the bottle to drain it.

Rita tugs off her T-shirt, unzips her shorts, and steps out of them. She has little inhibition about her long, lean body in her discreetly cut swimsuit. She kicks off her shoes and picks her way on tender feet toward the water's edge. She wades toward the middle and dives into the chilly pond. The tarnished-looking water rises shoulder-high as she crouches, her toes clinging to slick, mossy stones. Rita spies Andy bundling his clothing under his pack. His broad back tapers at the waist above the two pale globes of his buttocks. He turns and jogs toward the pond, and Rita averts her eyes as he splashes into the water. When he emerges, sluicing water from his hair and laughing, she stands upright, ready to stalk out of the pond.

He swims toward her. "What's the matter?"

"We're just swimming." The warmth of the wine drains away. "That's all."

"You think I'm putting the move on you because I'm skinny-dipping, right?"

Rita squints at him.

"Look, I don't *have* a swimsuit." Andy lifts his palms.

"Uh-*huh*," Rita says. "Corvette, mansions, even wine, but *no* trunks. *I* get it."

"I had to come here in kind of a hurry, you know."

"No, I *don't* know," Rita says, staring at him. "Why don't you tell me?"

"C'mon," he says, "not now. Let's just enjoy this, okay?"

Impulsively Rita scoops up a handful of water, tosses it in his face. She dives under and darts away before he can splash her back.

After that Sunday at the pond, Rita finds herself running into Andy nearly every day in camp. They arrive at the canteen at the same time, so it makes sense to share a table, sometimes joined by Rennie, but usually not. On weekends, when fine weather breaks the series of drizzly days, they hike to the pond. Andy always produces a bottle of wine. While Rita doesn't like the taste, she gets used to it, though she waves it off when her face grows numb. "Hmm," she says one Sunday afternoon, "leaves in a hurry, but packs a case of wine."

"Hey," Andy says, "I only had time to pack the essentials."

"And your mother's not going to notice the missing bottles?" Rita thinks of her father, who gripes when a single can of Budweiser disappears from the refrigerator.

"We've got a cellar full of wine," Andy tells her. "Not likely she'll go down there to count bottles. It'd take all day."

"Come on." Rita rolls her eyes. "I don't buy that."

"What?"

"That business about your fancy car and two houses—that crap you gave Rafe."

"You don't believe me?" Andy's eyes widen. "You think I was—what?—saying that stuff just to impress some *bus* driver?"

Rita doesn't like how he says this, the way it diminishes Rafe. She thinks of her father, the olive-drab coveralls, rubber-soled boots, and hard hat he wears to work. But she says, "Let's just say, I find it a *little* hard to believe."

"Why would I make all that up?" he asks.

"Like you said, to impress."

Andy snorts. "You're funny, you know that." He reaches, cupping his palm at the nape of her neck and drawing her close for a kiss. Rita struggles against his embrace. Andy releases her, asks, "What are you afraid of?"

She can't even begin to answer this. Instead Rita looks into his unblinking eyes and shrugs. She touches his cheek, surprised at the moist pliancy of his cool skin. *Orchidaceous,* she thinks, remembering the word from a horticulture text. She pulls him close. As they kiss, he slips the strap of her suit from her shoulder, reaches for her breast. Rita peeks at his face. Her eyes cross and his eyelids seem to merge over his nose at this range. He's still fine-featured, but the fishlike gobbling look on his face makes her want to laugh. She's had sex before, and it's never been painful—her uncle José had probably seen to that—or scary. It's no sheer sensual delight, either. Instead, she finds it awkward, even comic.

Rita spreads her towel over a sandy stretch before the pond. She isn't about to bump through it this time, scraping her tailbone. They lean back on the towel, and Rita squirms out of her swimsuit. Andy enters her with a shudder. Rita quakes, too, cupping his buttocks in her palms and guiding him into a rhythm. Her breath quickens and heart thuds as spasms of pleasure break over her like waves, and she cries out when he does.

Afterward, he holds her in his arms and draws a deep breath, as though preparing to speak, but Rita cups her hand over his mouth. She will hate it—and this moment will be spoiled—if he says something stupid or phony, if he says he loves her. She keeps her fingers over his lips and runs her hand along his bare thigh as they cradle each other on the towel, flinching with aftershocks of pleasure when he kisses her shoulder, the nape of her neck.

When she returns to the dorm, she remembers what Bette said about venereal diseases, but surprising herself, she doesn't race for a scalding shower. Instead, she throws herself on her bunk and sleeps. Without dreaming, she sleeps.

By the time Bette and Elena are due to visit, Rita nearly wishes they weren't coming. She dislikes sharing her time with Andy. In the presence of others, he adopts the boastful personality he revealed on the bus with Rafe. Rita winces inwardly as he natters on about his family's wealth, and the contempt and disbelief on the faces of his listeners—or worse, the pity in Rennie's gentle blue eyes—shame Rita. The prospect of Bette's visit also highlights how inexpertly Andy works in the medium her sister has mastered so well. She's sure his amateurish and self-flattering distortions will disgust Bette.

The day of her sister's visit, Rita wakes with shoulders knotted, her neck stiff. The frigid morning mist creeps up her shirtsleeves and pant legs, pricking her skin like icy needles, and as she trudges to breakfast, she can nearly hear her stiff bones creak. At the canteen, she finds Andy standing in line with Belinda. They're laughing together, their heads bent close, and a fiercer chill twists through Rita.

"Hey," Belinda says, "we was just talking about you, girl."

*Talking or laughing?* Rita grabs plastic utensils from the serving table.

"Andy says you guys go skinny-dipping over at—"

"He's lying," Rita blurts out. "*We* don't go skinny-dipping."

Belinda wrinkles her brow. "Huh?"

"*She* wears a swimsuit," Andy explains. "I swim in the raw."

"I get it." Belinda nods, smiling. "So, like, can anyone come?"

Lupe sidles up, bearing an odorous tray of scrambled eggs, butter-slathered toast, and bacon. "You guys want to sit with us?"

Rita shakes her head, but Andy says, "Sure," so she serves herself and takes a place at their table beside Andy. The eggs taste dry, rubbery, but the others wolf them down as Andy invites them to the pond, *their* pond, to swim on Sunday afternoon.

Rita interrupts him. "I'm not going."

"How come?" Lupe trades a look with Belinda and lifts a plucked-out brow.

Rita turns to Andy. "My sister's coming. Remember?"

"Bring her," he says. "We'll have a party. You or Lupe can get beer."

"Forget it. I don't want my niece around a bunch of drunken assholes." Rita balls up her napkin and throws it at her uneaten breakfast. She thrusts away from the table with such force, she nearly topples her chair.

"Ooh," Belinda says, "she's *pissed.*"

"Fuck you." Rita tells Belinda, and she stalks out of the canteen, banging the screen door behind her.


Bette promised to arrive by three, but knowing her sister, Rita automatically adds two hours to this and doesn't look for her until five. She's spent the day washing clothes, reading, and organizing her bunk area and locker. Despite trips to the laundry, Rita manages to stay clear of Andy, privately gloating over this until it occurs to her that he might be doing the same thing—avoiding *her.*

When Bette doesn't show up by six-thirty, Rita's throat thickens. Her inner ear clicks painfully when she swallows. She reaches for a book on forestry, which she's borrowed from the camp library, and thumbs through its black-and-white photographs of various trees, plants, and lichen, but a brownish quarter-moon stain mars one page. *Chocolate? Blood? Or worse?* Rita claps the book shut and drops it to the floor.

Rita has planned to take Bette and Elena to town and treat them to dinner with her sock money, but by a quarter to seven, she realizes she should get to the canteen before it closes for the night, though she isn't hungry. The empty dorm is impossibly chilly and dank in the way experts on the paranormal describe rooms inhabited by ghosts. Overhead, the tube lighting flickers and hums.

Rita stretches out on her bunk and pulls the blanket over her shoulders. As she dozes, Rita conjures an image of her mother wearing an emerald robe. Her large face softened with sympathy. She stands over Rita, stroking the hair from her forehead. Her hand is warm and dry. It smells of the earth—rich soil, roots, and manzanita. Her mother's image dissolves and Fermina appears. "Who are you really?" Rita asks, astonished by how desperate she is to know. Eyes glimmering, Fermina grins and emits high-pitched singsong: "Sana, sana, colita de rana, Si no sana hoy, sana mañana."

Rita opens her eyes to find Bette, holding Elena and leaning over her. "You okay?"

Rita shakes her head. "I don't feel good."

Her sister's cool hand rests on her forehead. "You're burning up. I'll find you some aspirin before we head to the hotel." Bette's round face is creased with concern.

"No!" Rita reaches out, grabs her sister's arm. "Don't go. Don't leave me here."

"I'll just be a minute."

"Take me with you, *please*, Bette."

"What about Elena?" Bette asks. "I don't want her catching what you have."

"Don't leave me here!"

Bette sighs. "I suppose if you're symptomatic, you're probably not contagious anymore. Come on. Get up, then. Let's go."

In the Sebastopol Travelodge, Rita spends a restless night on the double bed next to the one shared by Bette and Elena. Sweating, and then shuddering with chills, she kicks the covers off—rough nubbly flannel and starchy sheets—and then scrambles to yank them back over her chilled shoulders. Her joints feel leaden, and her head throbs. By early morning, exhaustion finally overtakes her, and she relaxes on the stiff, unfamiliar pillow, plunging into deep sleep.

Bette wakes her at ten, bearing toast and juice on a cardboard tray. She's got sixteen-month-old Elena strapped to her back in a child carrier as she settles the tray on the nightstand. "Can you eat?"

Rita yawns and scans the standard-issue double beds, chest of drawers, and bolted-in television set. The flat industrial carpet is the same bland shade of gray as the walls, which are decorated with imitation Ansel Adams photographs of redwoods. But compared to the dorm, this room seems downright homey.

Bette unharnesses the child carrier and lays Elena on the other bed to change her diaper. "So how'd you get sick?"

Rita startles herself by saying, "Maybe it's that venereal disease thing."

"Get real. You've got to have sex to catch that."

"I have," Rita says.

"You have what?"

"I met a guy."

"You have a *boyfriend*?" Bette's voice rises in disbelief.

Suppressing her irritation, Rita says, "Not a 'boyfriend,' exactly. He's kind of young and has some problems."

"Like what?" Bette rediapers Elena, who babbles and kicks in protest.

Rita examines the toast as if to pick out flaws before deciding where to bite. "He's a big liar, for one thing."

"Nothing wrong with that," Bette says as she zips up Elena's one-piece. "Shows initiative, imagination."

"Well, it works for you," admits Rita.

Bette looks up from the baby. "Honestly, it doesn't. Not that much. I mean, not since Luis."

"What are you saying?"

"I think we've been fooling ourselves, Rita. Really, think about it. I can lie myself silly and nothing is changed, and look at Sophie. She's not getting much of a laugh out of things these days."

But Rita thinks of Loretta. Her gift is propelling her through vet school with honors, and Rita knows what she can do with her curses. She wonders, though, about Bette and Sophie, seeks a common thread. "Maybe it fades when you fall in love," she says hopefully. "Maybe I'll get over it if I love somebody."

Bette pulls Elena into her arms, a skeptical look on her face. "I doubt it."

"You're probably right. You still tell good lies after all," Rita points out.

"Like I said, it takes initiative and creativity, an unwillingness to settle for the boringness of the truth."

"This guy lies about how rich he is, how his family has all this stuff."

Bette wrinkles her nose. "Oh, *stupid* lies."

"Yeah, and they're obvious, too. It's embarrassing."

"Yet you're sleeping with him."

Rita nods.

"And you're not using condoms, pendeja?" Bette pulls on the baby's pants.

"Where am I going to get condoms?" Rita bites into the toast.

"At the drugstore, any drugstore—I passed like three just driving into town."

"No, I mean in the woods. We go near this pond." Illness makes Rita more expansive with Bette than she's ever been, as though she's tipsy.

"You're supposed to have them, like, *before*hand."

Rita waves her off with the crust. "I know. I know."

"You say this guy's younger. How young?"

"Eighteen," Rita says.

"Look, it's doubtful an eighteen-year-old kid would have slept around enough to contract a venereal disease. I wouldn't obsess about it, but you should get tested."

"How?"

"I don't know," Bette says. "Ask a doctor. You probably just have the flu or something." She sets a few Cheerios on a paper plate for Elena.

Rita pops the last bit of toast into her mouth. "Maybe it's malaria."

"Don't be stupid." Bette sets the plate before Elena, who deftly picks at the cereal. "See how she feeds herself. She has great muscle control."

"She's perfect," Rita says. Her niece's plump pink cheeks and almond-shaped eyes remind her of a papoose or an Aleutian infant. "She looks just like you."

"Yeah," Bette says, "you can't tell at all that she has an asshole for a father."

Rita and Bette watch movies on television with the sound turned low and talk quietly while the baby naps. By the time Elena wakes, Rita feels strong enough to take her sister out to eat. She borrows a pair of shorts and a T-shirt from Bette, and since she doesn't have her sock money on hand, she has to ask Bette to pay for their meal, promising to repay her when they return to the camp.

After hamburgers and milk shakes at the diner, Bette drives her back to camp. She refuses to let Rita pay her for their meal. "All right, then, I got a long drive ahead of me," she says. "Take care of yourself, okay?" Bette hugs her sister, kisses her cheek.

Rita climbs out of the car, tempted to beg Bette to take her home, but instead, she says, "You remember how to get back?"

"I'll just go the way I came." Bette puts the car in reverse and releases the brake. "Rita Panchita, you be good!" she calls as the car backs away.

Rita is floored. This was her mother's pet name for her. She's forgotten almost all about it until now. Hearing it conjures her mother—big and beaming—on a sunny morning calling her indoors. *Rita Panchita, where are you? Rita Panchita, my sweet chiquitita.* How can Bette remember what Rita's almost forgotten? She stares after the car, wishing so hard that she'd asked her sister to take her home that it hurts as though she's taken a blow to her chest, aching like bruised ribs and a sore heart.

On her way to the dorm, Rita meets Rennie, who says, "Don't let it get to you."

Rita stops short. "Don't let *what* get to me."

"That beer bust—or whatever—out at the pond."

She'd forgotten about Andy's plans to party at the pond. "When?"

"Right now, I guess. I don't really go for that kind of thing."

Rita imagines the shaded pond littered with beer cans, crushed cigarettes floating in the coppery water. "Those assholes!" She turns toward the trail.

Rennie falls into step with her. "You aren't going out there, are you? You don't look so good."

"I'm fine," Rita says.

Rennie jogs to keep up. "I'll go with you."

As they hurry to the pond, the sun flares—a fiery ball that flattens before sinking behind the tree line. In the deepening shadows, the tall conifers are hunched and silent as hooded giants. Amplified voices and laughter reverberate across the water. As she and Rennie ascend the incline, Lupe lurches toward them, making her way back to camp. "Man, those guys are sick," she says, her painted face muddy with tears.

"What's going on?" Rennie asks her, but Lupe pushes past them in silence.

Rita races toward the pond. A thin voice pierces the laughter. "No, no, no, *please,* no, *please* stop!" A bonfire blazes near the water. Its guttering orange glow illuminates a circle of shining faces and an open sleeping bag, salted with foxtails and sand, on which two bodies twist and struggle.

"What the hell are you doing?" Rita thunders.

The group scatters; bodies scramble to gather clothing and race to the woods. The rustle of leaves and crackle of snapping twigs mask the clamor of voices. But Rita recognizes a few of these and identifies one person by sight—Jackie. She spies the back of his head, the skimpy mullet lock flicking as he hops into his shorts and stumbles away from the pond. She might have heard Andy's voice; though when she looks for him, all she can make out is the confusion of bodies hustling into the shadows. In no time, the party disappears into the brush, leaving behind a solitary figure cringing on the sleeping bag—Belinda, stripped from the waist down, her glistening thighs slender as a child's.

Rita rushes to her side and wraps the sodden, foul-smelling bedding around her bare hips. She tries to hoist the girl to her feet, but with a groan, Belinda collapses, her head striking Rita's collarbone. "Rennie, I can't carry her by myself."

"Okay," he says. "I got her feet." Together they heft Belinda over the rise and back into camp. Rennie cradles her like a baby while Rita raps on Noah's door.

The ambulance arrives just before the squad cars. Sirens howl through the woods most of the night. Rita answers the same questions again and again and signs her name after reading a deputy's report of her statement. At the first pink streaks of daybreak, Rita finally tumbles into her bunk, nearly slipping into the delicious blankness of sleep when a memory jolts her. Belinda. That morning in the canteen. Rita sits upright, draws her knees to her chest. "What have I done?" she whispers so no one will hear. "What have I done?"

Incredibly, the corps members taken that night by the police return to camp within a few days, wearing their khaki uniforms and riding out to work sites on the bus. Rita seeks out Rafe. The bus driver always seems to know the comings and goings in camp better than anyone else. She asks him, "Why aren't those guys in jail?"

"They made bail," he says.

"But why aren't they kicked out of the corps?"

Rafe shrugs. "They say it was just a party that got out of hand."

"What about Belinda?"

"Went home," Rafe says. "I drove her to the airport last night. She got early release."

After hearing this, Rita moves through the next day automatically, performing her work by rote and keeping her distance from the others. Jackie glares at her on the bus, but the others watch her warily. Andy's nowhere to be seen. She hadn't given his name to the police because she's not sure he was there that night.

When she returns from the work site that afternoon, she finds a note in her mail slot from Noah, the camp director, asking her to meet with him at once. On the way to Noah's office, she spots Andy perched on the short fence before the men's dormitory.

"What's going on?" she says.

He looks past her toward the canteen and pulls a harmonica from his pocket. He brings it to his lips and plays, "Pop Goes the Weasel."

"Talk to me," Rita says.

The harmonica warbles: *"Round and round the mulberry bush, the monkey chased the weasel."*

Rita draws closer to him, her heart hammering her ribs. "You stupid, lying fool." Her fist shoots out, and the harmonica flies, spinning to the ground.

Andy teeters, nearly toppling backward, but he catches himself. Eyes narrowed, he fingers his jaw, where she's struck him. She rears as if to lunge again, and he crouches behind the bars, his eyes round with alarm.

"You know what," she says, staring through him, as though he has vanished. "You're nothing to me."

In his warm, wood-paneled office, Noah urges Rita to take a seat. She sits in the chair across from the vast desk at which he is seated. Noah, a round-faced man with wire-framed glasses and a mud-colored beard spilling to his chest, has the habit of bringing the tips of his index fingers together, as though working out abstract problems through this act of spatial resolution. Rita stares at these long, knobby digits, pointing each to each, as he suggests she's misinterpreted what she saw that night at the pond.

"All accounts suggest inappropriate behavior, yes," he says. "Drinking while in camp is prohibited, true. Was this a party that got out of control? Absolutely. But did a crime take place? Hard to prove, definitively."

"What about Lupe?" Rita asks. "She saw what happened."

"She says she blacked out, doesn't remember a thing."

"Well, then Rennie. You should talk to him," Rita says.

Noah shakes his head. "He's been transferred."

"What?" Rita doesn't trust her hearing.

"He asked for a transfer after this unpleasantness."

"*Unpleasantness?* Belinda was drunk, helpless. She begged them to stop!" Rita's voice rises against a dizzying wave of disbelief.

Noah puts a finger to his lips, shakes his head. "This is bad, Rita, bad for the corps, bad for all of us. False allegations can destroy lives, destroy our good work."

Rita sputters, "But these aren't false—"

"I know you like being in the corps," Noah says, his index fingers meeting once more. "You believe in our work. So this is hard, Rita, but I have to ask you to transfer or resign your service. Even if you believe what you witnessed was a crime, no one will back you up. If this ever goes to court, the defense will make you out to be a troubled and vindictive young woman. This will only ruin lives and reputations, especially your own. My advice: let it go and move on." Noah draws his fingers steadily apart.

Rita shakes her head. "I can't do that."

"Then you force my hand," Noah tells her. "I'll draw up a separation order."

Rita rises, grasps the camp leader's desk, and leans in. "You can't *fire* me."

"We can't keep crew members who destroy camp unity." He pulls a folder from his desk, holds it before his face. "Thank you for stopping by," he says.

"You're as fucked up as those guys who raped Belinda," she tells him in a low voice. "And you know it, too." Rita glimpses a framed photo of Noah's wife and baby on his desk. Her own face is reflected in the glass, a holographic image superimposed over their smiling faces. She remembers her anger at Belinda in the canteen, what she said as she stormed off that morning. Rita cups a hand over her mouth and backs out.

Hurrying toward the dormitory, Rita plans to take change from the knotted sock and call Bette. Who else can she tell? Her cheeks burn when she thinks about telling her father. She slips into the dorm, grateful it's mealtime, no one around to see her packing. Rounding the bunk, she stumbles over a length of metal—a crowbar. Her lockbox has been ripped from its metal brace. "No!" she blurts, thinking not just of her savings, but of her few keepsakes—letters, photos, the one picture she has of her mother as a young girl. All of it gone. She longs to take the crowbar to the windows and mirrors. Her knees wobble, and she places a palm on her bunk to steady herself. The blanket feels wet. She lifts her hand to her nose and sniffs—urine. Rita's gaze travels from the bed to a heap of her clothes, also drenched and reeking. Nothing to pack, she scrubs her hands in scalding water and heads out to find Rafe hosing mud from the tires.

"Can you take me to town?" Rita doesn't have a clear plan, except to get away.

Rafe stands to regard her. "Sure, get your stuff while I finish here."

"I don't have anything." She holds up her hands, blinking hard.

Rafe looks away. "Come on then." He crouches to turn off the faucet and coil the hose. "You got someone there you can stay with?"

"No." Rita climbs into the warm bus.

"You know," Rafe says, sliding into the driver's seat, "me and my sister have an apartment in Sebastopol. I think she'd be okay with it if you want to stay with us for a while." He turns to give her a warm look. "You got the bad end of it, didn't you?"

Rita plans to stay with Rafe and his sister, Maya, just a few days, but those days turn into weeks, then a whole month. Rafe and Maya don't seem to mind, as long as Rita helps with housework and rent, which she does, after she finds a job in a Realtor's office. In a few months, she saves enough for her own place. Rafe offers to drive her around to look at rentals in the evenings and on weekends. They plan to meet for this purpose one afternoon at a café near Rita's work. But Rafe is half an hour late. As Rita finishes her iced tea, he rushes in. "Sorry, I got hung up." He slides into the booth. "A couple of those boys went missing—Jackie and that other little shit, that pretty-boy rich kid."

Rita's pulse quickens. "What happened?"

"Went on a hike last night and didn't come back. They got a search party going now. I had to take a bunch of volunteers out there to look for them at the last minute. The place is crawling with reporters and TV cameras and shit."

"Really," Rita says, keeping her voice calm.

"Yeah, I talked to one of them who asked if I knew that rich punk was serving in the corps because he and his friends assaulted some girl out in Marin, same as what you told me happened to Belinda." Rafe frowned, shook his head. "I said I didn't know about that, and the guy went off to interview someone else. You know it was Andy's old man that made bail for those guys that night. They were going to drag Andy into it, say it was all his idea. So some lawyer drove out in the middle of the night."

*"What?"* Rita's not sure she can trust her hearing.

"Yeah, turns out he really *is* a rich little son of a bitch, telling the truth all along. Nobody believed him. That's all." Rafe shook his head. "His old man's sending out some helicopters and shit, and someone said the FBI is on the way."

"Do you have to go back?"

"Hell no. I'm off the clock." Rafe picks up the menu, scans it. "After what happened to you, I don't care if they never find those punks. Do you?"

Rita shrugs, her heart thrashing so fiercely she's sure he can hear it.

"Another thing I found out," Rafe says, "old Belinda was connected and connected. Brothers, uncles, cousins—all veteranos, bunch of big shots in Eme."

"Eme?"

"You know, the Mexican Mafia." Rafe sets the menu down and nods. "I bet they took care of those boys, but good. They aren't too likely to turn up alive. I'd be very surprised if they ever find the bones." Rafe looks into her eyes. "What do you think?"

Rita thinks of her last day at camp, Andy and his harmonica. She clears her throat. "There's a duplex just south of here that I want to see before it gets too dark, okay?"

"You really don't care about that boy anymore?"

"Why should I?" Rita says. "He's nothing to me." *He's nothing at all, now.*

Rafe reaches across the table and clasps Rita's hand in his. Though she's startled by this gesture, Rita is more astonished by the unexpected familiarity of his touch, the warmth of his skin, and the strength in his long fingers.

SUBJECT: FERMINA/CHILDBIRTH
WPA: 7-14-38—DC: HMS
July 12, 1938
Words: 568

## FLOWERS BUDDING

Two years after Decidero's birth, Fermina was again with child. This time, Yrma was furious. She threatened to throw Fermina out to scavenge with the coyotes. Inocencio, though, hoped for another son to help with the farm. He convinced Yrma that he and Decidero would not be able to manage the work on their own, as their herds of sheep and cattle multiplied and the crops flourished.

But after childbirth, no one tore this newborn from Fermina's arms to dress in stiff lace and prop on embroidered pillows. Fermina's second child was a girl. The Gabaldons refused to baptize her in the church. They didn't even give her a name. Fermina called the infant *Shiamptiwa* (Hopi for flowers budding). Her pink face reminded Fermina of tightly bundled petals waiting to be coaxed open by the sun. When Fermina sniffed Shiamptiwa's fragrant scalp, the fine black hairs tickled her nose, and she grew dizzy, drunk with love. She swaddled Shiamptiwa to her chest as she worked and slept curled around her at night, her full breasts ready whenever the baby stirred.

Once after waking to feed Shiamptiwa, Fermina heard voices from the main bedroom. Yrma and Decidero rarely spoke to one another during the day, let alone late at night, so this alarmed Fermina. With the suckling baby in her arms, she crept to the hall leading to their bedroom. Fermina put her ear to the door to hear Yrma's low, persistent voice. She was telling Inocencio that he must take the baby away. She knew of a place, an asilo de huerfanos. It was not too far. Her voice buzzed on and on, like a hornet trapped under glass. Inocencio remained silent for a long while, but finally he grunted assent.

The next day, Fermina, the baby bundled on her back, stole away to visit Lucinda Aragon, a neighbor who was reputed to be a bruja. Aragon sat in a chair outside her house, puffing on a pipe. Fermina repeated what she had overheard, and Aragon told Fermina of a woman named Concha Gallegos, who lived near Santa Fe. Fermina knew Concha, who had grown up in Rio Puerco. She was a friendly girl whose plump face creased into easy smiles. La bruja explained that Concha married well, but had no children of her own. She took in those no one wanted. Concha fed and treated these children well. "Bring me a she-goat with milk," Aragon said, "and I will take the baby to her." So it was that Fermina's second child vanished, along with a brown-and-white spotted nanny. When asked about the disappearance of the goat, Fermina shrugged. No one mentioned the baby.

Over time, Fermina learned that Shiamptiwa had been renamed Patricia by Concha, who bought a piano to teach the children to play. Those who had known Concha in Rio Puerco clucked their tongues at the extravagance in having the expensive instrument shipped west just so children could hammer on it. Sin sentido, they called her, senseless and wasteful. Many years later, Fermina heard that Concha Gallegos de Obregon's children had contracted influenza, dying one after another, along with her husband in the bitter winter of 1918, all but la Patty, who never married and still lives near Santa Fe, as of this writing, where she looks after her mother and teaches neighborhood children to play the piano, which she is known for loving so well.

# SNAPSHOTS FROM THE MOTHER ROAD — THE GABALDÓN SISTERS: 1983

## NEEDLES, CALIFORNIA — SOPHIA

"Just whose stupid idea was this," you say for the second time since Barstow, leveling your gaze at the back of Loretta's head, her long dark braid. She's driving Woody, your father's old paneled station wagon, the one he bought after the red-and-white finned Impala died over a decade ago, the one he's about to give away (maybe to you) because he couldn't trade it in for "a shoeshine," he said, when he bought his new Buick earlier this year. "July in Needles," you say, fanning your five-month-old baby with the Triple A map. The raspberry flush suffusing his cheeks would alarm you if not for the sweat beading on his scalp. He's not feverish, just goddamn hot. "Need-*less*, California," you say as the car whooshes down Broadway past boarded-up storefronts, abandoned motels decorated with whitewashed truck tire planters that hold only dust and weeds.

"There's nothing wrong with Needles," Rita turns to say, "or this trip." In fact, Rita flew from Northern California to L.A. especially for this journey. She's more anxious than any of you to find out what Fermina meant by her cryptic promise. Your story is you're just along for the ride, eager to get away from your hot apartment and your job at the women's shelter day care, which Aitch attends free of charge, if just for a week. True, you're curious about Fermina, the gift business and whatnot, but you're not freaked out about it, like Rita, who now says, "I only have one week of vacation, you know, not ten years. So what's really stupid is not taking the interstate, instead of this Route 66 bullshit." But the rest of you know this is not about compulsion to return to work; Rita just misses her boyfriend, Rafe.

"It's the Mother Road," Loretta says as she brakes for an old man shambling across Broadway with a grocery cart. He's bare-foot, whiskered, and raving. He stops, midcrossing, to shake a bony fist at the sun.

"John Steinbeck," Bette reads from a guidebook in the back, the rear seat that faces backward—her window view: the reced-ing ribbon of blacktop parting scrub, yucca, Joshua trees, and date palms—"first named this 'the mother road, the road of flight—'"

"Mother *fucking* road," Rita grumbles.

Bette continues thumbing through the guidebook Loretta brought, until she groans and flings it over the seat. "Remind me never to read in the car."

You redouble your efforts to fan Harold Jr., whose name you've shortened to Aitch, so as to avoid association with his absent idiot of a father. "Turn up the air conditioner, tontas. We've got babies here." Oblivious of the flapping Triple A guide, Aitch snores in the car seat beside you, and two-year-old Elena, also flushed and dozing, is strapped into a safety seat next to his.

"Can't do it." Loretta shakes her head. "The car will overheat."

"Then open those windows all the way."

Rita scrolls down the glass, as does Loretta, after a pause, so she won't look like she's doing what you've asked. A warm gust flash dries your perspiration, and you sigh.

"Where's that tape?" Rita asks.

Loretta tilts her chin toward the floorboard. "In my purse."

Rita rummages in the bag and extracts a flat box, which she opens. "How come you never mentioned this before? I can't believe you just *forgot* about it until now."

"I never forgot," Loretta says after a pause. "I just didn't have a chance to play it back after the day I made it. It's a reel-to-reel. Those are kind of obsolete now."

"Where'd you find a thing to play it on?" you ask.

"My roommate's boyfriend is a musician. He had one." Loretta made the tape twelve years ago—an interview with Nilda in which she mentions a woman who wrote a book about Fermina's life. This journey taken together to find the author of that book, and to celebrate Nilda's birthday in Río Puerco, is Loretta's plan. The trip is the only gift she wants from you and your sisters—no party, no gifts—to commemorate her graduation last month from veterinary school. Since Nilda turns seventy-two at the end of this week, you've unanimously agreed to "kill two birds with one stone." Though you all manage to visit Nilda once every few years, you usually fly out on your own or travel in pairs, so this is the first time all four of you are making the trip together.

"What's her name again?" Bette asks from the back.

"Heidi," Loretta tells her. "Heidi Schultz Vigil. She lives west of Santa Fe. I phoned her son for directions."

You have few memories of Fermina, who you once thought was your fairy godmother, though you remember her more than your mother. "What's on the tape?"

"Nilda talks about her childhood, about the past, and she mentions that this Heidi used to visit Fermina to interview her for some book she was writing."

"A book about *Fermina's* life?" You picture Fermina as a child, then a young woman. You squint as you imagine a time before highways, trucks, dilapidated motels, and cafés—an expanse of sun-scorched earth, the emptiness of it. "Why?"

Loretta shrugs.

"Look," Rita says. "See that?"

Loretta slows, and we stare out the window at a café on Broadway and D Street. You stuffed yourselves with pancakes and runny eggs at the Denny's in San Bernardino not two hours ago. Even you aren't hungry yet. Anyway, the café isn't open, a hand-written sign explains: *We Are Seventh-day Adventists/ Our Only Closing Day Is the Sabbath/ What Was the Last Miracle That Jesus Performed? Do You Know the Answer?* You read this aloud.

"Water into wine," Loretta says.

"It's closed," you point out, "but there's a taco stand ahead."

"Not that, you dummies," Rita says. "There, *there*."

"What is it?" Bette asks.

"The sign for the I-40," Rita says at last, pointing at the blue shield. "Turn *here*."

"Can't do it." Loretta accelerates past the turn. "It's not the Mother Road."

"Mother *fucking* road," Rita says.

Loretta says, "We're committed to the Mother Road."

Rita asks, "Who put you in charge?"

"*I* did," Bette tells her.

## KINGMAN, ARIZONA—BETTE

Just before Route 66 becomes Andy Devine Boulevard, Elena and little Aitch kick the fussing into high gear. We stop at a Whiting Brothers, where Elena is fascinated by the curio shop attached to the gas station. She totters through the aisles, gaping at scorpions in resin, Indian dolls, licorice whips, postcards, T-shirts, back-scratchers, and other assorted crap. But my kid won't touch a god-damn thing. Instead, she stares, wide-eyed and openmouthed, keeping her distance, as though inspecting artifacts in a museum of incredibly breakable shit. I have to urge her to handle stuff. I show her a rabbit's foot key chain. "Come here, baby. This feels soft."

Elena opens her hand, and I run it over her pink palm. Her dimples deepen. "Tickles." But then she pulls away to examine her hand for microscopic traces of dirt. I toss the rabbit's foot on a shelf and scoop her into my arms. "Come on. I'll take you to wash." I lug her into the bathroom. A pestiferous cloud of stink hangs over the counter where Sophie is changing Aitch's diaper.

"Diarrhea," she says by way of greeting. We wash quickly— Elena recoiling from the sooty washbasin—and I hold my breath as we back out into the shop.

"For your information, Miss Knows-Everything," Rita is say-ing to Loretta near the register in front, "it was raising Lazarus from the dead."

"You're nuts." Loretta pushes a bill across the counter to pay for gas. "How can you compare reviving some corpse to changing water into wine?"

"Water into wine," Rita says, "was maybe the *first* miracle, if you don't count amazing the wise men in the temple with knowl-edge when he was just a kid."

"What are you talking about?" Loretta asks.

"No way was the wine thing the last miracle performed by Jesus Christ."

"*Last* miracle? I thought Sophie said *best* miracle." Loretta tucks the change into her purse. "Water into wine was definitely the best."

Sophie tromps up front with bald, gummy Aitch in her arms. "We better stop here for the night," she says. "He has the runs."

"Okay," Loretta tells her.

Rita says, "I only have a *week*. Can't you get it through your head?"

"Do you sell wine here?" Loretta asks the clerk.

"We have Coors."

Loretta draws back, wrinkling her nose.

"We should keep going." I turn to Sophie. "If he has the shits, he has them, whether we're on the road or in a hotel. You just have to give him applesauce, bananas, and rice cereal—the diarrhea diet. We can at least make it to Oatman for lunch."

The clerk shakes her head. "Nothing worth seeing there, except that open range."

"We can spend the night in Seligman or better yet, Flagstaff." I'd like Elena to see the Grand Canyon.

"Good luck finding a room in Flagstaff this time of year," the woman says, and reaches to squeeze Elena's foot in a playful way. "Aren't you cute?"

Elena wrenches away. "You got a *fill-fee* potty," she says, wagging a finger.

"I swear she's a throwback." My voice thickens with pride.

"I know." Sophie nods. "Nilda, junior."

## OATMAN TO SELIGMAN, ARIZONA—RITA

Rita's shoulders clench when Loretta pops open a Coors. She can smell the sickeningly yeasty belch from the can all the way up front. Rita's insisted on taking the wheel because the way Loretta drives, tapping the brakes every few minutes to make sure they work, is both driving her insane and giving her whiplash.

"Why didn't *we* bring wine?" Loretta says from the backseat. "We're from California. We should know better."

Rita grits her teeth.

"Look," Sophie says, "there it is — the open range, right there."

Sure enough, Rita spies a yellow diamond-shaped sign that reads OPEN RANGE, and propped against its post is a discarded white stove, the oven door gaping, an incongruous sight against the vast azure sky, biscuit-colored earth, and stubbly yellow grass.

"See that, honey," Bette tells Elena.

"That's just a stove," Elena says.

" 'Range' is another name for a stove." Loretta says she doesn't care much for children, but from the uncharacteristically warm tone Loretta uses, Rita can tell her sister has a soft spot for their niece. Elena goes silent, considering this information, when a plosive sound followed by rumbling emanates from Aitch's diaper area.

"Pull over," Sophie says, "as soon as humanly possible."

Rita flips on the turn signal. Her sisters roll their windows down and stick their heads out into the desert, until Rita bumps the car onto the shoulder and parks.

After this pit stop, she continues driving. Rita loves driving. She could drive all day and into the night, but her sisters complain she drives too slowly. Bette claims Rita drives too carefully, as if *that* were even possible. Around midday, Sophie says she's starving; so in Seligman, Rita pulls up to the Snow Cap, a drive-in next to Angel's Barbershop and a grocery.

Instead of sitting in the hot car and waiting for food service, the sisters climb out for what shade there is under the portico. A small yard near the drive-in is arrayed with a multitude of plaster lawn ornaments—gnomes, rabbits, cherubs, flamingoes, turtles, jockeys, and squirrels. Rita and Loretta stroll with Elena through these, while Sophie finds a table and Bette orders lunch. Rita's amazed at how carefully Elena picks her way through the sun-bleached figurines. The toddler is curious, but not enough to come too close or touch. Rita senses Elena's relief when Loretta lifts her to carry her to the table.

Bette approaches with two full trays, "I think that guy's in love with me." She points at the food. "Extra fries." Even at a plumpish twenty-eight, Bette's heart-shaped face is as cute as ever. The extra weight accentuates her curves, making her voluptuous. Against her white shorts and blue gingham halter, Bette's tanned skin is a rich shade of caramel. Rita glimpses the counterman staring after Bette and licking his lips.

Despite Loretta's pale-rose complexion and glossy black hair, she regards males with the same expression Rita imagines she wears when detecting tapeworm in fecal matter, and men don't exactly bask in the warmth of this gaze. With the exception of Aitch, Sophie glances away from any men she encounters, as though these sully the view. And Rita, as the corny song goes, has eyes just for Rafe. Of all of us, Rita thinks, only the deep-dimpled Elena is likely to give Bette serious competition when it comes to attracting male attention, but not for another decade or so.

Sophie cradles Aitch in one arm, a bottle of white grape juice held under her chin, so he can drink while she eats. "*Right*, he gave you free fries, so you'll grow bigger nalgas. 'Cause then, there'll be *more* of you to love." Her voice goes syrupy, and Rita trades a look with Bette. This is maybe something Harold the Disappeared has said to her. Rita calculates he dropped out of sight nearly two months ago. She opens her mouth to ask about this, but Bette shakes her head. It isn't the right time.

Rita turns away and spies two raggedy tumbleweeds wheeling across a vacant lot nearby. "So, tell us," she says, "the story of Dad and his girlfriend."

"Yeah, I want to hear about that," Loretta agrees.

Bette sets a burger and a few fries on a napkin before Elena. "It's a horror story."

A fly lands on the napkin, and Elena pushes the food away. "I'm not hungry."

"You have to eat something," Rita tells her, her voice deepening with sternness.

"*No.*"

"Good," says Loretta, reaching for Elena's burger, "more for me."

"Hey, that's mines." Elena snatches it back and takes a big bite.

Loretta's snuck her Coors to the table and gulps it surreptitiously, though the besotted fry cook couldn't care less. Rita's the only one who minds. "The story of Dad and the girlfriend," she says.

Bette glances at Elena, who's staring back at her, wide-eyed and expectant. "I'll tell you later," she says.


## FLAGSTAFF, ARIZONA — LORETTA


We take two adjoining rooms at the Mountain View Lodge, just off the highway, and Bette and Sophie settle the kids to sleep in their room before slipping across the threshold — the common door propped open — into our room, where I've filled the plastic bucket with ice chips and longnecks. Even Rita obligingly opens a bottle and sips from it. She says, "The story of Dad and the girlfriend."

"Ah, yes." Bette rolls a joint and glances at Sophie. "Where to begin?"

"What's she like?" In spite of myself, I'm curious about the woman.

"Let's see," Bette says with mock delicacy. "She's a woman of a certain age."

"A vieja, a drunken, cranky witch who's going bald," Sophie interjects, stroking her own thick mane. "Dad, for mysterious reasons, is nuts about her."

"They're getting married." Bette lights the joint, sucks in a toke.

Unfazed, Sophie continues her description. "She's a dead ringer for a Thunderbird puppet. Remember that show, those stiff-moving dolls? Pam's the bubbleheaded blonde exactly, except her hair's the color of dried blood."

Bette exhales noisily. "They already have rings and shit."

"She's reigning queen of the barflies. I, myself," Sophie says, "wouldn't know her without the stink of booze rolling from her pores, the constant nicotine haze."

"Can you imagine Mom smoking?" Rita asks. "Or drinking? Mom hated anything that made a person stupider than usual."

I drain my beer and reach for another. "She hated makeup, too. Remember how she used to say, 'Why do I need lipstick, when I've got brains?'"

"Pam loads that shit on. She must use a fucking trowel for the foundation cream," Bette says. "She even wears false eyelashes."

Sophie takes the joint. "And she calls everyone—even Dad!—'kiddo.'"

Bette says, "Cary thinks Pop's been brainwashed, says we should call in a deprogrammer, one of those guys that gets the cult out of people."

"This does not sound good." Rita's voice is grim.

"You *think*?" Sophie says. "Old Pam wants Dad to take her to Vegas. She says it'd be a 'real kick' to be married by an Elvis impersonator."

"I'd like to give her a *real* kick," mutters Bette.

"We have to do something," Rita says.

I clear my throat. "Look, he's an adult. If he wants to get married, let him."

"You only say that," Sophie tells me, "because you never met Pam."

"I'm not a violent person," Bette says, and we gawk at her. "Okay, I'm not *always* a violent person, but I want to smack the shit out of that old bitch."

"If old Pam has her way, they'll be married this summer," Sophie says. "Thank God there's divorce!" She sips her beer, and I wonder if *she's* filed papers yet. She ought to get some kind of support for raising Aitch; and the sooner, the better.

Rita yawns, and Bette pinches out the joint. "We better go to bed soon."

Sophie heaves herself off the bed, heads next door, and Rita lumbers for the bathroom, while Bette opens the outer door, lights one last Marlboro. I rummage through the paperbacks, notebooks, pens, and glasses cases in my all-purpose bag for my toothbrush holder and miniature tube of paste. My fingers brush the boxed reel-to-reel tape I keep with me so it won't be ruined by heat in the car. Energy surges from my fingertips, sparking me with the same giddiness I felt when I discovered it among my letters, photographs, and diplomas. I never forgot about the tape. That would be like forgetting my birthplace or middle name—things I don't think about every day, though they are imbedded in memory and identity. I always knew I had it, but rediscovering it after all those years in Georgia, as I was moving from the apartment I shared during graduate school into my own rental, time and place made the tape seem strange and new, unfamiliar as a relic from another world. But listening to it—the call and response of my high, clear adolescent voice combined with Nilda's animated, inflected tones—released a rush of familiar excitement, stirring up my old questions, and reawakening my longing to snap the pieces together so the whole picture finally emerges.

I tuck it in a deep corner of the bag and lower my voice to tell Bette, "The thing about Dad is that it's his life. Why shouldn't he be able to do what he wants? To love whomever he chooses?"

"You don't even know the worst of it," she whispers, expelling ragged streams of smoke, shredded ghosts escaping into the dark night.

## THE GRAND CANYON, TWIN ARROWS, TWO GUNS, AND HOLBROOK, ARIZONA — SOPHIA

At the lookout spot, you raise little Aitch to behold the Grand Canyon, and Bette lifts Elena into her arms so she can also see into the abyss. The iron-streaked crags and sheared rock plummet into a profound terrestrial gash. But Elena shields her eyes from the pale morning sun and says, "I don't see nothing. Where is it, Mama? *Where?*"

"You're looking at it, m'ija."

"I'm with Elena," you say as you cup Aitch's eyes against the light. He kicks his frog legs a few times, but is silent, unimpressed by the sight. "I hate to sound all Peggy Lee, but is that all there is?"

"It's the Grand Canyon," Rita tells you, coming up behind, her camera in hand. "It's a canyon. It's grand. What more do you want?"

"It's a little…" You pause, searching for the right word.

"Majestic," Bette says with nearly enough conviction to make this so.

"Picturesque?" suggests Loretta. "Panoramic?"

"No," you say, "*boring.* It's goddamn boring," and you yawn.

After the Grand Canyon, you again share the middle seat with the sleeping children, and Bette drives. Rita, who's wearing a red-and-white bandanna tied over her eyes, blindfold-style, rides shotgun, while Loretta is sprawled in back, reading.

Bette glances at Rita. "Will you take that thing off?"

She shakes her head. "I can't."

"Seriously, Rita, you look like a hostage," you say. "People will think we're kidnapping you."

"Take that damn thing off," Bette says between clenched teeth.

"No offense, Bette," Rita says, "but I can't stand the way you tailgate and steer with your knees. I can't even bear to look."

"Get rid of it before Elena wakes up," Bette warns her, "or you'll freak her out. So it's coming off, hear me, if I have to yank it off myself and strangle you with it."

"Like *that* won't traumatize the kid," you say.

Bette pushes in the lighter, fumbles for a cigarette.

Rita says, "You're not smoking while I'm up here."

*"Right,"* Bette says, and she lights up.

The second day of the road trip, you have to admit, is a jarring contrast from the first that was filled with goodwill, expectation, and nervy energy. After the first twenty-four hours pass, the car seems to shrink. The interior closes in, becoming tight and fusty, filled with a near-suffocating amalgam of odors — soiled diapers, sweat, spilled beer, stale Fritos, and melted chocolate bars. On top of this, Bette's smoking and Loretta's drinking drive Rita nuts, you know your voice is louder than Loretta can bear, Bette's sick of putting up with Rita's priggishness, and you wish they'd all disappear for a few hours, so you could take little Aitch in your arms and have a good solid cry.

But you say, "Look, *look*! It's the twin arrows of Twin Arrows."

Rita lifts the bandanna to peek out, emits a disappointed hiss, and replaces her blindfold. You reach for her camera, and through the window, you snap a photo of the two tall wooden arrows, their red tips angling toward the ground.

"Nobody better be using my camera," Rita says.

Loretta leans over the seat, reaches into the cooler, and fishes out an icy beer, which she pops open.

"Nobody better be drinking beer before noon," Rita says.

Loretta lifts her bottle in salute. "Your hearing is excellent."

"Hand me one, too," Bette says.

"Pull over this minute," Rita says. "You are *not* drinking and driving."

Bette snatches the blindfold off Rita and tosses it out the open window. "Will you *shut up*?"

"For the sweet love of Jesus," you say as Loretta hands you a dripping brown bottle to pass to Bette. Rita turns to face Bette, gape-mouthed, rigid with wrath. Bette wrenches the wheel, the tires squeal onto the shoulder, and she hauls out of the driver's seat. "You want to drive, pendeja, then *drive*," she says, and Rita scoots behind the wheel. Bette yanks open the passenger-side door, plops in, and slams it shut. "Just give me some fucking peace."

And everyone grows quiet for miles and miles until you can't take it anymore. "Look, it's the two guns of Two Guns."

Silence again, and then Elena stirs. "Are we there yet?"

Bette stubs out her cigarette, shuts the ashtray, and waves away the smoke. "No, honey, not yet."

You point out the window. "There's Holbrook. See the wigwams?"

"What's that?" Elena says.

"They're like teepees, Indian homes," Rita tells her, slowing so Elena can get a good look at the tall cement cones painted with crude designs. "They're motels. People can stay in them overnight."

Elena stares out the window. "I want to stay in one."

"We can't, h'ita," Bette tells her. "We have to get to Río Puerco tonight."

"But I want to sleep in a warm wig." Elena's lower lip quirks.

Bette shakes her head. "Sorry, honey."

"Why not?" Loretta asks. "Just for one night."

"I want to sleep in one!" Elena cries as we pass the Wigwam Village.

Rita gives Bette a sidelong glance.

"I thought you were in some big rush, Miss One-Week-of-Vacation. Besides, Nilda's expecting us," Bette says.

"So call her up," you suggest, "and tell her we'll be there tomorrow."

"You have any idea how expensive these tourist traps are?" Bette says. "Who's going to pay?"

"I will," Rita and Loretta say at the same time.

Your sisters can only afford one wigwam, but it's not too bad—a full bath, air-conditioning, and two double beds. But the conical ceiling does take some getting used to. To economize, your sisters stop at a market to purchase bread, cheese, and cold cuts for supper and peaches for dessert. Loretta, of course, buys a double six-pack and opens a beer as soon as she enters the room.

"You drink too much," Rita tells her. "What kind of doctor is always drinking?"

"I only drink," Loretta says, "when you're around."

"I wouldn't want a doctor like you operating on my hamster."

"I didn't know you had one." Loretta sips her beer.

Elena turns to Rita. "Let me see that hamster."

"I don't have one, honey," Rita says. "Ask your mommy if I can take you outside to look at the other wigwams."

While Elena petitions Bette, you strap Aitch into a front harness and regard his reflection in the dressing-table mirror; his thick, dimpled arms and fat-ringed legs dangle like chunky puppet appendages. "Can we come, too?" you ask your niece.

Elena sizes you up, thinking this over. "Okay."

"We'll call Nilda," you say, "from that pay phone by the front office."

Outside, Elena spots a rusted swing set at the heart of Wigwam Village and races for it. She brushes grit from the seat before putting her arms up so Rita can lift her into the toddler swing with straps. You lower yourself and Aitch onto a leather seat beside Elena. He's a quiet baby who smiles easily, but his eyes are a concern. They tend to wander and cross. Strabismus, the pediatrician says. He may outgrow it, or he might need surgery. When Aitch looks at you, he sees two mothers. Because you can't recall a single image of your mother, this doesn't seem like such a bad deal.

"Higher," Elena says. "Push me higher."

Rita shoves the swing with more force, and you say, "You need to lighten up."

"I know," Rita agrees, surprising you. "She gets to me. Loretta, I mean. It's like she's always laughing at me, mocking me."

"She's not mocking you any more than she is the rest of us."

"The weird thing is that when I'm up north and she's in Georgia, we get along great. We talk on the phone every week. I feel closer to her than anyone, as long as we're thousands of miles apart."

"You're not pushing," Elena says. "Push me, Tía, really push."

Rita tugs back Elena's swing as far as it will go and releases it to the little girl's squealing delight. "Something about seeing her in person—Bette, too, but not as much—just *irritates* me."

"You've got to let it go," you tell her. "Seriously, it's bad for all of us, but it's worse for you, all that negative *shh*—" You glance at Elena. "All that negative *stuff* is harmful for you, so let it go."

"Is that what you do?" Rita says, asking—in her way—about Harold.

"Yeah, sure, all the time," you say. "I just say, 'Okay, I forgive you; now get out of my face,' and I let it go."

"Hey, *I* know how to forgive people. I've let go of more than you can imagine." Her tone is sharp but she continues in a softer voice, "What I can't figure out is how not to let certain people bug me in the first place."

You cup the top of Aitch's head, his throbbing fontanel pulses against your palm. You imagine your mother holding you when you were this young. When he's cozy in your arms like this, you can almost remember her scent, her touch. You bend for a kiss and taste his warm, salty scalp. "You just make up your mind to be cool and let stuff go."

## HOLBROOK, ARIZONA—LORETTA

When Rita and Sophie march out of the cement cone with the children, Bette tells me, "Don't let her get to you."

"She doesn't." I toss the empty bottle in the wastebasket, reach for another.

Bette arranges bread slices on napkins. "I think she does."

But I ignore this. "We should have told them to get ice." I hand Bette a beer and fit the remainders into the slushy cooler. "What were you going to tell me about Dad?"

Bette says that Pam moved in with the old man for a short while.

"Dad was living in *sin*?" My voice rises with feigned horror.

Bette nods. "Just for a few months, but they didn't get along. They were both drinking pretty heavily and getting into all kinds of fights over stupid things, mostly over their dead spouses, if you can believe it. They're insanely jealous."

"Jealous of the *deceased*?"

"That's right," Bette says. "One time I went over, and they were in the middle of it. I swear, it was like something out of *Who's Afraid of Virginia Woolf?* but without any brains. And Dad had this swollen eye and scratches on his cheek."

I swallow hard, but say, "Still, he's a grown man."

"I *know*. I can't call protective services and say, 'My sixty-two-year-old father is in an abusive relationship.' It's not like they can step in and place him in foster care." Bette sighs, layering the sliced bread with bologna and cheese. "The best I can do is to be ready in case he needs me." She covers the sandwiches and gathers up the peaches. "Now, what did you want to tell me?"

I shake my head. "I didn't say I had anything to tell you."

"You don't have to." Bette stands in the threshold to the bathroom, cradling the fuzzy pink-and-gold orbs and waiting. "I can tell."

I wish Rita hadn't taken her camera. This would make an arresting photo: *Woman Holding Peaches in Wigwam*. Despite my resolve not to say a thing to my sisters, I blurt this out: "I think I'm in love."

"In love?"

"Yes, I think so. That's partly why I wanted to take this trip to get away and think it out, to see if it's still there when I go back to Georgia."

"Who are you in love with?"

"Chris," I tell her, "a doctor, but that's all I can say, or I'll jinx it." Really, I don't dare to say more, not even to Bette.

When she reaches to embrace me, the peaches tumble from her arms, bump to the floor. One rolls under the bed. Bette guards her own secrets so well that she will not press me to say more.

## RANCHO VIGIL, NEW MEXICO — BETTE

I don't completely agree, but Loretta insists we continue on to the Vigil ranch near Santa Fe before checking in with Nilda. We can travel on to Río Puerco afterward, she says. Loretta is acting so strange since her confession to me yesterday that I'm hesitant to contradict her. Rita's leery of her, too. So it's Sophie who says, "You know, Nilda was not all that thrilled that we didn't get there for supper last night."

"We'll get there tonight," Loretta tells her.

"For *supper*?" Sophie asks.

Loretta nods. "We'll aim for that, anyway." And after consigning Rita to the backseat facing rear, I drive steadily through the morning.

The Vigil ranch house is so much like our family's home in Río Puerco that it's nearly creepy: the sprawling rectangular structure, the sherbet-orange stucco exterior trimmed with white woodwork, the corrugated-tin roof, the screened-in front porch, the cuartito and adobe oven, the horno in back, and the kitchen garden separated from the drive by the clothesline. Was Heidi inspired by our grandparents' house when she and her husband built theirs? Though if one judged from the appearance of other homes in the area, this is pretty much the standard setup.

I steer the car over the unpaved road leading to Heidi's house, pebbles crunching under the tires and pinging against the wheel wells.

*"Wha-a-a-at i-s-s-s thi-i-i-is?"* The bumpiness causes Elena's high voice to vibrate, and this inspires Loretta to *baa* like a sheep.

*"We're tur-r-r-ning into she-e-e-ep,"* Rita says, joining in. Then all three of my nutty sisters and Elena make sheep sounds until I pull alongside the clothesline to park. "Okay, knock it off," I say.

"Where are we?" Elena asks. Loretta explains that we're visiting a lady here.

"Hand me a brush," I say, and Sophie tosses me my purse. Loretta opens the passenger-side door. "Wait!" I give my hair a few swift strokes, apply lipstick, and examine my smile in the rearview. "Okay."

We emerge from the car, blinking in the sunlight as though we've just stepped out of a darkened theater. A shadowy figure appears in the screened porch and the door yawns open. A lean man in Levi's and a denim work shirt emerges. "You must be the Gabaldón sisters," he says, and my sisters grow shy as real goddamn sheep, so I have to step forward and shake his hand. "I'm Bette Gabaldón. Thanks for letting us stop by."

His grip is strong and warm. "Clarence, Clarence Vigil." He's in his forties, trim and tanned, with graying hair and dark blue eyes. After the long trip with just my sisters and the kids for company, this Clarence Vigil looks as appealing as a dish of ice cream in the middle of the desert. I would not at all mind a taste.

I introduce las borregas, one by one, and the children. Then Clarence says, "Now, I got to warn you—Ma's had a stroke. She can't talk too well and gets mixed up."

He leads us into the house, which is cool and dark and smells of cinnamon and coriander. Deep inside, like a heartbeat, an unseen clock ticks. The front room is sparsely furnished—a rocker, a sofa, and a reclining chair. A piano stands in the dining room across from a table and six chairs. Beyond that is a knickknack-filled cabinet with glass doors. Clarence pauses before the door to a side room. "Her face is paralyzed." He glances at Elena. "Might be a little scary."

Sophie says, "Well, maybe I can wait somewhere with the kids."

"Sure," Clarence says. "Why don't you step through the dining room to the kitchen in back? I'll be right there." He leans toward Elena. "You like bizcochitos?"

Elena claps her hands. Sophie and Aitch lead her toward the kitchen as the rest of us file into the side bedroom. Like the front rooms, this one is cool and dimly lit. A queen-sized bed stands in one corner opposite an antique dresser set. In the bed, an old woman with shorn white hair rests against propped pillows. Her hands—liver-spotted but smooth, swollen with edema—rest atop the bedspread. She's wearing a white nightgown, cornflowers printed on it. My eyes travel to her mangled face, her slate-colored eyes. On one side, her expression is neutral, even placid, but on the other, she wears a stricken look. Her mouth is pulled down at the corner revealing tooth and gum, her cheek taut, her eye unnaturally wide and unblinking, her eyebrow arched and frozen in astonishment.

"Ma," Clarence says in a soft voice, "these are the Gabaldón sisters. They've come a long way to see you."

The woman nods.

He pulls up the dresser bench and a camp stool. "I'll leave you to talk," he says.

Loretta and Rita share the bench, and I take the stool, sitting closest to the bed. The sheep remain mute, so it's up to me to say, "I'm Bette, and these are my sisters, Loretta and Rita. It's nice of you to see us, Mrs. Vigil."

"Fermina's pearls," Heidi Vigil says in a deep slurry voice, a thread of spittle webbing her lips. "I know jewels."

Loretta clears her throat. It's about time she remembered this visit was her idea! "We understand you wrote a book about Fermina."

"Retorts," the woman says. "I wrote *retorts* for the project."

"Tell us about it," I say.

"Unmarried project, the unmarried writer's project, the double-you, pea, ay, but then"—she holds up her left hand, revealing a gold band embedded in the puffy flesh—"I quit."

"But you interviewed Fermina," Loretta says. "Our aunt Nilda says you made notes, so we're curious..."

"About Fermina," Rita adds.

Heidi stares off at some focal point beyond us. "Pepe, Pepe Gallegos, you remember him?"

Loretta nods. "He translated for you, for your notes."

I lean in closer. "What happened?"

"Mining accident, I think. Or was it his father?"

"What happened to your notes?" Loretta asks.

The old woman whimpers. "Ida never liked me."

"Did Fermina know magic? Did she practice brujería?" Rita's voice is strained. Of all of us, this inheritance from Fermina has hurt her the most.

Heidi crooks a finger for us to lean in. "Lucinda Aragón," she whispers, "was a witch. Everybody knew. She helped Fermina."

"Are we...," Rita asks, "...under some spell?"

"Pshaw, *I* can spell," Heidi says. "I am a good writer. But Ida... *refused.*"

"Refused what?" I keep my tone patient, even.

"All my work, my notes."

"Where are your notes now?" Loretta says.

"Ask Fermina." Heidi yawns. "I gave everything to her."

"What if we can't ask her?" I'm not keen to break the news of Fermina's death to this old woman.

"Then ask Nilda, she was there," Heidi says, but a doubtful look clouds her face. "She was just married. I remember she wanted to know about the work."

"Nilda read your notes?" Rita asks.

"Maybe," Heidi says, nodding. "I don't know. Fermina knows."

"Fermina's dead," Loretta blurts out. "She died a long time ago."

Heidi's blue-gray eyes fill, her chin wobbles. "Clarence!" she calls. *"Clarence!"*

When Clarence sees us out, he hands me a yellowed sheet, a carbon copy. "Here's something I found with my mother's papers," he says. "It might interest you."

I read it aloud as Loretta steers Woody back toward Río Puerco.

*Ida Saenz Pomeroy,*
*Director of the New Mexico Writers' Project*
*Work Projects Administration (WPA)*
*Santa Fe, New Mexico*

*September 9, 1940*

*Dear Mrs. Pomeroy:*

*I am writing to tender my resignation from the New Mexico Writers' Project as a data collector for the Work Projects Administration (WPA). I have recently become engaged, and when I marry, I will be ineligible for the work. My fiancé is a rancher who owns considerable property outside of Santa Fe. I wish to resign in good standing before I am terminated, as happened to one of my colleagues who inherited a sum of money.*

*I also wish to entreat you once more to reconsider the decision not to include data gathered through interviews with Fermina, a Pueblo woman who has lived many years in the Río Puerco Valley community that we are surveying for the recovery project. The insights she provides illuminate an important, and often overlooked, perspective on those early years in the territory. I know you have complained that my writing style is not suited for this project, but I suspect the information my subject divulges with regard to a leading family in this community is more the problem. You have also stated that the interviews veered notably from the set of questions that prompt remembrance of ceremonies, folktales, and such, but I must stress that Fermina's life story emerged whole cloth after the first few interviews. As a conscientious fieldworker, I would have been remiss in suppressing or omitting any of this valuable data. I will leave these materials in her care. If you have a change of heart, I believe she may still be willing to share the work with you.*

*Furthermore, I respectfully request placement for Pedro ("Pepe") Gallegos, the young man who worked as my translator on the project. Though he is only sixteen years old, he is remarkably fluent in both Spanish and English, and he is a sympathetic listener who encourages subjects to speak their hearts. He is well trained and would make another interviewer an ideal assistant. You may have heard that his father was killed in a mining accident, and his mother and sisters depend upon his earnings to subsist. I cannot recommend him highly enough.*

*Thank you for the opportunity to work as a data collector and writer under the auspices of this worthy project.*

*Yours truly,*
*Heidi Marie Schultz*

"Wow!" Sophie says. "Like, why couldn't he have given you the letter *before* you guys talked to her?"

Loretta says, "Wonder what she means about divulging information about a leading family? Do you think that means *our* family?"

I shrug. "Maybe Pepe Gallegos knows. Do you think we can find him?"

"Se murió," Rita says. "At least, that's what Heidi said."

"That was his *father*," Loretta says.

"We can ask Nilda." My stomach lurches and saliva floods my mouth. I should never read in the car.

"Speaking of Nilda." Sophie pulls a scallop-edged photo from her shirt pocket.

Rita takes it from her. "Where'd you get this?"

Sophie juts her chin in the direction of the Vigil farmhouse.

"You just *took it* from their house?" Rita asks, aghast.

"The son gave it to me, babosa," she explains.

"What is it?" Loretta, who's driving, asks.

I peer at the snapshot. "It's Nilda with some white lady." The faded photo shows two women—a young blonde with a much older woman—standing before the horno at the ranch house in Río Puerco, arms linked. Their faces are blanched in the sunlight, their eyes deep-set, shadowed, and their expressions unreadable.

"That's what I thought," says Sophie. "But Clarence says it's *Fermina* with his mother, with Heidi."

"No way," Rita says, examining the photo. "That's Nilda."

"Look at the date on the back, will you?" Sophie tells her.

"Nineteen thirty-eight," Rita reads.

"Nilda would have been in her twenties back then, ¿qué no?" Sophie points out.

"Looks *exactly* like Nilda." I'm sure of it. The upright septuagenarian in the picture bears little resemblance to the shrunken, wizened Fermina we knew.

"Pass that thing up here." Loretta glances at the picture as she drives. "Makes sense, though, they had the same diet, lived in the same environment. I notice a lot of seventy-year-old women in Río Puerco resemble one another."

"It's not a great picture," says Sophie. "I can't even tell if they're smiling. We should show it to Nilda."

"It's her birthday and all," I say. "You know how touchy she gets. I don't know if that's such a good idea..."

## RÍO PUERCO, NEW MEXICO — RITA

Rita helps Nilda set out Thanksgiving dinner in July. Her aunt has reheated the turkey, mashed potatoes, gravy, piñon and green chili stuffing, empanadas, calabazas casserole, pumpkin pie and pastelitos. As each dish appears, Nilda apologizes for it being "un poco seco," a reminder that she expected them the previous night. Rita eats second helpings of everything to assure her it's all perfect, and her sisters drink many glasses of wine made by her father's youngest brother, Santiago, a wine Loretta privately calls "vin de turpentine," for its sharp solvent-scented bouquet.

After dinner, Tío takes Elena out to see the lambs and Sophie settles Aitch in his traveling bed before helping the others clean up. While Nilda fills the sink, Rita clears the table, Bette puts food away, and Loretta scrapes food from the plates. Rita steps into the kitchen with a stack of dishes, and Bette mentions, in an offhand way, that they stopped to see Heidi Schultz Vigil on the way to Río Puerco.

"Pobrecita," Nilda says. "She had a massive stroke, I heard, the beginning of the year. How is she?"

"Not good," Rita says. She returns to the dining room to put away the unused silverware, and she spies a framed photo of her uncle José, suited and smiling from a credenza shelf. Rita freezes. She glances over her shoulder to make sure she is alone before removing the picture from the shelf and setting it — facedown — in the bottom drawer. Rita eases this shut before returning to the kitchen.

"Her son ain't bad, though," Sophie says with a wink.

Nilda swipes at her with a dish towel. "Bah, he's *divorced*," she says in a tone she might use to accuse someone of being an axe murderer. She glances at Bette, then back to Sophie, before adding, "There's nothing wrong with divorce for *women*. We put up with so much mierda. But it don't look good for a man to be divorced."

Mollified, Bette agrees. "Men don't wear divorce that well." Rita, though, knows her sister was attracted to Heidi's son. Apart from the geographic distance, it would never work. Bette's not interested in anyone as well adjusted as that Clarence seemed to be. She prefers to rescue a drunk or a criminal than to be with someone her equal. Rita checks her watch, wondering if it's too early to call Rafe.

"Anyway," Loretta says, "Heidi told us she gave her interview notes to Fermina."

"Did you ever see them?" Bette asks.

"I never knew that. I sure never saw any notes." Nilda plunges a glass casserole dish into the sudsy water and scrapes it with a steel-wool pad. "I don't know why you girls want to get mixed up with that old nonsense."

"We want to know about the gifts," Loretta tells her.

"Bah, ¡qué cosa!" Nilda wheels from the sink to face her. "You're so stuck on what that old woman said that you can't even see the things your mama left you."

"What things?" asks Sophie.

"You got that joking from her. She was always pulling jokes, looking for a laugh. And Bette inherited the way she cares for all of you and your daddy," Nilda says, counting off on her soapy fingers. "La Rita is honest, no matter what, just like your mama..." She turns back to the sink. "*She's* the one who gave you gifts."

"What about me?" Loretta's voice is low. "What did I get?"

"Brains, estupida," Nilda says. "You should be smart enough to know that."

Rita and her sisters stare at their aunt, stunned.

Nilda sighs and mutters, "I knew I should have bought a bunch of Barbies for you girls when Fermina died and told you they were from her. Then that would be that. Se acabó." She pauses to submerge a skillet. "Even so, I have told you everything I know about all that business."

"What about Pepe Gallegos?" Rita asks. "Where can we find him?"

"Over at the cemetery," Nilda says, crossing herself. "He was killed in a car accident about two years ago. She told you about him? Válgame, Dios. I'm surprised she can talk after a stroke like that."

"She wasn't real clear," Bette says. "She called us jewels."

"Pearls," Rita puts in, trying to remember the tiepin her uncle is wearing in the photo she's hidden—something glittery, she's sure, nothing opaque or lustrous. "She called us Fermina's pearls."

## ALBUQUERQUE, NEW MEXICO — SOPHIA

You and your sisters stay with Nilda and Santiago at the farm while you're in Río Puerco. From there, you all make the rounds to see your other relatives over the next few days. Midweek, your sisters begin planning the trip home. But Loretta insists on a side trip to Albuquerque. Specifically, she wants to visit the library at the University of New Mexico. She and Rita have been making some telephone calls, trying to find out more about the data collected by Heidi Schultz Vigil. Finally they've decided all of you should drive out there to examine the archives for yourselves.

After a long morning of scanning brittle pages in the dusty stacks and taking turns minding the children outside, Bette finally summons the librarian, Pat Coronado, a brusque woman with an iron-gray crew cut and a deep, gruff voice. "We're interested in finding WPA data collected by Heidi Marie Schultz," Bette explains.

"We're looking for her reports on a woman named Fermina," Loretta adds.

"What's the subject's last name?" the librarian asks.

You shoot your sisters a puzzled look, and Bette says, "What was it?"

Loretta digs in her bag and pulls out her wallet. From this, she extracts a plastic-coated holy card—why, it's your old compañera, the Virgin Mary, wearing a star-spangled navy shawl and standing on a purple crescent held aloft by a towheaded angel. Under Fermina's name and the date, the text on the back reads: *Queen of the Americas, pray for us. Queen of all Saints, pray for us. Queen of heaven, pray for us. Queen of Peace, pray for us.*

Bette shoots her a disbelieving look. "I can't believe you kept that all this time."

"It was starting to fall apart, so I had it laminated," Loretta says. "Fermina Hidalgo was her name. She died in 1967. There's no given date of birth."

The librarian is harried, busy updating the catalogue, she says. But she takes a shine to Loretta, so she disappears into her office to access internal files. Rita appears on the other side of the glass door, pointing at her watch to let us know it's time for someone else to take over watching the kids. Loretta says, "It's my turn."

But Bette shakes her head, saying, "Something tells me that librarian won't do jack for us if you're not here, so I'd better go," and she heads out.

"It's hotter than blazes out there," Rita says, joining you and Loretta as you wait for the librarian to return. When she does, she hands Loretta an ugly blue-and-orange book and says, "I have no record of that data collector. Often the data collectors aren't named. This book, though, contains some of the information they amassed."

The three of you page through *New Mexico: A Guide to the Colorful State,* but the dull, anonymous record of interviews makes no mention of Heidi Schultz or Fermina, holds no clue they ever existed. Looking at Loretta as though she's the only one in the room, Pat Coronado says, "I double-checked, and there's absolutely no record the woman worked for the New Mexico Writers' Project."

"But why would she resign," Rita asks, "from a position she never held?"

The librarian shrugs, and you thank her for her help. Then you three meet Bette outside, give her the news.

"We've run out of leads," Bette says. Her face is tired, uncharacteristically sallow and haggard. Loretta bites her lower lip, blinks rapidly. And you are stunned by the tightness in your throat.

"And we're out of time," Rita says, her voice breaking.

## SANTA FE, NEW MEXICO — LORETTA

I wish there was a way to stay on another day or so, maybe fly back on my own directly to Georgia. But between paying back my student loans and establishing a practice, there's no way I can afford to pay for a flight I haven't booked in advance. This letdown is as keen as a physical ache for me, and for my sisters. We collect ourselves to pack and say our good-byes to Nilda and Santiago. We don't talk much — our disappointment is too fresh, too tender. But we are polite to one another as we help Nilda clear away the breakfast dishes and then we gather our belongings.

Before we head back to L.A., Bette decides Elena should see Santa Fe, which we soon discover — as we stroll the streets lined with jewelry vendors, arts and crafts stores, galleries, upscale restaurants, and expensive boutiques — is no place for a cranky two-year-old and a baby, however agreeable he might be. Tourists and artisans glare at the troop of us as we block narrow sidewalks with the strollers and bulky diaper bags. By noon, I can't bear to look at one more piece of turquoise, spin another rack of postcards (*Greetings from Santa Fe! Wish you were here! The Land of Enchantment!*), or swallow another bite of green chili as long as I live. The enchiladas with sopapillas and honey that we order for lunch in a noisy tourist restaurant taste thick and pasty. I do not even have the heart to order beer. In fact, I feel something like the glass of water that the harassed waitress keeps filling for me, a reminder to hurry up and finish the meal so others can be seated:

Like that brimming tumbler, if you nudge me or even look at me too hard, I will topple, sloshing all over the place.

How is it possible to feel so overfull and empty at the same time? I glance at my sisters. Their faces are tense and drawn. No one makes eye contact. They also seem ready to spill at the brush of fingertips. The children are whiny and irritable. The altitude, Bette says, makes them touchy. We don't eat much. After we pay the bill, Sophie insists on hitting just one more souvenir shop. She says she wants a T-shirt for Aitch, but I suspect she's reluctant to return home without something to show for her trouble. We trudge the cobbled street for a discount shop Rita remembers seeing earlier.

Inside the shop, emptiness overtakes that overfull feeling, though the shelves of cheap gifts and racks of T-shirts here are packed so tightly it's nearly suffocating. Everything reeks of synthetic "newness," a polyester-plastic smell that makes my nose itch. Despite this, I rifle through the clothing, thinking of Chris. (What do you bring someone who has given you your first kiss, when you hope it will not be your only kiss? How about a hooded sweatshirt with a chili appliqué? A plastic backscratcher? Licorice whips? A buckskin-covered drum? The only thing that seems right to bring Chris is this question: *Why?*) But I keep fiddling with the T-shirts so my hands won't feel bare.

Bette sidles up. Hangers screech against the rod as she rummages through the rack. She murmurs, "Maybe they have one that says: *We drove all the way to New Mexico in a hot, smelly car, spent a shitload of money, almost murdered each other, and all we got was this stupid T-shirt!*"

"Wish they did," I say, thinking of why we made the trip, our failed mission. "I'd buy one for each of us."

As Sophie makes her purchase, a clerk playfully strokes Elena's plump cheek with a peacock's plume. "*Ahhh*! Feathers is *fill-fee*!" she screams, opening her mouth so wide I glimpse her tiny tonsils quivering behind the uvula. Bette scoops her into her arms and beelines for the restroom to wash her face, but Elena won't be subdued. She shrieks, flailing and kicking, all the way out to the car. Little Aitch, already wearing his new T-shirt, soon joins in, howling in sympathy. Weirdly, this racket comforts me. I'm tempted to egg them on: *C'mon now! Give it all you've got! More gusto! More, more!*

At the car, I take the wheel, steering this time toward the I-40.

"What about the Mother Road?" Bette asks, raising her voice to be heard over the squalling children.

"Been there, done that," Rita shouts, cupping her hands over her ears.

In the rearview, I spy Sophie pointing out the glittery Route 66 emblem on the turquoise infant top Aitch is wearing. "Even bought the goddamn T-shirt!"

"So let's see what the interstate has to offer." I press the gas pedal, accelerating to merge onto the highway home.

### EULALIA TORRES

When Decidero turned twenty, Inocencio and Yrma decided it was time for him to take a wife. In those days, parents decided whom their children would marry. The Gabaldons chose Eulalia Torres for Decidero. The girl's mother was a widow with much acreage near the river. Señora Torres was ill and going blind. The Gabaldons expected her soon to relinquish the land to Eulalia, her only child. No doubt they assumed that Eulalia, an inexperienced fourteen-year-old, would bend easily to their will.

Decidero's godfather was Inocencio's second cousin. This padrino was a schoolteacher's son, so he could read and write. He wrote the letter presenting Decidero's offer of marriage. As was customary, Inocencio and the padrino rode out to Eulalia's mother's farm, planning to arrive in time for the midday meal, when everyone would be home, including Eulalia's uncle who helped his sister on the farm. As Fermina recalls Inocencio's account, the visitors stayed two hours, discussing crops and livestock. When they got up to leave, the padrino handed Eulalia's uncle the letter.

For the next week, Decidero was nervous and irritable. If a letter arrived on the eighth day, he would know he had gotten "la calabaza," and his offer had been rejected. If no letter arrived after two weeks, it had been accepted. Just before suppertime on the eighth day, a horse clopped toward the house. Riding it was

Eulalia's uncle. He handed Inocencio a sheet of paper twice folded and rode off. They had to find Decidero's padrino to read it, but they already knew what it was: the squash. Inocencio and Yrma pressed the padrino to make an offer to another girl, but Decidero took no interest in this.

In a few weeks, Eulalia's uncle arrived with another letter. In it, the engagement was accepted, as if the first letter had never existed. The Gabaldons were puzzled until they learned that Eulalia's mother had suffered a stroke. She needed a doctor's care. The family had land, but not much money since Señor Torres' death. Decidero was overjoyed; he wanted Eulalia all the more since la calabaza.

After three days, the Gabaldons visited the Torres family, loading a wagon with gifts they had purchased over the years, anticipating Decidero's wedding. They brought wool bedding, in addition to the trousseau and fifty dollars for the bride. Weeks later, they rode out for the *prendorio* (reception for groom's family), bringing Fermina to help with preparations. Along the way, they were joined by relatives and friends invited to attend the celebration. By sunset, all had arrived at the Torres home. Fermina worked alongside other women—relatives and servants, some of whom she knew and had not seen in years—to prepare for the feast and dance. The next morning, the entire house was turned over to the Gabaldons to clean and cook. Meanwhile, Eulalia, her bedridden mother, and her uncle had nothing to do but wait for the wedding.

The Irina de casorio, an older married cousin that Eulalia had chosen as her matron of honor, helped dress and prepare the bride. Then the couple knelt before the Gabaldons at Señora Torres' bedside to be blessed by both families. Afterward, the bride, groom, Irina, and padrino de casorio rode out to the church for the nuptials, while everyone else waited at the house. Fermina and the other servants helped pack Eulalia and her mother's belongings, as they would move to the Gabaldon home after the wedding. Her uncle planned to stay behind to manage the farm.

When they returned, Fermina and the others served the wedding feast—tortillas, sopapillas, chiles rellenos, chili, beans, roasted chickens, blood sausages, pastelos, and wine, much homemade wine. The dance followed, lasting until daybreak, when *la entregada de los novios* (the giving of the bride to the groom's family) occurred. Not until after breakfast did the guests finally depart, wishing the couple many years of life and happiness.

## FISH AND FLOWERS — BETTE: 1985

After the trip to Río Puerco, Rita headed up north, and Loretta flew back to Georgia. They didn't travel to L.A. for the holidays that winter or this one, Rita claiming it was too expensive, and Loretta that she was too busy. The truth is — that trip was a setback, for all of us, and not just an economic one, though it ended up costing a fucking fortune, especially when Woody's radiator blew out in Indio. Ever since, my sisters and I have been a little...I don't know...tentative with each other, breaking into our comfortable pairs — me and Sophie seeing each other daily, and Loretta and Rita talking every week by phone. Cary's wedding will be the first time we're all together in nearly two years.

Though I can't stand wedding shit, I'm kind of looking forward to seeing my sisters again, and I do love the flowers. There's something about balancing muted buds and lacy greens with bright blossoms that's as soothing as firing up a joint in a bubble bath. So I've offered to do flowers for my brother's wedding, even though it means hauling out of bed early this Saturday morning to make it to Grand Central Market while it's still cool enough to deliver fresh blooms to the church.

I throw on a cotton shift, shove on my chanclas, and I'm out the door in minutes. The wedding's not until four in the afternoon, plenty of time to shower, and color my hair — that skunk stripe of gray roots that's plain absurd in a thirty-year-old woman. But I have to get home before Sophie arrives with Elena. I jab the key into the ignition, and I'm off, careening down Coates, Bostwick, Eastman, and Pomeroy all the way to City Terrace, which shoots off at Herbert and onto the San Bernardino Freeway.

My neighborhood streets are so spindly and twisted that if I meet another car winding toward me, one of us has to slam on brakes and reverse so the other can pass. There are zero sidewalks, and some people keep chickens, even a few goats. I have to watch out for these, especially backing out. The across-the-street neighbors are Santería people. They practically keep a petting zoo in their yard. When she visits me, Rita asks when I'm going to move back to the United States.

But my little rental house is so close to the law firm (specializing in custody cases) where I work that I may never move. I'm a field social worker. This means I log serious driving miles in deep traffic. I'd hate commuting to a distant office on top of that. But this is Saturday morning, and I don't want to think about work or even the voice-over narration for the infomercial I want to make for parents on how to prepare for a court appearance: *Remember to cover all tattoos of an obscene, satanic, or violent nature; come showered and sober, and please don't forget to wear your teeth…*

*Basta,* I tell myself, *Saturday morning, remember?* Now, what about that roach I stashed in the ashtray last night? Ah, here, it is. I clip that baby, spark a match — somehow my car lighter has disappeared — and pop in my Gloria Gaynor tape to sing along with "I Will Survive," a corny old song, but it sure picks a person up in the morning. A rooster with shimmering green-black feathers struts across the street. I open the window to a blast of boom-box mariachi trumpets. "Get out of here, you fucking cock!"

As I drive, I wonder why on earth anyone would want to get

married. My car glides past a series of cheap, crumbly houses flying U.S. flags in anticipation of the Fourth of July holiday. Never mind that the brown folks living in these stucco shacks are the first to be rousted by the LAPD on any whim. These residents are *patriotic* suckers. In the boulevard, I cruise past graffiti-scrawled liquor stores and pawn shops before nosing the car onto the ramp. I crank Gloria way up to blot out the freeway's roar. *Marriage?* I mean, *come on,* what with parents who can't hold on to their kids, the Third World lurking everywhere I look, and the LAPD busting heads, isn't there already enough trouble in this world?

At Grand Central, I slip into the cool, dank mercado, enjoying the citric tang emanating from fruit bins until stench from the fish stalls overpowers it. Underlying this, though, is the mealy aroma of fresh corn tortillas. With my mild buzz, nothing is as seductive as a steamy tortilla de maíz, butter-glazed and drizzled with lime juice. Nothing, that is, outside of Apolinario. As my eyes adjust, I wander from the tortilla and produce vendors toward the fish stand where my make-believe novio works. There he is, my dream lover, standing legs apart, as powerful and irresistible as his namesake, except that he's cleaving salmon steaks and wearing a blood-spattered apron. It's kind of hard to imagine Apollo—the god of youth, manly beauty, and poetry—hacking fish for a living.

"Hola, Apolinario," I call over the parsley-bordered displays of tuna, shark, and snapper near hillocks of pearly gray-shelled camarones spilled over ice chips.

He snaps off his rubber gloves as he approaches the counter. "¡Qué calor!" Because he's from Central Mexico, I'm surprised he finds the morning more than mildly warm, though it has been smoggier than hell. Climbing down the hillside in my car, I felt like I was entering, layer by gauzy layer, a recently gassed war zone.

He tells me he has no air-conditioning in the room he rents over Woolworth. At night, he showers and lies atop his bed, wet, with a rotating fan on. Now, as far as I'm concerned, Apolinario, the fish guy, could easily step out from behind that butcher's block and into a major motion picture. The guy could be as old as forty or just twenty-two. With his clear brown eyes, smooth cinnamon skin, and thick black hair, he could be an Aztec nobleman, an incarnation of Tezcatlipoca, old Smoking Mirror, the tempter himself, with four women to pleasure in the days before temple priests carve out his heart with obsidian blades to offer it, hot and throbbing, to the sun. As I picture him emerging from the shower, water droplets jeweling his lean body, I swallow hard, lick my lips. I'm almost queasy with lust — or maybe it's that I'm leaning over a tray of squid that's a little past its prime.

He asks when I'm going to take him away from all this, pointing at the stainless-steel buckets of bloody fish parts, blubbery innards, and silvery scales behind him. (We joke that one day I'll make an honest man of him — a U.S. citizen, that is — when we elope to Las Vegas.) In Spanish, he reminds me that men suffer, too.

I laugh and offer to bring him a cafecito with pan dulce from the bakery.

But he wants to know why I won't marry him. "¿No me quieres?"

I'd like to say, "Te quiero plenty." Instead, I fix my eyes on a severed trout's head at the top of one bucket. If I tilt my head, the dull eye seems to wink. And I mention that my boyfriend, Jaime, would not be cool with this.

"No me importa." Apolinario says *he* has a wife, insists she'll understand.

I do a double take.

"Yes, Girasol will be so happy," he says in English, but switches back to Spanish to promise she'll start packing the same day. We'll send her bus tickets express mail. With my sponsorship, she can apply for a work visa. He assures me I will die for her asopao. Her chiles rellenos, mole, tamales dulces are stupendous, beyond belief!

"¡Ojalá!" And I do wish I could. I don't like to admit I can no more afford to hire his wife than I have the means to "move back to the United States," as Rita says. And there isn't enough time to go into my feelings about marriage, even a marriage of convenience. "¿Quieres leche con tu cafecito?" I can never remember if he takes cream.

"Sí, un poquito de leche," Apolinario says, rubbing at a splotch on his apron. Without looking up, he asks me to bring him a cinnamon pig cookie, if they're fresh.

But before I step into the Panadería Cubana, he calls out, "Bette!" Early Saturday, the market is not crowded, but the stragglers gape at us. "Los hombres sufren." He emerges from the fish stall and stands under the fluorescent tube lighting like a character in a strange play, the kind that makes audiences uneasy. He holds his cleaver with the handle to his breastbone for drama. "Tú lo sabes."

I smile and point to indicate I'm headed to the bakery. If he's done embarrassing me, that is. Yeah, yeah, men suffer. You don't have to tell that to Jaime, my real-life boyfriend, who proposed to me a week ago at a dinner party in front of his friends and their wives. His glasses steamed and his cheeks flamed like I'd slapped him when I said, "Are you out of your *mind*?" That was a conversation stopper for sure—absolute silence until the waiter wheeled in champagne and Jaime told him to take it back.

After my cafecito with Apolinario, who behaves more sensibly once he has a little caffeine and pig cookie in him, I head for the flowers, bearing a carton in which Apolinario has placed a live lobster, saying "Langosta for you, because you are too nice to me." The thing bucks like a bronco in the carton, freaking me out, so I get a shopping cart to set it in, which I'll need anyway for the flowers.

Luckily, I don't have to do the bouquets or boutonnieres for the bridal party. Some florist will handle those, and we'll use the bouquets as table pieces at the reception. I'm thinking calla lilies, though, for the church. I pass on the usual sprays of baby's breath in favor of wax flowers. Carnations, cheap everywhere, cost next to nothing here, but I despise them. They look like balled-up tissue, reek like store-brand bathroom spray. My ex, who's in prison, sends me a dozen every year on my birthday. Maybe the carnations are supposed to induce amnesia about his never paying a cent of child support and *then* work as an aphrodisiac, making me all hot to see him when he's released. Really, that would take something more along the lines of a full frontal lobotomy.

Ah, peonies, sweet peas, lisianthus, and stargazer lilies. And hydrangea—how firm and dewy it is! I load the cart. The yellow rosebuds in the refrigerated case droop a bit, except for one in back. This beauty is red-veined at the base. When I touch it to the tip of my nose, the petals emit a lemon-tea fragrance, subtle as a whisper. Maybe I will make one boutonniere, the groom's. Then I pick some irises for my house. Finally I select a sunflower, its heavy head inclined toward a shaft of light pouring from a side door. I write out a small card: *Todos nosotros sufrimos,* and ask the florist's helper, a friendly cholito, to take it to the fish stall where Apolinario works.

"Why'd you buy lobster?" Sophie says as she takes the carton from me. She arrived as I was unloading the car. Since our kids' fathers are MIA, so to speak, my sister and I perform "visitation" for each other. I keep Aitch and Elena one weekend, and she keeps them the next. This way, we both have free time to party or date, but mostly we just catch up on housekeeping and sleep during our child-free weekends.

"I didn't buy it." I arrange the irises in a vase on the dining table, spreading them like a plumed fan. "Someone gave it to me."

Elena perches on tiptoes to peer into the box. "You better wash that big bug."

Two-year-old Aitch, busy removing plastic containers from the low cupboards, couldn't care less. His favorite activity is taking things out of other things and then replacing them, one by one. Give him a laundry basket full of socks, and he's happy until mealtime.

"Ugh." Sophie curls her upper lip. "*Giveaway* lobster?"

"It's alive, check it out." I step back for a full view of the flowers on the tile-inlaid table. The blooms cast violet reflections in the yellow enamel, like thunderheads before the sun in an impressionist painting by a brilliant, but demented, artist. "By the way, did Cary pick up Nilda at the airport?"

Sophie nods. "For once, he did something useful."

"Does Dad want me to take them to the wedding?"

"I'll get Dad and Nilda, since you're watching Aitch in the church," Sophie says. "When are you going to cook it? The lobster, I mean. There's the wedding this afternoon and the dinner after that. Aren't you supposed to boil it right up? It's not going to live all that long, you know."

"Sure, it will." I pull the hairpins out of my "fun bun," a style designed to hide the fact that my hair is unwashed and the gray is growing out. "Before we leave, we can fill the tub with cold water and let him loose in it. For now, we'll stick him in the sink." I wonder what, if anything, the across-the-street babalawo does for his goats before brandishing the knife.

"*Him?*" She stoppers the sink and twists on the cold water. "How do you know it's not a she-lobster?"

"Oh, it's a him, all right. His name's Apolinario."

Sophie uses salad tongs to lift the scrabbling crustacean out and plops it into the sink. Elena pulls over a step stool, climbs, and stares into the sink. "You okay?"

Apolinario waves a rubber-banded claw.

"You'll have more room in the bathtub." The way she says it, I know she won't let me forget to transfer the thing later. The hard part will be getting my four-year-old to agree that poor Apolinario has to be boiled later, cracked open, and dipped into garlic butter. Seriously, there's no way a live lobster is going to live out its natural life commuting between my sink and the bathtub. Like there's not enough trouble in the world.

Weddings bore the crap out of me, especially the church part. I settle into a front pew between Elena and little Aitch, imagining Apolinario's dripping body, ready for some heavy-duty daydreaming. I hand Aitch a wooden puzzle I bought so he doesn't get restless during the service. He's trying to fit the pieces together, while Elena fans herself with the church program.

I'm relieved as hell I'm not in the bridal party and didn't have to buy one of those garish lavender jobs, like the one Sophie's wearing as she trudges up the aisle. Those gowns cost a fortune and make anyone my age look like an over-the-hill prom date afflicted with color blindness. Sophie's struggled to shed pounds, but if you ask me, she ordered her dress way too optimistically. She looks like a great purple balloon ready to burst, yet she's smiling to beat the band, and her hair looks terrific—soft, shiny black waves tumbling down her back. Sophie's following some kid in white taffeta tossing rose petals, and behind them looms Rita, looking hot and pissed-off, clunking along in high heels she's clearly not used to wearing. A few other girls—stumpy as trolls in drag—tramp behind Rita. After these, lurches Rosa, the matron of honor. I wonder why she didn't do something about that hair, but short of shaving it and buying a wig, what can be done with hair so dull it should hang from a horse's rear, haloed by green flies?

Finally Aracely trails Rosa. Thank God she's outgrown her blue Mohawk days and now wears her black hair in a cute spiky cut. Her ivory dress, a miracle of silk vertical panels, actually makes her look more human than rodent.

Over the organ music, I hear a familiar honking. Elena tugs my purse strap. "Grandpa's crying."

I pluck a wad of tissue from my purse and hand it to her without taking my eyes from the side door. Where *is* that boy? Did he change his mind? There, now I see him in a slimming black tuxedo and — what's that? — a *carnation* boutonniere. What happened to my yellow rosebud? No doubt Aracely made him wear the cheaper flower to match the groomsmen.

"Uncle Cary looks *nice*," Elena whispers.

My mother should be here. She loved him best and never hid it, but she loved us all so well, it hardly mattered. How proud she would be, fierce with pride. My throat constricts and my eyes burn as my brother climbs the altar steps to take Aracely's gloved hand in his.

"See!" Aitch lifts the completed puzzle over his head, and the pieces tumble out, clattering to the floor.

In the church social hall, Nilda gasps when my first husband, Luis, meanders in with his second wife, Nancy, on his arm. "What's *he* doing here?"

"Relax," I tell her. "Cary invited him. They've been close for years." My brother's friendship with Luis outlasted my marriage to him by seven years.

Nilda, who feels no compunction not to outdo the bride, is wearing a trim cream-colored suit. For a seventy-three-year-old woman, she looks damn sharp. "I don't know about these ex-husbands showing up and bringing the *new* wife. Válgame, Dios."

"It's fine, Tía, really." I make my way to the door to hug old

Luis, who has truly aged. Though he's just thirty-six, he's already bent, withered as a scarecrow. I also reach to embrace Nancy, who's hobbling on a gilt-handled cane beside him.

"Glad you made it." And I mean it.

Nancy's mouth splits open, and she hee-haws with such force that I jump. Even Luis looks startled. Throughout the hall, heads turn, people probably wondering how the heck a donkey got in here.

"How's the hip?" I ask to make her less nervous, and I lean in to listen to her breathy tale of doctor's visits, X-rays, prescriptions, and physical therapy, until Aitch interrupts, crying because he's lost a puzzle piece. Grateful as hell to the kid, I ask Nancy to please excuse me.

"Where'd you drop it, m'ijo?" I scan the floor until Elena spots the wooden part. Then I grab a cup of planter's punch and soft drinks for the kids before finding a table. I prop Aitch in a chair, his puzzle before him, and I slip into a seat beside Elena.

"The floor is filthy," she says, "but the flowers look pretty."

"Thanks." The strategic arrangements of flowers left over after I decorated the church do look lovely. At Grand Central, I toyed with the idea of tying individual daisies to fishing line dangling from the ceiling, and, reasonably, decided, fuck that—*way* too much work. Who'd notice, anyway? I suck back the potent punch, feeling I earned it.

"Guess who I saw, Mama?"

"Who?"

"Pam."

I gasp, and sweet drink burns in my nostrils and windpipe. Elena thumps my back until I catch my breath. "You saw *Pam*? *Where?*"

"Behind us at church." Elena points. "Look, there she is with Grandpa."

I squint at her from across the hall. "At least, she looks sober."

The old woman isn't swaying on her feet, sputtering curses

and waving her knobby fists like she was the last time I saw her, months ago, when she turned up at Dad's birthday party, uninvited. In fact, she's marching—arm in arm with the old man—right toward us.

"Look who I got here," says my father, grinning like he's a kid who's just caught his first catfish. "You remember la Pam?"

Remember her? I still get night sweats when she pops up in my dreams. "Hello, Pam," I say. "How nice to see you."

Pam throws her saggy, freckled arms around me, glances down at Elena, and says, "Eva, my, how you've grown!"

"I'm *Elena*," she says, shrinking away from her reach. "Who invited you?"

Pam cackles. "Kids say the *darnedest* things."

"Why, h'ita, I invited Pam." Pops raises his eyebrows. "This is a family wedding, and Pam's part of this family."

"But Mama said you aren't married no more," Elena says. "She don't suppose to be here."

My father removes his glasses to wipe them with his handkerchief. Without the magnifying lenses, his eyes look smaller and duller than usual. "Don't be silly."

"She has a point, Dad." I don't like to remind him, but they about killed each other during the brief time they were married. That summer while we were visiting Nilda in New Mexico, they snuck off to Vegas like teenagers to be married by a man who resembled Johnny Cash. (They couldn't find an Elvis imperson-ator.) They fought like mad dogs and separated after less than a year. In fact, I was the one to put the paperwork through for the divorce, and it was just finalized a few weeks ago.

"Look." Pam takes both my hands in her cool, withered claws. "I know we had some trouble in the past, but let's put that behind us, okay?" She looks to Elena and back at me. "I'm not drinking anymore. I'm in A.A. now, and it's working for me, one day at a time, you know. Let's start fresh, okay, kiddos?"

"There's Nilda." The old man rehooks her arm. "Come on, let's say hello."

When Nilda spots the two, her mouth drops open, wide enough to hold a tennis ball between her teeth. Then she catches my eye and shakes her head, as if to say, *see,* this *is what happens when the exes show up.* ¡Válgame, Dios!

Cary and Aracely sweep in with the bridal party, having finished with the photographer in the church. Someone should throw a blanket over Cary because he looks like he's in shock, or maybe it's that his eyes haven't adjusted from the flashbulbs. His black sideburns are stark against his green-tinged jowls as he's gazing around in wonderment. The band cranks up, and Aracely leads him out for the first waltz.

Sophie rushes over, her panty hose rasping. "I need a drink." She's back in a flash, bearing two cups of punch.

"Thanks." I reach for one of the cups.

She slaps my hand away. "Get your own, pendeja."

"Real nice."

"Hey, you didn't have to stand around, grinning like the Cheshire cat for an eternity. I swear to God, my gums are chapped." She slugs back her first cup. "Ah, better. How's Aitch, my darling son?" She ruffles his hair as he snaps in a puzzle piece.

"He likes the puzzle," Elena says.

"The puzzle that Aracely says ruined the whole wedding?"

My face heats up. "She did not!"

"Yup, she did." Sophie starts in on her second drink. "I'm going to need more of these. They're *good.* Yeah, Aracely had a fit. She actually thinks you put Aitch up to it to get even for not being included in the wedding party."

Aracely glares at me over Cary's shoulder. I smile and wave. "Is she insane?"

"Deeply, I'd say." Sophie swirls the dregs in her cup. "She asked me if you were mad about not being a bridesmaid. I said you were more grateful than anything."

"Damn *straight.*"

"But she didn't believe me. She's truly whacked. You should have heard her barking at the photographer. When she told him to kneel in front of her—"

I gasp. "She told the photographer to *kneel* in front of her?"

"She told him to kneel in front of her and Cary to get an 'upshot,' whatever that is, and the guy clicked his heels and said, 'Heil, Hitler!'" Sophie laughs, but I'm thinking, *uh-*oh. The photographer can make her look runty, sideshow freakish in shot after shot, but how will our brother protect himself from her wrath in the years to come?

"Who knew she had it in her?" Sophie says with pride. "The nutty bitch."

"Tía Sophie, guess who's here?" Elena asks. "Pam."

"I *know.* I saw her in the receiving line." Sophie tosses back the ice, crunching it most annoyingly. "I wanted to say, so where'd you park the broomstick?"

"She's in A.A. now—one day at a time." I mimic Pam's gravelly voice. "Let's put the past behind us, kiddos."

"Like, isn't A.A. about making amends?" Sophie works at a shelter for battered women and, no doubt, sees plenty of ex-drunks begging forgiveness. "Isn't it about showing remorse, asking forgiveness, instead of just reappearing like some unkillable monster in a horror movie?"

"Maybe she hasn't gotten to that step yet." The band breaks into "La Bamba," and my knee involuntarily starts bobbing. "Say, where's Rita?"

"Changing shoes." Sophie drains her second cup. "You want another drink?"

"Hell yeah."

"Watch Aitch, will you?" Sophie says as she rises from the table.

The floor trembles under my feet from all the overdressed hoofers stomping to "La Bamba." I wouldn't mind a spin out there myself. After Sophie returns, old Luis, droopy moustache and sad eyes, shambles over to ask me to dance, but the song is nearly over. What the hell, I take his hand. Luis and I catch the last few bars, and I'm really moving to Luis's dogged two-step, when the band swings into a slow number for the out-of-breath oldsters, and Luis pulls me close for the waltz. There's an awkward moment before I remember that he doesn't like to lead. Then I steer us surely over the lusterless green linoleum. "Where's Nancy?"

Unnatural laughter erupts near the entrance to the kitchen. "Over there, somewhere." He nods toward the racket. "She doesn't dance because of her hip."

"Are you still playing in a band?" I know his original group, Sabor, disbanded years ago, and Luis took a job at the General Motors plant in Van Nuys, but I suppose he still sings with some band on occasion.

"Yeah, once in a while, I get together with these guys. We do, like, quinceañeras, high-school dances, stuff like that." He sighs. "Since they let me go, I got a lot of time on my hands these days, so I'm looking to do more with the music."

"Serious? You lost your job?"

"Like a few months ago."

"Wow!" I picture Luis in a bathrobe, scanning the want ads — a beer in hand — while Nancy's braying in the background.

"You remember that song I wrote for you?"

"You never wrote a song for me. I remember that freeway

thing, 'The 4-0-5 Blues,' right?" Laughter bubbles up as I recall the ridiculous lyrics, but hilarity wouldn't be cool under these circumstances, so I pretend to cough instead.

"I wrote a song for you, too. You just don't remember."

"Believe me, I'd remember something like that."

He starts humming something I can almost recognize and then he sings, *"Bette, oh, Bette, I'm so alone with you I could cry, so lonely I don't try…"*

*"The things you say push me away. Do you even know that I'm alive?"* I join in, suddenly remembering.

"See, you *do* remember." He glances around and kisses the top of my ear.

"How could I forget?" Sometimes my memory is like my answering machine at the office. It accumulates so much crap that I've developed a hyperactive delete finger. I throw shit out right and left. The crazy thing is, the more I try to streamline and cast out junk, the more junk seems to accumulate. I once wanted to be a psychologist, but working for the degree took so much time, I dropped out of the program to do fieldwork. Now, instead of listening to one lunatic at a time, I go into homes where I've got whole families of them to handle, simultaneously, several times a day, for the rest of my *fucking life,* or at least until I retire.

"I think it's one of my best songs. In fact, I cut a single—a demo tape—for this friend of Nancy's who knows some guy whose cousin works at a radio station."

Over his shoulder, I glimpse my sister Loretta stepping into the recreation hall. That egoista refused to come to the ceremony because she doesn't "believe in patriarchal institutions like the Roman Catholic Church." Apparently, her grudge doesn't extend to church social halls. But I don't see the mysterious Chris she's told me about. Last night, she was supposed to fly in with him from Georgia, where she started up a veterinary practice. "Loretta finally made it."

We circle. He faces the door. "She looks good." He lifts his hand to wave. "So, anyway, this friend thinks they might play it for 'Open Mike.' Wouldn't that be cool?"

"Huh?"

"My song—if they play it on the radio. This could even be like my big break."

I struggle to imagine the hunched and middle-aged-looking Luis breaking into rock stardom. "Oh, *yeah,* that'd be great." I circle us again to see if this Chris has appeared yet, but no, Loretta's just talking to this heavyset woman, actually smiling and looking friendly. Maybe this Chris, whoever he is, has had a socializing effect on my sister.

"I got a copy in the truck, brought it for you, actually, since you kind of inspired it." He laughs, releasing me as the band winds down. "Want me to get it for you?"

I give him a quick hug. "Sure, that'd be real nice."

I'm thinking I ought to go over to Loretta sideways, kind of incidentally. She wouldn't like me marching up to her, saying, "*Where* is this Chris?" So I work the hall like I'm running for city council. "Hi, there, Stella, how's Norberto? Sister Cleophas, *you* still alive? Rosa, how're the kids? Those gym shoes working for you, Rita? Really, they kind of go with the gown. Oh, hello, there, Loretta. When did you get here?"

"You saw me walk in while you were out there dancing with what's-his-name." She embraces me. "I want you to meet Chris." She turns to the large woman. "Chris, this is my older sister, Bette."

I slap that smile on, and draw a deep breath, waiting for someone to say something, anything, before I realize that someone should be me. "It's great to meet you."

"Same here," she says. Close-up, I see she's statuesque, not fat, just tall and full-figured, and that she's old, or older than I thought, with a pile of black hair twisted into an old-fashioned chignon. Her pink cheeks convey the clean life—likely not too much drinking, drugging, or rolling in gutters.

Once I'm over the stun-gun effects, I have to admit she's okay-looking, though her clothes are corny—brown *paisley* rayon. And who wears those crocheted vests with pom-pom tassels anymore? "What a *great* outfit!" My dimples start to ache.

"I feel like I already know you and your family from what Loretta's told me."

"She's told me about you, too." But I'm racking my brain to recall *what* Loretta has said apart from her name. Shit, I wish I wasn't so quick to delete stuff.

"I'll bet she didn't tell you she's dating a woman." Chris laughs as Loretta blushes, grinning like she's just been given a major award, but is trying to act humble.

I laugh, too, because what can you say? No, as a matter of fact, this is one of the greatest shocks of my life. In the periphery, a tall mass of purple tulle scuds toward us.

"Rita," Loretta says, "I want you to meet Chris."

"*This* is Chris?" Rita's voice is sharp. "You said Chris is a heart doctor."

"That's right. I'm a cardiologist." Chris extends her arm to shake Rita's hand.

Rita ignores this. "You're a *doctor*?"

"There are women doctors, you know." I step between her and Loretta, who is narrowing her eyes, tensing as if to strike. "Loretta's one herself, remember?"

"She *lied*!" Rita's huffing now, like she's just run up ten flights of stairs.

"Hey, what's your trip?" I say to calm her down, and I summon Rafe with a "get your ass over here" hand signal. This is not the time for a Rita freak-out.

"I'm sorry this upsets you," says Chris, reaching to comfort Rita.

"Don't touch me." Rita jerks away, her big old eyes all shiny and crazy. She turns to Loretta. "We're supposed to be sisters. We're supposed to trust each other. I tell *you* things, but you never tell me *any*thing about yourself. You just don't give a shit about me and Rafe and my in-laws."

Rafe's mother and father flew in from Michigan to meet our family for the first time at this wedding. So far, his folks seem like okay people, not the kind to require smelling salts at the sight of lesbian couples, but try telling Rita that, try telling her *anything* when she gets worked up like this. As Loretta opens her mouth to speak, Rafe puts his arms around Rita and turns her, so she's nestling against his collarbone, whispering angrily. He catches my eye and mouths, "She's pregnant."

"Whoa," I say to Loretta as Rafe leads Rita away. "What a trip! Who knew she was pregnant?"

"I did," Loretta says. "She called me right after she told Rafe."

"And yet you never told her about you?" I say, pointing from Loretta to Chris.

"I...couldn't."

By this time, I'm thinking about that glass of punch Sophie was supposed to bring. No doubt it's gone flat. "Boy, I need a drink, how about you two?"

"Maybe a couple soft drinks," Chris says. "We really don't drink alcohol."

The greatest shocks of my life are coming hard and fast now. I gape at my sister, but she lowers her eyes, smiling, but staring down at her shoes. "They're over here." I lead them to an array of sweating cans of soft drinks on a table near the kitchen.

Someone in the band pounds out familiar piano chords as I hand Loretta and Chris colas. My new sister-in-law has rustled onstage, and she's bobbing her head to the beat, holding the microphone to her mouth. She's singing and swinging her hips, snapping her fingers to Carole King, and beaming like a headliner in Vegas.

Chris says, "She's not half bad," and I finally understand exactly what that means when I see Luis's face, which is tight with pain, like he's just smashed his thumb with a hammer. Scanning the room, I notice everyone who loves music is suffering a bit right now. "Not half bad" means "not half good," either, but, hey, Aracely should get credit for confidence alone. No question about it—the girl's got huevos.

As Aracely sings, she points straight at poor Cary, slouching at the bridal table, looking like he could use a double shot of vanishing potion.

The song ends, and we clap like patients in an asylum where they've just announced an end to electroshock therapy. But Aracely takes this as encouragement, and after a brief whispered conference with the lead guitarist, she steps up to the microphone again.

This is my cue to excuse myself to powder my nose, as in *go out to my car and smoke a joint*. On the way, I hear retching from the ladies room, and I nearly collide with Rafe, who's rounding the corner with a glass of water. I should follow him in and hold back Rita's hair, stroke her back like I did when she was a little girl, but she has Rafe for that now, so I just smile and rush past my brother-in-law for my car and my lovely stash.

No sooner do I suck back the first throat-searing hit, than I hear *rap-tap-tap* on the car window. "Fuck!" I should have driven out to the park or something. I cup the joint under the dash and look up. It's just Luis. I roll down the window. "Hey, I'm just having a smoke, want to join me?"

Beer in hand, he shakes his head. "Nah, smoking makes me kind of stupid."

"O-*kay*." And drinking two six-packs a day makes him what— the village savant?

He hands me a cassette tape. "I want you to have this."

"Thanks, I'll listen to it right now." I pop out the Gloria Gaynor and put Luis's tape in the deck, but the key's not even in the ignition, so it's an empty gesture.

"We got to go. Nancy's hip is acting up." He grins. "It was great seeing you."

"Yeah, glad you came." The joint is going cold between my finger and thumb, and I used my last match to light it up. *Leave, baboso, leave.*

He looks like he's trying to decide whether or not to kiss me, but in the end, he decides to give my car door an affectionate pat. "Okay, let me know if you like it."

"I sure will. Bye, Luis." I roll up the car window. And shit, the joint's gone out.

Back in the hall, the guests are lining up for the dollar dance, when everyone who wants to dance with the bride or groom is supposed to pin a bill on their clothing. I find Sophie sitting by herself. She tells me Nilda has taken the kids around to introduce them to folks. I ask Sophie to fish a fiver out of my purse.

"All you have is a twenty." Sophie holds up a crumpled bill. "Cary's not worth twenty. Even five's kind of high. I think I have some change in my purse."

"You can't pin *coins* on anyone. Hand it over."

She laughs, balls up the bill, and tosses it at me. "Hey, guess what? Loretta's a lesbian now, a *sober* lesbian."

"That's yesterday's news. I bet you don't know that Rita's pregnant."

"Good God!" Sophie widens her eyes in mock terror. "Poor Rafe."

The line to dance with my brother moves quickly. Before long, I'm pinning the twenty onto his lapel. "This is almost a week's groceries, boy. You better be worth it."

He looks startled, but diligently twirls me around the linoleum.

"How's married life so far?" I ask.

He shrugs and releases me for the next partner.

"Hey, I want my money back!"

Cary takes the matron of honor Rosa's hand to lead her out onto the floor. As I head back to Sophie, I glance over my shoulder. The line has grown some for both bride and groom. Cary's already let Rosa go, and he's waltzing with somebody I don't know. They migrate to the edge of the dance floor, and he disappears into the sea of bobbing suit jackets and floral dresses.

The drive home is lonesome. Sophie still has "visitation," so she's keeping Elena overnight. It's just me and my car winding up the hillside. I know I'm always after peace and quiet, scoping out the nearest exit, wherever I am, but now I could almost stand some company. I push in Gloria Gaynor, but I get Luis instead—the demo, I'd forgotten all about it—moaning my name. Hmm…it's not half bad.

Just as I'm about to veer left onto Eastman, Jaime pops into my thoughts for the first time the whole crazy day. He's been incommunicado since he uninvited himself to the wedding. Clearly, he took my rejection of his proposal too personally. He's probably at Self-Help Graphics now, over on Gage. He teaches art during the week, but spends weekends printmaking. He'd probably like a break around now. Maybe he'll glance from his work and flush when he sees me, his eyes shining. Or he might turn his back, pretend I'm not there. Worse, he could start yammering about marriage, picking up where he left off. Like I've got so much leisure time I need another activity, like I don't have enough people eating away at my life that I need a husband, too.

I flick on the blinker. Yeah, there's plenty of trouble in this place—me raising Elena alone, my dysfunctional clients, my goofy sisters and besotted father, my poor, helpless brother disappearing from sight. More than enough trouble here and not enough time to delete half the shit that keeps piling up. Still, under this starless bowl of night and in these mostly empty streets, oil-stained and shimmering under the streetlights, this world seems hollowed out, bigger to me now, even capacious in its way. First chance I get, I swing a turn for the studio on Gage. "Hush," I'll say, "hush. Let's not talk tonight."

## LOS CAMBIOS

Soon after the wedding, Eulalia's mother died, and her land was passed on to the newlyweds, though they remained in the Gabaldon household. Over time, Eulalia gave Decidero ten children: five girls and five boys. With each successive birth, she grew more outspoken and determined until she was running the household like a stern and judicious cacique. While the aging Gabaldons struggled to keep up, Eulalia made decision after decision, working her will above all others. Decidero grew timid in her presence, for she would not hesitate to mock and scold him. But Eulalia raised her children to have respect for Fermina, whom she regarded as a confidante and ally, and Fermina took pleasure in these little ones.

Her favorite was Juan Carlos the second youngest. He was born in the seventh month of Eulalia's confinement. The family worried he would not survive, so Decidero, who had a Model T by that time, drove out to fetch the priest to baptize him. Afterward, Decidero built a small box in which to bury the boy. But Eulalia and Fermina used that box as a bed for the baby because it fit so neatly behind the stove. Within days, a violent snowstorm descended upon the valley. The baby survived that blizzard, and by springtime, he was fat and lively.

Juan Carlos remained healthy until just before his tenth birthday, when he contracted rheumatic fever. With the fever, he grew delirious before slipping into unconsciousness. Again Decidero

drove out for the priest. Eulalia sank to her
knees before her shrine to the Virgin, while
Fermina sat beside the boy, stroking his forehead
and talking to him in a low voice. Fermina told
him all she knew about her father, her brother,
her mother, but she said nothing about Inocencio
or Decidero. She talked all that afternoon until
it grew dark. By the time the priest arrived,
sweat broke on the boy's forehead. In the
morning, he was sitting upright and smiling.

Juan Carlos was known for obedience; he
would do whatever he was told to do. As a joke,
once when Juan was still a boy, Decidero told
him to stand in the cornfield to keep the crows
away. After the boy went out, a storm broke.
Thunder cracked and lightning scribbled down
from the dark skies. Fermina signaled him from
a window, but he refused to budge. Fermina
found Decidero alone in the sala, dozing in the
rocker. Yrma and Eulalia had gone visiting with
the girls. She drew close, listening to Decidero's
breathing—the peaceful rhythm of it. Then she
slapped him hard, nearly knocking him from his
seat. "You will do as I say," she told him. "Go
bring that boy inside." Without a word, he rose to
summon Juan Carlos back into the house.

Years passed and the children grew into young
men and women. First, Inocencio died in 1932,
and then Yrma passed two years later. Nowadays,
Eulalia's daughters handle the housework, leaving
little for Fermina to do, though she still enjoys
working in the garden. Eulalia's children continue
to treat her with kindness. They bring her candy
and small gifts from trips to Albuquerque and
Santa Fe. Though it is impossible, Fermina wishes
there was a way for these young men and women to
recognize her, as she does them, and one day call
her nuestra abuela.

# 13

# LAS POSADAS — LORETTA: 1987

When I flew home for my father's surgery in December, Cary and his wife met me at the airport. They would take me to Bette's house, where I planned to stay the first night. On the way there, Aracely claimed she was starving, and after the long, tense flight, and because Chris wasn't around to protest, I seriously wanted a drink. We collected my bags, trundled them out to the parking lot, and Cary drove us to a darkened Mexican restaurant in Inglewood before delivering me to Bette's. There, Cary and Aracely ordered dinner by courses, and I requested ceviche and a glass of house red.

"Listen, Loretta, we're going to have las posadas at my mother's house on Saturday," Aracely said after the waiter brought our drinks. "We want you to come."

I sipped my vinegary Chianti. "Me?"

Aracely explained that her new stepfather had planned the party to introduce his friends to her family, including the in-laws. "Sophie and Bette will be there. Even Rita might come."

"Yeah, it'll be like a family reunion," Cary said. My brother, always heavy, had grown stouter with marriage. Like Rita, he'd inherited our mother's height, but even at six feet, he wasn't tall enough to carry the extra weight with grace. He seemed awkward, bulky as a tamed bear stuffed into the booth across from me. Despite his girth, his thinning hair, and his five-o'clock shadow,

Cary's expression matched that of the apple-cheeked seven-year-old who'd twine his chubby arm with mine in solidarity. This was a face I could not refuse. "Will you come?"

Normally, I shunned things like this, but the wine infused me with warmth and magnanimity. "Sure, why not?"

Bette greeted us, wearing just a beige towel knotted between her breasts. Her hair, mucky with black dye, was piled atop her head. The tarry mess reminded me of seabirds rescued after oil spills. She hugged me and retreated to the bathroom to rinse. I stowed the carton of leftover ceviche in the refrigerator and made small talk with my brother in the kitchen—*very* small talk. Since his marriage, my brother had lapsed into grunts and monosyllables in place of whole sentences, even with me, his favorite sister. Aracely departed for the living room and flipped on the television.

In a short while, Bette emerged—hair wet, but indisputably black.

"Where's Elena?" I asked.

"It's Sophie's turn to pick up the kids from day care. She's giving them dinner and bringing them later," Bette said. "Are you hungry?"

"Sure," Cary said.

"We just ate," Aracely hollered from the front room, where she watched a sitcom with a hectoring laugh track. "Don't give him anything."

"Real charmer, no?" Bette opened the refrigerator door and handed Cary a pack of tortillas and a block of cheese.

"I brought ceviche." I pointed out the takeaway box. "Do you have wine?"

Of course, she had a case of California red, an opened bottle from it uncorked and breathing on the counter. She poured a brimming stem glass for me to take outside with the ceviche and a bag of chips. She followed me out to the patio, bearing her wine, stash box, and an ashtray.

"Sour," said Bette, after tasting the ceviche. "But not half bad."

"So how's the old man?" I asked.

"Oh, he'll be okay. They're just putting that thing in—what do you call it?"

"Carotid stenting." I'd already assured my brother and sisters by phone that this is a pretty routine procedure in which the surgeon inserts a tube—a stent—to widen the artery and increase blood flow in the area blocked by plaque.

"It's no big deal, as you know." Bette rolled a joint and lit it. "He'll be okay, really. Nothing fazes him."

Somehow sad, but true—nothing much fazed my father these days. Apart from floods, earthquakes, and fires that required him to turn on or shut off water mains, little disturbed him when we were younger. And now that he was retired, even natural disasters failed to excite anxiety in him. As I puffed on the joint Bette passed to me, I resolved to try harder with him. I would listen. I would laugh at the bad jokes and ignore the unintended slights. "I'm going to be better to Dad this time."

"You won't make it five minutes." Bette took the joint from me and drew on it.

"*You're* good to him."

"I never—absolutely never, *ever*—say anything truthful or important to him." She lit a joss stick and set it in the ashtray. "I bullshit. *That's* how I'm nice to him."

"I can do that."

"Five minutes *tops*."

A boom from the house startled me. Sounds of struggle and shouting, suggestive of a ransacking in progress, followed the explosive noise.

"Sister Sophie's here," said Bette. She gathered up the Baggie of grass and paraphernalia, stuffing everything into a cigar box she secured with a bungee cord. "She's got the kids," she explained. "I have to hide this shit."

Laughter spilled from the open windows. The entire house shook.

"She's doing shtick, la pendeja. We were supposed to go shopping this afternoon, but she flaked out on me. Says she doesn't *go* shopping anymore."

"Sophie doesn't *shop*?"

"Not for clothes." Bette stashed the cigar box in the crawl space and barricaded the opening with a cinder block, before returning to sit at the table with me.

"Why not?" I buttoned my blazer, glad I'd worn it for warmth on the plane. Bette's overgrown hilltop yard grew chilly in the evenings. Shadows shifted, yellow eyes glinting from their depths, as feral cats stirred in the bushes.

"Male odors."

Since Harold's disappearing act, Sophie had become cynical about men, but did their very smell offend her? I pictured my youngest sister sniffing at clothing racks for traces of . . . *men*? "She can't even stand their smell?"

"What smell?"

"Men — the way they smell."

"What the *fuck* are you talking about?"

"Male odors. You said Sophie won't shop because of male odors."

"Mail *or*ders, babosa, she buys from catalogues."

The back door flung open and Sophie's large body filled the frame, her hands on her hips as she shouted at the top of her lungs "¡Ay, borrachas!" before emitting a grito that sent the wild cats skittering.

\*       \*       \*

We checked my father into the hospital—a newly constructed facility in the foothills of La Cañada—the next afternoon. The old man was nervous in his overtalking, overfriendly way. Bette and Sophie were right behind him schmoozing everyone in their path, while Cary and I followed in awkward silence. It struck me that while my father and these two charmed the people they met, Cary and Rita tended to ignore others, and I spoke to strangers, here and in Georgia only when necessary. I imagined a sociability gene that somehow leapfrogged past me, my brother, and Rita.

"You can call me 'Speedy,' " my father told the nurse's aide.

"It's unintentionally ironic," I said, making a stab at friendliness. The aide wrinkled her brow. "O-*kay*."

"My sister's a doctor, a veterinarian," Sophie explained, cupping her mouth to deliver a stage whisper. *"No one understands her."*

"We get a lot of that around here." She glanced at me. "One hundred over seventy—pretty good, huh, Doctor? You're lucky, Mr. Gabaldón, to have a daughter who's a doctor."

"One thing I take pride in," he said, puffing up to boast—sad to say, I held my breath here—"is *good* blood pressure."

Sophie cast her eyes to the ceiling. "Yeah, Dad, you deserve an award, a golden blood-pressure-cuff thing."

"Sphygmomanometer," I said.

"*Nothing* fazes me," said my father, radiant at his own insensibility to stress.

After he had been prepped and gowned, an orderly arrived to wheel him through the sunlit corridors toward the lift to intensive care.

"Oh no," Bette whispered to me. "That's where they took Pam." Not too long ago, my father's second (and third) wife had succumbed to what her attending physician described on her death certificate as "complications due to alcoholism." One night, my father discovered her perched on the toilet seat, blood streaming from her urethra. It took four paramedics to convey her from their second-floor condominium to the ambulance. In this ICU, she had undergone an excruciating stint of renal failure before dying.

The elevator opened and the orderly rolled Dad through a short hall leading to the unit. We trailed close behind. The attendant then pushed the wheelchair into a room across from the nurses' station.

"It's the *same* fucking room," Bette said in my ear. The pale green wallpaper, glossy waxed floor, hospital bed, and beige visitor's chair suggested order and neutrality; no trace of Pam's agony lingered here.

The orderly helped our father from the wheelchair into bed. "This okay, Mr. Gabaldón?" He handed him the control to the wall-mounted television.

"It's good. What time is it, h'ita?" my father asked no one in particular. I remembered once hearing him call that corrosive crone Pam, "h'ita."

But Cary—his h'ito—answered, "Almost four."

"Oprah!" The old man grinned and switched on the set. "You can all go on, get something to eat or something, and leave me alone with my girlfriend." He never missed the talk show if he could help it. Once, Pam flung a bottle of bourbon (empty of course) at the television screen, shattering it, so he would pay attention to her while Oprah was on. Afterward, my father moved to Bette's until Pam replaced the set.

"You really want us to go, Dad?" asked Bette.

"You can come back after the show." He found the lever to elevate the head of the bed. The motor hummed until he sat upright. Oprah in a burgundy pantsuit loomed into focus on the screen overhead. "She looks good in red, ¿qué no?"

"Are you okay in *this* room?" Bette asked.

"Yeah, I'm fine. Nothing fazes me. Go, *go*."

That evening, we all stayed in the hospital waiting area until the surgeon emerged after eight to report that all went well, and then Sophie left to collect Elena and Aitch from the babysitter's, as it was her weekend to have them, and Cary headed home. Bette and I drove to our father's condominium, where we would spend the night to be closer to the hospital. "Now the *real* work begins," she said as we pulled out of the parking lot.

"What do you mean?"

"We've got to get rid of all that shit." Bette dug a joint from her bag and lit it.

"What shit?" I watched the road.

She passed me the joint. "Pam's shit. Dad hasn't thrown out a thing—those knickknacks and idiotic doodads, her clothes."

"What about her kids?" I remembered Pam's middle-aged daughter and sons. "Don't they want her stuff?"

"They more or less told us to junk it. Dad won't bother with any of it, not even to get rid of the clutter. So *we* have to do it before he comes home."

"Is this a different route?" After a drag, I passed the joint back. I didn't remember this many residential streets between my father's place and the hospital.

"I come this way after dark because I can't stand those stupid light displays on the main drag. Santa, reindeer, baby Jesus, and Christmas tree bullshit—you know I *hate* that ugly crap." Bette drew on the joint and spoke hoarsely while holding her breath. "I never want to see another fucking Christmas thing as long as I live."

"But aren't you going to las posadas at Aracely's?" I asked.

She let out her breath with a whoosh. "You're joking, right?"

The next morning after she visited our father, Sophie met us at the condominium to start "throwing out shit," as Bette put it, while the little kids were with the babysitter. Rita would be arriving with Rafe and their toddler, Danni, that afternoon. We planned to finish before she showed up and prolonged the process by hectoring everyone.

The second-floor condominium apartment looked as though it had been decorated by the manager of a gag-gift store: a dusty clutter of gimcrack, framed signs, and ugly craft displays, like the homemade rag doll—hanging in the kitchenette—designed for storing plastic grocery bags that had to be inserted between its dangling legs.

"Not what I'd call a 'feel-good' place." Sophie pulled a sign that read AVOID HANGOVERS: STAY DRUNK from the kitchen wall and chucked it into an empty carton she'd brought for trash. The glass frame shattered on impact. "Oops."

"Can we get rid of this?" I pulled a toilet magnet from the refrigerator. "It's always bothered me, right there on the refrigerator."

"Hey, I want that." Sophie snatched it. "It really flushes."

"It's yours. Just get it out of my sight."

She tossed it into the box with the sign. "I'm kidding, mensa."

"Listen, payasas, we've got to be organized, instead of running here and there throwing random things away." Bette tied her hair in a ponytail and pushed up the sleeves of her sweatshirt. "Where should we start?"

"The bedroom closet," Sophie said. "Those awful clothes."

Poor Dad had about four inches of space for his few shirts and slacks, his one suit, and a sports coat. The rest of the rack was crammed tight: Pam's dresses, blouses, skirts, jackets, and even T-shirts draped hanger after hanger. These were the kind of T-shirts a person sees in souvenir shops and wonders, *Now, who would be corny enough to buy one of these?* Pam would, that's who. She collected T-shirts that read: *World-Class Grandmother; Daytona Beach Bunny; Georgia's on My Mind; I Got Sloshed in Margarita-ville;* and *Kiss Me, I'm Irish!*

Bette brought a box of twenty-gallon-sized plastic bags to contain the clothes for Goodwill. I hesitated before shoving my pile into a bag. "You're *sure* her daughter doesn't want any of the clothes?"

Sophia pulled out a T-shirt with a cartoon image of pigs copulating on the front—*Macon bacon!* "Hard call, but I'm thinking, *probably* not."

"She said to throw it all out, but if there's anything nice, we can save it for her." Bette lugged an armload of dresses to the bed to sort through.

Sophie folded the pig T-shirt and reached for the Goodwill bag.

Bette glanced up. "Throw that out. I hate to think of some poor person having to wear that *grosero*."

"Hey, it's practically new," argued Sophie.

"Trash pile." I pointed to the heap of cracked and dusty shoes I'd started.

"Ooh, the formals!" Bette held up a long gown that reminded me of lemon chiffon pie: several layers of tulle and a satin bodice the color of a sunburst. I tried to picture the hatchet-faced Pam in it—maybe with her few tufts of rust-colored hair tucked into one of those turban things... but where would she have worn it? According to my sisters, the fanciest place she ever went was the track at Santa Anita.

"Feel the fabric, though." Bette handed me the dress.

The skirt rasped my fingertips like low-grade sandpaper. "Ugh."

Bette disrobed another hanger. "Here's something nice, though, this black dress."

"How'd she ever fit in that?" asked Sophie. "It's like a size six."

"Hey, that's mine." I grabbed it from Bette. "I hung it to get the wrinkles out before I wear it to that las posadas thing."

Sophie widened her eyes in mock horror. "You're going to *that?*"

"Aren't you?"

Sophie shook her head. "No *fucking* way. But it's nice that you're going, and that dress is perfect for it."

Bette handed me the hanger. "Definitely the las posadas look."

By noon, we'd finished with the closet, the entire bedroom for that matter, and we separated to tackle the smaller rooms — kitchenette, bathroom, hall closet. The plan was to meet again in the living room and lay siege to the cluttersome items with which Pam had filled every flat surface, including walls.

In the bathroom, I removed the cutesy acrylics of a little boy and girl seated on their respective toilets reading newspapers. I threw Pam's collection of joke books — *Lawyer Jokes, Polish Jokes, Dentist Jokes* — into recycling bins. Then, since I was there anyway, I scrubbed out the bathtub and sink. Scouring the toilet, I thought of Pam, who'd begun dying there. Apart from multiple indicators of poor taste, what kind of woman was she really? That she drank too much, everyone knew — everyone except my father, whose secret to never being fazed had much to do with not being observant. He had been shocked to find tiny bottles, airline-sized, stashed in hiding places throughout the house after she died. ("*Dozens* of them," he had told us, shaking his head. "But she was going to A.A.") What was it like for her that she had to numb herself with booze and cram her home with tasteless junk? How sad that her children cared little for her things, wanted no reminders of their mother's life, while we Gabaldóns scrapped over every trace — photos, recipe cards, even hair clips — that our mother had left.

"Poor Pam," I said, scrubbing under the seat with the toilet brush.

"What'd you say?" called Sophie from the hall.

"Goddamn, I said, *goddamn* this is a lot of work."

"No shit."


Later, as we were tying up the bags we'd stuffed—eight in all—a sudden pounding on the door jolted me. It was the same officious rapping that signaled police raids on television. I scanned the living room for Bette's stash box, thinking I should dive for it before the door was kicked in by narcotics agents.

But Sophie said, "Rita's here." She unlatched the door and held it wide.

"How come it was locked, huh?" Rita stepped over the threshold. "Are you trying to keep me out or something?" She laughed, fooling no one—that *ha-ha-ha* worked about as well as a smiley face on a T-shirt that reads: *I Am Intensely Paranoid*. Rita made rounds with the abrazos, though mine was a brief, mechanical thing.

"Where's Rafe?" I envied my brother-in-law's calming effect on Rita.

"He took Danni to the hotel for a nap."

"Well, you missed all the fun." Bette pointed at the overstuffed trash bags in the living room. She stretched, yanked out her ponytail, and mussed her hair.

Rita's eyes bulged with suspicion. "You didn't throw out anything important?"

"So we *weren't* supposed to throw out the important stuff?" Sophie scratched her head. "Gee, I must have misunderstood."

"You didn't come across any of Mom's things and take them for yourselves without giving the rest of us a chance, did you?"

Sophie ignored her. "What's for lunch?"

"When's naptime, is more like it?" Bette yawned.

"I'm hungry, too. I'll pick something up. What do you-all want?" I asked.

"*You-all,*" repeated Rita. "*You-all? Since when do you say 'you-all'?*"

I sighed. "Okay, then, what do youse guys feel like eating?"

"Ding-ding-ding!" Sophie said. "Break it up! Back to your corners!"

"Come on, Loretta." Bette grabbed her keys. "Let's get take-out Chinese. I know a place nearby."

"*Y'all* come back now, *heah*?" Rita called after us.

"You're letting her get to you again," Bette told me after we'd placed our order and slipped into a booth to sip mugs of beer. The tabletop and leatherette benches were bright red, the color that symbolizes happiness in China, but this shade reminded me of the flaming lakes that blaze when I shut my eyelids against the sun. A salty smell, the powerful aroma of chicken broth, emanated from the steamy kitchen.

"She's insinuating I'm some kind of fraud. By her logic, I'm not a Southerner, so if I use a Southernism, I'm a phony."

"Don't let her bother you."

"What's her *problem,* anyway?"

"Think about it," Bette said. "She can't let herself get angry, can't curse, so she's decided to piss you off instead, so maybe you'll blow up for her, and she can enjoy the spectacle from the sidelines. And, remember, she's still the same skittish kid who'd run from the TV when the organ music got too intense, way before the monsters showed up." Bette sipped her beer. "Except these days, she's not running. She's trying to act tough so no one knows how angry and scared she really is."

"Why is she in *my* face? I don't notice her treating you or Sophie like this."

"Well, you scare her more than we do."

Back at the condominium, we found Rita rooting through the bags of clothes, presumably searching for heirlooms we had been callous enough to chuck out. "Take it all, if you want," Bette told her. "You'll save us from having to wait for Goodwill."

"That's what *I* told her," said Sophie.

"I just want to know what you guys are tossing."

"Where does Dad keep the corkscrew?" I pulled open a drawer filled with a jumble of matchbooks, can openers, screwdrivers, pliers, pens, and loose keys.

Rita stood, legs apart and hands on her hips like a superhero. All she needed was a cape flapping behind her. "You're *not* drinking this early. You're as bad as Pam. All of you are."

Bette rolled her eyes, yanked wide another drawer and handed me the corkscrew.

In truth, I probably drank less than Rita, who enjoyed a beer now and again with Rafe. In Georgia, with Chris, I never drank. I never needed to. I uncorked the wine and poured it into three juice glasses. "I think Dad's got some soda and there's water," I told Rita, pointing at the sink.

By the time I had refilled my glass once, I felt mellow enough to turn to her and say, "Want to go to las posadas with me?"

"What is las posadas?" she asked. "Do you even know?"

"Sure, it's candles and singing, right? It's when they reenact Mary and Joseph looking for shelter just before Jesus is born, isn't it? Danni might like it." I pictured my niece's face aglow, her eyes shining by candlelight.

"When is it?"

"Tonight, at Aracely's house. Cary'll pick us up, if you want to go."

"Maybe." She speared a hunk of chicken.

"What I'm wondering is," Sophie said, "do they serve hard liquor at las posadas or just wine and beer?"

"Oh, hard liquor, I hope," I said.

"Forget it. If I want to see a bunch of borrachas, I can stay right here."

"Cary said it's supposed to be a family reunion, and that's the only reason I said I'd go. But now that I'm going, no one wants to come."

"Nothing to do with you," Sophie said. "Aracely, her family, even Cary (though he's our brother) singing and candles — that's some mighty boring shit."

"Why can't we make it like a family reunion?"

"You don't know because you don't live here and have to deal with Dad all the time and put up with your useless brother and his selfish wife," Bette told me, pointing her chopsticks for emphasis, "but we don't want to be reunited that much."

I stood to pour myself another glass of wine, but instead I said, "I guess I better call Chris." I headed for my father's room to use his bedside phone. As I shut the door, I could hear my sisters laughing and talking without me.

A few rings and Chris answered. "Hey, it's me." I smiled into the mouthpiece, as though she could see me. "The surgery went well. I'm just having lunch with my sisters now. It's really great getting together again."

In the aftermath of my father's surgery, the nursing staff enforced visiting regulations more strictly. Only two of us were allowed at a time in the intensive care unit. Bette and I took our turn first. We stepped into our father's room to find him chatting up a blond nurse with a Slavic accent.

"Hey, here's my daughters. Come on, girls, meet Magda." A gauze patch was applied to one side of his neck, and he looked pale, but otherwise he seemed the same as ever. "This here is Bette," he said, "and that one's my other daughter—"

"*Loretta,*" I reminded him. "Pleased to meet you."

"What nice girls!"

"How's he doing?" asked Bette.

"Great," Magda said.

"Magda talks Estonian," my father told us. "Now, that's one language I don't speak." He turned to Magda. "You know I'm a linguist."

Bette rolled her eyes. "Sure, Dad."

In the way some retirees give themselves over to golf or travel, our father had applied himself more rigorously to his lying when the pension kicked in. The bigger the whopper, the more of a kick he got. He said he was a parachutist on D-Day, a court reporter at Nuremberg, and a spy in Russia. Most of his imaginary exploits supposedly occurred during World War II.

"I speak six or seven languages."

"Is that right?" Magda said.

"During the war, I was a cryptographer, a code breaker. I had to learn French, German, Austrian, Dutch." He lifted his hairy, spotted fingers to count off the languages. "And I already spoke Spanish and English, not to mention American."

"American *is* English, Dad," Bette told him. She turned to give Magda a sympathetic smile, as if to say thanks for humoring the old coot.

"*Parlez-vous français?*" asked Dad.

"*Un peu,*" Magda replied, startling him.

"I used to ride in the rodeo, too," he said, changing the subject.

Bette sank into the one visitor's chair and sighed. "Not the rodeo story again."

"When was that?" I hadn't heard this one before.

"When I was first married, your mother and I were at the rodeo, and I went down to where they were riding the bulls."

"What rodeo?" I asked.

"*The* rodeo." He flicked his hand to show this didn't matter. "So I climbed the slats of a pen and got on this bull."

Bette took an emery board from her purse. "Emphasis on the *bull*."

"Yeah, I got on the bull. They opened the gate and *whoosh!* What a ride, man!"

"Wow, Mr. Gabaldón, that's incredible."

"Emphasis on the *in*credible." Bette worked the file over her nails.

"Good story, Dad." Though his tales never seemed to be grounded in any kind of shared reality or to ever have a point to them, I was glad to hear a new one.

"And my wife," he continued—quickly to show he wasn't done weaving this one—"was up in the stands, and she said, 'Hey, who is that guy riding the bull?'"

"How could you hear her from the bullring?" asked Bette.

"She couldn't recognize me because of the hat. One of the cowboys clapped this hat on me. So she goes, 'Who is that guy?' She didn't know her own husband!"

Bette stashed the emery board in her bag. "We get the picture, Dad."

"Wow," repeated Magda. "Well, I'll let you visit with your daughters, Mr. Gabaldón." She replaced the chart in its holder and backed out of the room.

My father sank back into the bed. He fumbled at his mouth,

and his dentures clattered on the swing-arm tray over his bed. His cheeks collapsed into his gums, making the stubble stand out on his chin like silvery quills. "What time is it?" he whistled.

"A little before four," I said.

"It's Saturday, Dad." Bette stood to look out the window. "Oprah's not on."


I showered and dressed before Cary was due to collect me for las posadas. After visiting our father, Rita and Rafe had picked up Elena and Aitch to take them to the carousel at Griffith Park. Bette and Sophie stayed behind at the condo, finishing with cleanup. When I stepped out of my father's bedroom ready to go, Sophie let out a wolf whistle and sang *"There she is, Miss Las Posadas"* to the tune of the Miss America theme.

"Knock it off, will you?" I smoothed my lipstick in the weird horse-harness-frame mirror near the entryway. "If you had any *decency,* you'd come with me."

"If you had any *sense,* you'd blow it off." Bette stood in the kitchenette, loading the dishwasher.

"I said I would go." I plucked a loose thread from the hem. "So I have to go, unlike some people who think nothing of disappointing their only brother."

"Qué brother, ni brother. He's a grown man, and I am way past letting a man tell me what to do." Sophie crossed her arms over her chest and chanted, "Hell no, I won't go. Hell no—"

"Stop," Bette begged. "I have a headache."

The phone rang, and Sophie lifted the receiver. "It's Cary. He's phoning from the security gate downstairs."

I pulled my blazer from the closet.

"Have fun." Bette waved a soapy spatula at me. "Don't be too late, because tomorrow the real work begins."

*"What?"*

"It's our chance to tackle the storage area downstairs before Dad gets back." She blew a stray lock of hair from her face.

"You're out of your mind." I opened the front door, headed for the stairs, taking slow, deliberate steps, so they could catch up. I kept this up long after I realized they weren't coming.

At this particular las posadas, they served margaritas and beer, but no wine. I debated these choices momentarily before settling on margaritas, thinking they had to be stronger than beer. "Uno, I mean, una margarita, por favor," I told Aracely's mother, Pilar, a petite woman, who looked young enough to be her sister. And, in fact, I learned she'd given birth at the age of fifteen to Aracely.

"Una margarita, yes." Pilar took my jacket and gave it to her new husband, a dolorous middle-aged man with thick, curly black hair. "I speak English. Him, no." She glanced at her esposo. "Only Spanish. I try to teach, but he no learn nothing."

The sad man smiled with modesty, as though he had been praised. Cary and Aracely disappeared through the hallway.

"Come in." Pilar clutched my elbow and steered me toward a spacious room that had an oversized Christmas tree in one corner and a dining table laden with food at the center. This room fed into a wood-paneled den, in which a large group of people stood about laughing and chatting in Spanish.

My brother and his wife reappeared, Cary holding beers while Aracely balanced an overfull margarita glass for me. "Here, drink this," she said, as though administering medication.

"What a nice place you have." I glanced at the unadorned white walls—no paintings, no bookshelves, no books—and tapped a toe on the polished wood floor, surprised by the hollow sound this produced.

"Come." Pilar urged me into the room filled with people.

The men had gelled and styled hair, leather jackets, tailored trousers, and crisp cotton shirts. The women were sleek and discreetly made-up, wearing black shifts with pearls or tight designer jeans and silk blouses. Many — men and women — smoked slender cigars. Cary had mentioned that Aracely's stepfather, before marrying and becoming a legal resident, had landed an engineering job downtown through the help of his friends, also expatriate professionals. Clearly, these sophisticated Mexican nationals were those friends. Listening to their confident voices and merry laughter made *me* feel like the alien — an awkward, solitary outsider with no legitimate business on the premises. I swallowed the remainder of my drink. Beer *would* have been stronger.

Pilar took my glass and called, "Ramón." Her husband reappeared and whisked the glass away. Then she parted a cluster of people, heading for a sofa on which three boxer dogs sat, wearing identical red knit sweaters with black-and-white-checked sleeves.

"Aracely say you like dogs." Pilar pointed at the trio of boxers. "Come meet. This is Dulce. Shake hands."

The dog she indicated glanced at me and yawned, but politely extended a paw.

The rough pad and cool nails rested lightly on my palm. "Pleased to meet you."

"This is Ynez, and this is Barbara."

I jiggled each dog's paw, and noting a space on the sofa near Barbara, I asked Pilar if I could sit there.

She turned to the dogs. "Will you be good?"

They wagged their stumpy tails and grinned at her, as only dogs can.

"Okay," she said. "But if they are bad, you tell me."

"Sure." After I settled beside Barbara, Ramón handed me a fresh drink. "Gracias."

"De nada." He bowed and vanished with his wife.

As soon as they were out of sight, the dogs began nudging one another, pulling on their sweaters, and whimpering. Barbara tried to stick her wet nose under my dress.

"Hey, hey." I pushed her head away. "Don't start."

At the same time as the dogs decided to plunge off the couch and make for the snack table, Aracely's voice rang out from the next room. I wandered over to find her quarreling with Cary near the kitchen. "What's wrong?"

"I told him *exactly* what to get me for Christmas." Aracely's lower lip trembled. "I even showed him the store, told him my size, everything."

Cary shrugged, his face blanched.

"And, guess what?" She blinked back tears. "He didn't get me nothing!"

Cary shoved his big hands in his pockets. "I told you we don't have the money." He had quit working as a typist to earn a teaching degree. My gentle, lumbering brother dreamed of becoming a kindergarten teacher. He was about to start student teaching, for which he'd receive no salary. The two had moved in with Aracely's folks, getting by on small paychecks from the dental office where Aracely worked as a receptionist.

"No fight," called her mother from the kitchen. "Come help in here, Aracely."

She moved off, glaring at Cary.

He set his empty beer bottle on the dining table and slunk from the room, his eyes on the floor. A chubby little boy appeared and tipped a drop of beer from Cary's bottle onto his tongue.

"Good idea," I said. "Think I'll switch to beer, too."

But Aracely burst from the kitchen, handing me yet another frosty margarita, which sloshed onto my knuckles. "I can't believe it. That *asshole*! He just took off!"

"What?" I dried my hand on my dress.

"Cary *left*. I saw him from the window." She stormed through the Christmas tree room and disappeared into the hall. Deep in the house, a door slammed.

"Um," I said to the little boy, "how am I supposed to get back?"

He shrugged, giggling.

Pilar emerged from the kitchen, hefting a roasting pan that she set on the table. "Having a good time?" Her face shone with perspiration.

I nodded.

"Can you give the velas? I don't know how to say."

"Candles," piped the chubby kid.

"Sure." I set my drink on the table.

Pilar produced a brown paper sack containing several three-inch tapers and a box of matches. "Give to everybody, okay? Light with these." She extracted a match from the box and demonstrated how to strike a flame, as though inability to speak Spanish indicated imbecility on my part.

"I think I can do that." I gave a candle to the boy. "I'm not going to light yours yet, so hold on to it." I headed back to the den, presenting a candle to anyone in my path, saying, "una vela," now that I knew the word, and lighting it.

A handsome man with longish sideburns jabbered back at me with a stream of Spanish so fast it made me dizzy. I smiled at him, saying, "Sí, sí, bueno," and put a candle in his hand. "Una vela." I lit it and moved on to the next person, who, I hoped, would just take the thing without comment. By the time I'd given everyone a candle and returned to light the little boy's and my own, my face felt stiff from grinning.

Soon off-key singing filled the two rooms as Aracely's mother brought forth a ceramic Nativity scene from under the Christmas tree. Much like the one Nilda produced during the holidays when we were young, this included a mismatched baby Jesus, one so large he could have more easily given birth to Mary and Joseph, both, than the miniature Virgin could have delivered him. People clustered near the tree and around Aracely's mother as she held aloft the crèche. Faces glowing in the candlelight, they sang in desultory voices while the dogs howled in pain. I didn't know the words, so I just moved my lips, hot wax tears dripping from my candle onto my fist, until the singing was done. Then, *poof,* we blew out the flames, and the dark room filled with smoke.

I set about retrieving the candles. "Gracias, gracias, gracias."

The talkative man with sideburns didn't have his.

"Vela?" I held open the bag.

He turned up his palms to show they were empty. His fingers rippled like a magician's. He pushed up his sleeves before reaching toward me and pulling out the candle as though it had been hidden behind my ear the whole time. Of course, this struck his friends as uproarious.

I thrust the sack at him. "Just put the vela in the bag, por favor."

After I had retrieved the candles, I found Pilar, handed them to her, and said, "Do you mind if I use your telephone?" It was time to call a cab.

"How was it?" Bette was stretched out on the sofa watching television, a glass of wine and lit cigarette in hand.

"Okay, I guess. They had dogs there." I took off my jacket and hung it in the front closet, which was now almost bare. The bags of clothing and junk had also been removed from the condo. "Where is everything?"

"We took it all down to the rec room. The manager said we could keep stuff there until Goodwill arrives." She muted the set. "Dogs? You must've loved that."

"It was all right." Vet school and then my practice cured me of my infatuation with animals. No room for sentiment in the lab, at the off-campus agricultural centers, or in the clinic. I never forgot they were sentient creatures, but there were so many that sometimes I handled them like matter. Long after my parrot, Saint Vincent, died, Chris discovered a stray kitten in our yard, so these days we kept a cat, but as a cat—not as a small furry being, anthropomorphized by my imagination.

"Oh, before I forget. Chris called." Bette set down the wineglass, as though mention of Chris's name conjured her censure of alcohol.

"What'd she say?"

"Something about a trip to Guatemala—she wants to check some dates with you."

I glanced at my watch. It would be nearly one in the morning in Georgia. "I'll call her tomorrow." I'd already told Bette we were arranging to adopt a baby girl from Central America. "She must have heard from the agency."

"I hope it's good news." She arched her brow. "But how will that be? I mean, a gay couple adopting a baby in the South?"

"It'll look like a single woman, a professional, adopting an underprivileged child from a Third World country." The adoption, we'd agreed, would be in my name, in case Chris's age might raise questions. "No reason to bring up our relationship in the proceedings."

"I hope that works out." Bette lifted the wineglass to her lips.

"Do you remember that time you told me to lie to Luis for you? You were going somewhere, didn't want him to know, so you asked me to say you were taking a nap?"

"Vaguely," Bette said, shifting uncomfortably on the couch.

"You said you owed me one—a lie, and I was just thinking, with the baby—"

"It's not a lie, Loretta." She smiled. "You *are* going to be a good mother."

*"Really?"*

"Yes, I'm positive." Bette rose to fill her wineglass. "You want some?"

"No, I'm going to bed." I was anxious to hear Chris's news. Because of the time difference, I could call her as early as I liked. "I'll sleep in Dad's room tonight so you can watch television." And deal with that lumpy couch, I thought. The previous night, I had tossed and turned over the loosened springs and hard metal frame while listening to the constant roar of traffic from the street.

"Suits me." Bette yawned. "Remember, tomorrow the real work begins."


I phoned Chris as soon as I woke, but she wasn't home or at her office. She probably had an early surgery. Claiming to be hopeless at names, Chris had insisted I name our baby. I teased her that I would call our daughter, Gertrude, Helga, or Madge. She said I may as well christen her "grunt," "helmet," or "mud," if I wanted ugly-sounding names. In truth, I had no ideas and was beginning to feel some pressure.

"What do you think of Ruby?" I asked Bette when she woke.

"Not really my color," she said. "It looks better on you or Sophie."

"No, the *name* Ruby. What do you think of it?"

"It's all right." She pulled the blanket over her shoulder and turned away.

After breakfast, we hurried down to the storage room — a cubicle near the laundry room — to sort through more of Pam's belongings before my father's release from the hospital, and, more important, before Rita showed up.

What we found in that dark, musty closet was more junk, but of the less interesting variety: Pam's old receipts, bills, and yellowed tax records, catalogues, *Reader's Digest*s, and even old telephone books. We loaded most of it into the recycling bin outside. But behind a short wall of boxes, we discovered the bird's-eye-maple trunk.

I wiped the furry coat of dust from it with a rag. "I forgot all about this."

"Nilda had it for a while," Bette said. "Remember? It was in the front room of her apartment. When she moved to New Mexico, she must have given it back to Dad."

"But why keep it hidden down here?"

Bette furrowed her brow, as though wondering how I could ask something so obvious. "Because it's exquisite, because it's tasteful. Think about it, how would something like this fit into Pam's decorating scheme? She'd have cluttered it with crocheted toilet-paper hats, porcelain shepherdesses, and plastic roses in no time."

"True." I lifted the heavy lid as Bette crouched beside me. The scent of cedar whooshed out at us. The trunk contained photo albums, baby books, yearbooks, and boxes of loose snapshots. Accordion files filled with papers and certificates lay atop plastic-wrapped piles of clothing.

Bette pointed to a sheathed bundle of yellowed lace. "Mom's wedding dress?"

"Probably." I lifted another parcel, a packet of papers, bound with twine. A thin envelope sailed out.

Bette reached for it and pulled out a letter to read its spidery script. "I don't believe it!" She took the parcel of pages from my hands and gently removed the string. "You know what this is, don't you?" She flipped through the pages once and then fitted them back into the parcel. "I'm going to make copies, one for each of us."

Part of me wanted to take the package from her and read the pages then and there, but another part suspected letdown. How could this stack of yellowed sheets possibly satisfy what I had longed for over all these years? So I was relieved Bette whisked the parcel away and tucked it into her oversized bag of "keep-ables."

In the afternoon, we retrieved our father from the hospital. It was no trouble getting him home, but he had problems after the catheter was removed, causing inflammation. This created a sense pressure, making him believe he had to urinate even when his bladder was empty. And since the surgery, he was moving even slower than usual, so we had a lot of false starts—trips to the bathroom, which he announced with a hollow, high-pitched whistling sound. *"Whoo-whoo-whoo"* followed by, "Man, I got to go!" Whoever was nearest leapt to her feet and helped him to the toilet.

By dinnertime, the condo was crammed. My sisters and I, Rafe and two-year-old Danni, Elena, Aitch, Cary, and Aracely—who was wearing a new rabbit's fur jacket to go with the smug look on her face—sat in the living room eating take-out pizza. I couldn't resist sidling up, pointing at her jacket, and saying, "I *hope* that's not real." She shrugged, but Cary gave me a tight smile, an apologetic look. Afterward, we settled Dad in bed for the night, and Bette pulled out the copies she'd made of the packet we discovered.

"What's this?" Rita backed away as though Bette were about to hand her a summons to appear in court. Rafe, though, took the sheaf of pages. Sophie accepted hers without a word, as I did. Bette even made a copy for Cary.

He started flipping through the pages, but Aracely snatched the stack from his hands. "Let me see that."

"Loretta and I found this when we were clearing out the storage area."

"We found the maple trunk," I said.

Rita narrowed her eyes at me. "Why didn't you call us?"

"*Any*way," Bette continued, "this was there—our *real* gift from Fermina."

Rita's mouth dropped open. "So none of that other stuff was true?"

Bette shook her head, grinning. "I'm a *natural* liar."

"But isn't lying unnatural?" I pointed out.

"Not for me," Bette said with pride.

"I *never* believed in that business." Sophie smirked. "I mean, what kind of a crappy gift was I supposed to have gotten—a shitty life, but ha-ha-ha, isn't it hilarious?" Even as a child, Sophie claimed to reject our ideas about Fermina's gifts. But from the look on her face, I could see she was stunned. "Is this the book then?"

"They're reports from Heidi Vigil's interviews. It's the story of Fermina's life," Bette said. "Read for yourself."

"Thank you, Bette," Rita said in a strange, low voice.

I cut my eyes at her to see if she was being sarcastic, but her expression was soft, her eyes shiny and full. She took her copy and disappeared into the bathroom for a long time. When she emerged, she took the sleeping Danni from Rafe's arms and stepped out onto the balcony. Through the parted drapes, I could see her under the mothy nimbus from the porch light, swaying back and forth, as though waltzing in place, her cheek against Danni's, her eyes closed, and a fullness in her face I had never seen before. "Has she always been so lovely?" I said.

Rafe nodded, but Bette said, "When she's not all uptight, that is." She drew Elena into her lap. "Are you getting tired, m'ija?"

Elena shook her head, but relaxed into her mother's embrace, nesting her head under Bette's collarbone. With a pang, I remembered my mother would hold me this way, and when she spoke, I would snuggle into the hollow above her breast to feel her words buzzing through my bones.

That night, my sisters left me alone with our father. I was to care for him over the next few days until I flew back to Georgia. After they went home, I found one of the copies that Bette had made. I had put mine in my suitcase and remembered seeing my sisters with their copies in hand as they left. This had to be Cary's. Just as well—Fermina never meant for him to have it. I shook off my reluctance to face disappointment, and starting with the letter, I settled into the recliner to read.

*Niñas Queridas,*

*Irina writes this letter for me in English for you. You call me Fermina, but my name is Nuvamsa. Nuvamsa means the flares of snow we asked of Nuvak'china, so we would have water in springtime. I am Nuvamsa, and my mother was Poh've'ha. This means lily blossom of the water. These pages have the story of what happened long ago. This is my gift, so you will know me, and my mother.*

*It was at the wedding of Decidero and Eulalia that I learned of my mother. There, I met a servant from Hano, on the First Mesa. She told me that my mother was not killed on the wagon road where*

*I was taken away. She rose up from the dust and walked thirty miles on that road to Fort Wingate. With blood in her hair, she walked to the fort. There, people helped her talk to the leader. She told what happened to us. A man named Shaw tried to help her get me back. They learned that Chato Hidalgo kept me, and they brought him to the fort. But he said I was given to him by a man who owed him money. I had to stay until the debt was paid. My mother asked to go to me, to work in his house, and he said that is fine. But he sold her to a sheep rancher. From there, she escaped that winter. She froze to death during a blizzard. They found her body on that same wagon road, where she was walking back to find me.*

*How could I know what she had done without hearing this? It was her last gift to me. Now that I have lost so much, I still have this, and through this, I have my mother with me. I close my eyes and I see her, with blood in her hair, walking through heat and dust and again through a snowstorm, walking all those miles, all these years, just to find me. I am Nuvamsa, called Nuva by my mother.*

*I am your great-grandmother, and this is my story, so you will know how far I have come to be with you.*

*Con cariño,*
*Nuvamsa*

I read through the photocopied sheets, numbly, as if I'd stumbled into someone else's dream that was nevertheless familiar and as powerful as a trance. When I reached the last page, my arms and legs tingled as though my father's steamy apartment had grown as cool and clear as a night in the high desert. A mesquite-fragranced breeze swirled past like a diaphanous veil. My inner ear buzzed with swelling silence that exploded into a cacophony of sounds: voices in an unrecognizable language, the snap of flames, hooves drumming the hard-packed earth, and weeping—the unbroken and copious wailing of a child borne away from home, from childhood. Then stillness fell. Light and shadow sharpened into distinct forms and clean lines. Holding the pages, I could see in the way I peer through my microscope, after twisting the lens for keen focus. The script on the page wavered, blurring as hot tears stung my eyes, but it was sure and true in the inexorable, undeniable way that one is at last confirmed in what one knows without knowing, feels without speaking about or thinking.

Though, these were only photocopied sheets, I set the pages on the nearby table so as not to blotch them. I stroked my warm, clotted throat, traced my jaw, long and sharp like Fermina's, and fingered my wide cheekbones, streaked now, slick with tears. I wrapped my arms about my sides as if to enfold and finally comfort that bereft and shuddering child who was Fermina, and who was also me.

Then I flashed on an image of Fermina as a lonely girl driven to send her baby away. I thought of my sisters and their children, the ferocious love binding them. They know better than I the devastation she must have felt in handing that bundle of life—*all she had*—over for another to raise, the courage it took and the *trust* she mustered in another woman's goodness. And I thought of our baby, mine and Chris's, in Guatemala—another woman wrenching herself from her own flesh and trusting, without knowing or seeing us, having faith in our goodness. We will have to earn this. For that selfless Guatemalan birth mother, for Fermina and my own mother, for my sisters, and mostly for our baby daughter, we will have to be better than we have ever been.

I doubted I was strong enough to have much faith and I was not sure where to direct it, but this is what I prayed that night: Like Shiamptiwa, called Patricia, our daughter will never have to wonder why she is alone, who her mothers are, and why they are not with her. We will give her music, stories, and art as companions for her spirit, and we, her mothers, will always be close at hand. We will show her through our acts and tell her often who we are—all of us through the generations—and how abundantly blessed by fortune we are to be with her.

After his grogginess the first night, the next morning it was as though someone had thrown a switch, activating my father's tongue. He yakked incessantly from the first light of dawn. I guided him to the couch, where he grabbed the remote control and flicked on the television, ostensibly to warm up the set for Oprah's show. We sat through a series of soap operas, show after show dealing with the mysterious paternity of certain characters. My father gabbed through them all. At one point, when a brassy blond actress confided to the stiff actor portraying her husband that he was not the father of their child, my father hooted, "I'm the father! *Heh-heh-heh*! I'm the one!"

I grew alarmed and phoned Sophie, who had the morning off. "I think Dad's stroked and compromised."

"What's he doing?"

"He's watching soap operas."

"Is he claiming to be the baby's father?" she asked.

"Yes, he is."

"Relax, he always does that, thinks it's funny. Since Pam died, he's been acting sillier and sillier—anything to get attention." Her voice was quiet, her tone somber.

"Hey," I blurted out. "Are you okay?"

"I think so," Sophie said.

"Did you—"

"I did," she said. "I read it last night."

"And?"

"It's crazy, because I just stepped off the scale, so I know better, but I feel lighter than ever right now. I feel free, like I can finally climb off the damn stage. I'm incredibly relieved, but sad, too, after reading about Fermina, what she went through. It's like I've got all these backed-up tears in me for Fermina and from a lifetime of doing stand-up, and I don't know how to let them out yet," she said. "I'm really glad I have some time off today with Aitch, just me and him. I wouldn't want to be anywhere else right now."

We hung up, and my father raised a brown-speckled fist from his nest of blankets on the couch. "He's not the father. I am!"

"Ha-ha," I said. "That's pretty funny."

He thrust his cup at me. "Get me some more coffee."

"Do you think that's wise, Dad? We nearly didn't make it in time last trip." My father's bladder was still acting up. Instead of false alarms, he was now unable to tell when he really had to go.

"Well, get me a soda, then."

"You should have something to eat."

"No, no, no." He shook his head stubbornly.

"How about some oatmeal, Dad? You can eat a little oatmeal."

"Hey, did I tell you about the time I was in the rodeo?" And he was off, with the television blaring in the background. As though stored in a loop in his brain, one story triggered another and that sparked the next. There were the ubiquitous World War II stories, stories about neighbors, about cousins, and several tales of winning money at the track, at cards, and in the lottery.

I interrupted once to ask, "Do you remember Fermina leaving something for us?"

"Bah, how would I know? I was busy. I had responsibilities. I had you kids to take care of. Nilda handled Fermina's stuff. I couldn't do everything."

"Did she say anything about—"

"That was so long ago, h'ita. Can I have a soda now? I'll eat some oats with it."

I rose to get his drink. "I'm going to be a mother," I blurted out.

"It ain't easy, raising kids. I raised five and look at me now." He pointed to his bandaged neck and shot me a shrewd look. "Are you married now to that woman?"

"Something like that." Wariness crept over me. My father had never before asked about my relationship with Chris. He'd met her, a couple times—Cary's wedding and a holiday get-together. Ever appreciative of a fresh pair of ears for his stories, he seemed to enjoy her company. "Why?" I asked.

"Well, you always did things your own way," he said. "You get that from me. Now, take your mother's family. They got no imagination, and they're boring, too. They couldn't tell a good story if they wanted, except for your mama."

"Mama told stories?" I remembered her reading books to us, one after another, during the long days of her confinement, during pregnancy and illness. But I couldn't recall her weaving a tale of her own invention.

"Esperanza told five of them—you, Bette, Rita, Sophie, and Cary." He laughed. "Hey, h'ita, did I tell you about the time I was in the rodeo?"

"When were you in the rodeo?"

I listened from the kitchenette as he told the tale, beginning to end, winding in the loop to the place where he's disguised from my mother by a hat. "She didn't know me," he said. "She didn't know me at all." Story into story, his voice quavered without tiring that morning and into the afternoon. Each narrative apparently purposeless, certainly convoluted, and likely untrue, but one after another pressing my father's point: Here I am. Look, *look* at me. *I'm* the father, and I'm still here!

*     *     *

After I helped him to bed that night, I stood in the dim kitchen and emptied the dishwasher, stacking dishes, bowls, and cups in the cabinets. But the woodworking had warped, and some cabinet doors would stubbornly creak open as soon as I shut them tight. The rag doll that stored grocery bags between its legs watched me, wearing a look that was both insipid and triumphant, as if mocking and challenging me. After closing and reclosing the poorly fitted doors a few more times, I gave up and pulled every cabinet, every drawer, wide, absurdly thinking that things should breathe. The kitchenette had a stale smell, so I thought more reasonably of dankness, of mold. Things should be exposed to the circulation of air and what light there was. Then I wiped my hands on a dish towel and phoned Chris, waking her, I'm sure. "Hi, it's me. I heard you called. I tried you earlier, but I couldn't reach you. Busy day?"

"Ridiculously," she said.

"So we're going to Guatemala?"

"Everything's set for mid-April. You'd better be thinking of names," she warned.

"I have one," I told her.

"Oh, really? I hope it's not something like Brunhilda or Myrtle."

"I can't tell you now because you have to hear the whole story," I said. "But this one is a real name, a family name."

# READING GROUP GUIDE

1. The Gabaldón sisters lose their mother at an early age, and much of the book is about trying to regain her through recovering her memory. It is also about their attempts to find out who their late housekeeper/servant Fermina was. What dilemmas are faced by the sisters in seeking secrets from the dead? And in what ways do the dead speak to the living in this novel?

2. The WPA reports about Fermina appear as interchapters in the novel. These are written by a fieldworker who apologizes to her superior for not writing "correctly." How does this unauthorized history work to provide connective tissue between the chapters that chronicle the sisters' lives?

3. With the exception of Rita, the sisters are happier and stronger when they are without male partners—husbands and/or boyfriends—in their lives. In fact, Rita theorizes their "magical gifts" are diminished when they fall in love, as though men draw strength and wisdom away from the women. Bette and Sophia even perform "visitation," helping raise one another's fatherless children. What shapes their belief that they are better off without men? And what is gained and/or lost by this conviction?

4. The novel suggests that love is being seen for who one is in the context of family. One's traits—strengths and weaknesses—show up only because these are what the others don't possess. Family isn't about getting along; rather, family is the source of self-definition: the brain, the angry one, the caretaker, and the clown. How is the Gabaldón family a

microcosm of the larger cultural tensions explored in the Los Angeles area of the girls' youth and the historic Southwest of Fermina's past?

5. The novel reveals the horrible and hilarious ways in which siblings betray each other. They collude, create factions, and intentionally drive one another out of their minds. How do the multiple perspectives affect the complex and ever-shifting strands of familial connection and disconnection?

6. Much of the conflict in the novel arises from misunderstanding related to the idea of a "gift" or "legacy." Attached to the idea of receiving a gift is responsibility or obligation. What does this responsibility entail for each sister?

# Una Guía para Grupos de Lectura

1. La hermanas Gabaldón pierden su madre cuando son niñas y, por mucho del libro, tratan de recobrar la memoria de ella. También tratan de descubrir la identidad verdadera de su criada Fermina. ¿Qué problemas encuentran las hermanas cuando buscan secretos de los muertos? ¿Y cuáles modos usan los muertos para hablar con los vivos en esta novela?

2. Los informes del WPA sobre Fermina aparecen entre los capítulos de la novela. Éstos son escritos por una investigadora quien se disculpa por escribir "incorrectamente." ¿Cómo trabaja esta historia no autorizada en proveer el tejido conjuntivo entre los capítulos que narran la vida de las hermanas?

3. Con la excepción de Rita, las hermanas están más felices y más fuertes cuando no tienen esposos y novios. Rita piensa que sus "regalos mágicos" se disminuan cuando las mujeres se enamoran, como que si los hombres les roban la fuerza y la sabiduría de las mujeres. Bette y Sophia hacen "visitation" para auydar a criar a sus niños sin padres. ¿Por qué creen que están mejores sin los hombres? ¿Qué ganan y qué pierden a causa de esta idea?

4. La novela sugiere que el amor es ser visto por quien uno es, en el contexto de su familia. Las características de una persona—las fuerzas y las debilidades—solo aparencen porque son las características que las otras personas en la familia no tienen. La familia no es de llevarse bien; sino la familia es la fuente de la identidad: La Preparada, La Enojada, La Guardiana, La

Payasa. ¿Cómo es la familia Gabaldón un microcosmo para la tensión cultural más grande que existe en Los Angeles durante la juventud de las hermanas, y del suroeste histórico de Fermina?

5. La novela revela los modos horribles y chistosos que las hermanas usan para traicionar una a la otra. Conspiran, pelean, y se vuelven locas. ¿Cómo influyen las perspectivas múltiples a las conexiones y separaciones complicados de la familia?

6. Mucho del conflicto de la novela es debido a un malentendido de la idea de un "regalo" o una "herencia." Con un regalo viene responsabilidad y obligación. ¿Cuál responsabilidad tiene cada hermana?

# ACKNOWLEDGMENTS

This book could not have been written without the practical help and encouragement of my patient and trusty readers: Beth Bachmann, Lauren Cobb, Teresa de la Cardidad Dovalpage, Maura Mandyck, Justin Quarry, the splendid Kathryn Locey, and the luminous Heather Sellers, whose encouragement and wisdom benefited the work more than I can say here. And I must acknowledge the benevolent intercession of my wise mentors: Judith Ortiz Cofer, Mark Jarman, William Luis, Tony Earley, and Peter Guralnick. I am also grateful to those who urged me on with friendship and empathy, my dear colleagues and friends: Tina Chen, Blas Falconer, Tayari Jones, Janis May, Karen McElmurray, Lynn Pruett, and Nancy Reisman. I am likewise indebted to my calm and sensible agent, Lauren Abramo, to Andie Avila for seeing the promise in the work, and to Selina McLemore, an astute close reader and supportive editor. I owe a fresh bouquet of thanks to Manuel Muñoz and Stephanie Finnegan, whose careful scrutiny benefited the work more than I can say. I thank my children, Marie and Nick, for putting up with my writing life for many years. For inspiration, I must recognize all the López Lovelies—aunts, cousins, and nieces, as well as the men with the courage to love them. My most profound appreciation goes to Louis Siegel, my husband, who has read this work almost as many times as I have and is unfailingly honest and kind in his insights each time.

Finally, I attribute the following books for the wealth of research material they yielded: *Captives and Cousins*, James F.

Brooks; *Hopi Animal Tales*, Ed. Ekkehart Malotki; *Hopi Stories of Witchcraft, Shamanism, and Magic*, Ed. Ekkehart Malotki and Ken Gary; *Hopi Voices*, recorded by Harold Courlander; and *Recuerdos de los Viejitos*, collected and edited by Nasario García.

# About the Author

Though born in Los Angeles, California, Lorraine López comes from a large extended family with long-standing ties to central New Mexico. The austere and haunting beauty that characterizes the Land of Enchantment has long captivated the author and inspired her work. Several years ago, López discovered that her "adopted" paternal grandfather was the biological son of his adopted father's brother (his uncle) and a Native American servant, a Pueblo woman who worked as a maid in the family home. After bearing this son, the woman subsequently gave birth to a daughter, who was surrendered by the family to an "asilo de huerfanos," an orphanage. When López learned this bit of information, a life bloomed in her imagination, and this novel is an attempt to recreate fictively and to comprehend the heartbreaking circumstances of such a life.

Currently, Lorraine López is an assistant professor of English at Vanderbilt University in Nashville and associate editor of the *Afro-Hispanic Review.* Her stories have appeared in *Prairie Schooner, Voices of Mexico, CrazyHorse, Image, Cimarron Review, Alaska Quarterly Review, StoryQuarterly/Narrative Magazine,* and *Latino Boom.* Her short story collection, *Soy la Avon Lady and Other Stories* (Curbstone, 2002), won the inaugural Miguel Marmól Prize for Fiction. Her second book, *Call Me Henri* (Curbstone Press 2006), was awarded the Paterson Prize for Young Adult Literature. She is completing a second short story collection and editing a collection of personal essays and memoir by women writers from lower- and working-class backgrounds. She lives in Nashville, Tennessee, with her husband, Louis Siegel.